THE KATAGI MAN-EATER

BRENT DeHAAN

Print ISBN: 978-1-66780-4-668

eBook ISBN: 978-1-66780-4-675

THE FULL MOON HAD RISEN OVER THE HILLS SUR-
rounding Natali district as easily as night follows day. The jungle in its natural habitat found itself illuminated by the light that spread to every corner of the country. The sight of countless plants indigenous to India came into view. Nocturnal animals went about their usual business in collecting food or mending nests. Diurnal animals slept away in a lazy slumber content to let time roll on.

It was July eighteen hundred and ninety, and the monsoons had come earlier than usual this year bringing a natural relief from the sweltering days before the rains. The jungle had taken on a new form with the inundation of water, and for two months the surrounding regions flourished. Now they had left as swiftly as they came.

The area was beginning to return to its dormant hot humid weather as the great cat moved silently through the foliage. Its dark black stripes ran vertical like daggers dripping from an unknown cavern. The deep orange set against them contrasted for one of the world's most prized and beautiful animal coats. Few people realize that these beautiful stripes go clear to the skin with stripes forming the unusual pattern unique to each cat. In the daytime with lush green tropical plants in the background, the sight of one of these magnificent cats was both rare and exquisite. It was for this reason that these animals were hunted by the sportsman and royalty that lived and came to India. To claim to have bagged a tiger was quite an accomplishment. Routinely, hunts were organized just for that purpose. Quite often the sportsman were amateurs, and the result would be tortured animals who were injured and would likely die later of an infectious wound, A slow tortuous death unfitting for the true king of the jungle. Such was nearly the fate of a magnificent male Bengal tiger.

As the cat moved with gracious dignity, every muscle slightly tensed with each sinew while the tiger glided effortlessly through the interior of India. It had not always been this easy. It had now fully recovered from the gunshot wound received six years previous. It was in perfect health, having learned to feed off of an easier prey, a prey in which hunger had been the catalyst, but now it was the taste it fancied. That prey being human flesh.

It had been very close to death soon after the injury, in its weakened condition, it was unable to mount a successful kill on any of its former prey. It had grown weaker every day as it watched potential food feasting on the succulent green leaves in the lakes. The cat wasn't accustomed to being unable to do anything that would result in a kill and food for itself, in desperation it retired to one of the many footpaths which led between the villages and hamlets in Northern India.

By chance a young girl had been sent to fetch water for her family and had the unfortunate experience to be the first in a long list of horrific and often heinous murders between man and beast. For no other animal has killed with such ease and intent as has the royal tiger turned man-eater. As the girl walked casually to the water, the wounded tiger had stayed concealed near the footpath, the girl approached nearer with each step.

It was over in a matter of seconds as the great cat swiped its massive paw across the terror-stricken face of the young girl. The swath and the razor-sharp claws easily removed the skin from the front of her face and continued across her neck with five precise lines where blood was beginning to pulsate with each beat of the young girl's heart. The blow to her head was with such force as the tiger somehow wound up the majority of its weight into a powerful massive blow that immediately killed the girl.

The striped cat barely had enough strength to drag the victim the short distance from the path so it could eat its meal in peace. The meat was different, a new taste unfamiliar to the animal. It ate as quickly as possible. After an hour had passed the family of the victim came looking for the missing girl. They quickly found the sight of the kill with blood already congealed as it covered the path. The trail led into the dense jungle. The cat could hear people approaching and after eating what it could, was forced to abandon the kill. But it was enough, it was no longer faced with starvation.

That had been nearly six years ago. And since that first kill, it had established itself as the Katagi man-eater named for the hamlet where it had made its mark. By eighteen hundred and ninety-six, it had established an astonishing two-hundred eighty-three victims that were confirmed and attributed to it. Now was the time that the beast reigned within its own realm.

Within those six years since the first casualty and more precisely within the last four, it had earned a reputation of the most feared man-eater India had ever known. The tiger had set down a curfew that extended in a radius well over and beyond its possible range. No one dared be outside their hamlet or village past sunset, and when darkness came everyone quickly retired to their huts, closing all doors and openings. People traveled between villages in large groups for safety, often with a few men carrying primitive weapons. The fear of the tiger infected people of far reaching territories and stories of tiger attacks, greatly exaggerated spread like the flames of a windblown wildfire throughout the districts. Everything from Gin traps to cyanide poisoning had been used to try and eradicate the tiger from the surrounding country. Even the British government had reluctantly publicized the affair and had asked various sportsman to hunt the beast down for a reward. With each year the reward got larger, and the hunters fewer, some of them becoming victims themselves, but none had been successful. Many tigers were hunted and killed but never had one matched the enormous pug marks of the Katagi man-eater.

During those years, the tiger became wiser and more intelligent sensing danger before it became lethal, and now in the prime of its life was the most feared entity in all of India.

The tiger moved through the tall grass that separated the dense jungle from the village of Danira. The sun had already set and the sky showed beautiful shades of orange, yellow, red and violet. As the villagers gathered in their huts and the darkness settled in, there was a quiet that permeated the countryside. Within twenty minutes there would be nearly two hours of total darkness before the moon began to rise over the surrounding hills. The village began to descend into a tranquil peace. Occasionally there was a barking dog or a bleating goat that broke the silence but for the most part the village was sedated into a growing slumber. It wasn't a large village, only about two hundred people stirred, half of them already asleep following the evening meal and a hard day's work tilling the land or gathering wood.

The big cat approached with a steady canniness, studying every foot of terrain for anything out of the ordinary. Its eyesight like that of all big cats was excellent and even in darkness was four times greater than mans. With no moon it could still make out every detail with distinction. It chose its steps carefully, drawing stealthily closer to the village with each step. The hind paws were carefully placed in the prints which the front ones had just made reducing the chances of stepping on a twig or branch that might give its position away.

Abruptly, a Himalayan sheep dog began to bark savagely as the wind carried the unmistakable scent of the danger that was approaching. The owner had tied it close to his hut with a wooden peg driven deep into the soft dirt and some hemp cord made from braided strands of vines. The tiger, sensing a loss of surprise began to pick up its pace bringing it closer to the yapping dog. It cleared the jungle that separated the village from the dense cover and within seconds was upon the hapless canine.

The dog took the full brunt of the six-hundred twenty-five pound tiger. It was over in a matter of seconds as the cat quickly sank its teeth into the neck of the dog and shook it with such force that everyone within two-hundred yards could hear the snapping of the dog's neck. The cord securing the collar was broken and the peg was brought out of the ground by the amount of force exerted. Undoubtedly the owner had heard the final yap of his dog and was now gripped with a fear that penetrated every fiber of his body.

Everything was deathly quiet as the tiger circled the nearest hut. The man was trying to be as quiet as was possible, but the old man could still hear the sniffing from the tiger and the low raspy breathing. His heart was pounding like a drum. It was difficult to keep his own breathing at a whisper knowing what was outside.

As the big cat closed in on the far wall it reared and put its full weight on the wall with its front paws reaching up to the peak bamboo support beam. With little effort the wall came down and most of the roof came with it. The small man within was now in such a state of shock that it seemed he could do nothing as the tiger quickly entered the hut dodging fallen bamboo.

The cat and the man's eyes quickly met, as the tiger began to curl back its ears. The mouth opened and emitted a snarl as the cat bore five inch upper canines white as ivory contrasting with the already blood stained face. Its mouth opened wider as saliva dripped from each canine with the low growl that was bellowed from deep within its throat.

Within a second the tiger was on the old man batting him around like a kitten plays with a ball. But it was real, deathly real as you could hear the sound of a skull being crushed when the cat clamped down on the old man's head. The head had broken open like a crushed melon. Bits of the old man's brain were oozing out as the tiger lifted the body clear off the floor and carried it outside disappearing into the dense jungle.

The cat feasted well that night after dragging the hapless victim nearly a half mile into an area it felt was safe. It did not like to have its meals disturbed. The tiger ate half the body that night and although it was a small man, there was still around twenty pounds of meat left. It covered the body with leaves and some small rocks and after getting a drink from the nearby brook found a grassy area and laid down to let its body digest the meal.

This had been a good kill, it would not need to eat for another three days with the amount of meat it had consumed and with what was left over. It was a kill that was far easier than any other game, and it had an abundant supply.

Most of its former victims had been paralyzed with fear. All rational thinking had left them and any means of defending themselves had quickly been forgotten in the terror of the magnificent beast which they beheld with the last breath of life they were to hold. But the kill was made, and there would be a reprieve for at least a couple of days.

India was a country like no other. Since sixteen hundred and eight the English had gradually increased their trade with India. After minor setbacks due to competition from the Portuguese, the British had, by seventeen-twenty, established a solid business interest in the country. India by that time accounted for nearly twenty-five percent of England's total imports, saltpeter, sugar, indigo, rubber and pepper were the most popular exports to the mother country.

Fort St. George was established around sixteen forty, followed shortly by Calcutta, Delta, and Bombay. The British influence was beginning to spread over the land like a sun shedding its rays.

The Indian Mughal empire had reached its apex during the second half of the seventeenth century during the reign of Awrangzeb. Although ruthless as a ruler, he was able to unify the people in ways others could not. But the days of the Indian empire were numbered.

India at the time lacked the cohesiveness that molded a country. For too long princes had fought one another and only weakened the country. At the height of population there were a hundred and eighty million subjects, accounting for twenty percent of the world's population. With the advancement of technology and warfare in Europe, it was only a matter of time before India became part of the British crown. Conflicts between the British owned East India Tea Company and the ruling princes, or Nabobs as they were called, forced England to take matters into their own hands.

With the treaty of Allahabad, the English, through the East India tea company, began to establish themselves as the Dwain of Bengal with the right to impose and collect the revenue of the provinces. A fixed tribute was paid to puppet rulers in Delhi, but everyone knew that the real power now belonged to the British government and their representatives. As the dew is swept before a rising sun, a rich and resourceful India came under British rule.

Competition for resources in Asia was intense between England and France, as both moved to monopolize regions and resources. In eighteen fifty-eight, the British passed the act for the better government of India. Eventually they hoped that India might serve as a springboard into entering the more lucrative Chinese trade market.

As England had set up governments around the world, they were quick to establish departments under the new laws. One of the new departments established in India was the Office of Natural Resources.

Natural disasters like floods and earthquakes had devastated the economy and subsequently cost the crown quite a sum. The new office was organized in an attempt to stymie the losses and restore order. Small dams were built to control flooding, and improvements were made to reduce crop losses.

Recently, the new government had received numerous complaints and reports about the growing menace which kept a large portion of the countryside at bay during the twilight and evening hours. The menace was dismissed at first as a mere nuisance, but now the threat had become very real with nearly eighteen deaths a month being reported. The annual production of crops was down due to the shorter work day in some fertile providences.

Although a portion of the deaths could be traced to snake bites, crocodiles or other predators, nearly half could be directly traced to the man-eating tiger called the Katagi man-eater. It was solely responsible for the second greatest number of deaths in India, with only the mosquito causing more fatalities by spreading the disease of malaria.

The complaints were often directed to the office of Natural Resources.

In the largest room in that office was a rather large map of the entire country. It was one of the most recent illustrations showing the most current elevations, contours, lakes and rivers. Some areas of the country remained uncharted, and despite well trained native topographers trying to infiltrate other forbidden countries in order to find the sources of the rivers, their attempts were largely unsuccessful. Nevertheless, some progress was made and the map represented the most complete one to date. The large map had just been hung in the main room of that office the year before.

In addition to the many responsibilities the office was handling, pressure was coming from higher authorities whose complaints came directly from the people and from the hierarchy of the crown. They wanted all of its possessions free from any disturbance that could upset the balance of trade which was considered utmost of importance to England. Not only was the office responsible for organizing relief from natural disasters, like floods, tidal bores, earthquakes and landslides, but it also had the responsibility to avert such disasters by overseeing the actual building of dams.

The director over the office held a powerful position, and in fact the office itself was only third in power behind the office of the military, and the viceroy. The various reports and complaints about the tiger menace were passed along rank and file until the majority of them ended up on the director's desk. The previous director had tried unsuccessfully to pass them back up the lines, but the Viceroy eventually intervened and made it clear that this new threat was the responsibility of the director and its office.

As casualties began to rise and as the people began to panic, it became clear that the director would be replaced. That replacement had happened only three months ago. The Viceroy had appointed a new leader by the name of George Smythe. Although he took the task very seriously, very few in the office liked him. In the three months he had taken over the department he had managed to alienate many. There was no doubt that he could do the job, but it was difficult to put him into the position in such a trying time. The government itself was receiving an enormous amount of pressure from the people who seemed to look to the British to now solve their problems. A very known and indescribable fear had gripped the country from border to border. The pressure was being felt in the director and the office itself. George both loved the challenge and hated it. If he could rid the country of this plague, he would be considered a hero by the government and a god by the people.

But if he failed like the last director, that failure would follow him around for the rest of his life.

In the building of the Department of Natural Disasters was a large room where most of the department workers had their desks. The office was lavishly furnished with mahogany wood and relics from India. On the wall at one end of the office was the enormous framed map of the country, showing the present borders. It was the old map that used to hang in the front foyer. The map was covered with small red flags that jutted out from various geographic locations. Every flag represented a death attributed to the Katagi Man-eater. On each one was the name of the person killed and the date on which the attack occurred.

An attempt had been made by the office to verify the accuracy of all the reported deaths. Many kills attributed to the man-eater had been found to be false reports. Most of the victims listed were women whose job it was to gather firewood for their families to cook their meals. As firewood became scarce, it was necessary to wander further from the village to get the wood. The women would often become easy victims of the man-eater, the dense foliage providing excellent cover for the beast as it dragged its victims into the jungle never to be heard from again. Even the bravest of men would not dare venture into the thick protection the jungle offered the cat. There was no shortage of male victims as well, some having primitive firearms that were never fired.

The flags on the map were more common within a three hundred twenty-five mile radius in the northeastern part of the country. Unfortunately for the director, this was one of the most primitive and underdeveloped parts of the entire world, with few roads and no railroad. The most common way of travel was to walk one of the many footpaths that led from one village to the next. There were a few flags in Burma, but they had been among the early reports and were now about five to six years old. There were now two hundred ninety-two flags on the map with another death reported every three to five days on average. The Viceroy had been under considerable duress for failure to rid the country of the menace. Only recently had political forces, both from the crown and wealthy investors, come to have influence in getting rid of the problem. Everyone would need to come together in a cooperative effort in order to be successful.

The Viceroy and his right-hand man George Smythe, the head of the office of Natural Resources, was optimistic the job could be done quickly. The new director was given the primary duty of riding the country of the Man-eating tiger responsible for creating the fear driven frenzy that gripped the entire country. As investigations continued and facts were brought to light it was found that the tiger was an unusually large specimen, and it possessed a very keen intelligence that had allowed it to become astoundingly elusive. It had a very uncanny ability to survive like no other cat. All efforts of the government to rid the country of the problem had so far failed. Now the situation had exploded into proportions larger than the cat itself. Every day George would have to force his way through throngs of protesters wanting relief and vengeance for relatives killed. The situation had become grave indeed.

George was a perfectionist in every sense. Even the mugs in his home had to be organized in a very systematic way, which often drove his wife batty. He was often the brunt of jokes around the office. He rarely put in an honest day's work being on so many committees and enjoying his wealth and his personal interests. George had decided earlier that day to hold an emergency meeting to talk specifically about the problem of the tiger. At the desired time, everyone with any clout in the office began to assemble into the large conference room. When everyone was there and seated, George surprised everyone by slamming his fist into the table and saying in no uncertain terms that they would not leave until they had a plan for killing the Katagi man-eater.

His gesticulations were everywhere, he looked at everyone, not waiting for reactions he bellowed, "People we have a very serious situation here. There is considerable pressure coming from the mother country and the viceroy to rid ourselves of this nuisance. There is no other mammal on this planet that has been responsible for more deaths than the tiger. It has been a problem before now and it will continue to plague us until the end of time. But we will take care of this one. It is only one cat. How hard can this be? It is our job to come up with a workable solution to eliminate this fiend from hell. Heretofore it has been classified as a menace, but now it is classified as a natural disaster for all intents and purposes and has been assigned to our office."

George then asked the group for suggestions. This was indeed a new development. George, although in the office for only a short time, had never asked for suggestions before; it just wasn't like him. There was silence for awhile as he waited for anyone to reply. Pipe smoke ascended to the rafters as Charles Whent spoke up.

Charles had been keenly aware of the problem for some time. He had worked at the office for nearly a year and a half and had followed the story enthusiastically. He thought the entire situation was quite interesting and he had ideas of how to solve it.

Charles was British through and through. He had graduated from Cambridge and had come to India for adventure. Although he was young at twenty-five, he possessed an intellect that few men or women could match. He had an unconquerable spirit and had even climbed such mountains as Mount Blanc and the Jungfrau in Europe. He was hoping to get some time off and enough money to start a small expedition to the Himalayas and climb some of its high and mostly unnamed peaks. He had a special interest in a peak called X29 which may prove to be the highest mountain in the world.

Many women were left with broken hearts in the hopes that Charles would somehow single them out and settle down, but not Charles. He had an untamed personality within him that reached out for adventure wherever he was. As he had spent time in India, he had grown to love everything about the country including the people, the food, and even the smell.

He spoke with a strong confident voice that seemed to resonate with authority.

"We have tried everything, traps, tracking, even poison."

He then let some moments of silence pass.

"I think it's time we hired a real professional, someone who knows tigers, someone who has experience with this sort of problem, someone who knows the jungle and everything about it in order to stay alive."

Heads began to nod in agreement. Charles looked around the room, admiring many of the stuffed mounts of various trophies adorning the walls.

Then he said, "I believe I know just the man for the job."

George spoke up "Yes, I believe I know who you are talking about."

George knew that he was speaking about Winston Jamison, a renowned big cat hunter that was now semi-retired but still living in India. George despised the man. He had met him at one of the state balls. George remembered he had joined a conversation with Winston and a few ladies. At one point Winston had gone to get some punch for the ladies and looked back to see George pointing in Winston's direction as the women laughed at something. Winston was no fool and guessed correctly that George was making fun of him in some way. When Winston returned, he corrected George on some issue and the ladies were impressed with Winston's insight and his humorous way of telling stories. Winston had intentionally embarrassed George. It was just Winston's way to give back what was being given. Winston generally treated the politician and the beggar the same way. He would insult, intimidate or simply be direct and without tact to anyone depending on how they treated him. But reflecting on the problem at hand, George knew it was the best solution, and perhaps he could rid the country of the problem while taking the credit for himself.

Winston Jamison was a man known by many people, and those people either had great respect for the man or deep envy and jealousy. He had many nicknames which translated meant "White reaper" or "white death" because he always had a thing with death or death had a way of following him around. He was in his fifties, but there were few with greater stamina or a nose for the jungle. He was born and raised in India though his parents were from England. His father had worked for the East India Tea Company. He was once in love, but the relationship had never worked out. He had already established something of a reputation for eliminating the Jangii man-eating leopard that was responsible for killing twenty-three people including two men who were sent to exterminate it. Many felt that the cat's cunning and violence was due to demonic possession. A combination of skill and luck prevented Winston from becoming another victim. Although it had been nearly ten years since the incident, people still passed stories of the sahib who killed the cat responsible for so many deaths.

George finally spoke up.

"Do you know where we can find him?"

"Some say he has retired to a summer home in the district of Agrada," said Charles.

"Well, let's send for him straightaway," replied George.

"We can send a cable immediately, but I don't think it will do any good," said Charles. "I think we had better send someone personally, don't you, sir? I mean I've never met the man, but I believe we will need someone to convince him."

"Yes, I suppose your right."

George was gazing out the large window as silence fell on the room, he was thinking of the repercussions of hiring Winston. The smoke from his pipe was wafting up through the window. Finally, George spoke up and asked if anyone objected to hiring the Jamison fellow. No one spoke as pipes were raised and lowered throughout the room although you could hear some murmured whispers.

"Very well, you had better get going Charles."

"Sir, I couldn't possibly go at this time."

"Oh, you can and you will. You can give your responsibilities to Sarkee for the time being. And Charles, I expect success or you will find yourself taking a children's census in the northern providence for the next couple of years. Do I make myself clear?"

Reluctantly Charles agreed and silently nodded.

Charles took longer than normal getting ready for the field. He wanted to make sure everything was perfect, he didn't want to forget anything. He tried to think of the most minute detail of what Winston needed. He knew if he could convince Winston to go that they would likely leave immediately, the result would be that there would not likely be a large city to draw needed supplies. He sent couriers to the markets to get key items. He would send an expense receipt for the most important items and he would pay for anything else. He figured he would have to catch the first train out the next morning.

How did I get myself into this? he thought, I walked right into it.

But he only expected to stay a week at the most as he was just planning on trying to talk Winston into the hunt.

The sun was rising over the hills as Winston Jamison lay slumbering on a late spring morning. He was snoring slightly as he lay sprawled out in his enormous cotton hammock that was strung between two large beams on the front porch of his summer home. The hammock was handmade and was a gift from one widow of a victim of the Jangii man-eater. It had taken her nearly eight months to finish, but it was beautiful and functional unlike any gift he had received. His name was carved in the wooden support ends as well as some intricate artwork of elephants and tigers which made it different from other hammocks. Occasionally, when the mosquitoes weren't bad, he would sleep an entire night in it. He loved to be outdoors and hear the sounds of the jungle, and feel the nightly breeze acting as a salve, soothing his body and keeping him cool.

Something woke him early this morning. It was the scent of sweat and he could smell it blowing in the breeze. He opened his eyes and began to get accustomed to the surroundings of his familiar front porch.

It was still several minutes before Charles arrived. A native child had already pointed in the direction of Winston's home and made off, perhaps feeling that Charles was close enough to Winston's home that if he couldn't find it he shouldn't be in the jungle.

As Charles arrived he could see Winston staring in his direction. Charles took a few more steps and was soon staring down at Winston.

"Good morning."

Winston mumbled something like "morning" back.

"My name is Charles Whent, and I'm from the Ministry of Natural Resources."

"Well you certainly don't look like someone from some ministry," replied Winston.

Charles knew it was joke and an insult but had been warned of Winston's dangerous tongue.

Charles spoke immediately as though the insult wasn't heard.

"I'm here to offer you a very promising and lucrative job."

"You don't say," replied Winston. "I'm sorry to inform you that I'm retired, have been for some time now."

"Yes, I know. But you and I know that you're only good at one thing, and I think you know what I am talking about."

This time Charles was insulting Winston.

Charles couldn't help but think that Winston was nothing like he had imagined; small, about five foot seven and one hundred sixty-five pounds and well-proportioned for a man in his fifties. A perfectly shaped and sculpted goatee hung on his face. His eyes were as blue as the Indian ocean and he had a weathered complexion. He was bald on the top of his head which showed no hair at all as if it was closely shaved. He had large upper body proportions to go with his taut body. He was in shorts and his legs looked massive to Charles. There were several severe scars on his legs and arms indicating some wicked accidents.

"Let me guess. You want me to hunt and kill the Katagi man-eater," replied Winston.

"Yes," replied Charles with a sigh, as he wiped the sweat from his brow with a handkerchief. "We've been unable to eliminate it. The others we hired have been killed, maimed or just given up. We know you're a professional and can take this job if you're interested."

"You should have come sooner," replied Winston.

"It's killed nearly three- hundred people so far, and it's seemed to pick up an appetite over the last few months."

"You are wrong on the statistics," replied Winston. "If you count the deaths in Nepal it's killed over three hundred and fifty people. Well we've tried everything and now we are asking for your help. You and I both know you're the man for the job. No one else can do it. Those who thought they could are dead."

Winston, knew deep down that Charles was right. He also knew many more would die if he refused to take the offer.

"What does it pay?"asked Winston.

"Well I'm prepared to offer you one thousand pounds now and another one thousand when the job is finished."

"Plus expenses," replied Winston.

"Well I don't know ab…"

Charles was quickly cut off by Winston.

"You can either take my offer or people can continue dying. Two thousand pounds plus expenses, and I'll need your help as well."

"Oh no, I'm not going with you, not on your life, no sir."

"Do you have a family?"

"Well no, but what does…"

Winston interrupted him again.

"Well then, you are going with me whether you like it or not. That's the only way I'll agree to do it."

It seemed that in just a few moments Winston had made a friend, and he didn't make friends easily. Charles didn't reciprocate the feeling but was concerned and Winston saw it.

"Don't worry chap. My last assistant is retired and doing just fine. Of course, his leg had to amputated due to gangrene, but he's been doing fine with just the one. Just remember to stay between me and the cat at all times."

Winston laughed and slapped Charles on the back with enough force to move his upper body forward. Charles didn't know if he was joking or not.

"Come on in, your just in time for breakfast."

Charles couldn't help but think it was nearly eleven-o-clock by now and it was almost lunch time, but he followed him in. The summer cottage was quaint, but neat. On the walls hung various game heads indigenous to India. Charles had seen other mounts of the same species, but these were remarkable animals many of which would be records for India if recorded, and for the world as well. He stood in awe and just stared at them. Over the doorway two enormous tusks curved over the opening from the floor. They were so immense that they towered over the archway leading into the kitchen. On the floor was a beautiful leopard skin with the fall coat as vivid as a summer sunset. Winston noticed him staring at it and said, "The Jangii man-eater. It nearly got me you know. Excuse me a moment."

Winston left the room.

Charles noticed a skin that seemed to dwarf the leopard. It was a magnificent tiger skin further into the room. The incisors on the beast were at least four inches long. It was the largest tiger Charles had ever seen.

Winston was asking his servants to make something for Charles. Most of Winston's servants were widows or orphans who voluntarily served him out of respect and thanks for killing the animal responsible for the deaths of their loved ones. It was a symbiotic relationship as Winston in turn provided food and shelter for them. One of the servants was a widow who had a daughter in her twenties that was very fair to look at. There seemed to be an unspoken language between Winston and her.

Charles noticed on the wall the guns that Winston used. They were beautifully polished and one had a sling hanging from it. Charles was looking at the caliber when Winston came back in.

"It's the four-fifty nitro express double-barrel. It will kill an elephant with one shot. Here's one of the cartridges."

Winston pointed and went to the cabinet, opened the door and handed Charles what looked like a small cigar. It was immense to say the least.

"They're expensive, and no one would steal this gun as they likely can't afford the ammo. It's my favorite," Winston said, without being asked.

"It's a nice gun," replied Charles.

After a brief pause, Winston replied, "Yes, that gun has saved my life on a number of times. It has never misfired on me yet. I've needed the second barrel on a number of occasions."

The guns were flanked by two drawings in charcoal of two cats. On the left was a drawing of the Jangii man-eating leopard and on the right was the Tanchi man-eating tigress. They were done by Arlett Hatami, a famous gifted Indian artist who had studied in Paris. He was half Indian and half French and all of his works were expensive.

As Charles looked away from the drawings he could sense that they had taken Winston back in time, and he was reminiscing about the good times and good luck he had been blessed with.

Winston came back to reality and offered Charles a seat. Charles sat on one of the finely crafted, woven reed chairs covered with black antelope skin. He noticed other stools made from elephant legs. Winston took a seat on his favorite chair.

"I know you've hired others, and the cat got some of them eh? Why did it take you so long to come get me?"asked Winston.

Charles had always been a straight shooter and was always direct.

"Well I guess you've caused a few wrinkles with the directors haven't you?"

"Me? You've got to be joking. I'm not the kind of chap that would purposely insult someone, unless of course they absolutely deserved it."

Both men smiled. Neither men had met prior to that day but they knew that their lives were somehow intertwined.

Charles and Winston were talking about politics and the empire when Winston's servant came in and told them that breakfast was ready. The servant was Indian and possessed some of the most striking features he had ever seen. "Good. We'll take it on the deck."

Both men arose and Winston led Charles back to the rear of the cottage. They walked onto the deck which held a beautiful view of the jungle. The area was lush with vegetation and giant trees which could have supported several large tree houses. In the distance one could see a small stream with vines and other vegetation hanging over it. One of Winston's servants had a pet monkey and it paced back and forth on its bamboo pole, curiously looking at the new occupants on the deck.

As soon as Winston's servant poured some tea, Winston asked for the latest news on the cat. Charles pulled out a rough map that was folded several times and told him that the last report was near a village called Caritti. Charles pointed to the village on the map. It was still about three hundred and fifty miles from their present location, but they could take the rail part of the way.

"How soon can you be ready to start?" asked Charles.

"We can leave first thing in the morning, and with any luck this menace will be gone within a fortnight."

"Good."

The next time Winston's servant came out Winston instructed her to go and fetch Sarvi, an expert tracker who was a good friend of Winston's. Winston quickly scribbled a note and gave it to his servant, and that was it.

Charles told Winston that he needed to go and get his things, but Winston told him that there wasn't time. He could wire someone the next day and have his things sent to Jaipur, which was the closest city to Caritti.

"In the meantime," said Winston, "you can wear some of my clothes."

Charles was going to disagree but Winston had a good point.

They finished their meal and Winston sat back and lit up his pipe. He took in the jungle air and the pipe smoke with deep breaths. Charles neither smoked nor drank which many found unusual, but it had always supplied him with nearly endless entertainment as others would inevitably take too much.

Winston said, "You had better savor this moment and enjoy it, because over the next few months you'll never have another one."

"You can't be serious," replied Charles. "We'll surely be home in less than a fortnight."

"You should never underestimate a man-eater."

Winston started to make a thousand-yard stare and finally said, "Wherever you think they are, they won't be there. Whenever you think you are safe, you're in danger. Even some of the simplest tasks can turn upside down and become lethal. There's only one thing that you can count on, and that's the unexpected."

Following the smoke Winston took Charles inside and led him to his gun cabinet. He opened the case with the key he had on his neck that was part of a necklace that held impressive claws nearly three inches long. Charles could see several rifles and a few handguns. Winston took out his second favorite rifle and handed it to Charles.

"What do think of that?"asked Winston.

"Very nice," replied Charles as he looked down the barrel at one of the stuffed heads at the end of the room.

All of Winston's guns were left handed and, as such, were usually specially made and ordered. Winston was right handed but left eye dominant which would explain why he shot left handed guns.

"It ejects automatically once breached manually, so be careful of hot cartridges hitting you in the face. Of course, you may need only one shot."

Both men smiled.

Winston took out two knives that were still in the sheaths and handed one to Charles.

"You may need this as well."

Winston then took out several boxes of cartridges and handed one box to Charles and kept three to himself. He also gave Charles a small pair of binoculars.

They left the room and Winston went and fetched his favorite rifle that was hung on the wall in the front room. A ladder was needed in order to reach it. He retrieved one and was climbing up to the rifle when Charles asked him about the Jangii man-eating leopard. Winston looked over at the cat spread across the floor and slowly came down the ladder.

"Yes, he was a smart one alright. It was eighteen-eighty-seven, and the beast had already killed almost two dozen people when the government called me up to track it and kill it. I can remember that night as if it were yesterday," he recalled. "It was my first man-eater you know. I bought a young goat and tethered it to a tree about thirty yards from a large sycamore that I had climbed and was in perfect view of the goat. A large horizontal branch offered the optimum perch from which to shoot, although at the time I wondered if the branch was high enough on the tree to be completely out of harm's way.

"The moon was three quarters full and it was just enough to see the goat and not much further. The goat began to bleat around two a.m. which kept me very attentive. I never sleep during watches and at that time all senses were tuned to try and figure out where the leopard was. The goat was frantically trying to escape the rope which held him, but fortunately I had tied it very securely. Fifteen minutes passed with nothing changing and then, all of a sudden, the goat stopped bleating. I could still see the animal and it was still standing there. I waited another thirty minutes with nothing happening and decided that the cat had somehow seen me and left the area.

"As I climbed down the tree I had a very eerie feeling that something was amiss. I can always tell this as the hair on the back of my neck sticks up. When I came to the bottom of the tree, I noticed in the torchlight fresh pug marks behind the tree. I could not have seen them from my vantage point.

Thoughts raced through my head. *Was it still lurking behind some bush close by, or had it left the area?* For the first time in my life I felt vulnerable.

"Somehow, I knew the cat was still around and that made me nervous. I can't really explain the fear, although anyone who has been near death will know what it feels like. Cats have eyesight four times better than humans in the dark and I was at a disadvantage. I tried to think about anything I had heard while in the tree but could not think of anything. I knew that if the leopard wanted me in the tree it could have had me, for as you probably know leopards are known for their tree climbing skills. On many a day I would see leopards with their kills hanging off branches in the trees where they preferred to take them. But why was he prowling around the tree? Surely he had known I was there.

"I quickly came to two conclusions, I could either climb back up the tree and wait for dawn, or I could try and make it back to the village about one and a half miles distant to the south. The thought of staying all night up in the tree didn't appeal to me and I had thought that the leopard had seen me and moved on, so I decided to make for the village.

"I had only gone about a mile when I saw with the torch fresh pug marks made not too long beforehand and they were heading to the village. I knew where it was going, and I knew I had to move fast in order to intercept it. The problem was that I had a lot of adrenaline in me, and it's difficult to be quiet when you are hurrying as fast as you dare to go. I paused for a minute to make sure cartridges were in the chambers and the hammer's for the triggers were set. I started again for the village, but I had scarcely gone a couple of hundred yards when I noticed in the light of the torch more fresh pug marks, but this time they had left the trail and they indicated it had returned from the village. There was no doubt about it. The beast knew I was there and was in all likelihood stalking me right at that very instant. It sent shivers down my spine and gave me a feeling I had never before experienced. The fear was overwhelming. I began shaking and picked up my pace back to the village.

"There were no sounds anywhere, very unusual for the jungle, and it made me even more uneasy. I couldn't leave the path, for it would surely put me at a disadvantage by giving away my position. Hell, it would be like ringing the dinner bell. Occasionally I would squint into the darkness, but I couldn't see a thing. I knew an attack would probably come from behind, so I was constantly turning around to try and see it. I was sweating profusely and I kept wiping my forehead to clear the perspiration. I could just barely make out the lights in the village, but it was still some distance away. I finally heard a langur call out, and it wasn't very far behind me. I knew the cat was close.

"Rounding a bend I remembered there were some ledges higher than the trail that I had passed earlier, but it was a good four-hundred yards to clear them and I had a premonition the attack would come somewhere near them. What was I to do? Should I wait for it on the path? What would be my best option? I couldn't think straight. I could only see about five yards in front of me with the help of the torchlight. I quickly looked back behind me and then I heard a twig snap off to the right side of the trail. I was already crouched low and couldn't see up the sides of the ledges.

"As I was looking down the path, something caught the corner of my eye. I quickly turned to see the leopard lunging at me, claws extended, mouth agape with a roaring hiss that would have sent the devil hiding. There was no time for anything. I reacted with my reflexes and swung my rifle up. There wasn't even time to aim. I pulled the trigger at the last moment from the hip, and as luck had it, it passed through the head of the beast killing it instantly. However, the momentum carried it onto me knocking me over. With its last lease on life it gave me this."

Winston pulled a scarf down off his neck and there were four white streaks about three inches long.

"He came at me from the right. If I weren't left handed, I wouldn't be here. Every time I think about that experience it gives me shivers up and down my spine. I can still see and taste the awful breath. It nearly cost me my life, but I've learned quite a bit from that first encounter, each encounter has given me a little more wisdom. Of course, there is the unknown. You can never predict what's going to happen, but it's the confidence and absence of fear that I have now. Now I'm not saying I'm not afraid, because I am. Hell, who wouldn't be? That's a beast out there deliberately trying to kill you! but I've learned to manage the fear much better. That's what separates the amateurs from the professionals; knowing what needs to be done in a moment of utmost critical fear and danger and being able to suppress all those emotions in order to get a good, accurate shot."

Charles had never heard the story but was completely fascinated by it.

Most villagers lived among several species of animals that were considered lethal and dangerous. Some invoked extreme fear while others seemed harmless. The mosquito may be a seemingly harmless insect, but it has been responsible for more deaths than all other animals combined. In India salt water crocodile's account for several hundreds of deaths each year, as well as the hamadryad or king cobra.

Most of the deaths result from unexpected encounters where the animal was only using self-defense as a way to survive. It was just a problem of being in the wrong place at the wrong time. Most everyone accepted this fact. These animals did not actively seek their victims or constantly feed on them for survival. Those occurrences were rare indeed.

Salt water crocs had accounted for twenty-seven deaths that year and poisonous snakes had claimed several thousand, most of which were caused by the Krait. The problem with the krait was that as it entered huts looking for mice, people were sleeping on the floor, they would mistakenly turn in their sleep only to be bitten, they would never wake up. The king cobra caused many deaths because the venom was not only toxic but injected in large amounts. News of these deaths and casualties, when spread, caused increased panic. However, additional deaths rarely involved the same animal.

Now things were different. Now there was a rogue tiger hunting humans as it's only food source. Sometimes it killed for pleasure only, leaving the uneaten corpse for family members to find and mourn over. One thing proved factual, and that was that it was an efficient killer if there ever was one. This invoked a fear in the population that other predators did not inspire.

The previous year it was widely known that the tiger had killed sixty-seven people and wounded another twelve. Most of the victims were dead within a few seconds, but some were not killed instantly, lingering on, paralyzed, having the stoic shock of a realization that they were being eaten alive. Those that survived would be handicapped for the rest of their lives.

The tiger's normal method for killing its prey was to snap its neck through a well-placed bite. The tiger was the largest of the big cats and only the South American Jaguar had a stronger bite, being able to crack the shells of the turtles they fed upon. On larger prey the tiger would clamp down on the windpipe and strangle the victim, but on humans it was different. Humans stand upright, so the cat would usually either pounce on them and clamp down on the skull, crushing it, or tear them open with teeth and claws until they were a bloody mess.

The government and its heads could not afford to look the other way. Random killings were one thing, but a rogue man-eater was another. With the kind of statistics that the Katagi man-eater was putting up, the government could not wait another minute. They had to cull the animal and as quickly as possible. Having every amateur kill every tiger in the region was bad for India as well. Princes and statesman would pay good money to hunt these beasts, but how many would be killed before the man-eater itself?

Winston was barking orders at servants as they readied for what seemed like a month-long expedition into the Himalayas. He planned on taking along two servants including his tracker which he had sent for already with instructions to meet him at Linblad on route. Kinta was a trusted servant of Winston's who had been with him for more than twenty years. Not only was he a great cook but he was also a likable fellow. It was apparent at once that Winston treated him with the utmost respect, and it seemed Kinta followed every order with exactness but also had a foreknowledge of what was needed. He didn't speak any English except for a few words and continually called Winston "Sahib."

Charles helped pack that night as they would leave for the train station in the morning. After all necessary business was taken care of Winston asked Charles if he was up to the trip. He pointed out that if he was afraid or felt he couldn't be counted on, he needed to know now because their lives may very well depend on the support of the one another. Charles, never one to back down from a challenge or a fight, felt he was capable and told Winston he had nothing to worry about.

Winston's reply was, "I'm not sure how long this is going to take but I'd like you to see it through with me to the end. The monsoons will be here in two months time. If we don't get it by then we'll have to wait till the rains end. The cover will just be too dense and we'll never have time to get a shot even if we see it, so we're going to have to give it everything we have."

Charles realized he was starting to relish the adventure and thought perhaps he had been involved at his desk for too long. Winston told Charles again not to worry about things and that with some luck they could be back in a fortnight.

If Charles knew what he was about to embark on he would have resigned right then.

The royal Bengal tiger had traveled only a short distance since its last kill, but it was on the prowl again already feeling the pains of hunger. Although it yearned for human flesh there was none to be found where it was at. The bamboo clumps and dense vegetation gave it the perfect disguise as it constantly looked for anything to eat. It came to an open clearing where there was a small waterhole. It noticed some sambar coming down to drink. Although this deer species was large, it didn't pose any problem for a tiger. It began to stalk its prey. Slowly, taking all the time in the world, it crept ever closer always stopping when a sambar raised its head. It would slowly raise its head every few steps to make sure that the deer hadn't moved. Finally, after what seemed like an eternity it was within twenty-five feet of the closest sambar. With no cover left it was as close as it could get. It crouched lower getting ready for the last lunge and waiting for the opportune time when the sambar had its head down drinking. When it did the tiger broke cover and bounded towards the deer in just a few leaps, it had covered half the open distance before the deer discovered what was happening. The deer nearest was a marvelous stag with impressive antlers, it began bounding away with wide eyes, realizing its very life was hanging by a thread. By following the yellow and orange flash it instinctively knew it was a tiger. Every muscle was trained and determined to escape what was bearing down on it. The big tiger was gaining with each leap and when it was within eight feet, it lunged at the stag.

A well-placed maneuver to the left or right could have achieved a getaway but seeing the flash coming, the stag was running a straight course. The tiger was on it in seconds and the momentum carried them both to the marshy ground. The cat had missed the jugular and now they both struggled to their feet. The sambar was first and was starting to get away, but the tiger had few matches for speed at short distances and was on the sambar's lower back in no time. It reached up with its forepaws and raked the back of the deer with its claws fully extended, bringing bits of flesh off the animal with each claw. There was over six-hundred pounds bearing down on the rear of the sambar, but it remained on its feet and gave a last jump as the tiger lost its hold and came off. The big cat continued to give chase until it realized it was futile. It stood there in a foot of water realizing the mistakes it had made and the meal it had lost. The massive stag with powerful legs had managed to keep on its feet. The tiger was not used to natural prey, and the intended victim proved much more difficult than any human.

It began to retreat back into the jungle hungrier than ever, craving the human flesh it had become accustomed to. It hadn't traveled far when it realized from scent markings, that it was in the territory of another large male. A male tiger may have a range of up to seventy-five square miles and will often patrol and mark its territory by urine markings spread on trees or bushes or on well used animal paths. Any other male intruder on its territory would be expelled or face a very dangerous and real fight which would often lead to the loser sustaining a serious injury. The katagi man-eater sniffed the markings and could tell that they were no more than a few days old which would indicate that the male could possibly be within several miles. It stretched its massive body up on the tree where the scent markings were and could see the scratch marks of another large male. The resident was a indeed a large tiger, but the man-eater could reach further up the tree and started sharpening its own claws above the markings of the other ones. With the close proximity it would be very likely that they would find each other in the next couple of days.

That night as the tiger laid down it could hear the male roar, the sound traveling over the miles between them. It answered as the two drew nearer. It only took another day before the two tigers met.

It was twilight when the two finally came face to face as if two great warriors were destined to come to battle. Although the man-eater was larger, the resident tiger had not come to own this territory easily; it too was experienced. Scars were visible on its face as the two began to growl menacingly at each other with ears laid low and canines showing. Like two great boxers they began to circle in a small clearing. Both had been in this game before and it was clear they would come to have some very serious wounds. Aggressiveness was a great trait to have as a tiger or any other cat.

The resident male charged at the man-eater with everything it had. The man-eater tried to sidestep it, but with all its weight, it couldn't completely get out of the way. Both reached out with claws extended. The man-eater blocked the closest paw and was able to reach in briefly to the head with the other and let a swath go across the face of the other cat which had connected as well. It was no use biting unless a cat could get to the throat because it took too much time. Experience for both of them would lead them to use blows from the paws as much as possible. It would be like having a knife fight with five outstretched razor blades.

Within seconds they were back at each other locked in close fighting. The man-eater used timing and its weight to force the other to the ground. The other male kicked back with all four legs in succession ripping through the flesh that was bearing down on it. The man eater got off quickly but left a little distance between them. The other tiger came in again but this time the man-eater waited patiently for a well-placed blow. Using most of its weight it struck out, slightly twisting its foreleg to give more power, and knocked the other tiger down.

To the other animals in the jungle that night it sounded like the very jungle would divide asunder from the growls and roars of two animals possessed with the vilest of smells and noises as they fought for their lives. They came together a couple more times, but each time the man-eater was patient and landed more effective blows. The resident male was bleeding hard and it was decided to get out and it did quickly.

Although the man-eater was thirsty, it was exhausted and decided to lay down enjoying its victory, before finding a stream to quench its thirst. It had now gained supreme confidence that nothing was its match.

It had laid down a short distance from a well-worn path. Sleep would not be interrupted here, and the short distance would also provide ample time to get away if anyone approached. It could imagine the taste of humans and knew that it could find someone tomorrow or the next day, it was just a matter of finding the settlement and the paths leading into the jungle. It had been craving human flesh again, having been at least a week since it had last eaten, but now it needed rest.

The next day as it walked the jungle path, it became weary and moved off to find a stream somewhere to clean itself and drink. There were some deep wounds on its underbelly but it felt supreme at having vanquished the opponent from the area.

Winston, his servants and Charles were up at the crack of dawn and getting supplies organized from where they had placed them the previous day. They needed to be at the train station no later than eleven a.m., even though the trains were not known for their punctuality. They would need to cover about seven miles to get to the village where the train would leave. Winston sent a message by a local native to have his friend bring some tracking dogs to where they would depart from the train, further instructions could be obtained there. After a quick breakfast they were off traveling the small path which led to the village of Mataba.

The railway had been completed a year earlier and was one of the bright points of having British rule. It connected most parts of the country with the main villages, but the northern part of the country was another matter. The normal departure and arrival times were posted, along with the routes and fares in the rail station. Most of the main routes had newer quality steam engines and rail cars. The lesser routes had engines and cars that were in disrepair and breakdowns were common.

Since most of the recent tiger attacks had come from the northern providences, that's where they were headed. It would take two days by rail and another two days on foot or waterway, depending on where the most recent attack was, in order to get to the area. Fortunately for them there was a cool air car available that utilized a large piece of ice placed in a compartment just under the car with large vents, which brought the air up to the sitting area as the train rolled along.

They arrived at the rail station without incident and as usual the train was running late. The tickets were purchased, and the group went across the street to get something to eat. Charles was amazed at the people who gawked at Winston. Obviously, he was well known in this area and his popularity bordered on a successful arctic explorer. He wasn't bothered at all by it, but there was a sort of awe about him which made people keep their distance, yet admire the great hunter. It was apparent that the word was out that he was going to kill the man-eater and people were glad for it. There were many people who either had relatives or knew friends that were affected one way or another by the striped cat, and everyone wanted it dead, the sooner the better.

Someone mumbled something in Hindu and Winston replied back.

"Everything about this man is impressive," thought Charles. "Is there anything he is not good at?"

Charles decided to ask Winston what he thought of the Katagi man-eater.

Winston took a sip of calamanchi juice, thought hard and replied, "it will be either the easiest kill to make or the most difficult ever encountered. I don't want you to get any ideas that this is going to be a walk in the park. If it turns out to be the latter, there's a very good chance that one of us will not make it back alive."

The last sentence shook Charles to the very core, but he was no coward and was committed, like it or not.

They had finished lunch and the train had still not arrived, so Winston motioned to Charles to follow him and gave some instructions to one of his servants. They went to the edge of the village and sought out a clearing. The servant arrived a few minutes later with the hunting rifles and several bottles. Winston gave some instructions to have them set up on a log about one hundred and fifty yards away. There were six bottles set up three on each side. Winston handled Charles the rifle he would be using and the servant gave him three bullets.

"The three on the right are yours."

Charles loaded the weapon and set the iron sights on the far right bottle. He squeezed the trigger just like he had been taught in military school and the bottle broke to a thousand pieces scoring a perfect hit. With meticulous precision he cleared off the other two but the last was barely nicked.

"Not bad," Winston said, as he rattled his three off in very quick succession.

The servant ran up and set six more smaller bottles up about half the size of the others.

Winston spoke up.

"Why don't we make this interesting? I'll bet you a months wages of yours you can't do that again. However, if you lose I'll want twenty weekends while you build me a second bungalow." Winston possessed a great deal of wisdom and probably would not take a bet unless he had the odds in his favor.

Charles thought hard about it, constantly looking at the bottles. He had been in the top five of his class in marksmanship, but could he do it? There was some doubt. That was a heck of a lot of money but if he lost he would be sweating away half a year's weekends not to mention travel time. He wanted to take it, knew he could do it under normal conditions but there was just too much doubt.

He told Winston, "No thank-you."

Winston looked at him and replied, "Your wiser than I thought, however, just for fun go ahead. You and I both want to know whether you would have done it."

Another three cartridges were handed to him, and like before he nailed two of them and just barely caught the side of the third one as he slightly jerked the rifle. Winston spoke almost before the echo of the third cartridge was spent.

"It's a lot easier with no pressure. The trouble is learning to harness that pressure when it really counts. I've seen many an experienced hunter miss the monarch stag or the biggest cat they have ever seen because they have thought too long about it, wanting it, yearning for it, envisioning it, but when the time comes, nerves gets the better of them and they miss the kill shot or more often than not miss altogether. In some cases, with man-eaters, it has cost the lives of several people. If you've done it as long as I have, you'll get used to it. I've had the nerves before and it nearly cost me my life once, but after a series of experiences you learn to harness that energy, that excitement, that fear, and you suppress it, quell it. If you were to hunt man-eaters for a living, you too would overcome it."

"Do you have any advice for suppressing it in a quick lesson?" asked Charles.

"Only to remember to breathe, don't get excited, and squeeze the trigger."

They walked back to the train depot where there was a rather large crowd by this time. Soon after they arrived they could hear the train whistle in the distance. Winston's servants began to assemble the baggage near the loading dock. Winston made some last-minute purchases and he and Charles began to move over to the dock. Winston spoke as they moved closer.

"This is where it begins chap, a great adventure, not knowing the outcome, you can live a full life to the age of a hundred and you will always remember this experience as paramount. All I can promise you is hardships with a few seconds of excitement like you've never experienced before."

Then he made as if quoting an advertisement for help.

"'Wanted: young man with courage and tenacity, with a desire to rid India of the Katagi man-eater, hours long, depravedness common, danger high, safe return doubtful.' It's not too late to turn back you know."

Winston was making certain Charles was dedicated to the task at hand. Charles thought back at the consequences, gave it one last thought, and knew he could do it.

He thought about the fine line between being a coward and a hero and replied, "I'm as ready as I'll ever be and quite up to the job."

Winston smiled as that was the answer he was hoping for.

Winston said, "Relax. That cat will only eat you one bite at a time."

Both men began to laugh heartily.

The train began to slow as it pulled into the station and Winston and Charles made for the dock as people began to disembark. The air-conditioned cabin held no one as they climbed up and into the cabin. Winston's servant took care of the baggage and took his place on one of the other cars. Winston immediately sat down, stretched his feet out and put his safari hat down over his face, instantly going to sleep. Charles looked at the hat with one side pinned up and a band of tiger skin wrapped around the rest of it. The train stopped only long enough to take on passengers and to take on water for the next leg of the trip. Charles looked again at the tiger band around Winston's hat and couldn't help but think which man-eater it was from. He too put up his feet and relaxed, looking out the window at all the hustling that was going on as time seemed to stand still.

The great cat had washed itself, gotten a long drink and was again on the prowl. This time it wanted a human victim. It began by walking down one of the jungle paths that meandered through the countryside. Occasionally it would cross a stream or there would be a waterfall, and it would continue on, constantly sniffing the air, raising its whiskers for the aroma of humans.

Mile after mile ticked away.

It took quite some time but eventually it caught the unmistakable scent of a fire as someone was cooking dinner. It followed the scent until it could hear the sounds of laughter. It turned its attention to this new sound until it came to a small pool of water not far from one of the villages. In it were three young girls taking a bath although still wearing the long sun dresses which covered them. On the bank was an older man with a white beard and turban. He had a musket which must have been at least a hundred years old. Where he had obtained it was anyone's guess.

The tiger crept closer and got to a point where it could see the pool and the young girls in it. One of the girls thought she had seen some rustling in the tall grass, but the others were teasing her saying it was the Katagi man-eater over there.

The older man spoke up, "Don't joke about such things."

The girls quieted down and began to splash on one another. The tiger crept ever closer, moving slowly with each step. It was able to see the old man as well and crouched down with its tongue rasping outside its mouth at the succulent meal it was witnessing. It didn't want to take a chance with the guard there. It waited, bidding its time, until one of the girls emerged from the water and walked up onto the bank. There were some dry clothes there. Some words were exchanged as she quickly got into them while the old man's head was turned. One of the other girls was getting out too. The remaining girl looked over into the vegetation and there, staring at her with yellow eyes narrowed to slits, was death itself. The fear paralyzed her. Just then the cat burst upon the scene, leaping from the opposite bank into the stream as if the very gates of hell had burst open. It gave a blood curdling roar as water seemed to go everywhere.

The old man turned around and froze for a second as the beast knocked the remaining girl senseless and picked her up in its jaws with blood dripping into the once clear water. The cat carried the girl effortlessly as it quickly turned around and made for the jungle. The old man regained his wits and fired his ancient musket at the cat and the girl. Pellets stung the striped cat as it dropped the girl and turned around giving another snarl that sent the old man backward, tripping over a vine. He lost his turban but continued to run with the girls in the direction of the village raising a cry for help along the way. There was nothing to do for the victim. She was dead from the initial blow.

The cat dragged her down the trail for awhile and then pulled her into the thick brush to enjoy its meal. The flesh was soft and tender and although there was not a lot of meat there was enough.

Back at the village hysteria was rampant. Everyone was seeking shelter in their huts. The wailing and moaning from the mother of the lost daughter could be heard throughout the village. Torches were lit and placed outside the huts. Fear was on the face of everyone there. Even the bravest soul shirked at the thought of venturing outside the village. A large bonfire was built in the middle of the village in the hopes of keeping the man-eater at bay. Sleep was out of the question as families huddled together in their respective huts. The curfew had been set by the cat and no-one challenged it. It was only the big cats who had turned man-eaters that were the only animals driven to pursue humans relentlessly for food. Just as a human was possessed with certain talents and intelligence, so it was in the animal kingdom, and it seemed this cat not only had the intelligence but also the demonic attitude that possesses every murderer. When it prowled the jungle, a village, a road, it held its own in knowing it feared nothing. Not even the hunters that were previously sent to kill it managed to avert the fear. It out-maneuvered them, out-thought them. It was as if it possessed a greater intelligence; one equal with man. It was the most lethal killing machine the earth had known, and India was its footstool. Now it was at its peak and had yet to be properly challenged.

The office of natural resources was beginning to get more and more pressure from the Viceroy to remove the problem of the man-eater and George was nearing exhaustion from anxiety and pressure. No word had been sent from Charles since he had left, and it seemed more and more people were protesting outside the office to do something about the man-eater. Things were explained that they were doing all that they could but the people continued to harangue the office. The viceroy was in a constant bad mood, always checking the mail for any news of progress made. He thought about sending some detachment from the military up to handle it, but when he mentioned it to his cabinet they thought that there may be more accidents if they went into the jungle with so many firearms. He looked at some of the portraits of former viceroys and thought of the difficulties they had in dealing with their own problems. Somehow, they had gotten through it all. Some of their problems were just as great, but they had persevered. Perhaps he could too. But then the negative thoughts took stage and he thought about setbacks and having to explain to his superiors why he had failed. He didn't have a lot of confidence in himself and was rarely at the office. Somehow dinner balls or tiger hunts were always on the agenda and he was milking the country out of some serious revenue. All his shoes and clothes were imported from London as he wore hardly anything that was made locally.

It was getting time for lunch and he pushed the thoughts aside to focus on what was being brought to him. He had gained quite a bit of weight since he arrived in India, some of which was due to indulgences, but some was the result of the problems he was facing and how he had to handle them. His wife was equally plump, but the two seemed destined for one another. No one seemed to like them but themselves. She treated the natives like dirt and couldn't wait until they left the dreadful country and the god-forsaken heat. He was indifferent to the locals and never acknowledging them as equals.

While the viceroy was eating lunch the mail had arrived from England. He had instructed his servants to interrupt him with any news at all. One particular letter had the royal seal affixed, and he quickly retired to his office to read it. It was from the House of Commons asking him how the situation with the Katagi man-eater was coming and requesting an update immediately. It seemed a little more stern than the last one he had received two months ago. It took letters about two months to arrive from England and it was apparent that they had received some news, other than his, to warrant such a reply. He could only think that someone was leaking information, but who could it be? He was doing all that he thought he could and began thinking deeply about how he was going to respond. As he tried to think, his mind kept creeping back to who it might be that was leaking the information. He could order a censor on all outgoing mail, but somehow he thought that would be found out as well. Besides it would be much too difficult to control all ports. He had to think of a way to pacify the House of Commons and let them know that he had everything under control. He read the letter again trying to read between the lines. It was starting to give him a headache. He returned to lunch but only ate sparingly picking at a few bits of mango and grapes. He eventually ordered in a scribe to dictate a letter. He also inquired as to the departure dates of the soonest ship to sail for England, so he could make a reply as quickly as possible. Other matters, he had been able to solve with relative ease but this one was proving to be more of a challenge. However, if he could possibly solve it quickly he may be promoted. In the meantime the protestors should be dealt with immediately. He ordered some gendarmes to keep the gates to the Office of Natural Disasters clear of protesters.

As the slow train rolled away mile after mile, Charles looked out at the countryside and how beautiful it was. The whole country was a green paradise with an occasional river or lake to be seen. You could also catch glimpses of wildlife as well. Sometimes the trees or vines were so close that you could see them touch the train as it rambled on. The cool breeze would come up through the floor and cool the compartment.

It wasn't long before Charles found himself dozing off as the rails made a constant drone like a metronome which put him to sleep. Winston woke him up by kicking his feet down off the bench. Winston went straight for the basin of water and quickly undid his scarf from around his neck and dipped some water onto it, then re-wrapped it around his neck. He mentioned to Charles that he had requested his tracker come to this car where they were to discuss the upcoming strategy concerning killing the man-eater. Charles was still wiping his eyes as he pulled his pocket watch from his pocket and realized he had slept longer than he had thought.

Within minutes Winston's servant had arrived and they all sat down around a table in the train car. Winston pulled out a folded map, which was very detailed, and showed the northern providences. It was as good as the ones Charles had seen in his offices and he wondered how much it must have cost. Some of the markings were in Hindu and Charles didn't understand them.

Winston pointed to the village of Cirimbe and indicated that the most recent attack had come from there. He mentioned that three girls were bathing in a river when the man-eater attacked. He said that had been two days ago and he would expect another attack within a couple of days. He pointed to another village and said that the attack before that one was here, and it truly showed a western migration. He then took out a small pencil with a string attached to it and put the end of the small string on the Cirimbe village and traced a perfect circle around it. He said that this represented a one-hundred mile radius which was the likely territory that the Katagi man-eater could cover in a fortnight.

"Now, if we believe it will continue in a western direction we should set up shop here, in Hatawi. From there we will wait until the next attack and direct our efforts from there. It is near a logging village and we should be able to utilize some of the trained elephants for a flush. Unfortunately, Hatawi is in a very remote part of the empire here in India, and it will take us another three days overland to get there once we depart from the train. There is a real chance we may miss the next attack, and in addition to that, we will be in the possible area where it is and thereby our party may be vulnerable to attack. Does anyone have anything to add?" asked Winston.

Charles spoke up.

"How many locals will be required for the flush?"

"Well we'll need at least fifty men and we might have to ask several villages for help. As mentioned, it's very primitive country up there and we can't expect a lot of help. We'll have to ascertain the situation once we get there."

Another question was raised by Winston's servant who had asked in his local tongue if the most recent deaths could be the work of a second man-eater.

Winston explained the question and then answered that he doubted it, but it was not altogether impossible.

Winston spoke again.

"It's extremely thick cover out there following the monsoons. If you see the man-eater it will likely only be for a brief moment, therefore, you must be ready with your gun at all times and ready for the opportunity. If we're lucky we'll get one good shot and we need to make the best of it."

With that said, Winston folded up the map and put it in one of his over-sized shirt pockets.

"We'll have to hire a few porters once we get off. They will need to watch over the Indian tracking dogs I have brought along."

The dogs were a unique breed that originally were bred in Italy, they were bred for one purpose only: to track game, and only hound dogs were better at it.

"It's going to be a long haul and we'll have to cover close to thirty-five miles each day."

Charles mentioned that he would need to cable his office once they arrived at the rail departure station since that would be the last area with a telegraph.

Just then Winston's servant arrived with cold glasses of Calamanchi juice and it was a welcome respite.

Charles glanced over at Winston's leg which had a small knife lashed to it. Its handle was made from Rhino horn and was black as the night. On its handle was carved Winston's name. From what he could see of it sheathed it was a beautiful piece.

Charles felt his own knife, a much smaller one, on his side. A fine piece itself, carved from obsidian.

Winston sat down and stuffed and lit his pipe, the aroma filling the cabin.

They had small talk for another hour or so, speaking of England, India and various political topics. The train continued to roll on.

Winston spoke up again.

"So, Charles why did you really accept my demand to come with me? It couldn't have been because you enjoy the safety of the city. Is there a young woman you need to get away from for a couple of months?"

"No," replied Charles as he looked away out to the countryside.

A paused moment later he said, "I guess I just wanted something different. Something with danger, and a way to do some good for the country perhaps."

"You're not vain, are you?" asked Winston.

"No, I don't think so .It just seemed like I could help out and at the same time get away from the George and the office."

"Yeah, I can see that. You know, I've never really gotten along with the sea cow that wears a suit. I don't see how he can effectively run the country, let alone keep all the Dwains in check."

Changing the subject Charles asked again about the elusiveness of the Katagi man-eater. Winston replied, looking Charles straight into his eyes.

"There's no illusion here and I'll be frank, I believe it will kill someone in our party, maybe more."

He continued slowly, "It hasn't survived this long by pure luck. No, this is a very intelligent cat indeed, and if we expect to pull this off we're going to have to be at the top of our game. It's just a matter of numbers. We're going right after it, into the heart of where it was last seen. It could be you, it could be me. We don't know, but someone is likely to die. And if not us, how many more before it's stopped? Now we may get lucky of course and get it the first week, but I've learned never to underestimate these cats."

Winston had earlier dispatched a runner to have Jano bring his dogs to the rail station the day they planned to arrive. Jano had offered to care for Winston's dogs for him and Winston gave him a small allowance to do so. He only used the dogs for hunting, and they were also excellent trackers, especially his favorite named Badge.

By eleven a.m. the following day the train began to roll to a stop at their desired station. It was as far north as the rail line went and the village was bustling although small. Winston's servant woke him from a long slumber and told him that they were at Tibulo. Winston gave some quick instructions to have the luggage unloaded and to hire two additional porters to carry the gear. They were to meet after lunch at the trail leading north out of the village.

There was a wire station in the village and Winston mentioned to Charles that he might want to get a last dispatch off since they would be in primitive country from here on out.

"I'll meet you at the Tindahahn across the street from the station when you're done."

"Right," replied Charles and off he went.

Winston's servants were busy unloading supplies and finding help to organize the gear. The train started to take on water as everyone busied themselves.

Winston put on his hunting jacket, which was rolled up on the sleeves, and stepped off the train. He strode right over to the Tindahahn and began to order some buffalo meat cooked on small bamboo spears over charcoaled coconut husks. The smell was making everyone's mouths water.

He moved outside on the boarded sidewalk and took a seat at one of the tables with a nepa leaf umbrella shading the sun. There was a small railing that he put his feet on and leaned back in his chair. It was going to be a hot one, he could already tell.

Soon Charles joined him and they enjoyed their calamanchi juice while waiting for lunch. Charles asked how far they were going today. Winston said that he hoped to get to Coetaia by sundown. It was nearly fifteen miles away, mostly uphill.

"Hopefully we'll be able to start as soon as we've eaten."

They chomped down the food once it arrived and they enjoyed the change from the train's menus.

Soon Winston's servant showed up and said that they had two porters for the next leg of the journey and asked when they would be getting started. Winston asked if he had eaten anything yet and the servant answered no. Winston told him to get something and they would leave as soon as he had eaten as he handed his servant some money.

While they were waiting, they strolled into the dry goods store and Winston saw a beautiful waterbuck antelope belt with the white and brown fur tanned and sewn on the outside. He bought it and immediately took off his old one and gave it to someone out in the street who seemed pleased to be the recipient. The store was glad to sell the item as it was expensive, and no one had purchased one in over two months.

Winston and Charles began to make their way out of the village and towards the path leading north. Winston's servant and porters showed up shortly afterwards and they started hiking towards the small village. It was about one in the afternoon and the intense heat began to make sweat pour down from their foreheads as they moved slowly along the path. The servants were setting a regular pace as the sun began to rise in the sky. Occasionally they would pass under a canopy of trees which sheltered them from the sun's rays. The trail was well traveled with beautiful views of the lush green jungle and an occasional stream meandering through the countryside. At times one was required to cross a stream on a primitive bamboo bridge which creaked with the weight of each person. There was an abundance of wildlife, which on occasion could be seen in the meadows and at other locations. The animals would spring from cover as they approached, more startled than anything. It made the walk a lot more enjoyable despite the heat. Winston commented on the lack of people on the trail as they would normally have seen several by now, but the nearness of the man-eater dictated that few ventured out, especially on trails like the one they were on.

After a few hours they met a group coming from the village and Winston asked them if they knew of any recent news of the Katagi man-eater. They replied that they did, but the news was a week old and Winston had already heard the majority of it. They were traveling together for protection with a group of about ten individuals. Some of the porters were worried about the man-eater but the pay had been too good to pass up. They could feed their family for an entire month for the wages of ferrying supplies in a week. It was too lucrative. The big cat had not killed in over a week and the thought was on everyone's mind whether or not they were walking right into a trap. No one seemed to want to talk about it. With no one vocalizing their fears, concerns showed on every face and in the behaviors of those in the group, one could see them looking into the dense foliage or around corners.

Winston continued to lead on at a regular pace, not showing any fear or discomfort. He would occasional shift his gun to the opposite shoulder. He was in great shape and Charles marveled how fit he was for his age.

"Obviously, he thought, "he must work out on a regular basis."

Sweat continued to form on Charles forehead as he continued to wipe it away with his handkerchief. He would at times look up at the sun and shade his eyes. The few stream crossings offered cool water to drench a head in or get a long cool drink. Sometimes one could see a tree python hanging from the trees or vines that dotted the trail.

As they hiked through the jungle, Winston explained that in most cases the man-eater attacked only single, isolated victims, but within the last year it had become more brazen and daring and had come upon small groups and in bright daylight. It seemed that it was not afraid of anything anymore, yet still possessed a keen sense of intelligence whenever it did kill. This bold new brashness was responsible for the fear that now permeated all of India. Stories of the man-eater were circulated, and most were not true, but they still contributed to the paranoia. The porters had heard many of the stories, and they wondered if they would be the next victim. Every sound they encountered along the path would arouse suspicion.

The miles ticked away as the sun gradually fell into the horizon. They were anxious to reach the village before nightfall as undoubtedly the porters would be frazzled with their nerves. Sometimes, as they would cross a river or small stream, they would see leopard tracks or pug marks in the soft mud. This would incite some consternation among the group until Winston would indicate that the pug marks were too small for the tiger. Even with these reassurances, the group of porters were still agitated.

They were within a few miles of Coataia when darkness fell and with it all the sounds of nocturnal animals enveloped the surrounding jungle. Occasionally one could hear the roar of a leopard or tiger in the distance. A few torches were lit to guide the way as they continued on the path. The moon was not up as of yet and darkness prevailed everywhere. Winston had to admit that they were extremely vulnerable in the darkness as a tiger could kill at will and it would be near impossible to follow. They would round a bend and look anxiously for the lights of the village ahead. Sometimes vines which they could have easily seen in the daylight would brush their faces and cause them to jump back or to curse. Although the heat had abated, the humidity was constant as they continued to perspire with the quickened pace. Winston wanted to send some of the men forward to begin preparations for dinner and sleeping but thought that it was better to stay together. Sometimes one person or another would hit their foot on a root or a rock which caused considerable pain. They finally came to a point where they could see the lights of the village and were required to cross one last stream. Winston held one of the torches while everyone looked where to put their feet. Within another half hour they were safely within the village and asking where they could procure sleeping quarters and food.

Winston sat down and let his guide make the necessary arrangements as he usually did. Charles joined him, as they were both tired from the march. They ate some of the dried antelope jerky they had packed as they waited for word from the guide. The guide came back and informed Winston that the village chief insisted that they dine with him for the evening meal. The long trek had made them all ravenous.

Winston's reputation had preceded him, and they sat down on cushions to a scrumptious meal with roasted water buffalo, fresh fruit, river shrimp and a special custard. The village chief asked Winston questions about the man-eater, and he, in turn, asked questions about the last known whereabouts of the tiger. They were now close to the area of the last victim and no doubt everyone was one edge. The arrival of Winston and his party did give some hope to the people, but they were scared none the less.

Winston's party was pampered with every sort of convenience that could be obtained in that region. They were provided with separate huts that the villagers vacated, and they were fed sumptuous meals and waited on day and night.

Following dinner Winston was noticeably dozing off and excused himself.

They were close enough now that they would have to wait for another attack to see which way the tiger was heading and to get a little closer. That attack was expected any day. They could still stake out this current village in hopes the man-eater was close.

Charles stayed up a little later than Winston, but also soon felt the effects of exhaustion and retired to bed.

The hut was well furnished with wicker chairs, a table and mosquito nets for Winston and Charles. Charles could hear Winston snoring lightly under his net.

Early the next morning they were awakened with another fine breakfast and an invitation to go on a pheasant hunt with some of the local leaders. Winston had accepted the offer because they still needed more precise information on where the tiger was and it would be considered rude to refuse such an offer. The pheasant hunting in this region of the country was supposed to be fantastic.

The locals only had two shotguns so one was given to Winston and the other was given to a local tribesman named Cho-Cho who happened to be the best shot in that region. It looked like it was turning into some sort of shooting competition to Charles. The locals were saddling up four work elephants to be used in the hunt. Behind the scenes there was some sort of organized gambling going on. They explained to Winston that he would have one mount and the local magistrate another with judges on the other two. The rules were explained to Winston and he indicated that he understood them.

The elephants were working beasts which had been used to haul timber in that region over to the Fataloe river where they were floated down to a logging camp and then into a larger river and on to the coast where they were processed for export.

When the elephants and contestants were ready, the trainers had the large beasts drop to one knee and the men mounted into the mahout by first stepping onto the knee and then climbing into the basket. The great beasts then arose and started for the bush to await the blow of the horn.

They would be out in the field for approximately two hours after which the horn would blow again signaling the end of the hunt. The game shot would then be counted, and a winner declared. The locals took the event very seriously, and due to the gambling that was established in the logging community, many were fronting their money. Most bets were placed for the local village leader. Winston had put up a large sum for he hated to lose. The elephants started for the dense foliage just outside the village. They arrived within ten minutes and waited there for the horn to blow.

Normally a hunt like this would involve days or weeks shooting anything that moved. The bag may include deer, antelope, or perhaps a leopard or tiger, but due to importance of the man-eater, the hunt was reduced to a couple of hours and limited to fowl.

Once they were in the tall grass those with guns loaded up. Within minutes the horn sounded and the hunt was on. The beaters kept close to the elephants helping the hunters by making noise in order to send fowl into flight. Almost immediately five peafowl flew up and Winston unloaded both barrels in succession as two peafowl dropped to the ground. They were gathered up and noted by the judges. Within minutes shots broke out from the magistrate as two more peafowl were downed. Cho-Cho looked over to Winston and, as the sun caught his gold teeth, one could tell he had a very large smile on his face as he knew they were in for a great contest.

Birds of all kinds would occasionally take flight. Both Winston and Cho were very selective on which birds they aimed at and which shots they took, almost always downing the bird closest, knowing that it was a better shot than the birds further away.

Both groups realized it was going to be close and that it might come down to which group flushed the most birds.

The first hour was relatively even as Winston had bagged thirty-two birds to Cho-Cho's thirty-five. Occasionally Charles would be required to duck as Winston yelled out for him to move in order to get a shot off. Charles thought that Winston was getting hyped up too much and realized how badly he wanted the win. Both of the barrels were getting warm about an hour and a half into the match. Finally, the elephants and the people began to funnel into a valley bringing them closer together. There were still more shots that rang out and by now it was too close to call. Winston looked over to Cho-Cho and for a brief moment their eyes met, and smiles were exchanged as they returned to the chase. This time a chinese pheasant flew up and was closest to Cho-Cho, he fired but it was a rare miss. The bird was moving further away when Winston decided to take a very long shot. He fired and the bird went down. It was an astonishing feat considering the distance involved. Cho looked over at Winston and looked astonished.

Charles said to Winston, "Nice shot, buffalo Bill!"

Winston just laughed and considered it a very lucky shot.

A few more birds were taken before the bell rang out ending the competition.

The elephants began heading back to the village with the outcome still in doubt. Winston had indeed performed better during the last half hour of the competition due to more birds being flushed, but it was going to be close.

The locals were already talking among themselves about the incredible shot that Winston had made. It had been a great hunt and it was very beneficial for Charles who began to relax a little, having been wound tight as a violin. When they got back to the village the judges began to empty the booty on some bamboo tables and count the birds. When the birds had been tallied a judge arose and began to announce the outcome.

"Before we announce the winner of the competition we would like to thank Winston Jamison for accepting the invitation for such a meet. Now as far as we know the amount of birds downed by Winston totaled forty-three birds and from what I am told one of those was quite a shot. The total for Cho-Cho has amounted to forty-nine birds."

The crowd that had gathered screamed with excitement as Winston went over to congratulate Cho on such a fine match. Surely Cho was a natural in an area that had limited supplies and income for shells. It was a great sacrifice for the locals to supply such means. Winston gave them enough to pay for the lot.

It was a great match for the locals and, although Cho-Cho had won the match, it was still questioned who was the better shot after seeing Winston make such an outstanding kill.

Everyone involved sat down to a sumptuous lunch that had been prepared for them. Winston had asked if he could visit the last victims kill spot since he would need to make plasters of the pug marks for identification. He was told that a young man could lead him to the spot that was approximately twelve miles away as soon as he liked. He was also told that the pug marks were very large, and they would be dealing with a very large tiger. Winston informed the magistrate that he would like to inspect them as soon as possible. Perhaps after lunch if it would be alright. The magistrate indicated that their resources, though small, were at his disposal and bowed his head to Winston. Although the local magistrate had won the bird competition, he knew that the tiger was Winston's specialty and respected him immensely for what he had previously done and what he could do now. He asked him if there was anything else they could do for Winston. Winston replied that they would likely need to organize a beat if it was discovered that the cat was still in the area. The Magistrate indicated again that they would do whatever was necessary in order to get rid of the menace.

Winston wolfed down his lunch as quickly as politically possible without insult and indicated that he would need to start as soon as possible in order to get to the last attack site and examine the pug marks. A young man was already ready to go, with previous instructions when they set out.

Winston went with his servant and the guide as Charles waited until they got back either late that night or possibly in the morning, depending on how long it took them. There was a small chance that the cat was still in the area but, based on previous kills, it was unlikely as the striped cat usually moved on, rarely staying in one place too long. Winston brought along his gun just in case as he always did. They moved at a quick pace in the heat of the day and just before sundown they found where the kill had taken place. Usually, it was common for tigers to hang around a kill for several days while continuing to feed on the victim. But the man-eater had less meat to deal with on humans and as a result it usually ate its prey in one sitting and never or rarely returned unless the victim was a portly soul which was indeed a rarity in India.

The first thing that Winston noticed was how immense the pug marks were for this tiger. In all the years he had hunted them he had never seen such large pug marks. He judged from the width and depth of the tracks that the beast would likely be a new record in and of itself, possibly tipping the scales at six-hundred and seventy pounds and probably ten feet over curves on its length. This would be both beneficial and difficult because it obviously presented a slightly larger target to shoot at, but it would also be more powerful having survived that long to grow to its fullest proportions.

They found a good pug mark in which to make a cast, and when they extracted it Winston measured it at eight inches across. With the claws extended there was no doubt that one hit from a paw like that could create enough openings in a body to make something bleed to death if they hadn't already died from fright.

Winston's servant had followed the tracks a little ways when he came running back to Winston out of breath. He indicated that he had found new pug marks from the same tiger indicating that it was still in the area. At least, it had been there since that morning, which is how old he estimated the tracks to be. The servant was never off by much when it came to these matters, and Winston quickly pulled the hammers back on his gun after ensuring it was loaded. They were in a difficult situation as it was beginning to grow dark and the cat could possibly be waiting for just that before attacking. Winston got a bad feeling about the whole idea and asked in what direction the tracks were going. The servant followed them just briefly enough to know that they were heading northwest.

Winston thought it prudent to retreat with the darkness as they began to make their way back to Coataia. Winston knew that if the tiger was still in the area it would attack at the first sign of darkness, which was approaching rapidly. They were trying to put as much distance between them and the victim's area as possible.

Winston was amazed how the cat had stuck around for nearly a week and a half.

"There must be a reason," he thought to himself.

Perhaps the killings were easier here or maybe there was an abundance of prey. He didn't know. All he knew for sure was that his heart rate had jumped up to nearly a hundred and twenty beats per minute.

Winston, his servant and the boy were moving as quickly as possible. Night had now overtaken them and they had lit their torches which gave some light into the darkness. Even more disconcerting to them was a tiger's roar heard only a few miles away. If it was the man-eater, returned to the scene of the last victim, it would no doubt pick up the scent of new prey and it would be a race to see who would become victims or who would get to the safety of the village.

Winston had to slow down the pace several times because they simply could not jog the remaining ten miles and still be vigilant of the tiger. Every noise the jungle made was amplified due to the high alert they were on. Winston still had his cartridges chambered in the gun as his hands continued to perspire around the stock, and now he had it off his shoulder in anticipation of a quick defensive shot. Several times he caught himself shining the torch back on the trail behind them.

Charles was relaxing back at Coataia when a runner came running up to the village well after dark. There had been another killing that afternoon, this time in Sanari. This was only a short distance of fifteen miles away. It had taken an incredible amount of courage for this man to get through the jungle paths in order get word to Winston, who wasn't back yet.

What was Charles to do? He thought about it and was very uncomfortable with the whole idea. He had no experience with man-eaters, and he could very well be the next victim. However, it seemed time was of the essence. If they could somehow find out which valley it was in they could organize a beat and likely get a good shot at it.

Charles made a quick decision that there was nothing they could do that night, but they would immediately leave first thing in the morning with or without Winston. Deep inside Charles was hoping that Winston would be back as planned that night.

Charles knew that they would be traveling in the area of the attack and there would be a very good chance that the tiger would still be there. This was what he had come for, the excitement, but it was very nervy for him. He had to struggle to control his emotions and fear as Winston had instructed him.

After he had time to think about it he realized he had made the correct choice. To have ventured over to Sanari in the dead of night, even with a force of men, would have been suicidal. All he could do was to wait for Winston to return.

It was about one in the morning when the torches of Winston's party could be seen just outside the village. They were exhausted and when they finally brought their heavy feet into the village, Charles wasted no time in filling Winston in on the situation. Winston told Charles to get the village leader, ready for a meeting while he washed up.

Everyone was assembled in Cho's hut, which was large enough to accommodate a host of people. By the light of a few candles Winston got out the map and asked the runner exactly where the victim was killed. The man didn't know how to read maps and so they began to ask him questions about the terrain and how far from the village the attack had taken place. After several questions there was no doubt as to where they were looking on the map. Winston said that there was a very good chance it would be sleeping off the meal the next day, and it would likely head to a place of water for a drink first thing in the morning. He explained that this gave them an incredible piece of luck.

Winston spoke up again grabbing his small backpack.

"Just so you know what we are dealing with."

And saying that, he pulled out a plaster of paris cast of the pug mark. There was astonishment all around.

Charles picked it up and said, looking at Winston, "Good lord! How big do you reckon he is?"

"At least ten foot over the curves, maybe bigger. But I'll tell you this, we won't have a hard time identifying this animal. It's a one of a kind."

Charles passed the cast around for the others to see. As each individual received it, he zoned out of the discussion, just staring at the cast.

Winston spoke again, "I believe we are dealing with a very intelligent creature which most likely turned man-eater from a gunshot wound or porcupine quill, but it really doesn't matter because it's been living good for too long. It may take a little more to bring this one down, but we've got to do it. Don't even think about shirking from your duty here. It's probable that one or more of us will be killed, but you must perform your duty well enough for us to get a shot. That is the only way we will succeed. If you succeed, glory and honor await you. I know, for I have experienced it and don't care for it, but all the accolades can be yours for a moment of courage, of temerity, of vigilance. Don't let anyone forget that we are going to succeed, and to do so will take the courage and determination of every person taking part henceforth. You will need to dig a little deeper to put aside fear and find courage. You are all here for a reason. I have handpicked each of you based on your abilities, if, and *only* if, we work together can we hope to end this menace once and for all. I've told you before that this is a dangerous assignment. There's no other way to put it. You may be mauled or killed or you may come out of the mess unscathed, focus on the task at hand and do it. We cannot have any slip ups. God help us all come tomorrow. I'll expect to leave around four in the morning .Be ready."

He looked to Cho and mentioned that he thought they would have a better chance surprising the tiger, so they needn't worry about rounding up beaters. Cho understood.

One final look around and he said, "We have a job to do so get some sleep and be ready in the morning."

There was a silence from the group as Winston left to get some sleep. He walked away with a saunter, like a man with a mission and all the confidence to boot.

There were some last-minute arrangements being made but this was the start of it. The group would be jumping right into the fire by tomorrow.

Charles was concerned for Winston, he had hiked a tremendous distance the last couple of days and seemed fatigued. If he hiked again early in the morning how was he going to be when they got to the valley where the tiger was? He expressed his thoughts to no one, but he wondered.

The group went to bed and it seemed only hours before Winston's servant woke everyone up and gave them hot tea with bread and honey. They would be leaving in a matter of minutes in hopes of reaching the valley in the morning when the cat would likely need a drink from the river in the valley.

Winston was up and ready and with his gun on his shoulder. He mentioned to Charles that he should have his as well and instructed him to chamber a round once light hit because he didn't want the sound scaring off the cat. They left immediately with all men tired, but they couldn't let a chance like this get away. There was a three-quarter moon which illuminated the jungle somewhat. Luckily for them the trail leaving the village was, for the most part, a gradual decline into the lower valleys. They had lighted torches and were lead by the messenger who had come the previous day, his job being to identify the area where the victim was killed and to identify the valley where Winston thought the cat would be. Everyone's heart was skipping a beat or two even though they still had some distance to cover. On and on they marched like some military detachment going forth into battle or to report to some commanding officer. Not many words were spoken. Everyone knew the danger and kept his thoughts to himself. There was no use trying to be quiet. They were trying to make as much distance as possible in the time that they had. But there would be more astonishing news when they approached the village. It appeared that the cat, which had not gotten enough to eat from its most recent victim who was old and had little meat, had made an effort to get another victim the previous night. Having tried in vain to get more, it became ravenous wanting another human.

The villagers had ringed the village with torches put on bamboo stakes which stood to the height of a man. They were spread about fifteen feet apart and the villagers hoped that it would keep the cat away from the village. The ring of fire kept everyone feeling a little safer. Of course, the torches only lasted about six hours being wrapped and soaked with a treatment of sap and lamp oil. But no one could be convinced to soak them again and re-light them. To do so, would be a suicidal mission. But during the night the striped cat was again on the prowl and the little inconveniences proved to be of no worth.

The beast quickly ran into the perimeter of the village between two of the torches that were still lit. It could smell the flesh of humans, being acquainted with it over the years and possessing a smell several times greater than man. It was around two a.m. and most people were already asleep. The cat surveyed the area close to ten minutes before even making a move. It was unusual to strike near the same area of its last kill and it was taking no chances. Slowly it began to prowl the area going from cover to cover. The doors and windows of each hut were closed or barricaded. At last the tiger came to a hut that was slightly smaller than the rest, and it could smell the scent of a man inside. It circled the hut once and found there was no easy entrance.

Most of the huts in this region of India were simple nepa huts made with fronds of palm trees that were prevalent throughout the country. The roof and outer structure were made from bamboo with the nepa leaves woven together to form the walls and the roof. There wasn't a lot of strength to them, but they did keep the occupants dry and warm. The cat could sense that the wall was weak as it exerted some strength in pushing up against it. The old man inside was nearly deaf and so could not hear anything that was happening on the outside. But the hut began to move ever so slightly as force was applied to it which awoke the man who thought there was a slight earthquake happening. Within seconds he began to realize that it was not an earthquake but something trying to get in. The man looked for his lamp and lit it with a shaking hand and began to look to see where the creaks were coming from. At that point when he shined the light in the direction of the sound, his body shaking, he looked right into the face of the biggest tiger he had ever seen. For a brief second they both looked at each other. A second later the tiger's ears rolled back as its mouth came open showing a perfect set of canines at least four inches long with saliva dripping off each one. A low, piercing growl began to emanate from the dark recess of its throat, and with it every hair on its thick neck began to stand on end making it appear even larger than it was.

The man turned frantically and tried to clear the barricaded door, but it was of no use. His machete was lying near the door but in his hysterical state he didn't think to use it. He was fumbling and tripping over things in order to get out and into the safety of another hut where someone may have a gun. The cat was by now boring a larger hole with each passing second as nepa fronds and bamboo were being sent everywhere. The old man was just pulling off the leather latch to the door when a powerful swath came across the back of his neck. It whirled him around and he looked with the fear of the damned at the sight of a huge head coming down on his own. With a bite force of over twelve hundred pounds per square inch the tiger crushed the old man's skull with ease as the hapless victim died almost instantly.

By this time the villagers had awoken to the sounds of barking dogs. Everyone was up now and knew with an uncertain premonition that something was definitely awry. The only possibility was that the striped cat had returned to the village and claimed another victim. Even those with guns delayed coming out of their huts until enough courage was gathered to see what had happened. Some would peek outside their huts to try and see anything at all, but although there was still a three –quarters of a moon in the cool night it didn't illuminate much. Then a woman peeking through a fist sized hole saw something move in the shadows. It moved again into the moonlight where she could see a body being dragged across the ground by a huge beast. The cat rested for a bit and looked around. There was still a little bit of steam exiting from the crushed skull which looked like a melon which had been dropped from a considerable height directly onto cement. She gasped at the sight and quickly covered her mouth, but she couldn't turn away from the scene fixed before her. She watched as the cat continued to drag the victim out of the village and into the dense jungle.

For fifteen minutes most people didn't do anything, they just waited inside their huts like frightened children. The silence was unbearable, for many had a feeling of what had happened. After a while some with guns began to explore the village. The dogs were still barking once they saw the cat, being unable to run from the chains that held them. Once they lost sight of it, they began to bark more vocally again.

Eventually people began to gather around the victim's hut and examine the large hole the tiger made. There was a lot of blood everywhere including where the victim had been dragged out of the hut. Some of them followed the trail until it reached the jungle and stopped there.

A man who took charge of the situation asked for a meeting of leaders. When they were gathered it was decided that they needed to send someone again to inform Winston, as they knew from word of mouth that he was coming to their area, as to what had happened and the most recent whereabouts of the cat. They also discussed raising a group of men with guns to retrieve the remains of the old man, but no one volunteered. Although there was a need for burial there was still a good chance that the cat was still in the vicinity and they could not afford another victim no matter how strong a group they sent out. They came to the conclusion to wait until Winston arrived and let him handle the situation. After all he was the professional, they reasoned.

In the village itself work had come to a standstill. No firewood was gathered, no water retrieved from the small stream near the village and no one ventured into the jungle. They talked among themselves and each had a reason for the devilish creature being sent to torment them. They discussed how long it would take for Winston to get there and whether or not he could truly rid the country of the beast. There wasn't a lot of mourning in the village, the old man not having any relatives and being somewhat difficult to get along with in his older years, nevertheless they respected him and helped him when they could. But the reality was that the beast was still alive out there somewhere and so the anxiety continued to permeate the air. The people just wanted their lives back. They wanted to return to a state of normalcy. All they could do was wait.

There was some cleaning that was done to the hut and the damage was being repaired as well, for the people were industrious in this region and it was hard for them to stay idle for long. They didn't have a lot of food stored up, having lived each day by gathering the food they needed or hunting for it, but they made do with what they had, and everyone shared. It was during these times that everyone seemed to pull together and help each other out when they could. Many would chant their prayers and asked Buddha to help them through the difficult times.

Winston and those with him were making excellent time due to the downward slope they were covering. They were getting close to the village and everyone was on edge. There was a very good chance that an attack could come at any time and at any place. Both Winston and Charles had unslung their rifles and carried them ready to fire quickly. Sometimes they would patiently wait while the tracker would investigate any tracks that could prove to be the man-eaters. They only slightly lessened the pace wanting to get to the area as soon as possible. They ate on the run only pausing briefly at streams to get a drink of water and refill their canteens. Other animals could be seen occasionally as well.

At last they came to a spot where they could see a small amount of smoke coming up from a village. The man from the village indicated that it was indeed his hamlet. They were within a couple of miles and it was just after eight a.m., which indicated they had made excellent time.

As they approached closer the point man noticed a fresh blood trail. The tracker came up and examined the drag marks and the blood. He thought that there was another victim, likely human due to the impressions in the earth, and that it had happened probably early in the morning being only a couple of hours old. Some of the others who were gathered around the spot began to be extremely uneasy about the whole thing. Winston quickly gathered everyone around him and indicated that his servant and Charles would remain with him and the others should go into the safety of the village while they continued to track the animal.

There was no doubt as to what had done this when they found the pug marks. They knew right away that it was the Katagi man-eater. Some of the blood had collected in pools when the tiger had stopped for a rest. The fact that it had not coagulated indicated that it was fresh. Heart rates on everyone went up nearly double with the others beating a quick pace into the village Winston gathered his servant and Charles down on their knees. Winston's voice was barely a whisper.

"Here's how it's going down," he said. "Keep absolutely as quiet as you can. We are going to follow the trail until we can see some of the victim. Hopefully the tiger will be resting close by. Once we can see the cat we'll fire and kill him. We need to make sure to approach downwind. We might not get another chance like this. The jungle in this part is much too thick to try anything else. We might only have one chance so let's make the most of it.

"Charles pull the hammers back on your gun. Be ready for a quick shot."

"Right," whispered Charles.

"Ok. Let's do it."

Winston double checked his own gun and also undid the leather latch holding his knife in place. He took one more wipe of his handkerchief slowly removing the sweat from his face. He wiped off the gun and started off very carefully moving to follow the trail into the jungle. The bloody trail could easily be seen and for now there was no need for Winston's servant although he followed behind Charles.

Winston's servant had been through the thin and thick of things with Winston on most of his cat hunts, including some of the more difficult man-eaters and like Winston, was a man possessed with single determination and had little fear. Or if he did, he failed to show it. Charles on the other hand was sweating profusely, trying to calm his fears. They moved at a snail's pace making no noise at all. Winston knew from experience that the victim would not be too far into the foliage. He knew that the cat was just trying to get a little privacy before starting on its meal. They could be coming up on it any minute now. Of course, a tiger that size would have little difficulty dragging a light victim such as the old man. Who knew how far it had dragged him. Surely this was a cat that defied what was normal. Charles could hear his heart beating close to a hundred and thirty beats a minute and was sure the sound could be heard, but Winston said nothing. He just kept creeping along. Winston would peer around every plant or tree before going any further, it was very slow and taxing on the knees but there was no other way to do it. It took them close to a half an hour to go less than one hundred yards. Silence was so important their very lives depended on it. Winston carefully removed every bit of twig that might make a noise. The trail seemed to be harder to follow but there was still enough blood to see quite easily.

Winston's eyes and his gun barrel moved in one continuous motion as he would simultaneously look around a bush with the gun barrel pointing in the exact location he was looking, his finger on the trigger ready to fire.

The wind had been favorable when Winston had checked it before they started tracking the beast, but now due to a change in the terrain; the cat had begun to drag the victim in another direction. As a result, the wind was slightly with them, and with the amount of sweat they were producing there was a good chance the cat would smell them before they could even see it.

Winston had stopped and was deciding what to do. It would take them a good couple of hours to circumvent the area and approach from the West, but they had to do it. They could not take a chance on losing this opportunity.

Just as they were about to retreat they heard a very unusual sound. Winston motioned silently for all to be quiet by pressing his finger to his lips. There it was again, faint, but they could hear it. They weren't sure what exactly it was but they knew it had to be the man-eater. The sound seemed to be a crunching and rasping noise which was more intense at certain moments and they knew that it was the sound of bones being crushed. With a bite second only to the jaguar it was easy for a tiger to crush the weakened bones of a malnourished native. The sound made earlier was probably the cats tongue rasping on the bone trying to get the last bit of meat. How far it was they couldn't tell, but they knew it was probably within one-hundred yards in jungle so dense you couldn't see ten yards in front of you. If the terrain was more open they would have an excellent shot, but the foliage was still quite thick as the summer heat had not yet wilted many of the plants, which had received abundant rain from the monsoon months before.

The wind began to pick up again and Winston knew it was just a matter of time before the cat picked up their scent. But what would it do? Would it stalk them and kill them or turn and run? Obviously, it wasn't hungry, but this cat killed for pleasure as well.

Winston motioned for Charles and his servant to beat a retreat and to do it as quick as possible. They started to move without making too much noise. Winston was in the rear and continued to look around behind him to see if he could see anything. Within three minutes the cat picked up the scent and everyone knew it because you could hear the snarl that sounded, indicating it knew its privacy was compromised and it didn't like it. It immediately left the kill and began to sniff the air trying to pick up the scent's direction. It could still smell them, and it would be just a matter of time before the cat found their last location and the trail would be much easier to follow. Winston instructed Charles to get up and pick up the pace. Once they got to the regular trail they started running towards the village. There was a long straight path just before reaching the village that afforded a long look at the trail for nearly five-hundred yards. Winston yelled to the others to get to the village as he ducked behind some bushes and looked down the trail where they had just come from. Charles looked back, saw what Winston was doing and returned with him, while the servant kept going into the safety of the village.

Charles rushed back to Winston who told him to take the opposite side of the trail and to look out for the cat which was expected on the trail at any moment. Both men had their rifles trained on the spot where they hoped to see the cat. The trail gave just enough sight in a straight line to perhaps get one shot off. Perspiration ran down both their faces and sometimes into their eyes as they refused to wipe it off. They were still breathing hard from the exertion of running so far and were trying hard not to vocalize it. Both continued to stare down the path, not daring to remove their eyes from the trail for fear they may miss the opportunity.

The cat by now had found the place where they had been crawling and the trail was easy to follow. It knew that it was only a few minutes old. It was confused. Who would violate its privacy? Somehow it realized it was being followed just like it had tracked so many of its victims. Although it was extremely curious it was also cautious, realizing with natural canny that there was danger in the presence that followed it. Yet it continued to track the trail until it led to the main path. Here it was extremely careful, recognizing the way they had come earlier and the way they had recently left.

Another disagreeable snarl sent shivers up Winston and Charles' backs. From their vantage point they could not see if the cat was on the walking path. They had to wait until it showed itself and hopefully it would not follow another course to get around them. They continued to wait, minute after minute.

Meanwhile the tiger had been both curious and apprehensive enough to investigate further but refused to follow the walking path that led to the village. It placed every step with caution as it moved through the foliage in the direction of the village.

Winston was impatiently waiting for a glimpse of the cat. It was taking too long. It should have been there by now according to when they heard the snarl, he thought to himself. What was it doing? Had it given up? He began to be very uneasy and to look in other directions. He was frustrated at the other areas which only opened up a few yards and would definitely necessitate a shot from the hip and only one at that. There was a very good chance either he or Charles, or possibly both, would be mauled to death. He whispered to Charles to watch the brush on his side carefully.

The cat had been stalking in the direction of the village using its sense of smell. It sensed someone was near, but *where* was the question. One thing it knew for sure was that whatever it was, it had to be close. It was drawing stealthily closer when a peafowl took flight giving its call and warning everyone of its presence. Winston immediately jumped up and fired a shot in the direction of the sound and quickly readied the second barrel.

"It's not on the path!" he yelled to Charles. "Let's get back to the village as quick as possible!"

Without a moment's hesitation Charles surprised Winston by bolting ahead of him and had a pretty good pace about him. Winston was close behind and was right on his heels. He looked back as he ran but saw nothing. They continued to run and when they were about to leave the long straightaway Winston looked back again and saw, running at him on the path at a pretty good pace, the largest tiger he had ever seen. He turned around and shouldered his gun, but as soon as he did the cat was gone, having seen him and what he was up to. It had left the path once again and Winston started running again to get up with Charles. He was wondering if he would make the village before the cat reached him.

The tiger realized that someone was hunting it and wanted to pursue the attackers, but instinct was also telling it to break off the attack.

Winston had double timed it to get up with a slowing Charles as they entered the village together, which wasn't hard once he saw the cat pursuing him.

"That was bloody close," said Charles. "Do you think you got anything with that blind shot?"

"I really doubt it," replied Winston. "But one thing's for sure; that cat is a smart one and its got experience. We've got a game going on here and someone is going to get killed. It's a good thing we both escaped that one."

The rest of the group came up to them and began asking what happened. Charles hadn't understood Winston back in the jungle when he had said to back off and retreat, so he wanted to know as well.

"The wind shifted, and the cat picked up our scent. If we hadn't of broken off the track we would be dead. In fact, we're lucky to be alive now. We barely made the safety of the village, and if it wasn't for that peafowl I'm sure one of us would be dead."

It was a sobering thought for Charles. He would have plunged headfirst into the fray, and if it wasn't for Winston's experience he probably wouldn't be there. He thanked Winston but he said not to worry about it because there was no doubt he'd get another chance. Charles asked what they needed to do next.

Winston thought about it and said, "Well, he knows we're after him, and if he's done anything similar to other kills he will leave the area, and we need to try and predict where it's going to go. Let's get some lunch and meet under those coconut trees."

He instructed his servant to bring the map and asked his cook to get lunch ready. A little later they ate a quick, simplified lunch and then went over to the shade and coolness of the coconut trees. Again, Winston, his servant and Charles were there along with the village leader too. Winston spread out the map and began looking at it.

"Here is where we are," he said, pointing to a section on the map. "Here," pointing again, "was where the cat dragged its victim, approximately. The terrain indicates that he will either head north or south and we will have to try and guess correctly the right direction, any suggestions?"

The village leader spoke up and indicated that the foliage was much thicker on the southern way but that had never stopped a cat before.

"Yes," replied Winston. "It would not stop the cat, but it would make it very difficult to follow and get a shot off. If it's an intelligent creature it would head that way, but then again it may not make a difference to the beast which direction it goes. The topography would indicate that there's little chance it would cross the mountains to the east and west. What do you think Charles?"

Charles looked at the map for a few seconds and then said, "It's just eaten a good meal and will likely look for the easiest route out of the area.

That would indicate that it would head south even though it's thicker. The contour lines on this map indicate the gradient is easier."

Winston thought for a few moments and then said, "There's also a good chance we'll be traveling in areas now where the group could be attacked."Again, he indicated that if anyone wanted to leave, now would be the time. There was silence but no one left.

"It's a toss-up really," he explained. "There's no way of knowing for sure which way it's going, and it will likely be another week before it kills by which time we want to be in position, hopefully better prepared, you had better get a good sleep tonight because we're going south in the morning."

As Winston left the group, he came to a few villagers who asked him in the local dialect to please rid the place of the evil spirit possessing the tiger. Winston said that he would do everything possible within his means. They thanked him and shook his arm chanting the whole time. It was like they were concerned about him and were putting some spell of theirs on him to protect him.

Winston thought about the experience and realized he should have had a shot at the cat on the trail. The cat was a lot smarter than he had thought and it would be wise not to underestimate it again.

Charles hadn't had that kind of excitement since he had nearly hit a water buffalo on his motorbike at high speed. He was surprised his heart could beat that fast. What a magnificent beast .It had to be a record based on the pug marks alone. Maybe its unique diet, made it that large, who knew, but surely a trophy he thought. The news and photo of anyone bringing it down would make a sensation all over the world.

He made it back to the tent and staggered in wanting a well-deserved rest. He had paid some of the villagers to clean his clothes and they had left them outside hanging on the rope supporting the tent. The mosquitoes were quite bothersome, and it took him some time to get to sleep, but soon he was dozing like a caboose operator.

Winston was making plans to get all the equipment moved the next day. He came in after about an hour and soon was asleep as well.

It was near dinner time when Winston's servant woke the men for the prepared meal of fresh sambar and pineapple. It looked delicious and Charles now knew why Winston couldn't part with his servant for any expedition. The steam rose in a twisting manner as it came off the meat when Charles was served. It had a distinct wild taste to it, but Charles loved it. Winston asked him where he had obtained it from and the cook indicated that the village chieftain had supplied them with everything that night. Winston reminded himself mentally to thank him when he got the chance. It wasn't long before the events of the day were long forgotten in the laughter and frivolity of the men and their experiences.

Charles was awake just after sunrise smelling the wonderful breakfast aroma that was permeating the air. He did not look forward to another hike through the heat of the day. They were served with fresh fruits of every kind as well as scrambled eggs. As usual it was tasty. A few porters were hired to haul some of their gear and Winston was forced to double the pay once the porters found out where they were going and the danger involved. For some of the porters the loads were light and it was a welcome respite.

Charles had a bad premonition about the trip but said nothing to anyone. The day was hot and humid, and the summer heat was beginning to peak although the vegetation was still green throughout most of the region. Everyone, after a few hours, was continually wiping the sweat from their faces, and drinking huge amounts of water. Charles had to admit that he wasn't in the kind of shape Winston was even though he was considerably younger. He had just spent too much time in the office and failed to regularly exercise. Despite this he managed to keep up. Winston was a man who seemed at ease in the jungle; a person who relished the wild and everything about it. Occasionally he would point out poisonous plants and warn not to touch them. There was no doubt he was in his element.

The dull and monotonous hike was broken up by screams coming from up the trail. Winston and Charles thought it might be the tiger, so they unslung their rifles and ran to the front of the group. There they met pandemonium as people were quickly moving back from an object that was on the trail. Winston soon saw that it was the Hamadryad, or king cobra, and this specimen was extremely large with its hood drawn out and swaying back and forth. Winston wasted no time in drawing out his revolver, quickly aiming and pulling the trigger. The snake dropped right where it was and Winston moved up to examine it. It was a magnificent specimen and still going through some convulsions. Winston got a large stick and clubbed it for good measure then they began to lengthen out its body. The girth was the size of a native's leg and when they got it stretched out it measured sixteen feet long. Winston asked his servant to skin it and get the meat. The snake would either be eaten by them tonight or they would give it to some of the villagers. Cobra was a very delicious meat and most everyone would want some.

They decided to take a break there while the servant did the job of skinning it. They walked a short distance down to the stream that was nearby to fill their canteens and wet their handkerchiefs. The rest was a welcome time to Charles who had been struggling the entire morning. It seemed every day since he had left was coupled with some sort of life-threatening danger and he had escaped it thus far. But would his luck run out?

After eating some dried jerky and drinking enough water to fill a camel they were off again, like a roman contingent marching to their destination. Not much was said, just a constant walk through trails that went through the country like giant slithering pythons. Sometimes the terrain was sparse with little to see but small plants living alongside the trail but mostly there was lush vegetation just starting to give way to the heat of the summer. Occasionally there would be vines and trees overhanging the trail and a machete was needed to completely clear the way. Everyone was thinking of the cat in one way or another. If it was in the area, and if it attacked, how many of the party would it go after it, would Winston be able to kill it?

After several hours they began to near the village of Aaten. The sun was just setting over the hills casting a warm orange glow over the entire valley. Charles had to stop for a few minutes to admire the glow. He wiped the sweat from his brow and took a swig of water, then continued on, hoping that the village was less than a half hour away. Winston and the others kept plodding on almost like something mechanical, varying little from early on in the day.

They arrived in the village within the hour just as the darkness was setting in. Winston asked to see the local chieftain who he met a few minutes later. Winston explained the events of the past week and the possibility of a tiger attack in or around the village. The news of the last killing had already reached them and they had taken precautions just to be on the safe side. Winston continued to discuss what could be done to minimize the danger. It was a double edge sword to give the chieftain the advice. No doubt it would lessen the danger to keep everyone inside but on the other hand Winston needed to know for sure if the tiger was in the area and that could only happen by sightings or pug marks. They needed to be where it would attack next, and hopefully this area was where it was. It was a dangerous game and Winston insisted on having the upper hand at all times in order to be successful.

Winston and Charles were assigned another hut to share in the village and the chieftain assured them that they would have all the help and supplies they needed, all they needed to do was ask. Winston was feeling good about the area and was pleased with the willingness of the people to help him. All they needed now was a good chance to get a clean shot off. The only thing to do now was wait for word that the cat was in the vicinity. It might be as short as four days before an attack and it could be another fortnight, but they really couldn't do anything until they knew for sure where it is.

Winston asked to meet with Charles and his servant before dinner.

They sat down a few hours later to the delicacy of cobra meat. The snake was given to some locals to prepare and it tasted great although there wasn't a lot of meat to go around. It was supplemented by antelope meat and fresh fruit.

Before dinner Winston again held a meeting with the local chieftain along with his servant and Charles. Winston laid out the plan, If the tiger was in the area, they would isolate the valley it was in and form a beat with the help of the local villagers in order to drive it to one end of the valley where Winston and Charles would be waiting for a good shot. Winston asked the local chieftain how many men he could muster for the beat and he replied that he could probably produce about eighteen or nineteen, but if they petitioned the help of some of the other villagers as well they could possibly have about thirty-five to forty men.

"Great," Winston replied. "In the meantime, we can go to the other villages and ask for their help if and when we need it."

"Also, have the tracker see if he can check the best possible areas for signs of the cat's pug marks, and we can try to determine that it's in the area that way as well, make sure there are a couple of brave men to go with him ."

"Tomorrow, Charles and I will head to Ralsta and Nager. A few men can head to Qiuta and ask them for any news on the cat and whether they could help us if need be when it comes time for a beat.

"The tracker will need to make sure he checks out the river for any signs down there and along the bank?"

Better yet lets have Charles go with the tracker and a few men. I'll take a few men with me."

"Fine then, it's settled," said Winston, "If you could leave first thing in the morning and be back here by nightfall. Don't dally too long in the village you will need to start back as soon as possible."

Charles agreed and was already quite tired, so he headed off to the hut to get in a good night's rest. As he retired, he could hear a roar from either a tiger or a leopard in the distance.

Before Charles could get into his bed Winston came in with both rifles and told him that they needed to be cleaned. Charles reluctantly rose from his chair and took the rifle Winston had lent him. It was covered with dust from the trail and it was a good thing Winston told him to clean it.

Soon after cleaning the guns both men settled down to get a good night's sleep. There was going to be another long day tomorrow. That night both men slept soundly due to the days hiking. In the early morning Winston was up before the sun and quietly woke Charles and told him they needed to get ready. Winston gave some last-minute instructions and they ate a quick breakfast prepared by some of the villagers willing to help out. They were off within thirty minutes of waking up, each going off in separate directions with their hired help.

Charles was very refreshed from a good night's sleep and a hearty breakfast. Both parties were making good time and had arrived at the villages by noon and one o'clock. Both parties knew that the man-eater could be in the area and so took extra precautions.

The village leaders assured them they could send as much help as possible if and when it was needed. Charles felt good about the success they had and, following a good lunch, he headed back to Aeton.

They had been instructed by Winston to check out the small lakes in between Horn Mountain and Qi valley on the way back. When they arrived, they made way down a well-groomed trail that led down to the lakes. Charles wasn't expecting to see anything out of the ordinary there, so he casually followed the tracker. They got down to the first lake and had started to stroll around to the other side when the tracker became quite excited and agitated and motioned Charles over to where he was at. Charles went over and found himself looking at the exact pug marks they had taken plaster casts of a few days ago. It was unmistakable; there was no other tiger big enough to make those marks.

"Can you tell how fresh they are?"

"Probably this morning," replied the tracker. "If we were a little earlier we could have been its first meal. There's a good chance he's still in the area."

Charles got up and started looking around, taking the gun off his shoulder.

"Yes, we better get back to Aeton as soon as possible. He could be watching us right now waiting to spring onto us."

They made their way very carefully around the lake the way they had come, pausing to look around every few moments. The vegetation here opened up a lot and one could see for some distance, but they would need to enter back into the jungle with its cover of plants and trees. It was there that the likelihood of an attack was greatest. Charles began to sweat and his heart rate jumped up to one hundred and twenty. They didn't talk much, just moved very carefully and deliberately, always listening to see if any monkeys or other animals gave a distress call.

It took a long time to cover the distance back to the main trail but finally they were on it and picked up the pace back to Aeton. The discovery was exciting, but they also wished it were somebody else who discovered it. Knowing the cat was in the area and Winston wasn't around was not a very comforting thought. Still they pressed on with a faster pace, sweat pouring off their foreheads in the hot afternoon sun. They only could hope that the tiger had settled down in the heat under the shade of a tree and was sleeping away the afternoon.

The distance seemed like it had tripled from the morning's hike. They had finished off their water without bothering to refill it at any of the streams they crossed. It would have made a lot of sense for one of them to return to a closer village in order to facilitate a party for the beat the following day, but they were too afraid to break up and go back to the territory where the tiger would likely be patrolling in a few hours.

They were within a couple of miles of Aeton when they heard the unmistakable alarm call of a monkey not far away. They both stopped in their tracks and looked at each other.

Charles spoke first and said, "I think we had better double time it back to Aeton."

The tracker agreed and they began to half run half jog back towards the village. They continued to look around everywhere looking for any sign of danger. Charles thought about calling out to the village for anyone to help them but then realized that the call would alert the tiger as well.

Within thirty minutes they arrived in the village exhausted. Some of Winston's group came up to them asking what was the matter. They explained that they had seen the pug marks of the tiger and there was no doubt as to its identity. Charles asked if Winston was back yet and of course he wasn't but was expected within a couple of hours.

Charles began to organize at once and asked the chieftain if they could possibly muster everyone for a beat in the morning. He also asked if they could summon some help from Ralsta for the morning. A runner was asked to spread the news of the cat and get help from the small village. He was likely to pass Winston on the way back, so he was to get the information out that they were trying to organize a beat for the morning unless Winston thought otherwise.

Charles started asking how many they had that were willing to help. The chieftain thought they could get at least nineteen men from his village and it was possible they could have another fifteen from Nager. They agreed that the best they could do would be to wait for Winston to arrive before they made their final preparations.

Both Charles and the tracker downed a large quantity of water and wolfed down a well-prepared supper.

It was an extraordinary piece of good luck to have found the pug marks, and with a good beat in the morning they may even be lucky enough to get a good shot at the tiger.

Both of them were exhausted and fell asleep waiting for Winston to arrive. Charles was asleep on the chair he was sitting on, slouched over like a drunken sailor. The tracker had the presence of mind to at least retire to an unused hammock he had seen hanging between two trees.

Winston had been intercepted by the runner and concurred that the best option was to organize a beat in the morning. He asked the runner to make sure they were in Aeton as early as possible and to make sure that they traveled as a group with torches in the morning before sunup. He also indicated that they needed to bring as many noisemakers as possible. Winston and a laborer then hastened back to Aeton where they found Charles napping in the late evening. Winston roused Charles and also asked the village chieftain and his assistant to come to a meeting in their hut.

The sun was setting fast as everyone invited gathered in the hut. Winston began to eat pieces of his dinner that was brought in while asking Charles and the tracker where exactly they had seen the pug marks and which direction they were going. As people arrived Winston welcomed them with a warm handshake and then went directly over to the map. With everyone listening intently he indicated with a pencil on the map where the pug marks were found.

"It's likely that the cat could still be in this valley here," pointing to the large valley where the two large lakes were. "We can position hunters here, here and here with the beaters working down from this end of the valley to the narrow opening here at the southern end. There's a chance that it could exit here as well so we'll need to place a hunter there too."

Winston asked if they had a gun in the village. There was one gun, but the person only had a few cartridges to go with it.

"There may be some more with the other villagers," said the chieftain.

"That's ok," said Winston, "because he will likely have only a shot or two anyway if he manages to see it."

A question was asked whether the owner was a good shot or not and it was affirmed that he was a very good shot.

"Alright, we'll place him here, pointing at a spot on the map, just in case the cat tries to exit there, and Charles and myself will watch the southern escape route. The beaters will continue to move down the valley at a leisurely pace making as much noise as possible. The big cats usually sleep in, so if we're lucky he will still be there. How fresh did you say those tracks were?" "Very fresh, this morning said the tracker." Can we use your friends tracking dogs? Asked Charles,(the dogs and the owner had arrived a day earlier and were constantly yapping at each other). I don't want to risk sending the dogs into the valley and springing the tiger early." "I think there's a good chance he'll still be there in the morning, you can count on it. Now, in order to get into position without disturbing it, we'll need to leave much earlier and get into position by following this ridge down. There's less chance it will be sleeping up on a ridge, but just to make sure we will need to be as quiet as possible."

Winston turned to the chieftain and indicated that they would need a forty-five minute head start in order to get into position on time before the beat started. He gave instructions to have his men stationed about ten to twenty feet apart depending on how many beaters they had.

"It's very important to keep the line straight and to keep moving at a leisurely pace through the valley making as much noise as possible. Someone will need to make sure the line is moving at the same rate and that the people are evenly spaced in order to prevent the tiger from getting through the line. You will need to be in position at the head of the valley by sunup."

The chieftain asked if any of the men could carry guns since there may be a few from the other villages. Winston said that would be fine, knowing that there were maybe three or four guns in the whole group, and also mentioned that they were not to take a shot unless they had a completely clear view. The last thing they needed was a wounded tiger and forty to fifty beaters.

As soon as Winston finished he instructed everyone to get things ready for the beat.

As people shuffled out of the hut Winston grabbed Charles's arm and said, "We might only get one shot. If it's you, make sure it counts."

They also discussed a few hand signals and animals sounds which they could use to communicate if they spotted the cat. Charles asked Winston what he thought the chances were tomorrow.

Winston thought for a minute and said, "If that cat is still in the valley we've got probably a forty percent chance of bagging it, and probably a sixty to seventy percent chance of briefly seeing it."

They went out and had a bite to eat as people were already starting to come in for the beat. The chieftain was explaining some things to those who had arrived and making arrangements for their sleeping quarters. The women were busy preparing food for the following day and it already looked like it was going to be a good turnout.

Winston and Charles began to retire over to their sleeping hut and Winston made sure when they got there that they looked over the guns to make sure they were well oiled and free of dust. With that done they turned in to get ready for the long day ahead. There was some apprehension on Charles' mind knowing they would once again go head to head with the cat. He had already had some close calls and wondered how much longer things would last.

The crickets from the jungle began to chirp louder the darker it got, until there was a chorus of them. He couldn't sleep but he could hear Winston snoring up a storm and wondered how anyone could sleep with that racket. Hopefully he wasn't a sleep walker too or he might be a midnight snack sometime.

Three a.m. came pretty quick for Winston and Charles. They ate a quick breakfast and Winston gave some last-minute instructions to the chieftain and the gun handlers. There were sixty-five people available for the beat with two working elephants. Winston was instructing the chieftain to make sure the elephants were on opposing sides of the line. Charles couldn't understand the language but could tell from the gesticulations the gist of what was being said. They were to blow their horns if they saw the tiger. Winston and Charles would be able to see which direction it was heading by how they adjusted the line.

Everyone wished each other good luck as Winston told them to give them a forty-five minute head start. There was some confusion on this until Winston gave his watch to the chieftain and told him not to leave until the longer hand reached the two on the dial. When it looked like he understood they left.

Charles asked Winston if they should say a prayer and Winston replied that any help they could get would be good. Winston removed his hat as Charles uttered a quick prayer. There were three of them and as they started off. The gun bearer from the village looked a little concerned but knew his job from the previous night's meeting and exactly where he needed to be. They kept up a brisk pace as Winston explained how the horns were to be blown and what it meant.

The tiger was in the valley and had been sleeping there during the day and the night. Winston and Charles came to the area after several hours of hiking.

"This is where we separate. I want you to follow this ridge until it starts to descend at the end of the valley. Try and position yourself where you have a good view of the exit route out of the valley. Don't get too low on the valley floor, but don't get more than three-hundred yards away from the valleys exit either. Winston gave similar instructions to the man who had the gun saying "You go with Charles until you get to your assigned spot. It's on that side of the valley. If you see the cat just relax as much as possible and squeeze off a good shot. It will take about an hour for the beaters to get through the valley. About thirty minutes from when they start you'll start to see every kind of animal that can move. Make sure it's the man-eater before you shoot. It should be easy to distinguish because of its size. Don't smoke either, it will smell it. I hope the wind is with us today. I'll be on the other side and hopefully we'll have everything covered. Good luck and Godspeed."

After thirty minutes, as they descended the ridge, they could see the torches of the other men starting to come down the trail. It was an eerie sight. The vegetation was still thick as the summer heat had only just began to wilt the valley and Winston wished there was less growth, but just knowing the cat was here was good enough luck. At this point the sun began to come up and Winston instinctively pulled out two cigar shaped cartridges and loaded his gun leaving the hammers down for safety. The tiger had not heard anything and was sleeping in the valley just as Winston suspected. It slowly awoke with the sun and began to stretch its forelegs out extending its claws and yawning, showing stiletto-like canines. It needed a morning drink and the stream that ran though the bottom of the valley provided the necessary water. Animal calls were occasionally heard as the big cat moved cautiously down to the stream unaware of the trap that was being set up. The beaters had not begun yet and the tiger was still in the middle of the valley.

As the three men struggled to get into position the sun was already beginning to warm up the valley. They could, by this time, see their positions as to where they wanted to be. As they began to descend the ridge they became more cautious and alert trying not to make any noise. Winston's ridge fell off first and he was able to obtain a great view into the exit area where there was a large opening only two-hundred yards away. Charles too was in position a few minutes later. Unfortunately, the sun coming up was sending rays straight into his eyes. The man from the village was also soon into position. As everyone settled in, the sweat from their hiking started to bead on their foreheads and roll down, occasionally being wiped free. They could hear by this time the faint sounds at the far end of the valley and strained to see anything moving into the exit areas. Winston had said that the tiger would likely wait until it was just ahead of the beaters to move, but one could never be sure.

As the beaters continued to move down the valley they started to glimpse a few animals running out, mostly antelope. Then Charles saw a leopard dart out the exit area and his heart began beating a hundred times a minute. The valley was still pretty dense and there were only a few areas open enough to allow a shot. Winston hoped that Charles has chosen his spot well. A fleeing animal would likely take the easiest route out through the open areas Winston and Charles were watching. There was a chance that some of the animals or even the tiger would try and go over the hill but that was a lot of work.

The noise from the beaters was growing louder every few minutes and they were roughly in the middle of the valley. It amazed Charles how well sound could travel as he could hear voices.

The tiger was on the move and being pushed exactly where they hoped, but no one had seen it yet. The tension was growing with each passing minute like something spectacular was about to happen. The adrenaline was pumping into the veins of not only the three shooters but the men doing the beat as well. Everyone kept moving, making as much noise as possible, driving anything and everything through the exit areas.

From where they were at, neither Winston, Charles or the other man could see each other. But if the tiger choose one of the routes, someone would see it. Winston was by far the best shot, especially under pressure, and he seemed to excel at moving targets. Charles wasn't bad himself and better than most. The man from the village was a crack shot too, so they had an excellent chance if a good shot could be made.

More animals kept coming through the end of the valley including tapir, antelope, wild pigs and other smaller game, but no sign of the tiger. Then Winston spotted a cat coming his way and looking back towards the beaters. He lowered his gun and put iron sights on the animal. He realized fairly quickly that it was another leopard and a large one at that.

"Too bad," he thought to himself as he continued to watch it for a few seconds.

The cat kept looking back trying to figure out what was happening.

The tiger had been keeping just ahead of the beaters, not panicking but more annoyed than anything else. At this point in the valley there was still a lot of cover to move within, and it had managed to keep out of sight of everyone, but it had no idea what was waiting for it.

Winston and the other shooters were more attentive as game continued to filter through the trap. Charles was looking at some of the animals coming through his area when the great cat appeared like a ghost in the opening. The tiger was huge compared to the leopard that had come through. The sight you always imagine was right there in front of him. His heart started racing. Reflexes took over as he raised the gun's sights on the tiger. The cat was moving a little faster than a walk and mixing it up with short jogs. The adrenaline was at an all-time high for Charles at this point and it was difficult keeping the gun steady.

He was thinking to himself, "Keep it together. Squeeze the trigger."

The cat was about two-hundred yards away and would soon enter cover again and be lost to view. He had to act quickly.

Everything up to this point had only taken a few seconds but seemed an eternity. The sights were on the cat's shoulder and the trigger was being depressed with each millisecond. The high-powered rifle cracked with a boom that made everyone stop. Time seemed to stand still. The recoil forced Charles body back about six inches as smoke from the barrel wafted up to the sky.

The tiger had leaped high into the air and came down running effortlessly to the dense cover a few yards away. It knew from previous experience what had hit it and was trying to get away as quickly as possible, while at the same time thinking of doubling back to attack the shooter.

Charles had fired the second hopeful shot into the brush where it had disappeared from view. He didn't think the shot had a prayer but he had to take it nonetheless. He stood there breathing hard not believing what had just happened. Was it real? Was he dreaming? The cat was gone, but the first shot definitely hit home, but where? He thought that he had slightly jerked the gun.

Winston was running over to where Charles could be found making efforts to stay in the open as much as possible. There were still several animals running the gauntlet and Winston kept a sharp lookout for the big cat as he ran over to where Charles was. Charles' heart was still pounding as Winston came running up to him.

Winston was out of breath but he quickly asked, "What happened?"

"I hit him on the first shot. It was the same brute no doubt about it, I'm sure it was him. He continued to run after being hit."

Winston sounded his horn signaling that the beaters could call off the beat. A few minutes later a runner found them and Winston communicated that he wanted a message sent to Aeton to have the tracking dogs brought up to meet him at the bottom of the valley. He said that Charles hit it and they may have to track it.

They started off towards the clearing, with Winston asking more questions as they moved down. When they got to the area, they examined it closely and could see small drops of blood from where it had been hit leading into the dense underbrush where Charles had taken the second shot.

"Well, you hit it alright. Good shot."

There was a pause.

"But it's probably not good enough."

"What do you mean?" asked Charles.

"Well there's blood here, no question about it. But it's just in drops and the drops get fewer and fewer towards the brush. Now, that may be the speed at which he was moving, but I think we have a wounded tiger which makes for a very dangerous animal. It may just stand and fight now, which may mean an ambush if we're not careful. It's possible you may have hit him in the belly passing all the vitals. If we're lucky you could have hit him in the heart, in which case we just track down the carcass."

What Winston was saying was the truth. Charles had done the best that he could, but the fact of the matter was there was no carcass laid out in front of them.

Winston indicated that he wanted to track him. It would take a couple of hours for the dogs to arrive. He asked his servant for advice and he said they could do that, but if it wasn't wounded too badly, it could go on as if he was never hit. The blood would coagulate if it was a minor wound.

The servant tracked it a little into the brush but could tell fairly quickly that it was moving well and out of the area. They had a little time to wait for the dogs and so they took their lunch there.

It was two hours before the yelps of the dogs could be heard. When they arrived, Winston spoke to the handler and indicated that he wanted the tracking to be done with leashes on for now.

They started out, apprehensive at first, not knowing how far the cat had gone and how wounded it was. It was evident after an hour of tracking that the trail was getting extremely cold and very difficult to track, but as long as they didn't get any rain they should be able to follow the trail fairly easy.

They decided to pull back. The trail was still cold and it appeared the cat was putting some distance between itself and the valley where it was shot. Charles had entertained hopes of being the one who had killed the famous man-eater but now he realized it was still in pretty good shape and the wound was not fatal.

It was a good decision to turn back anyway, the brush and vegetation had gotten thicker the more they ventured out. The Italian bred dogs were specially trained for tracking game and they made things easier once they got close to their quarry by warning Winston where the cat was.

The news spread far and wide that the tiger had been hit and rumors started to fly that it was dead, that it was wounded, that it had killed three men before dying, the only thing missing was the truth.

The weather continued good with no rain in sight. With some luck they may catch up to it before nightfall. Winston knew that it could take anywhere from an hour where they left the trail if it was hit in a vital spot to several days. The entire group was a little fidgety. Tracking a man-eating tiger was bad enough, but a wounded one was twice as dangerous. Actually, they were still in good shape. Even though the tiger was wounded, they knew the general vicinity and the dogs could hopefully pick up a good trail. They could eventually corner it and finish the demon once and for all.

The group retreated to a large clearing where they camped for the night. A few men keep a large fire going all night. Early the next morning at daybreak the dogs picked up the scent pretty quickly and the pace picked up. Winston allowed the quick pace. The dogs seemed to pull their handler along. After another couple of hours Winston made them slow the pace down and became more concerned. Both Winston and Charles had their rifles unslung and ready for any emergency. The tiger had been moving in an easterly direction toward the village of Amaki. The trail was devoid of blood but the scent could still be picked up by the dogs. In the lead with the longest leash was the handler's favorite dog named Badge who had the tenacity of a badger and the endurance of a hound. Badge had been on other significant tracks and was the most experienced dog. He had survived when others around him were sliced open by the razor-sharp claws of tigers or leopards. He was a survivor and knew not to get too close to the cats. His agility was incredible and Winston had seen him sidestep a tiger with the ease of a matador dodging a bull. A leopard on the other hand is a bit more agile than a tiger, and the one time he nearly got killed was at the claws of a leopard, which would have finished him off if it hadn't been for another dog distracting it. Badge took a full six months before he completely recovered, but he was still the best dog in the group.

The men were not oblivious to the fact that an ambush was possible. They had already covered close to seven miles from the valley and everyone was getting tired. The dogs gave no indication that they were nearing their quarry. Winston called a halt at a stream where everyone guzzled the water from their canteens and refilled them.

They sat down for a pow-wow to discuss their options. Winston went over the plan, for when they neared the tiger, one more time. Repetition was good, especially in this case. They would go as far as they could with the light they had. If there was any indication that they were getting close and it was nearing nightfall they were to back off, especially if the wind was blowing in the tiger's direction. He didn't want to take any chances that the tiger was on to them when they were at a disadvantage. Winston was surprised the cat had traveled this far already and it was apparent now that it wasn't wounded too badly. The tracks, when they did come across them, indicated that it was walking fine and they hadn't seen any blood for several hours now. Of course it was impossible to keep the dogs quiet as they tracked the quarry.

They traveled several more hours, and it was about an hour before sundown when they heard a loud roar from about three miles away. Winston was pretty sure it was their cat because the roar sounded a little deeper than other tigers but there was no way to tell for sure. They had to make a decision. If it had stopped and it took them an hour to get there they would likely be ambushed in the dark, or near dark, where the tiger's eyesight was six times greater than a man's. But if they camped there that night they would likely not be detected and could resume the tracking at first light. Hopefully, the dogs could be kept quiet enough, and anyhow Winston didn't think the cat could hear them from three miles distance even though they could hear the tiger.

Winston decided, wisely, to wait there and camp until the morning when they could resume the tracking. It was a good decision endorsed by everyone. Since there was no rain expected they had brought with them lightweight hammocks which they began stringing between the trees. Charles couldn't help but think they would be nice little dinner appetizers if the tiger knew they were there. They ate a quick dinner without fire, which Winston would not allow, and quickly went to bed and slept soundly due to the day's labors. It looked like tomorrow was going to be another very long day.

Charles was a little more concerned than usual, being that they were out in the jungle in the tiger's domain, and if it decided to back-track they would all be tempting targets for retaliation. At least he had hopes that the dogs would bark at anything approaching and give him enough time for a last wish. Even with all the anxiety, everyone fell soundly asleep, even the dogs. For someone unaccustomed to sleeping in the jungle it could be overwhelming, but luckily those that hadn't experienced it had fallen asleep.

Charles was awakened just before sunrise. They knew that they still had at least three miles to cover and Winston wanted to get a head start before it got too light. It was just barely light enough to see when they set off, the dogs picking up the trail once again. Hopefully the cat had slept through the night as well. The dogs were still kept on their leashes because they could cover ground much faster than the men, but once they got close they would turn them loose to distract and maybe corner the cat so they could come upon the scene unnoticed and maybe get a shot off. Four dogs with two to a split leash were about all that the handler could handle.

As they got into the day a couple hours it became apparent that they were getting close. The dogs were yapping constantly now and it seemed they were on a fresh trail. Winston called a halt and conferred with the handler to decide if they were close enough to release them. They felt that they were very close and so the dogs were released. This meant that the men had to do double time to try and keep up. Hopefully, they would catch them soon and all this would be over.

The dogs were running hard and fast without the leashes to hold them back. Their ears waved in the air as they ran, bringing the fresh scent of the tiger up to their noses. Winston and Charles were just hoping to keep within earshot before the dogs caught the big cat. The tiger by this time was no doubt hearing the dogs and was on the run too. The dogs had opened up some distance on the men, but Winston could tell from the barking that they were nearing the quarry.

The tigers strength was beginning to wane and it decided, after clearing a large downed tree, to stop and make a stand. The lead dog had instinctively jumped the tree only to have the tiger waiting there patiently. With a well-placed swath of its claws it quickly cut the jugular vein of the lead dog. It went down, gasping for air, bleeding to death. There were only three dogs left now and as they came over the tree they were nearly dispatched too. There was a vicious fight to the death now as the remaining dogs worked together to hold the big cat until the guns arrived. The cat was pretty agile for its big size, but the dogs were a little quicker, always moving out of reach, never getting too close. One wrong move and they would be dead in their tracks.

The big cat's instinct told it to run again, so it bolted with the dogs hot on its trail. Another ten minutes and Winston would have arrived with

Charles. The dogs were starting to tire as well, as they had been on the trail since before the sun came up, but having caught up with the prey they relentlessly pursued their quarry with renewed vigor. The dogs wanted the cat cornered but it just wasn't happening. Occasionally Badge or another dog would nip at the hind quarters of the tiger and the cat would turn and charge, but the dog's agility always kept them at a respectable distance.

Winston and Charles hadn't been gaining any distance since the cat started running again, but they weren't losing ground either.

The dogs were following closer, getting anxious, when the big cat turned again and caught one of the dogs by surprise. The first swath of its paw caught the dog just on its nose with enough force to throw it off balance. Like a seasoned boxer it followed that up with a swath from the other paw which was a well-placed blow that caught the jugular of the dog with a few extended claws. It was enough. The neck was sliced open and the dog was gasping and wheezing for air with blood dripping and spattering everywhere. It lasted a few more minutes but then it was dead.

There were only two dogs left and Winston could tell that something had happened from the reduced number of barks that were silenced. The tiger was still being harassed by the remaining dogs but being unable to catch them, it again turned and ran. Both the dog's and tiger's fur was wet with sweat from the exertion made having to run longer than they were used to, but both the dogs and the cat were in remarkable shape. Winston and Charles were struggling themselves having been at double time for the last hour.

Winston and Charles rounded a small hill which gave them an unusual vantage point with a clearing of about four hundred yards ahead. They quickly saw the animals running up ahead and Winston immediately dropped down to his knee while at the same time pulling back both hammers on his gun. Charles followed suit as well. The cat and the dogs were heading back into the trees and there were only a few seconds before they disappeared. Winston and Charles were about to squeeze off their shots when the tiger charged into the woods.

"Damn!" cried out Winston, "We almost had him! Another few seconds was all we needed. There isn't much time left. We've got to finish this in the next half hour or it will be too late."

Even though they were at the end of their tether they somehow knew that a chance like this may not come their way again, on they pushed. As they came down the small hill they passed the dead dog lying in its gore. There wasn't any time to attend to it. Time was running out as they continued to hear the barking of the remaining dogs. There was nothing to do but push on at an even quicker pace with Winston leading the way. Another fifteen minutes had passed and Charles didn't like the idea of not being able to see anything in the dark until it was too late. If they didn't get it soon, it could track them at night with greater vision and perhaps take one or all three of them. The thought of falling asleep somewhere with a man-eating tiger clamping down its jaws on your neck was not a comforting feeling.

The tiger was getting extremely tired when it came to a good-sized stream and rushed in sensing that this water would be advantageous to it. The dogs, hot on the trail, hesitated momentarily. Then Badge jumped in first, determined not to let the tiger escape. The sly cat was making for the opposite bank and was three quarters of the way there when it looked back and saw that the dogs were halfway across. Its giant paws were turning the water like it was a polar bear in its element. The cat made a quick turnaround and was making fast progress to the dogs, which realized their predicament and were making for the shore they had just left. The stream was a little deeper than most but near the shore it began to shallow out. The tiger felt bottom first and used its massive muscles to propel itself out of the water and onto the closest dog. Its front paws caught the dog's hind quarters and the dog had started to yelp when its neck was pulverized with a bite force of eleven hundred pounds per square inch. It was instantly dead.

Badge had come to the rescue of the other dog but had slightly misjudged the distance and quickly the tiger released its grip on the dead dog, which floated down the stream, and made a quick swath of its paw, catching

Badge on the head and throwing him off balance. However, it didn't follow up on the attack but moved again back into the deep water with an incredible leap that nearly covered a quarter of the stream.

Winston and Charles were now within five minutes of arriving on the scene, but it seemed that the sun had already set and there were only a few minutes of light left.

Badge instinctively knew that the game was up with it being the only dog alive. As Winston and Charles came to the stream out of breath, there was Badge with blood covering his face and with eyes that seemed to say, "I'm sorry."

Winston looked around and knew instantly that they had lost their chance with the thick jungle on the opposite side. Charles was more determined and wanted to follow with a little light left. Winston told him to forget it. "In a few minutes it would kill one of us."

Charles recognized the danger, having forgotten about it during the heat of the chase. Winston tore up his undershirt and wrapped Badge up to prevent further bleeding. Winston never would have imagined that a cat would take out three of the four dogs so easily. It was a cunning one and had managed to isolate each one enough to deal a death blow to them one by one.

Charles was carrying Winston's gun as he carried Badge back to the handler who had been trying to keep up with them. They made a quick retreat, trying to put distance between themselves and the cat, and were hoping it hadn't back-tracked and now they were the prey.

The big cat could not run anymore. It was spent and It rested near the large stream enjoying not being pursued by the dogs. It was smart enough to realize that there was only one dog left, and darkness had set giving it a very distinct advantage. It started to rise and went to the stream where only moments before there was death and chaos. It leapt back into the stream letting the water cool its vibrantly colored fur. It continued swimming to the other side, shook itself of excess water, and there it picked up the unmistakable scent of man. That eternal enemy that had hounded and attempted to destroy it since it was young. Relentless, ruthless and cunning instinct led it to know that they would never stop pursuing it, even to the ends of the earth.

The trail was fresh and easy to follow. The heightened pace made the men sweat profusely, which made them all the easier to follow. Stealthily it stalked, seeing the foliage better aided by a sliver of a moon.

On and on the men went looking for a giant cypress tree to gain sanctuary. They had brought a few pine torches and they stopped to light them. Winston had never seen Charles unnerved but now he could see his hands shaking knowing the danger they were in. This was no ordinary tiger and only Winston seemed to know that. During the tracking Winston had noticed the large cypress trees that would benefit them. They were about fifteen minutes away at a good run. During this time, they all knew how vulnerable they were.

They were still moving as quickly as possible with the dog handler bringing up the rear. They had been taking turns carrying Badge and Winston was carrying him now. The tiger was picking up its pace as well and was gaining on the men. The dog handler would turn around at every sound that was made, half paranoid. The jungle was alive with every noise imaginable. The trail wasn't easy for the men to follow and the tiger was gaining rapidly, ready to exact revenge as if possessed with the fiendish spirit of the underworld.

The men could see the large outlines of the cypress tree as Winston said, "Look, there."

They moved out again but as they did a ferocious roar sank into the very fiber of each being as it rang out behind them.

The dog handler was screaming in his native tongue for all he was worth, for the tiger had knocked him over and as he fell into the underbrush it clasped its massive jaws onto his shoulder, crushing the bones and dragging him off.

Winston and Charles immediately went into defensive positions pointing their cocked guns into the nights darkness where screams continued for a few seconds more. Winston didn't lose a second.

"C'mon, we've got to move! There's nothing we can do for him," he said, and moved out again at a quicker pace.

Charles was right behind him, nearly paralyzed with fear himself. Winston had dropped Badge in the fray, and he was running with them too, somewhat recovered.

They were at the base of the large cypress when Winston yelled at Charles to get his pack off. Winston made a quick inventory and found a rope. They shined the torches up into the branches which were about twenty feet up in the air offering places for their lightweight hammocks. They continued to watch the clearing as they tossed the rope over the lowest branch. Winston told Charles to tie one end to some stout bushes close by while Winston quickly made two small prussic or climbing knots from two pieces of cordette taken from the pack.

"I hope a leopard hasn't already claimed this one for the night said Winston with a nervous smile."

Winston gave the prussic loops to Charles and told him to get up as quick as possible and to loosen them and slid them back down. Charles was shaking like a leaf in the wind but managed to tie the prussic's and inched his way up to the branch and passed the cordettes down to Winston. He shimmied his way up in haste.

Winston kept thinking to himself to hurry. He was the only one on the rope and the tiger had to be close by now. The packs were left on the ground. They did feel somewhat safe being at least twenty feet up in the air, but not safe enough to sleep so they climbed higher until they reached several large branches about thirty-five feet off the ground. There was no question a tiger could easily leap twenty feet, but tigers weren't known for their tree climbing skills due to their weight. They went to work finding a place to sleep in the various parts of the tree which offered the most comfortable position. They wished they had grabbed some water and food but were lucky to be alive. It was safer than staying on the ground and getting killed. In their haste to get up the tree Badge was left behind on the trail and managed to scurry into some dense foliage on the ground and although wounded still had enough sense not to sleep in the open.

Winston and Charles were dead tired. Not much was said, and Winston and Charles were down with the loss of the tracker. Charles kept thinking there was something they could have done but Winston was right. He was gone the minute the tiger caught up with him. Charles kept thinking it could have been him. Like King Hezekiah caged up in Jerusalem, they were holed up in the trees.

The tiger had killed for vengeance, if an animal could possibly possess such a trait, for the cat didn't eat anything after killing the dog handler but retired from the area.

The night came and went like all the others through the eons of time. Now they were forced to get down from their perches and deal with the man-eater once again. Was it near? Was it waiting for them? Had it left?

Winston lowered himself first by twisting the rope around his body and slowly lowering himself. If the cat was still around he would rely on adrenaline to get him back up if possible, but it would likely be too late.

They were again at a disadvantage although they did have light now to see in.

Winston instructed Charles not to come down until he said it was safe. Winston noticed pug marks from last night surrounding the tree and knelt to feel them. They were several hours old but there was no doubt the cat knew where they had stopped for the night. The only chance they had was if it had returned to feast on the dog handler. It had to be somewhat hungry, but maybe it was waiting for them right this moment.

Winston looked around for any other signs or warnings. He didn't see any and quickly motioned for Charles to get down without saying a word. The pug marks moved over in the direction where Badge had gone, and although Winston didn't go looking for him, he knew from the dogs personality if he was well enough to move he would have been there waiting for them at the base of the tree. In fact, the tiger had tracked him down in the night and while he was weak from the loss of blood and the rigors of the day the tiger killed him without a sound or yelp.

Somehow Winston knew the tiger had killed Badge. He wept within himself trying to think of what he could have done, but there was nothing. Even himself and the others were lucky to be alive. The great cat would have killed Badge either way; whether it happened last night or from the earlier blow he didn't know, he just knew that his favorite and most experienced dog was dead.

There was no time to dwell on it as they were still in grave danger. They had to get to the safety of a village before the cat wreaked further havoc.

Charles came down as Winston motioned for him to remain as quiet as possible. They gathered up just essential gear, leaving a lot of food behind. Winston had taken a compass bearing up in the tree and had looked at the map as well. They were heading for the closest village, not in the direction of where the tiger had attacked last night. They would have a large body of men return and bring the tracker back and have a proper burial.

They started moving quickly, anxious to get to safety. From Winston's estimates they were about ten miles away from the closest village. At that distance it would take them about four to five hours to get there, and it was through man-eater territory. The guns were unslung and ready for an ambush.

The tiger itself was doing well despite a gunshot wound which had narrowly missed it vital organs. It didn't seem affected by the wound at all. It had returned for the time being to the dead tracker, which it ate at its leisure.

Winston and Charles were paranoid getting back, pointing their guns at every sound imaginable. Most men would be locked up in an insane asylum after what they had been through the last couple of days. They were both longing for the comforts of semi civilization and better food. It was another hot, muggy day and sweat poured down their faces. They were both constantly wiping the perspiration from their heads with a cotton handkerchief kept in one of their pockets.

Luck was bound to change sooner or later for that tiger, thought Winston. It was as though it did indeed have nine lives. If things had gone just a little differently they would have been spreading that skin over pegs by now. And it had to be a record, a cat that size. Winston had never seen one that big, not even stuffed.

After a couple of hours hiking through the jungle, Winston was fairly certain the tiger wasn't following them, but he couldn't be sure. After all, this cat showed unique initiative. It was almost as if it was human itself, being able to foresee danger and eliminate it.

Charles asked what the next plan was, mainly just for conversation, but Winston didn't quite know and answered that they would likely have to return to square one and try and guess the next village to be attacked, or maybe try a tied up animal. It was apparent that he was frustrated, but that was the nature of the game.

Even though neither spoke of the incident with the dog handler, it was on both men's minds. Here was a tiger which had killed hundreds, but they were all unknown faces until now. The tracker was a family man, well liked among everyone. It would be presumptuous to assume that in getting into a business like this there would be no casualties. But once it happens there's bitterness and vengeance and it's hard to keep emotions in check. Winston thought about this and realized that he had to keep a clear and thinking mind, because intelligence was the only think keeping them ahead of this cat and he had to figure a way to outwit it.

Like Napoleon's army returning from Russia they marched on in despair. Unbeknownst to the men, they had been watched early on. The tiger had tracked back and picked up their scent soon after they left, and although they didn't see it, the cat had seen enough of them to know them by sight. It was instinct that held the tiger back. It could have easily killed one but the other, no doubt, would have gotten at least a shot off and perhaps killed it. Like all intelligent animals it had learned lessons that enabled it to survive all these years.

The men came into the village of Katarim like drugged sailors from a long ocean voyage. They were hailed and asked what had happened. They were fed and the news of another death quickly spread through the village, and by tomorrow it would run through the countryside. They quickly ate and retired to sleep, weary from being exhausted which had been accentuated by fear.

All of Winston's asking and directions were accounted for promptly as he and Charles spent a restful sleep away from danger. The murmurs and gossip were, even at that time, starting to spread with exaggerated exploits already in the works. The villagers didn't mingle long. There was a man-eater around and people quickly went to their huts.

Charles woke up the following morning to see Winston looking at the map. He had marked spots where attacks had occurred and was tracking the progress of where the tiger was heading. He estimated that they would have another three to five days before another attack occurred, in the meantime they could recover their friend.

Breakfast was announced and the two men sat down to what seemed like wonderful food compared with what they had been eating the past couple of days. Hopefully, another group of the men would be here by tomorrow. Until then they had to formulate a plan, one that would work this time.

Charles was putting together his progress report to the office, hoping they would realize they were making headway and getting chances, but he knew his boss too well and guessed they would be pulled from the project soon unless they could deliver results.

Winston and Charles both went down to the river to get a well-deserved bath in the stream. It felt good to wash the dirt and dust from their bodies. It was particularly pleasant as the temperature was hot and the water cool. Animals and birds played around them like there wasn't a care in the world.

Some villagers seemed to be the shaken from the closeness of the man-eater. They had a constant, wild eyed stare. Winston thought they would eventually get over it.

Winston focused on the future and what they could do, Charles on the other hand thought about what they could have done differently to achieve expected results.

It was too difficult to predict what the cat was going to do next. They could be close with generalities but specifics were something different altogether.

Whenever one is away from his home the thoughts eventually return there, to the comforts enjoyed, the friends or family that is missed, the particular bed or hobby that makes life just a little more enjoyable. Those thoughts kept hounding Charles as he continued to sacrifice. Winston on the other hand was used to it and it was second nature to him. He had been in positions like this before and he knew what it took. He never complained but just improvised the best he could.

Charles caught up with Winston later that night. "I hear you do a lot of charity or volunteer work with digging water wells for outlying villages when you're not hunting big game?" Winston took a big puff from his pipe and answered "You know Charles service is an interesting thing in and of itself, I guess I could sit back and do nothing, take all the favors and invites I could and give nothing back and I did do that for awhile, rather enjoyed it". He looked out to the jungle as he took another puff from his pipe, "but then a friend of mine convinced me to donate some funds for a needed well, I decided I wanted to see where the money was going and I went to the village where it was taking place, I saw the people and their faces, I heard the stories of how far they had to fetch their water, I actually got in and started digging too, stayed there until the project was finished and felt good about it, that I was actually doing something worthwhile. You see if you don't take the time to give something back to help others, you become a little more concerned with yourself. Doesn't the bible say something about that if you are in the service of your other beings, you are only in the service of your God"? "I didn't know you were religious" asked Charles. "I'm not, but that doesn't mean I don't believe in God, I'll have to answer to him sometime, and if I didn't help people out that just makes it that much worse when I meet Him. You should find a worthwhile cause; it does wonders, I'm telling you". Charles thought it was good advice and said "Is there anything else about you that I should know"? "Only that I'm extremely difficult to work with" With that both men gave a hearty laugh.

Charles began to reflect about things back at the office and he thought about the map now covered with a few more flags, some of them now known to him personally. With all those flags he mused, how had the tiger had such an incredible amount of good luck? How many times had it managed to slip away, to use its instinct, when it should have met death? A few of the deaths were accidental, which was a direct result of tactics used to try and eradicate the tiger. There had been numerous disasters greater than this over the years, but this menace held the country captive with fear and paranoia. It was more than all the other disasters combined because it hadn't ended. With other disasters, the catastrophic event happened, and people mourned and then they began to rebuild. This disaster kept feeding upon itself growing larger every week.

Charles was trying to think of something new they could use against the striped cat, because everything else had failed. He longed for a long hot bath and a comfortable bed. He missed the company of women. But he had no regrets thus far. He had seen some wonderful parts of the country he wouldn't have seen otherwise. Maybe someday he could publish his memoirs of the whole adventure. This is what he lived for. This was why he had chosen to come to India.

The days were getting hotter with the advent of the summer. This meant that the foliage would dry up and there would be less cover for the tiger, but they only had a couple of months, for the summer monsoon would return like clockwork twice a year and with it the foliage would return as green as ever, hiding the presence of the beast so many hated.

They waited patiently for the others to arrive, looking over the map, studying it, trying to predict the next move. It was boring most of the time. One teenage young man came up to Winston and presented him with a beautifully carved tiger with stripes etched into the wood. It was remarkably good and Winston, in turn, gave him his pencil and pad so he could sketch.

Charles had begun his weekly report to the office but had rewritten it several times before settling on a final draft. It needed to be somewhat positive but with the setbacks it was difficult to put things into the correct light. Although there were some thoughts that he could be fired, in which case Charles would have to return to the office, he didn't want that. Even with the danger he wanted to see this through to the end.

Early the next morning Winston met with the local leaders. They brought news that had come up from the outside world, along with letters that had been sent in their direction and forwarded to them. One of the letters Charles recognized immediately as being from the government and most likely his office. It had the official state seal of wax which had been used for centuries.

Charles quickly broke the seal and opened the letter and began reading. Winston glanced over and realized it was important news from the look on his face. Winston asked what it was, and Charles told him that he had been recalled to Bombay immediately. Apparently, there was a very distinguished guest attending the Jubilation ball held in a week and a half. There would be questions of the man-eater and Charles was being recalled to answer any questions they might have for him. He sat down in a chair while telling Winston the news.

"I probably won't be able to get back here for at least a fortnight."

"Well, that's alright. It probably won't attack again for a few days and we'll just have to wait for it anyhow. Maybe you could tell them that you've caught it alive and you'll be presenting it to His Majesty in honor of the jubilee of India!"

Charles gave a slight laugh.

"Yeah, maybe we could feed him politicians we're not particularly fond of. I don't suppose I could convince you to come as well?"

"No, you couldn't. We're too close, I can feel it. All we need is some luck on our side. Besides I'd probably get fired for some remark."

There was a pause in the conversation.

"Well, I'd like to rejoin you in a couple of weeks if that's ok with you and if the cat's still alive."

"Well I hope to have a say in that."

The men shook hands as Winston said, "Godspeed."

Charles went to pack and within the hour was on his way to Bombay. It would take several days since they were in areas which were quite remote. Charles was upset he had been ordered back to the offices. Couldn't anyone do anything there without his help? he thought to himself. Perhaps if he had been a better shot, he would have been returning in glory. But it seemed like the tiger had fully recovered from the wound anyway. There was no way it could have handled the dogs that way if it was hurt. The more he thought about things the more he realized they had underestimated the cat's intelligence. Round one goes to the Katagi man-eater.

As the time came and went he admired the slow pace that allowed him to see the beautiful countryside and the people. He truly loved this place. With his position, he was truly treated like a king. It was difficult to shake some of the techniques learned from Winston, even though he was clearly out of danger. He found himself looking at the jungle closer, occasionally feeling for a gun that wasn't there.

After a short boat ride, more miles on foot, and a day later, he was at last on the train bound for cities leading to Bombay. He found a compartment and put his feet up and his hat over his eyes and fell asleep. The train would arrive at the first major stop in the morning with several more stops scheduled along the way.

Somehow in the morning he managed to wake as the train came into the station. He was hungry and grabbed a little food from a street vendor once they disembarked. Later in the afternoon he arrived in his home city and went straight for the office with his report. He found everyone working like normal when he entered. Some of the office ladies giggled when they saw him disheveled and unshaven for several weeks. They were used to seeing him impeccably dressed and groomed, but there was something about the wild man look that made less than pure thoughts come into their heads. He wondered how bad he smelled.

He noticed the map and the flags were already up to date. Charles thought that the office was getting their information from more than one source.

Some people saw Charles and came to greet him and ask particulars. He told some of them the highlighted version and then made it to his office, which was exactly as he had left it. He turned on the fan and began to type up his report up to the time he left. It took about an hour. Sarkee, a very close friend and colleague (and a native to India) who, through his intelligence, had secured a position in the office, knocked and parted the door and looked in.

"Can I come in?"

"Only you," replied Charles.

It was good to see a friend, especially one that cared.

"I hit him you know."

"Yes, I heard," speaking in his heavily accented English. "And I hope that you will have a magnificent tiger rug to lay on your floor"

"I said I hit it. Killing it is an entirely different matter. So, I understand the Prime Minister is in town?"

"Yes, that's why George recalled you. And he hasn't been pleased with your reports."

"Now, why am I not surprised at that?"

"Well, the jubilee ball is in a couple of days. Do you want me to get you a companion for the evening?"

"Are you suggesting that I may have a problem getting a companion on such short notice?"

"Well, if I remember correctly, last year your exact words were 'yes, I have my choice of three women,' and then you showed up alone!"

"Can I help it if it slipped my mind completely?"

"Well, just say the word and I can line you up with several of the most beautiful women in all of India"

"English or Indian?" asked Charles.

"Well that depends on what you're looking for. You can have the English woman who will relate to your homeland and can talk politics and may have a mind of her own, or you can choose the native woman who understands the man and can attend to your every need?"

"Make it the Indian woman this time and she better be shapely and beautiful."

"By the way, George wants to meet with you right away."

"Yeah, I expected that. I'll drop off my report and then we can catch some lunch down at the Monsoon café."

"Sounds good, Just come and get me when you're finished."

Charles went back to typing up his report as Sarkee left his office.

The constant pecking of the typewriter of someone used to typing reports three days a week could be heard through the office. In a way it was good to be back, but he wished he was still out there.

He hadn't been typing long when George opened his door and strolled in. George asked him if he was starting a new dress code. Charles replied that he had come straight here.

"Yes, someone told me that you had arrived."

"Just an hour ago. I'm finishing up the report now. I'll drop it off at your office as soon as it's done."

"Thank you. I must expect that you'll be at the ball as well. The prime minister is in town and I'm sure he'll have a question or two on how we are handling the Katagi man-eater."

"Yes, that's why I was recalled I understand. I would also like to return to the field as soon as the ball is over and the prime minister is satisfied with how we are doing things."

George answered that he didn't see a problem with that.

"Fine. Make sure that report ends up on my desk, won't you chap."

With that said, George left the office and Winston thought about how pompous George was and went back to his report. It was done in another fifteen minutes and he left the office and dropped it off with Smythe's secretary, telling her to make sure that he got it as soon as possible.

He went off to catch a rickshaw to his cottage on the edge of town and to get in a quick bath before he joined Sarkee at the café. Luckily, his servant had heard that he had arrived and was already getting the water boiled and the tub filled. He arrived at his home to find the steam already permeating the rooms. He quickly undressed and jumped into the tub without feeling the temperature.

His cottage was modestly furnished, but definitely there was a masculine motif everywhere. He had a few stuffed animals that he had shot while on hunts, which were impressive mounts themselves. There were various paintings of mountains and jungles around the room, most of them by local artists, and some pictures with dignitaries. Wicker furniture was everywhere as he purchased it locally. The whole cottage took on a native look that was quite different from the other Englishman's homes who lived in the country.

Charles woman servant was a great help to him, she always knew what he wanted and would anticipate everything with impeccable timing. She had no doubt little to do over the last few weeks, but he had kept her pay the same regardless and she was even more determined to make up for lost time or to get back from her vacation. She was bored not having Charles to talk to and tease her. In a way she loved the Sahib and would do most anything for him. As Charles sank into a well deserved bath he heard his servant comment through the door that several of his lady friends had called on him. He thought who they might be and blissfully sank further into his bath.

After about twenty minutes Charles's servant knocked on the door telling him he would be late for his appointment. There were some fresh clothes laid out for him and before long he had dried himself off leaving a large bath full of muddy water which represented a cumulative total of several weeks of dirt. Then he was off to the café.

He caught a rickshaw and rode it into town, taking in the smell of a city with inadequate garbage removal. He took a new notice of all the people doing their mundane errands and knew it was a part of his life.

Meanwhile, George was looking over the report Charles had typed up and was wondering why they couldn't close the deal when they were so close. He began to wonder if bringing him back at this time had been the best thing to do. *But it's too late now,* he thought. *He's already here.*

He barked some orders to his secretary and she was off making some arrangements for dinner that evening with the Prime Minister. Somehow, deep inside he knew that if he didn't solve this problem immediately he was going to lose his position. He couldn't stand the thought of it and quickly got it out of his mind. Now he had to arrange for someone to meet with the Prime minister's wife to help her shop the best places in town and to show her the ropes while the Prime Minister was off on an elephant hunt. Anyone else in the same position would have assigned a savvy feminine shopper weeks before to help her out, but George Smythe didn't have the foresight nor the tact. Handling the problem of the man-eater and presenting it in the right way to the Prime Minister was going to be a difficult and delicate matter in and of itself, and handling multiple tasks was not a talent that he possessed. Perhaps Charles could sway the minister about how they were properly handling the situation. One thing was for certain; Charles was going to tell the truth. He didn't know if that was going to be good or bad, but he thought to himself that he had better be prepared for anything that may be asked, either way he wasn't looking forward to it.

Charles was hungry for lunch and one of his favorite meals was roast chicken smothered in a tasty oriental sauce prepared in a special way by the cook. He could already taste the fresh baked bread that came with each meal as well. It was one of the things he had missed most while out in the jungle. He met Sarkee, who was several minutes late, and the aroma of the food made him forget everything.

There were a few ladies at the café who knew and said hello to Charles and asked him to call on them.

He was reflecting on the sweet smell that permeated the room when they walked by and he asked Sarkee, "So who are you setting me up with?"

"Oh, just some homely woman from the countryside with the face of a cow, you know, one of those courtesy dates that make women feel good when they have a date."

Charles barely cracked a smile.

Sarkee continued, "You know cows are venerated in this country."

"Yes, an idea I find to be preposterous."

Both men grinned.

"I've missed your jokes."

Charles had a very fast and humorous wit.

"So, tell me about the Winston Jamison fellow."

"Well, he's everything of his reputation and more. Quite intelligent you know, and unequaled in the jungle. He's well worth the money. If it had been him with the shot instead of me we would be reading about the tiger's death by now."

"Is he hard to get along with?"

"No, not really, once you get to know him. Well, I guess it depends on whether he likes you or not, demanding though. But he has a right to be you know. We lost a man to the beast about a week ago. It could have been me."

"What about eccentricities?"

"Well he's got them, there's no doubt about that, but then again so do you. What about the freshly pressed white shirt that you wear every day? Wouldn't that be considered an eccentricity? Anyway, some see it that way, but I think its confidence; he exudes it, and he can back it up."

"Sounds like he's rubbing off on you?"

"Maybe he is. Anyway, I want to get back as soon as possible"

"Why? I thought you said you were almost killed?"

"Yeah, but its different out there. There's a sense of doing something good, something for the people, a greater sacrifice for the whole."

"Well if you want to get yourself killed I know a number of ways that are less terrifying. Weren't you scared? I mean, one wrong move and you're being ripped to shreds, alive!"

"You only think about it when the danger is gone. It's quite strange, but when in the thick of things, you are focused to a point where all your senses are finely tuned to accomplish the goal. Sight, smell, hearing, everything is trying to give you a slight advantage. Now, I'd be lying if I said my heart wasn't going at one hundred and twenty beats per minute, but you ignore it because your looking out at the danger, the threat. I think that's why Jamison is so good at it. He's been there before and knows exactly what to expect. The fear is there for him too, he's just learned to subdue it better than anyone else.

"Now tell me what's been happening at the office while I've been out."

"Well, you know George took his lessons from the Egyptian taskmasters, the only thing missing is his whip. I think he takes some of the pressure and frustration out on us. You're lucky you were not at some of the meetings we've had. And you know he lacks true leadership. How he connived his way into that position I'll never know. Other than that not much has been happening. Katy asks how you are on a constant basis; wants to see the reports and all."

"Are they trying to do anything else on the Man-eater?"asked Charles.

"No, not really, they are leaving things up to you and Jamison for now, as far as I know. To tell you the truth, without you there I think George is like a boat without a rudder."

"Thanks. That means a lot from someone who doesn't give many compliments. Anyway, I'm wasting precious time here. You know we only have a couple of months before the summer monsoons come back. I'm heading back to the jungle right after the ball you know."

"Yes, I figured as much. You're not turning this thing into a personal vendetta, are you?"

"Why do you say that?"

"Because you had a look I've never seen in you before, very determined, almost like you're taking it personal."

"Well maybe I am. It killed the dog handler who seemed like a decent chap, is it wrong to have a vendetta against an animal?"

"I don't know. You remember Captain Ahab. His determination to kill that whale cost him his life. He would stop at nothing for vengeance. What about you?"

"Well, you don't see me going around asking people if they've seen the white tiger, do you?"

Both men laughed.

"Just be careful. Don't let this thing cloud your judgment. You have a bright future you know."

"Well, it almost sounds as if you care about someone other than yourself."

"Yes, but don't let the word get around."

"Well, are you going to tell me who you're lining me up with? You know an Englishman and an Indian as a couple may cause quite a stir around here."

"That's why we have to make her the envy of every woman in attendance. I just wish I had a couple more weeks to work on her manners."

Charles gave a look of concern which quickly gave way when he knew Sarkee was joking again. Inside, Charles was appreciating the simple things that he had always taken for granted which weren't there when he was out in the jungle, something simple like his freshly squeezed calamanchi and orange juice which he was holding up and looking at. He drank it slowly savoring every drop. He couldn't remember when a meal tasted so good. And the great thing would be a normal bed for the night. How he was looking forward to that.

Sarkee excused himself and Charles stayed on in the open air at the table. He was starting to feel sleepy after a few minutes so he got up and caught a rickshaw home where he fell into his bed, too tired to take his clothes off.

It was several hours before he woke up and realized the sun was setting on a beautiful horizon. Tomorrow he thought he would go to the library and see what he could find out about big cat hunts and traps. Perhaps something new was needed to get the wily creature.

His servant was already beginning to prepare the evening meal and he was looking forward to it. When the meal was ready, his servant called to him that the food was ready. He always looked forward to her cooking although it was a little on the spicy side as most Indian dishes were. He ate at his leisure and when she came back to fill his glass he told her he wouldn't need dinner tomorrow as it was the jubilee ball, and asked if she could pick up his tuxedo in the afternoon from the tailor. She said she would be happy to and asked who the lucky woman was who would be accompanying him. He mentioned that Sarkee was lining him up and he didn't know the woman. He left out the fact that she was Indian.

Following the meal he went for a stroll around his bungalow. There was a full moon out and he wondered if Winston would be tracking the man-eater in the illuminated night. He realized he was getting sleepy and returned to his home, climbed under the mosquito net and went straight to sleep. It was one of pure slumber appreciating the comfort of home and a well made bed.

He woke late the next morning, having left no instructions to be awakened. His breakfast was quickly served and following that he dressed to go into the office to catch up on a few things before heading for the library and hopefully the next day back to the jungle. He arrived at the office where there was a message to see George right away. He walked straight over to his office and took a deep breath before knocking on the wood and opening the door to see George looking over some papers.

"Ah, come in Charles, I wanted to see you. There was a pause as he pretended to look over some papers. I'll come straight to the point. The prime minister will likely ask you some questions tonight about the Katagi man-eater, and I would appreciate it if you answer him in a positive light and let him know that we have the situation under control and well in hand."

"So, you want me to lie."

"No, I don't want you to lie," there was a slight pause in his speech. "I just want you to convey that we are doing all that we can to eradicate this menace. You *do* believe that we are doing all that we can, don't you?"

"Well, I don't believe we ever received the requested supplies we asked for in my second report."

"Yes, yes of course, but you must understand that the budget has been stretched to the limit this year and we are already over budget by thirty percent. We have to conserve in places you know."

"Yes, but not in this place, we need to utilize every resource we can to eliminate this threat."

"So, what you're saying is that you're going to give him a negative report?"

"No, I didn't say that, but I will be candid and forthright with him."

"Well, I know he's anxious to talk with you. I'll see you there at six sharp and don't be late. That will be all."

Charles was wondering why he had been recalled if George thought that he would render a negative report, but then realized that he had probably already informed the Prime Minister that they were doing all that they could at the moment and wanted Charles to reiterate that, that made sense, things were starting to come together now.

He went back to his office and a secretary quickly brought in a telegram from Winston which read,

"Hope you're having a ball. Tiger being quite elusive. Join us as soon as possible and bring necessary supplies." Winston

He decided to leave and head over to the library to see if there was anything else they weren't trying. Before doing so, he dropped by Sarkee's office to see what time he was picking up his date and where. Sarkee was working as hard as ever, but glad to see Charles as he came into his office without knocking.

"So old chap, who am I going out with tonight?"

"You'll find out soon enough. Why don't you plan to be ready at four-thirty. I'll pick you up then."

"Alright I'll be ready, but she better be pretty."

"I've told you before not to worry about that. You do have a reputation you know."

"Yes, and I need to keep up appearances."

"Four-thirty, don't be late."

With that Charles left the office and caught a rickshaw down to the library. He walked in and asked for assistance with anything to do with tiger attacks. The librarian was most helpful. Libraries, roads, bridges and schools were some of the benefits that the British had brought to India and it helped thought Charles as he wondered how much information he would have if the British hadn't helped. Articles started pouring onto the table he was sitting at. He had no idea there was so much news about it.

One article blamed the destruction of natural forest, which was then used for sugar cane fields which tigers frequented. As the tigers lay sleeping they would be disturbed by the workers, the tiger would then attack which usually proved fatal. Methods to eradicate the tigers lead to other accidental deaths. The numbers were alarming even before the Katagi man-eater. There were two hundred deaths attributed to one district alone. Sometimes tigers worked in pairs and created pure havoc. Maharashtra's were bragging about how many tigers they had bagged, some upwards of over one-thousand cats exterminated by one man. Some attacks occurred while a man or woman would leave the trail to relieve themselves only to be attacked from behind and severely mauled or killed. One article talked about a missing postman who was not heard of for some time until some old unopened letters were found near a rotting skull.

Some of the methods he read about astounded him. One in particular was a carcass rigged with an exploding grenade which had the pin attached to the rib cage and when the rib cage was spread apart to get more meat the animal met an untimely death.

Charles was enthralled and forgot about the time until he looked at his watch and realized it was three forty-five. He left as soon as possible and caught a taxi to his cottage. He would only have about fifteen minutes to prepare. It was a good thing he stopped by the barber earlier to get a shave. He was thinking about the articles as he rushed home. So many deaths, why? Why had they turned to eating humans?

Charles servant had his tuxedo out and ready when he arrived. Charles quickly changed into the tuxedo and wetted his hair, combing it straight back. He asked his servant how he looked and she replied that he looked great. He reminded her that all his clothes and ordered supplies were to be ready for prompt departure in the morning. He grabbed his hat and looked at his watch. Just a few more minutes before Sarkee and his date arrived. Charles servant asked again who he was taking to the ball and he replied that Sarkee was lining him up and he was a little concerned about it. He thought about the meeting with the Prime minister and figured it would only be about a half hour. He looked again at his pocket watch and tried to remember if Sarkee was always late.

The cab soon arrived, and Charles quickly said goodbye and rushed outside to enter the cab. Charles came around and saw one of the most striking Indians he had ever laid eyes on. She was absolutely beautiful. The introductions were made outside the waiting cab. In a flash they were off to the ball.

Charles asked his date, in Hindu where she was from. She answered that she was from Calcutta, and spoke in perfect English. Charles was impressed and asked where she was educated. She told him that she had attended school here, but that her mother was Indian and her father Australian. It was a rare combination that produced slightly brown skin with green eyes and chestnut hair. Charles indicated that he might need to excuse himself for part of the evening because he was meeting with the prime minister. Charles date spoke up and indicated that she hoped he wasn't in too much trouble. They all had a good laugh about that one.

They were dropped off at the royal palace and escorted by guards up the steps to the spacious front doors where they presented their invitations. Their names were announced and at first all eyes were on Charles and his date. It was rare to see a native as an escort, but most were jealous of the curvaceous figure and beautiful countenance that seemed to radiate to every part of the room.

Charles had no sooner sat down with his friends then he was summoned by an official and asked to join George and the Prime minister in the orient room. Charles excused himself and was led off like an ox to the butcher. He entered the room as the door was opened for him and saw the Prime minister and George, who were the only individuals in the room. George saw him and beckoned him to come over where he was introduced to the prime minister.

Once the introductions were over, the prime minister began to ask questions about the man-eater, some of which he already knew. Most of the questions were easy and were answered without much thought.

Then the prime minister said, "You know, the news of the man-eater has already reached London and the House of Commons are very concerned. India has been a very profitable commodity for the empire, perhaps their biggest thus far, and any threat to that status quo must be handled and dealt with immediately. How long has this tiger been killing people?"

George began to answer but was cut off by the prime minister.

"I am asking Charles if you don't mind. Is he not the expert you told me about?"

George was beginning to regret embellishing the credentials of Charles.

Charles himself was surprised to hear the words as well and looked over at George.

"No, I'm not an expert on these things. But, in answer to your questions, we believe it has been operating for several years now, perhaps up to six, but the last two years we've seen an escalation."

"Six years, and no one has been able to kill it yet?"

"Yes, that's correct. But we are trying everything possible at the moment."

"Well it's not enough. This cat should have been made into horse meat by now. This is making news back in England and the queen and the House of Commons want their investments protected even if it takes a legion of dragoons. We will not have hysteria gripping every part of this country.

"I understand that you have a professional in the field right now, but I'm sending you another one. Perhaps they can work together."

"Sir," said Charles, "I'm not sure that's a good idea."

George looked at Charles intently, letting him know with his eyes not to disagree with the Prime minister.

The prime minister eyed Charles and asked directly, "And why not?"

"Well sir, you can imagine the chaos with other hunters all trying to bag the same animal. You may have several accidental killings, and you may also have some conflicting personalities with different egos and such. They may try and out-do each other and resort to brashness instead of safety. They may not be as harmonious as you would think."

"Well, I see your point Charles. It's good to have an opposite opinion once in awhile instead of having everyone agree with you all the time," the prime minister glanced over at George, "However my mind is set on having another hunter join the chase so to speak. I've already sent for him. His name is Bart Hawthorne."

"The African big game hunter?" asked Charles.

"Yes, one and the same. Hopefully he can get along with your Jamison fellow and together they can kill the striped beast. Perhaps we need to increase the reward money as well, what is it now?"

George told him that it was up to five-thousand pounds.

"Well double it. We need to take care of this quickly."

Charles politely asked if there were any more questions that he would like answered and was told there were none, so he asked to be excused.

He quickly joined his friends and was determined to have an enjoyable evening despite the fact that he could not dance well.

The Prime minister and Smythe continued their boring conversation about politics or this or that. The fact was the government had always been run by those with high birth and positions and not necessarily by those with experience or natural ability.

The ball was a splendid affair where no expense was spared. The food was wonderful and Charles couldn't ever remember eating so much and so well. Perhaps it was his meager foodstuffs in the jungle that contributed to his voracious appetite and an appreciation for good food. His date was congenial and pleasant, a welcome surprise, and Sarkee himself was a little jealous. He kept eyeing Charles with an approving look.

Charles hadn't had such a good time for quite awhile. But just as all good things must come to an end the time flew and it was starting to wind down. Charles opted to get a second taxi to be alone for a few minutes with his date. They cuddled like kittens in a storm and expressed how good of a time they had. They had one glorious evening, it had been heaven for both of them. Charles dropped her off and gave her a kiss. He was sure they would be the talk of the town on the morrow, but he liked controversy. Otherwise he wouldn't have agreed to the lineup.

He started to think and focus on the task ahead of him. He had procured everything Winston had wanted and had a few more items as well. He wanted to make sure he was well prepared this time and wanted the finest items money could buy. After all, the coming days might be his last on earth. Many of the items he had purchased himself. He returned home to try and get a little sleep before having to get off to catch the morning train. He laid down to rest, appreciating the soft mattress and the imported feather pillow, and knew he would be without for a few more months. He quickly fell asleep and was awakened by his servant at the appointed time.

He felt as though he had just fallen asleep although he had been asleep for at least five hours, he was exhausted and didn't want to get out of bed, he realized he could sleep on the trains as well, so he pulled himself out of bed and began to get dressed.

All the arrangements had been made as far as logistics for the equipment and he had acquired a few more natives to help with the portage of the items.

He departed on time from Bombay. He left a brief note with George that he was back with Winston trying to eliminate the tiger. The last telegram from Winston indicated where they were heading but to check with the last station as there would be instructions if plans had changed.

The people within close proximity to the killings had been on edge for more than a week. As the jungle sounds began to filter through the nighttime air, every sound, every call was listened to by all within range, whether it was a howl from a monkey or a bird call, all ears were pricked and people stopped what they were doing to listen further. The question on everyone's mind was whether the striped beast was around the area, but of course no one knew for sure.

Unbeknownst to the people of Gatine, the tiger was indeed around and studying their village for anything out of the ordinary; anyone walking alone. The cat circled around to the back of the village where the jungle lay as a backdrop. Again it waited, looking for anything strange or unusual. Patience was one thing the cat had and it used it well.

In the darkness it could see a large hut a little on the outskirts of the village. The tiger broke cover to investigate. The doors and windows were shut and bolted but as it sniffed the air it could discern a human scent from within.

The hut was raised on stilts, characteristic of many of the huts built in the flood plain of the region where monsoon rains can bring heavy amounts of water into the village and the surrounding streams, which can occasionally overflow.

It went under the hut easily and began sniffing the floor area above its head. It made no sounds at all and the occupants were still unaware that there was any danger. It found an area where the people inside where sleeping and went to the other end of the floor. The floor was made of stout bamboo latched together, it couldn't break through without making a lot of noise.

It moved outside and leaned against the walls of the hut on the opposite side of where the occupants slept. It easily pushed through the thin nepa walls and stuck its head inside. It sized up the situation, including the bamboo poles that offered support for the walls, and within seconds it was in the hut and moving across the floor to the occupants on the other side.

Not a sound was made as it smelled a teenage girl and clamped its jaws tight around her neck, there was no way the girl could scream as the cat dragged the victim back the way it had come. Within a minute or two the girl was dead and all that was left was a bloody drag mark on the floor and a large hole in the wall of the hut.

Once down on the ground the tiger picked the girl up in its jaws and disappeared back to the jungle.

The rest of the family awoke with horror to find that the girl had been taken sometime during the night and no one had heard or seen anything. With such stealth they attributed it to the were-tiger with its enchanting powers.

The family was in shock. It could have been any one of them, but the daughter was loved by everyone in the village.

Word was quickly spread that a new victim had been taken in the village of Gatine and Winston wasted no time in getting there as quickly as possible. He left instructions by telegram at the nearest rail line to have Charles join him at the village of Gatine.

Charles had been making good time, catching the necessary trains and boats just before departure, and was relishing the chance to get back into the action.

Some of the family of the victim, and some of the villagers, were visibly upset, the keening of the mother was understandably present. Some of the villagers were accusing others of being were-tigers.

Such were the circumstances when Winston arrived and had to quell things down and restore order. The crowd wanted to hang one person accused of being the were-tiger right then and there. Winston was able to convince them to put the person in a holding room that was guarded so a trial could take place. Of course, he knew the cat would kill again and the man would be set free. He had saved his life for the moment.

The people began to quiet down, and he was trying to get as much information as possible. It had been twenty-four hours since the killing and he was hoping the cat was still in the area. The tiger had carried the victim a little distance and had consumed twenty pounds at the first sitting. There was enough meat for two meals since the victim was on the robust side.

This information was gathered by Winston and he knew there was a good chance the cat would be back for a second feeding, probably that night. Since there were only a few hours of light left he needed to work fast. Luckily the trail was fairly fresh and the added weight of the girl in the tiger's jaws in combination with a light shower made the pug marks deeper than usual and easy to follow.

There was a village tracker that came to help who was a relative of the victim and wanted to help in any way he could. They got their needed supplies to stay the night and began tracking the tiger.

The trail was easy to follow at first with the deep pug marks and an abundance of blood that had dripped at the beginning of the trail. The big cat had not taken the victim far, perhaps a quarter mile.

They found what was left of the girl soon enough and there was still an hour of daylight left. It was a difficult sight to behold but Winston had seen this thing many times and it no longer affected him like it used to. The tracker on the other hand was sobbing and Winston had to remind him to keep quiet.

The corpse had been eaten from the torso with strips of flesh hanging outside the body. The eyes were frozen in some comatose state that surely registered for a brief second what the girl had seen or felt before dying. The arms and the legs had been picked clean by the rasping tongue which all cats possess. The head was crushed and the gaping hole in the torso was a ghastly sight.

Winston observed that the cat had been feeding recently, in fact much more recently than he expected, and there was a chance that they had disturbed the eating although he couldn't tell for sure. There was an absence of dirt and leaves which a tiger usually will use to try and cover a meal that it was planning on returning to.

Winston quickly pulled back both hammers on the gun. He started looking around for any signs of the tiger or exit points from the small clearing to the tall grass. They left the remains undisturbed. Winston had a very uneasy feeling that he was being watched that very second. He was scanning the grass on the far side of the clearing which wasn't more than about twenty-eight feet away, enough for probably one or two shots from his side by side gun if the tiger decided to charge.

He told the tracker to slowly back up and not to say a word unless he saw something.

He started to notice fresh pug marks around the victim which had remained unseen before because of the gruesome scene they were witnessing. He noticed them now and how they went directly to the other side of the clearing, just where he surmised he was being watched. He would continuously watch that area while scanning other places for clues.

His gut feeling was not to move any closer and he was glad that he had pulled the hammers back when he thought he should. Instinctively, he began to retreat slowly, keeping an eye on the foliage on the other side of the clearing. The gun was ready to be shouldered and shot in an emergency, and if there wasn't time a hip shot was still possible.

They came to an area where they would no longer be able to see the clearing and Winston decided to stop there for a moment and assess the situation. He would alternate looking behind him and looking at the clearing to make sure the cat had not broken cover.

The tiger had been watching them for some time when it decided to circle around and try to get at Winston without being seen. It was moving very slowly and deliberately.

The big cat had made it nearly half way around them when a langur spotted it and gave the alarm call. Winston and the tracker stopped immediately and looked in the direction of the call but were unable to see anything in the dense foliage. Winston knew exactly what it was trying to do and needed a quick counter move if they wanted to see another day.

The tiger although agitated continued to stalk the men. Winston knew he had to get out of there. The cover was just too thick to get a good shot off quick enough. Winston made hand signals to retreat to Gatain and they started to make their way as quick as possible back to the village. There just weren't enough odds in their favor to continue. If he was going to get this wily cat he needed to surprise it or somehow get the odds in his favor.

The big cat was nearly to where it had seen Winston last when it picked up the scent of men. By this time it was a race to get out of the thick cover where they could get a better shot or get back to the safety of the village. The tiger instinctively picked up its pace and was running at a slow trot to try and cut them off. Winston had also picked up his pace sensing the dangerous predicament they were in. He took his rifle off his shoulder and began to run with it in his hand to increase their speed. How many times, he thought to himself, had he been forced to look over his shoulder to see if this cat was coming. He vowed to change things around and sometime in the future the cat be looking over its shoulder. The heat didn't help as they ran, for sweat was running off their faces and sending the scent into the air. The big cat had no problems picking up the smell and was slightly gaining on them to within three-hundred yards. Winston knew once they hit the large clearing they would have more favorable terms and was making for it with all haste. The tiger covered the distance a lot easier and was within one-hundred yards when Winston broke cover and raced to the center of the clearing. It was just large enough to perhaps give him two good shots. It was, he felt, the best choice. To have continued to the village would have been suicide, especially if the tiger was tracking them like he thought it was. The tiger had caught up to the clearing in no time and stopped short of breaking through the foliage instinctively. It peered through the foliage without revealing itself and could see Winston and the tracker making a stand in the middle of the clearing. It decided to move around the perimeter and see if there was a spot that it could get closer.

As it moved around it found the best spot for an attack and, like a poker player having all the cards, decided to wait until dark to increase its chances. Winston was thinking that it would be best for the cat to strike once darkness fell, and although they possessed several torches in the back pack he was certain they could not last the entire night. He remembered the moon and knew that it would be at three quarters strength tonight and could give them a little more light.

The tiger laid down in the grass where it could still see through to the trapped men. It was a waiting game now and still several hours before night-fall. Winston told the tracker that they were being watched by the tiger, he was sure of it. The tracker began to tremble and Winston had to calm him down. Winston checked his gun and made sure the hammers were pulled back.

The hours of the evening were oppressive in the muggy heat but on and on they waited. At last the final light of the bright orange sun was starting to be dispelled from the area and the moon began to rise.

When it got sufficiently dark Winston had one torch lit and the tiger saw it. It was not good for the cat, for the light would reflect off it eyes and give its position away. It didn't understand this but knew that the torch was not good because it gave temporary light to the scene.

The tiger continued to pace back and forth deciding what to do. It wanted to get rid of this menace that had hounded it for weeks, that had prevented it from eating when it wanted. It wanted an end to the relentless pursuit. Everywhere it went, there was this man trying to kill it. The torches made the tiger uneasy and unwilling to attack, but it had no idea they didn't have enough to last the night. It continued to pace around the perimeter. But it wasn't going to wait forever. It was frustrated and it left the perimeter and started out for the village.

Winston and the tracker were at an impasse. They couldn't leave until it was safer, and that was in the morning, and they had no idea that the tiger had left. For all they knew it was still there waiting for them. The tracker continued to keep a sharp look out with neither of them sleeping, for how could they, with a man-eater patrolling their area waiting for the slightest mistake which would result in a very painful death for both of them. Like two shipwrecked victims they lay there waiting, hoping for some rescue which would never materialize.

The tiger continued to prowl towards the village picking up its pace. There was no need for food as it had eaten earlier in the day, but it was hell bent on revenge, if that was possible in the animal world. Some say that animals, at times, can be very human or possess human characteristics. But can they possess traits such as hate, envy, jealousy, or vengeance? Do they have murderers among their own kind? Do they have individuals that have mentally broken down and defy the norms?

Winston was thinking about that, knowing that at times this cat had killed for fun. But could this striped death be taking out human lives purely for vengeance? Could it be doing it from the constant tracking, the wounding, the hounding that it had experienced in the last month?

On it went as it continued into the night making for the village like a long distance runner always with the prize in mind. It did not worry about silence, for the one person who could dispatch it was in some invisible prison being held by fear. They had no idea the cat was gone. All they could do was wait it out until morning.

The tiger knew that the one danger to itself was holed up out in the jungle. It was making no stops in its quest to reach the village and take another victim. It was only a couple of hours after darkness that the tiger began to approach the outskirts of the village. There were some torches lit, but that did not prevent the tiger from coming straight into the center of the village. There were still some members of Winston's camp in the village and some people were expecting him shortly, for he had not taken camping supplies with him. Much to the astonishment of those who were milling around was at once heard the ferocious snarls and roars mixed with screams as the tiger swept in like an unsuspecting wolf leaps into the fold of sheep. There were no guns ready as no one was suspecting such a bold venture. Screams could be heard everywhere and at first it was difficult to tell where the attack was coming from. Bamboo doors were being bolted shut as quickly as possible and people who were left out were asking to be let in at the closest huts. But it was already too late for one young man. He heard a swoosh and turned around to be knocked out cold by the paw of the lord of the jungle. The tiger quickly picked up its hapless victim and left as quickly as it came. Villagers tried to light torches to see what was happening and came too late to the scene.

The village was at such a distance that Winston could not hear the noise of the pandemonium.

The tiger had the victim in its jaws when the young man awoke from the earlier blow that had knocked him unconscious. He came to his senses at once and began to scream and twist to try and free himself from the massive force that had him bound. Within seconds the tiger had a death grip on his neck and a loud crack could be heard as the tiger used its jaws to crush the man's neck. Then it thrashed the man to and fro like a rag doll.

Blood began to ooze out of the large canine holes clamped down on the man's neck. The cat, knowing that the man was dead, left him in the middle of the trail to be found and left the area.

Winston and the tracker were getting tired and everything was beginning to look like a possible attack. Calls from animals throughout the night kept them edgy and nervous. Bushes and foliage looked like the waiting tiger as their eyes played tricks on them. They were both very sleepy but neither would yield to sleep knowing that their very lives depended on their ability to fight off an attack.

The torches and pine tar started to fail at about two in the morning and Winston knew that if the tiger was still there the attack would likely follow soon enough. The moon still gave out a little light and they strained their eyes to see anything. They hadn't heard the tiger for some time and as the torch went out, Winston was convinced that the tiger wasn't around anymore.

However, it could still be in the area and it would be foolish to return to the village at night. They went looking for a good tree to climb, all the while trying to be as quiet as possible and straining to see anything that was moving. They made it to a large mango tree and Winston unloaded from the pack his special climbing spikes that attached to the inside of his boots. With a small rope around the tree he began to shimmy up the trunk to where he secured a spot on a large branch and tied off the rope. He threw the remaining coil down to the tracker. With no light he could only hope it was free of leopards and that if there was one that it would find another home for the night.

Both men tied themselves off and began to sleep twenty-five feet off the jungle floor. They awoke without incident at sunrise and with enough light, they began to lower themselves down to the jungle floor.

They started back for the village immediately but after an hour they came across the victim from last night just outside the village. The mangled body lay right before their eyes. The scalp was nearly removed and there was a large hole in the stomach area with intestines reaching up as if suddenly seeking freedom.

The body had not been eaten in the least which indicated that the cat was out to kill for vengeance alone, as if to say, "I knew you couldn't do a thing last night, and for your troubles this is what I can do."

Winston began to think that it may be a trap with the cat waiting around to ambush them. He pulled the hammers back on his gun as they approached the victim.

There were hundreds of flies already congregating on the body. The eyes showed extreme fear which indicated that he was alive before being killed and knew what was happening. As they approached within about twenty-feet, Winston stopped them and whispered to the tracker that in case the cat was waiting they can't stop but must run quickly past the victim when he fires his first shot. Winston fired and they ran like mad past the victim and continued on for a spell. It became apparent that the tiger was not waiting in ambush and after a small rest to catch their breath they headed for the village only a short distance away. Winston was angry that there was another victim and told himself that somewhere, someday, that cat was going to make a mistake that would cost it its life.

When they got back to the village Winston was greeted by the man thought to be a were-tiger and was thanked and bowed to excessively as the man had been set free once another tiger attack had happened last night. There were a few apologies, but the village was still mourning the victim from last night and began to question Winston as to what happened.

Winston was reluctant to tell them that the tiger had indeed outwitted him yet again and confessing to the fact that they cowered out in the jungle while the tiger circled them would do little good at this point. All they could do was re-group and try yet again and hopefully the cat would make a mistake this time.

There was a telegram waiting for Winston from Charles telling him that he was on his way.

Winston showed little emotion if ever, but inside he was seething over this latest incident. It had shaken him a bit and he was determined to get the cat at any cost. It was no longer a job for him. He, like the cat, wanted vengeance too. This striped cat had made him to look the fool. Money didn't matter anymore. He reasoned he would do this job for free if it ever came to that. Deep down he knew it was either going to be the cat or himself that died in the end, and he was going to put his money on himself coming out of the fray unscathed. He knew he could do it, it just required a little more patience and a little luck.

He moved over to a hut to catch some needed sleep, but he still continued to entertain thoughts on the situation. It was no accident that he had a third sense for knowing or guessing where the cat would show up next, and he knew he would have another chance or two before the rains came. He thought about his luck, especially with the Jaangi man-eating leopard, and how lucky he was on that occasion. How much further could he push his luck? Was it destined to run out soon? One thing was for sure, and that was that this cat was head and shoulders above the rest except for the leopard possibly. Already it had showed some human genius in outwitting them, a very smart and elusive cat.

Maybe he could use that against it, he thought. Maybe he should start thinking like a tiger instead of trying to figure out the cat's next moves.

Before going to sleep Winston sent word to see if the tracker could help them track the tiger again. The pug marks could still be followed with no rain and they may catch the cat unaware and perhaps kill it. The tracker was a little shaken from the whole experience and refused to help, knowing that if the cat sensed or saw them coming he would be the first victim in the line since he was doing the tracking. Winston respected his decision and immediately gave word to the chieftain that he would need another tracker if they were to kill the tiger. He mentioned that he wanted him for the following morning. The more time they wasted the more the trail would grow cold.

Winston still had a couple of volunteers in the village and he picked one which agreed to go with him along with the tracker. Winston gave the volunteer the gun Charles had been using and instructed him to make sure he knew how to use it.

They could track easily in this part of the country due to the soft soil that was everywhere despite the dry season.

Winston then spent the next several hours getting things ready for the morning, then ate a hearty dinner and went to sleep. The rest of the group were still making preparations.

Morning came quickly for the men. The tracker arrived an hour later and agreed to help Winston. They made last minute adjustments to their gear and supplies and headed off in the direction of the last victim. The trail was easy to follow and they wasted no time in tracking the cat.

They broke for lunch around one in the afternoon under a large shade tree by a small stream.

The tracking was becoming more difficult but not hard for an experienced tracker to handle. They could tell they were gaining on the cat when the pug marks indicated that it had slept for the night. They were picking up the trail only a half a day old.

As the sun began to set, they were onto tracks only a couple of hours old and Winston thought it best to camp for the night and continue first thing in the morning.

As the hammocks were being set up, Winston got out the map and realized they were within about fifteen miles of another village.

As the others were a little nervous, Winston had to reassure them that the tiger was not that close and was unaware of their presence. A fire was forbidden just in case, and they all ate cold food before settling in for the night. They slept soundly as the jungle noises reverberated through the night.

The first man up was Winston and he started to brew some tea. The others began to stir as they knew that Winston was a man who liked to get an early start.

Winston looked at the men and realized from yesterday that he had an excellent tracker and they were a formidable force to be reckoned with. The tiger may be in for a few surprises.

The tracker was a wily man named Manchio who had lost his right arm in a tiger attack nearly a decade ago. The tiger at the time had severely bitten his arm and before medical attention could arrive, gangrene had set in and the arm had to come off to save his life. Unable to continue farming in the traditional way he had turned to tracking, and his specialty was cats. It was a miracle that he only lived one village away. He never gave up a chance to track a man-eating cat and take a sort of vengeance on them.

With a short breakfast they were off and Winston was hoping that the cat had stopped for the night so they would be that much closer. Hopefully they could catch up to it by early afternoon.

The area was lush with ample foliage and at times they had to cut down the plants and vines with a machete. The tiger no doubt passed easily underneath without trouble.

Winston was always amazed at how trackers could find the trail in such thick foliage, but there was always a broken branch here, a small pug mark there, and on they continued. At times the trail was lost, but only for a few minutes as the tracker would invariably find it again.

The jungle was a little thicker here than the previous day and it was taking a little longer to gain on the tiger, but the trail was still fresh as they continued on.

The tracker indicated that they were still about eight hours behind the big cat. A few minutes later they came across the area where it had bedded down for the night. This was great news for they could gain several hours based on how long it had stayed there.

The site was impressive indeed. The long grass was depressed under the tiger's weight and Winston was already getting measurements. He hadn't yet seen the tiger up close but knew from the pug marks that it was big. The matted grass showed that it was nine feet, not including the tail. This would put it in the record books for sure. Rarely had Bengal tigers achieved that sort of measurement. This would put it on par with many Siberian tigers, which were generally larger.

There wasn't any dew on the matted grass and the tracker said they were only a couple of hours away from it. They started to pick up the pace, although they were still careful not to make too much noise which might give them away.

Thoughts raced through Winston's head, this could possibly be one of the biggest Bengal tigers on record, and the fact that it was a man-eater made it even more valuable. Museums would pay a fortune for the stuffed beast. The sheer size of the pug marks made it stand out from other tiger tracks and made it easier for them to follow.

After a few more hours they realized they were getting close as the trail was only about a half hour old. The adrenaline was pumping in all of them in anticipation that something was about to happen.

Winston stopped everyone and gave them last minute instructions. He told the tracker when they got within ten minutes of the cat that he was to take over the lead. Winston made sure the hammers on his gun were set and on they continued.

The wind was in their faces which was good, for the tiger would not be able to pick up their scent as easily. Everything was in their favor except for the terrain which was still as thick as molasses in the wintertime. The machetes were put away as they needed to make little or no noise at this point. Everyone was sweating in the afternoon sun and the high heart rates were caused by the close proximity to the tiger.

Up ahead about three-hundred yards, a pea fowl took flight giving out an alarm cry which everyone recognized as warning of the tiger. Winston took over the lead at this point. While the pea fowl was making its alarm cry, Winston was busy using the noise to mask his movements, however once the cries stopped they needed to return to stalking quietly.

They had managed to narrow the gap to perhaps one hundred yards but because the terrain was so dense they couldn't catch a glimpse of the tiger. Things were going well for them, perhaps too well. Everything seemed to favor them and Winston truly believed that he had the element of surprise. They heard some more alarm cries and they could tell they were close.

Just when they thought they were going to have a chance Winston noticed that the wind had changed directions. How long had it been that way? Did the tiger already have their scent? They were sweating profusely, so the aroma would have to be great. If so, it would only be minutes before the tiger would smell them and possibly attack. The alarm calls stopped altogether and there was a very uneasy feeling about the situation they were in. The tiger had no doubt caught wind of them and could be prowling back to investigate.

They could still see about ten yards ahead of them and Winston decided to venture forward to see if he could see the tiger. He quickly and quietly ran up to the bush blocking their view from the tiger's trail. Not wanting to waste time if it was coming back, he slowly began to part the bush and peer through it.

At first, he didn't understand what he was looking at, but then a movement caught his eye as he noticed a large snarling face looking directly at him from the other side of the bush.

There was no time for reaction. In a millisecond it was lunging through the bush and he saw a flash of orange and white as he tried to swing the gun into play. The tiger wasted no time and didn't even bother to circumvent the bush. Instead it half jumped, half pushed its way through the bush with such speed and power that one of its paws caught Winston square on the forehead and knocked him out cold.

The remaining men saw what had happened. In a second fear had caused them to flee. They dropped whatever they were carrying, including weapons, as they ran pell-mell for their lives.

The tiger saw them running and pursued with a vengeance of a cornered wolverine. Within seconds the cat was on the nearest victim and there was a blur of orange and black fur. It was over as soon as the tiger crushed his skull.

Winston was still unconscious as the tiger was pursuing the next man who had gained some distance based on his speed and heightened sense to live. However, he was no match for a cat that could reach speeds of forty miles per hour. The tiger quickly ran him down and killed him with a quick bite to the neck.

Winston by this time was slowly coming to his senses. He felt a pain on his jaw and neck where he was bleeding from some of the claws that happened to come across his neck.

He was a little dazed and was still trying to figure out where he was, when everything came together and he remembered what happened. His gun was somewhere close but in his haste to get it he was looking too hard and couldn't see it. Finally, he forced himself to get a hold of himself and then looked around. It was under one of the bushes and he quickly retrieved it and made sure it was still functional. He then started to look around sensing that the beast was still close. He could taste the blood in the corner of his mouth and wanted to attend to it, but couldn't because the tiger might still be around.

He started to examine the scene and then heard the screams from the other men. He started to follow the noise and hadn't gone far when he came across Manchio, lying in his blood, eyes wide open with fear written all over them. His face was covered with blood and you could see the puncture marks of the canines and part of the crushed skull.

Winston began to look around again with his rifle at the ready. No noise could be heard at all, which caused him a little concern, but still he pressed on slowly retracing the trail listening too for screams of terror. All his senses were heightened. He needed them if he was going to manage to kill this beast.

He tried to put out of his mind the thoughts of seeing the beast eye to eye and being a little too slow in bringing the gun to bear. That was the last thing he remembered, but he was thankful to be alive and to have another shot at it. Maybe this was it. He could end it all with a well-placed shot.

He continued to follow the trail wondering if he would find anyone alive. But he realized he still may be able to catch the beast unaware.

It didn't take long for Winston to find the place where another man had died. The blood was still quite fresh and the body had been dragged further into the jungle. The wind was against Winston and it was futile to continue.

Winston was tired and the dried blood on his face was becoming a nuisance as he headed to the nearest village on the map. He was famished with hunger and thirst slaked his mouth.

Because he had lost some blood, he blacked out resting against a tree. He was awoken about a half hour later as a very large reticulated python was slithering over one of his legs.

He located where the head was, as it had been sniffing the air with its tongue to determine if Winston would be a good meal. Given a few minutes more he may have been in the coils unable to free himself and may have died the death of suffocation.

He acted quickly by removing himself from the snake, and to make sure the snake didn't harm anyone again, he took out his machete and simply cut the snake in two with one blow.

The heat was now unbearable as he trudged along a path going in the direction of the village he had seen marked on the map. He constantly rubbed the area on his head where there was pain and continued to open the gash on his face as blood trickled down his cheek. He was a little delirious.

Occasionally he would see a woman gathering sticks and would give out a warning that the Katagi man-eater was in the area. This would cause some alarm as the women would scramble to the path and run to the village.

Winston was the last to come into the village being extremely tired. He was hungry as well and he beckoned a few villagers to make him some dinner, for which he paid handsomely.

Everyone knew that something had happened and that he had probably survived a tiger attack based on the gash on the side of his head and throat, along with his dried blood. Some of the villagers were already preparing some hot healing ointment and balm which they applied to his face. They then sent for the village codari or medicine man who came quickly.

The codari barked that the wound should be cleaned again as he got out what appeared to be a crude needle and some coarse thread. The needle was so large you could easily see light through the eye.

After cleaning the wound he applied some special herb that deadened the area and then made Winston lie down with his arms and legs held by other men. A cloth was placed over his forehead and the ends were threaded down through the bamboo floorboards. A person was instructed to crawl under the hut and to tie the cloth together as tight as possible. Winston grimaced as each stitch was made but eight stitches later the job was finished. He fell asleep while they were still attending to him.

Charles had obtained the latest telegram but was still out of the loop when he didn't receive word from Winston's party at the last rendezvous point. He passed the time reading from his pocket bible and relished the story of when Samson killed a lion with his bare hands. *What strength he must have had,* he thought.

Winston had failed to return to the base camp and was overdue. Charles still had a little traveling to do but was moving as fast as possible.

The boats and the trains all seemed to move at a snail's pace for someone wanting to get back into the fray of things.

An unfortunate accident occurred as well when Winston was warning some of the wood gatherers about the man-eater being near in their area. One woman, who was extremely afraid of tigers and big cats, began to run back to the village. She was some distance away from the trail gathering wood for the evening meal when she heard the calls from the other women to get back to the village because the tiger was in the area. She began to run hard towards the trail but was still in a thick area of the jungle when she began to panic and flee towards the safety of the village. She surprised several animals and birds as she raced through the underbrush.

She came into a clearing and sunning itself on a small anthill was a king cobra which felt threatened. It flared up and instinctively struck out catching its fangs in the foot of the woman who had nearly run over it. Its venom being one of the most dangerous in India, the woman did not make it far before she began to have muscle spasms that affected her heart and she died within a few minutes.

Although the snake actually killed the woman, the whole ordeal started from the panic of the man-eater being in the area.

The jungle is unforgiving at times and its rule is simply: kill or be killed. The woman never returned to the village and was found a few days later with the characteristic discoloration on the leg as it had swollen up suggesting a toxic bite. The sheer volume of swelling which had caused the leg to balloon to four times its natural size was an unsightly scene. She was only discovered because of the close proximity to the village and had the characteristic signs of a poisonous snake bite.

Life outside the danger of the man-eating tiger continues and there are many ways to die in the jungle besides the tiger. People understood this and accepted the fact. They obviously could not go out and kill every venomous snake in the country. If they were to do that there would be a gigantic increase in the rodent population which the snakes help to regulate. But a man-eater like the tiger could be killed, although it has had a spell of extremely good luck.

Life continued on in the countryside, but the tiger was still at large and Winston had a score to settle with it. Winston asked the villagers, once the tiger had been thought to have left the area, to go back on the trail and to venture off to where he had placed three frond leaves to bury the dead men where they lay.

His head still ached as he could feel the crude stitches made on his cheek. *So much for good looks,* he thought as he rubbed his fingers again over the rough stitches.

That damn beast, he thought, but an adversary none the less. He had to respect it and give it credit, for it had outwitted him again. The thought constantly pushed itself into his mind. He kept thrusting it out, but it was always there, presenting itself like the time he had witnessed a rape in Calcutta and was injured coming to the girl's rescue. The memories remained, ugly, pressing thoughts that you wish you could rid yourself of, but they keep coming back, always to be forced into the recesses of the brain.

However, he was a survivor, and one of only fifteen from the Katagi man-eater. Of course, most of those survivors were mangled and permanently disabled, while some had long deep scars that revealed both physical and mental stress. Many of the survivors lived their nightmares over and over again in their sleep, constantly waking up yelling and screaming at the top of their lungs. They never ventured far from the village and some seemed like they were alive physically but otherwise they were walking cadavers. Some felt pity for them, others thought that it would have been better for them to die rather than live in constant fear and have the emotional distress.

For Winston it had been a humbling experience, he had come through each and every other hunt without a scratch and now he was to bear these scars for the rest of his life. He looked again in the small mirror he used for shaving and realized he looked like a scoundrel, but didn't care at all. He thought to himself that he would just have to rely on his charm with the ladies. But of course the ladies wanted a man who could stand up for them and defend their honor. Winston fit that bill exactly and many men not confident in their own masculinity envied him for it.

Somehow deep down he knew his luck was changing, and with that he knew the striped cat was going to live to regret not finishing him off. Perhaps, he thought, he was going about it all wrong. Perhaps there was something new he needed to try, something unorthodox. One thing was for sure and that was that the monsoon season was only two months away by now, and that would only give him a small window in which to kill the beast before the grasses returned in abundance and he would have to wait another year. It was frustrating to say the least since he had had several very good chances to date.

The big cat left its kill early in the morning of the next day having eaten nearly twenty-five pounds of flesh and sinew. Its belly protruded nearly to the ground like a basket-like net of fruit, swaying back and forth with its gait.

It moved slowly and was taking everything in from its surroundings, not wanting to miss anything that could do it harm. It was becoming more cautious with all the attempts on its life in the last few months. It continued to look for a stream to slake its thirst and knew it would be near the bottom of the valley as they all usually were. It found the stream about twenty minutes later and began to drink from the cool, clear, early morning water. The liquid was helping with the digestion. It soaked itself as the sun was starting to beat down on the jungle valley floor as it had just crested the hill. The tiger pulled itself out of the water and began to clean its paws with its rasping tongue.

The bank near the stream had high elephant grass and it began to get drowsy as it laid down in the grass to get some sleep. It didn't think it would be bothered in this part of the valley, so it slept from the affects of the meal.

There wasn't much left on the victim as certain parts were picked as clean as a northern snow. The vultures would scavenge the rest as they always did. There would be no decent burial this time.

A call suddenly came from a bird in the area which awoke the tiger. It went toward the sound to investigate. The tiger was being as cautious as ever, as the sound turned out to be nothing. It had no desire now that it was up to return to the soft elephant grass, but continued on going south.

The cat was extremely wary since it had had more than one experience in the last few months with it being tracked and wounded. So now, every sound was taken with alarm and caused it concern. It wasn't getting the long rests in the daytime that it was used to and it seemed that it had been on the prowl for several months.

Charles was used to having questions asked of him, of what he was doing in that part of the country. It didn't bother him at all but he casually took it in stride and was basically still amicable to the people for the most part. He could not quite speak the language like Winston, but there were others who had been educated and knew enough English to get by. However, on this hot and humid day while traveling by boat he was intrigued by an old man telling a story about a were-tiger. Oh course, he did not believe in such rubbish and sensational stories, but this one was told with such gesticulation and livelihood that he was astonished at the story teller and intrigued by those that listened, many had heard it before but were still frightened each time it was told. It was apparent that everyone believed in it except Charles.

The story, as mentioned, was known by most everyone except himself and was told with little variation in each village. The fable was recounted by an older man who indicated that he knew one of the men in the story from his childhood. Although he was very advanced in age, he vouched for its veracity.

"Long ago," he began, "while the Indians had been fighting the foreigners around the ancient city of Daspurin, deep in the interior of the country where the cities walls, although crumbling and forgotten are still intact today, but yet no one resides there now due to the superstition and bad luck that abounds in that cursed city. The armies of the foreigners had brought massive weapons of war which operated from gunpowder. They annihilated the local troops who beat a retreat and tried to get away from the destruction. The foreign troops followed them and decimated their ranks. There were only a couple hundred survivors.

"There were four particular tired soldiers who had made their way to the valley and city mentioned. They had been so tired from their march and the fighting that they decided to camp in the valley for the night and resume their journey in the morning.

"During the night they heard roar after roar coming from the valley. All of the sounds were coming from tigers and a few leopards. They were all very afraid and, despite the possible pursuit of the foreign army, they decided to build a large fire to keep the wild animals away, especially the tigers they had heard during the night.

"They had unfortunately not gathered enough firewood prior to nightfall, and in the late darkness the fire was beginning to wane because there was no more wood. They realized they needed more fuel for the fire, but it was really only necessary for two individuals to gather the logs or wood to keep the fire burning, so they decided to draw straws to determine who should venture out into the night to gather the wood. The two who had lost the draw went out immediately with one of the last burning sticks to light their way.

"It wasn't long, and they had not gone far, when the men who remained behind started to hear the terrible screams of the men who had gone for the wood.

"What they think happened was that many of the surviving soldiers had made it to the valley. There were not a few who had endured hardships, including receiving multiple wounds. Many were dying and the moans and cries from the soldiers were heard by the tigers in this forbidden and cursed city.

"It was believed that the ancient city they were in was inhabited and haunted by reincarnated people who were entirely evil and sadistic during their lifetime, and that this city was a punishment for damned souls which could take on other forms of life or transform themselves. Once bitten by the animal that caused their death, they would then take on a form of man or tiger depending on whether it was day or night, the animal form taking place at night and the human form taking place during the day. The only difference was that even when they had transformed into a tiger they remained and walked upright. There were some who had claimed to see the actual transformation.

"Well, the two soldiers, once they had heard the shrieks from the other men, started to panic and run for their lives. While running they thought they heard the voices, somewhat muffled, of their compatriots, calling to them to halt and wait for them. Because of the situation, and the unfamiliar sound of the voices, they refused to stop despite their exhausted state.

"They had been running for some time and were about to leave the valley on the well-worn trail they had taken on the way in, when they both saw what looked like a haggard person, beckoning them to come to him, standing in the trail. Excited to see another person they continued to run to him.

"In the night things aren't always as they appear, sahib, and as they came running up close to the person, the moon cast its light on the figure standing before them. Of course, it was too late by that time. Their momentum had carried them to the figure, it was just too late to stop.

"The figure was a were-tiger, sahib, still in half transformation, which can take some time I am told. The facial features were mostly human with some puffy cheeks with whiskers growing longer by the second. The were-tiger tried to smile at them but the teeth and the canines were already starting to lengthen and curve, and the smile turned into a snarl and hiss.

The creature was standing on two legs, but they were curved legs like an animal, with fur already growing before their eyes.

"An arm or forefoot was raised as if to say hello, only to come down on the first man with tremendous power, knocking the man senseless. The were-tiger was on him in seconds as the other man, the only survivor, ran away and was only saved because the were-tiger was busy feasting on his friend.

"The valley remains haunted to this day and no one has returned to inhabit it. The tigers still patrol the valley and the were-tigers have passed on their genes to other generations so that they are still there today. If you don't believe me, sahib you can go and check it out for yourself, but it may very well be a one-way ticket."

Many in the boat were frightened, the stories weren't told often for the fear that they incited.

Charles didn't believe one word of it, but the locals all believed with every fiber in their body. It wouldn't have surprised Charles at all if some people, walking between villages at night, were killed from fright alone based on an unknown sound or animal that may have inadvertently crossed their path.

As Charles watched the scenery go by, he thought of the story and how fabulous it was. *And yet the people believe in these things,* he thought.

It was amazing how much meat was needed to sustain the tiger. Its taste for human flesh required more killings than a person would think. It wasn't that the tiger required human flesh, although the tiger preferred that, but it wasn't going to turn down an easy meal by any other animal as well. It was an opportunistic carnivore, eating what it came across but preferring the salt-like meat of humans.

It continually prowled the jungle, knowing that it was lord of its domain, unafraid of anything yet cautious enough to stay alive.

It had learned long ago that humans could inflict serious harm with their weapons. All its life had been one learning experience after another. It was one of the most intelligent animals in the jungle.

There was a certain amount of respect that every animal had for the tiger, even up to the mighty elephant. Tigers have been known to prey upon baby elephants and only a watchful and diligent mother can avert disaster by keeping a close watch over her young.

Needless to say, the tiger was given a wide berth in the jungle because it had earned its right to be there. Anything that had a problem with that could seek the tiger out and attempt to become the new lord, but there was a reason it was lord of the jungle and it retained that honor through time. It was the law of the land that you either eat or you're eaten; a simple but deadly fact of life.

Winston had sent out messages with people who were already traveling to different villages. All news between the villages, no matter how big or small, was brought to the attention of the chieftain of the village. In this way word was spread quicker than the mail itself.

Winston had recovered from his wounds enough to stage another attack as soon as the tiger was located again. The gathering place was an area he believed was close to where the tiger might attack again based upon the information they had already gathered.

It was becoming increasingly difficult to find local work in the field. Who could blame them? The loss rate for the local population that was hired on to go with him into the jungle was over thirty percent. Those with less meaningful jobs such as around base camp were better off, but the fact remained that it was a miracle that even he was alive. Winston had to up the ante on the pay for help which he needed and was enough for an indigenous man to live off of for several months and feed his family as well.

The fact was that without Charles helping him he had to rely on others, and he couldn't handle all the gear and equipment needed in the field without some help. He was expecting Charles back at any time but couldn't just wait for him. The monsoon rains would be coming in about six weeks and that didn't give him a lot of time.

They had several advantages at this point since they knew the general whereabouts of the cat and were already in a position to launch another attack. The noose was beginning to tighten around the elusive cat, and it was just a chance moment that Winston felt he needed to get a good shot at the tiger. Then things could return to normal. But he couldn't have any more mishaps. He was on borrowed time as it was. Another mistake and he knew he would be dead. He also couldn't take responsibility for anyone else's death. This was a deadly game of either kill or be killed. Everyone knew the consequences before they came out. If they didn't, they were imbeciles.

Winston sat back in his wicker chair and enjoyed his Tea. There was nothing to do but wait for another attack. He hoped it would come sooner than the end of the week. They were running out of time. Soon the monsoons would make conditions impossible. This part of the game was the hardest for Winston, waiting, not doing anything, feeling like you were powerless.

There were some benefits, such as good food and bed, even in the most remote of villages. People were always wanting to do something for you or bring something to you. Yes, someone like Winston could enjoy king-like status out here, but he just wanted to do his job and get back to what he called home and a normal life.

Winston let his thoughts run. What was it like for Charles?

Was he as content about life with its trials and tribulations as he looked and acted? It was strange for Winston to think of anything but himself. Winston thought of his own life and how things might have differed if he had married and raised a family. Would he have more appreciation for life? Obviously, one cannot have joy without feeling pain, he thought to himself.

The fear that was over the region had now doubled with the news that the man-eater was in the area. No chances were taken with anyone venturing out alone. Often, women would gather sticks for their fires under the protection of a man who was on the lookout for any danger.

The tiger had sensed the heightened security and had decided to travel some distance to where prey was easier to get to. It could easily travel up to sixty miles a day, and within three days it was nearly one-hundred and fifty miles from the last kill it had made. No opportunities presented themselves during that time, but it made every effort to remain hidden so that no one could see it. It was by this time getting hungry.

It had traveled in a western direction across uninhabited country even more remote than where it had come from. It had made such good time that Winston would have been hard pressed just to keep up with it. The big beast moved through foliage and jungle with effortless precision. Having fully healed from the gunshot wound several weeks earlier it was back in full health.

The grasses and other plants were already turning yellow from the lack of rain and the tigers tawny coat blended perfectly with the new countryside.

After covering such a distance, it was confident that it wasn't being followed and let down its guard somewhat.

Winston had no idea it had given him the slip and thought that it was in the area still. He was waiting for the next kill and also for Charles, since there was little local help. All he could do was wait.

Charles had made it to the latest rendezvous point only to find the news was old. He was given fresh news that the new meeting place was in a village another thirty miles away. It would take another day before he met up with Winston.

He was getting anxious and despite the dangerous circumstances he wanted to get back into the fray as soon as possible.

There was no hurry since they had to wait for the next attack in order to pinpoint where the cat was. Winston thought that it was close to where he was, and began thinking of tying up a goat with an all night watch in hopes that the obnoxious animal would attract the man-eater.

Unbeknownst to Winston the cat had indeed given him the slip and it would take another week for Winston to get into position for another track. Time was of the essence now, and like the sand that pours through the hourglass, the summer killing time was quickly slipping away.

Winston was also anxiously awaiting the required items that Charles was bringing, at least he hoped he was bringing. They were falling short on some supplies and out there in the jungle or in primitive villages many things were in short supply.

Everywhere else in the jungle, things had returned to a normal state. The jungle was absent of humans except in large wood gathering parties. There was a sense of quiet as animals were not calling out like usual.

Charles decided he was too tired to try and get to the next village that evening. He had been traveling some distance in the last week and decided on a nice meal and a long sleep before venturing out again in the morning with the supplies.

After what seemed like a fortnight he was finally sleeping on somewhat nice accommodations with a mattress filled with straw and a feather pillow loaned to him. The long nights traveling in railway cars or on river boats had added up to the point where he needed a good long rest with decent furnishings where he could sleep the night away without fidgeting or waking up every half hour, and where he wouldn't wake up with a sore back in the morning.

He splurged a little on dinner as well. He asked the local villagers what kind of meal he could get and for what price. There had been an antelope killed the previous day and he salivated at the thought of antelope steaks. He had been going hard for several days, and he knew Winston and knew once he joined him they would be going full tilt until the job was accomplished. *That man is a hound dog on the trail of a fox,* he thought to himself.

Charles took off his boots and paid a young villager to wash his feet and legs, as they were dusty from the days traveling. He also ordered a hot bath in a worn out tub which was heated underneath by a small fire. He nearly went to sleep relaxing and enjoyed resting from his labors.

The steaks were grilling close by and the aroma of savory wood smoked steaks filled the village. He could almost taste the meat already.

He had already given orders for his group to get some sleep that night as they would start again early in the morning.

He was very tired that day and had to be aroused once the meal was prepared. The steaks were excellent and he was filled with the delicious food and fruit of the area. He immediately went to the assigned sleeping hut and fell asleep within a minute of laying down his head. He would need all the sleep he could muster for the upcoming events.

The night's sleep was very restful for Charles. He awoke early in the morning and started getting things organized and ready for the hike to the village. If things went well he would be back with Winston that afternoon, provided he hadn't moved on again.

He was anxious to get back and made as much haste as possible.

There was some sort of magic in the whole ordeal, dangerous magic that dealt the ugly hand of death. He could envision the death angels having their hands full just following them around, plucking hapless victims here and there, sending them to heaven or hell. All they had to do was follow their camp, for death followed it. Everyone knew it and knew they could be next. It wasn't the sort of subject anyone brought up. Those with experience live with it but it never goes away, it was always with you. At least that was how it was explained by Winston and he ought to know.

Charles started before the sun was rising in the east. The oppressive weather never seemed to change until the rains came. Usually it was a welcome sight but now it would mean the end of their quest if they didn't get the striped cat soon enough. He continued trekking with his entourage, having to cover nearly thirty-two miles before sundown and still being well within the so-called killing zone where the tiger could possibly attack at any place along the way and at any time.

He had a few hired hands with him and just for good measure he had his gun on the sling or occasionally in the crook of his arm for added insurance. He needed to pay his porters double the usual wages just to get them to pack his supplies and come with him. Every sound and every bush that moved was cause for concern, increasing the anxiety everyone already felt.

The season was almost over and the grasses were dying out. The thick grasses made it difficult to see the tiger and as they grew browner it blended in with the tiger's coat.

The cat had not attacked for nearly a week and that had Winston concerned. Had it moved on? There was no way of knowing. They had to pinpoint its area before venturing out, there was just too much territory to cover.

But time was running out for this season and Winston could only hope that the rains would be late this year.

Everyone was anxious including the usually patient Winston. He continued to study the terrain from the maps he had at his disposal.

While they were waiting for the next attack Winston had some of the villagers dig a tiger pit, it was more of an effort to let the people know that he was doing something to get rid of the menace rather than nothing, but there was still a slight possibility that the cat could be in the area.

On the following day the pit did indeed yield a tiger which the natives thought was the man-eater and had come to tell Winston of the incredible luck. Winston was skeptical and when he came out to see it he knew right away that the cat was too small to be the villain. He had the villagers let down a log and the cat scampered up and away.

The villagers were disappointed to say the least. Winston managed to convince them that they were doing a good job and maybe the next time they would have the killer.

Winston thought again of putting up a goat as bait and thought of waiting all night in the event it would come and he may get a shot off.

The only good thing happening was that they were in an area that was sparsely populated. The cat was going to have a more difficult time finding victims. Still, Winston wondered what else could be done. The heat was stifling to say the least, and as he thought about things the sweat poured off his forehead as he occasionally wiped his brow.

He was expecting Charles any day now. He had realized, once he was gone, how much he had come to rely on him and had to admit to himself how useful he had become. He was beginning to trust his opinions and had more respect for him, which he had undoubtedly earned in the time he had spent with him.

He began looking at the map again showing the last victim's location. He needed some luck and he knew it. He had to be right where it was going to attack again, and he had better be good and accurate because he may not get another chance until next year. He pushed the thought out of his mind.

"When will the rains come?" he asked himself, thinking. "How much time do I have?"

Every little thought, every doubt was coming into his mind. He picked up the compass in frustration and threw it out the tent. He took a deep breath and ran his fingers through his thick hair, calming himself as he thought *OK, just get a hold of yourself, there's still time. We will get another chance and this time it's going to make a mistake that will cost it its life. Now I've got to make my best educated guess on which village or area will be hit next.*

He looked over the map again and saw that to the south was Bakarin village, to the north was Saptaan, and there was only one other village to the north-east. *Of course,* he thought, *the cat could bypass these altogether and hit further.*

He looked at the information he had for the previous ten attacks and started looking at the dates between the attacks and the distances between them. Then he had a thought. *This is what we have been doing all year and we have only been successful half the time. We need to change our thinking. Perhaps it's been in this area before and knows the villages.*

He would need information on the attacks from previous years and maybe he could see if the cat had been in the area. But how could he get the information that quickly? By now Charles should have left the Ministry office. Maybe he could find someone close by to relay the information, maybe he could do that in a sizable city or two, but not out here. He just had to get a message out as soon as possible. It might be five days before he got a reply, but he thought he needed the information.

Charles was getting exacerbated with each slow cart and every person that got in the way to slow him down. He was more than anxious to get back to Winston and time was of the essence. Who knew how early the rains could come this year.

Travel was congested now because the cat was known to be in the area.

Even though it was an area so vast that it was impossible to cover, still people traveled during the daylight hours and made sure they were home by evening.

He was traveling through one of the last villages before Bakarin and he stopped briefly to buy some fresh pineapple which seemed to quench a growing thirst as the heat continued to permeate the country with each growing hour.

He continued to wipe the perspiration that was constantly building up on his forehead or brow. His clothes had the common signs of sweat under the armpits and down the small of his back.

The porters were performing their jobs well, but he was still miffed about having to pay double wages even though it was a pittance compared to what he had. He was becoming like them, haggling over trivial prices the same as an old woman barters for the best price for melons or vegetables in the market. He had always been very frugal with his money, or even the governments money, but he had to pay them out of his own pocket since the minister had refused to pay them in an effort to get him to stay in Bombay.

Charles was well enough off in India, but he had become accustomed to the conditions and thought, that things were getting expensive. Ever since the East India Company had raised the cost of spices the entire food market had followed suit, as well as everything else.

It was such a long arduous journey and he wished again that he did not have to make it, but it was nearly over now and he would be joining Winston for supper and the next day be back to work with Winston, who despite his eccentricities was becoming a likable chap.

As time passed, they continued to hike to their destination. Charles un-sheathed his new purchase from Bombay: a bowie knife, as the Americans called it, of gargantuan proportions. Made of stainless steel and imported from turkey he had paid extra to have it finely honed and razor sharp. He ran his thumb slowly down the blade. It was eighteen inches long and needed an extra tie in the sheath just above the knee. It was something that could come in handy sometime and secretly he hoped he would never have to use it, but it made him feel more confident and safe. As he looked at it he thought that it could double as a mirror if he was concerned about his looks in the bush. Perhaps on down time he could practice throwing it. It might prove to be a good skill.

The porters traveling with him began to pick up a tune and started singing to try and quell their fears of the man-eater. Night would fall within a couple of hours and they were far from the protection of a village. It was good Charles had remembered the torches and the pine tar that would be lit that night. He was tired as it was and he was tempted to call it a day right now, but he knew it would only be that much more distance to cover on the next day.

The path they were traveling on showed no signs of a tiger's pug marks which the porters were keen to look for. Charles was sure that if they had seen them, no amount of wages would be able to convince them to continue on.

The rays from the sun were beginning to stretch out into the countryside as they trudged on. About fifteen minutes after sundown, and while it was still light enough to see, they stopped and began to make preparations for camp.

Charles wiped the sweat from his forehead as the others busied themselves. He had picked this location in hopes that the abundant bird calls would notify them of any approaching danger.

Torches were lit and the glow they gave added to a nice ambiance seldom enjoyed in the jungle.

Charles unsheathed his machete and began to help the others cut down palm fronds to sleep on. They were getting to bed early, but they were also very tired so sleep shouldn't be too much of a problem.

As they lay down that night Charles couldn't help but think of the times he had camped in the jungle and the first sounds he heard. It is an unusual cacophony of sounds; some familiar, some not. Here they could hear the occasional roar of a leopard or tiger which only amplified the fear they were experiencing. Everyone felt it, yet no one spoke of it. To do so would be to show cowardice. It was something only a younger child might speak of, yet all experienced it.

As Charles looked around into the night he seemed to see the vines as snakes, the rocks as rabid animals. All his fears came from his imagination, yet he was learning to subdue those thoughts as Winston had already taught him. Now he was more confident, more assured than anyone else in the camp that evening. He knew that statistics were on his side. It would be unusual for the man-eater to attack a large group. His mind was beginning to analyze the surroundings and handle the fear much better.

It wasn't long before he was snoring loud enough to keep all the animals at bay.

The night proved uneventful as everyone began to awake for the next leg of the trek. The water was gathered in twos as nobody dared venture anywhere outside the group without a companion. Everyone knew once again it was going to be another hot humid day.

There wasn't much preparation as Charles wanted to get away as soon as possible. He was hoping optimistically that he would meet up with Winston that evening.

After a quick cup of tea, everyone was off. They would be able to snack upon wild bananas and other fruit found along the trail. They still had provisions for lunch when they would take about a forty minute break.

The jungle was beginning to come to life as it always did, with sounds everywhere. Charles was beginning to remember what Winston had begun to teach him about the sounds of the jungle and what they can mean. There was still much to learn, and Charles wondered if he would be able to learn enough to survive this whole, bad ordeal. How Winston had put up with similar conditions time and time again was beyond him. The negative thoughts of quitting came into his mind as he slowly entertained, then dismissed them.

He instinctively began to oil his gun and wipe the morning dew from it as Winston taught him. He was beginning to find things as second nature now.

Thoughts of his last date were constantly on his mind and he knew he had to stay distant somehow if he was to keep focused with his mind on the job at hand.

As he sipped his tea, he fingered the new knife he had and pulled it from the sheath, looking at it again almost like it was some sort of forbidden object not to be looked upon. He touched the blade lightly and as he had done so before on purchase, he thought how sharp it was. He cut a few whiskers from his days old beard and put it back in its sheath, comforted that it was there but realizing it might do no good.

The group was beginning to pack up and start. Charles returned his cup to the hired porter and began to make preparations on his pack. After a quick break to a small tree, he too rose and shouldered his gear.

The news reports were again being more and more focused on news of the man-eater. Word had spread about Winston being attacked like a fire that was out of control. Winston paid no attention to it but continued his preparations while the people around him admonished his verve and dedication.

It had been several days and no word had come about another attack or even a sighting of where the cat was. He was thinking it could be as far as seventy-five miles away for all he knew, or it could be watching him right now as he paused to look up and into the vast jungle with a thousand yard stare.

He hated playing the waiting game but he wasn't going to give the beast another easy chance. He needed the rest desperately. He thought of sending a telegram to Charles letting him know what had happened, but knew he would be reading the papers keeping up on the events. Winston thought how fast the news actually spread when they were in such primitive country.

He changed his mind and sent instructions to have the telegram sent from the nearest telegraph station. The telegram would read, "Encountered tiger a few days ago. Still at large. Moving out to village of Cagidemorra. Several hounds dead. Will need your assistance as soon as possible. Winston"

It didn't say much, but then again, he was never a man known for his lengthy conversation. He would have a native dispatch it the next morning.

Winston had thanked the man who had stitched him up, and though it wasn't a neat hospital stitching, it was well enough and he should have a good scar to show because of it. Perhaps it was now his largest one, having surpassed the one he got as a child from a vicious boar.

He and his entourage began moving out to Cagidemorra.

He couldn't remember much of the ordeal, in fact everything was a bit of a blur to him. The stitches caused him to constantly feel the wound, and he thought to himself what a lucky man he was. He wondered if there was anything he could have done differently, but his head began to hurt and he focused more on the task at hand.

He began to methodically make preparations for the next venture into the jungle. The people of Cagidemorra seemed alarmed at his arrival and rightly suspected that the man-eater was operating very close to the village. Some of the leaders tried to extract information from Winston as to the man-eaters whereabouts, but he didn't know for sure and it was questionable whether he would have told them anything knowing that the truth sometimes hampered his work. He didn't say that it was his best judgment that the attack would come to this very village.

He thought and thought of any new means to take the cat down, but it always came back to the tried and true way of killing man-eaters, which was to track them down and kill them or to wait with a tethered goat or another hapless animal. He thought about how he needed only one clean shot, and how could he get that shot. This was what was constantly occupying his thoughts.

How many times had he cheated death now, he thought to himself. Sooner or later it was bound to catch up with him. He brushed the thought aside and continued to make preparations.

Charles had arrived at Bakarin village expecting Winston to be there, only to be told he was another village away. It was too late in the afternoon to make it, so he made the decision to stop and rest there and they would head for the new destination in the morning. He was also weary from the last few days and needed some rest.

Things were indeed quiet in the village as everyone knew the where-abouts of the tiger had to be close.

Charles was able to purchase a last-minute meal for him and his servants and then quietly went to sleep, trying to get as much shut eye as possible.

Winston had already begun making preparations as if going to war. He had decided on a tethered goat until they received news of the next attack. His servants were rushing around making the necessary arrangements in order to put things in motion while he scouted out the near countryside in hopes of finding an adequate tree from which he could shoot from.

There wasn't much time. The monsoons were expected in about two weeks time and he prayed they didn't come early.

He could sense they were close, and the noose was beginning to tighten around the cat. If they could only get it before the rains came, otherwise they would have to start all over again.

He wondered where the hell Charles was. At least he knew deep inside that Charles was doing everything he could in order to get back as soon as possible.

He eventually located a suitable tree for the stakeout not too far from the village. He would give instructions to have the goat tethered during the afternoon and wait in the tree before darkness fell and stay throughout the night. His thought was to catch a couple of hours sleep before darkness came so he would have the ability to wait up all night in the tree stand. The chances of the tiger taking the goat were next to nil, but it was something he could do instead of waiting for the next attack.

He asked a local man if he could use his hammock for a few hours and as soon as he shut his eyes he was gently swaying into a deep snooze.

It seemed he was only asleep for fifteen minutes before his servant woke him up and informed him that the tree stand was ready and it was time to go.

He took a small tin of dinner and a canteen along with his gun, and went with his servant to the tree stand. About half way there he sent the others back because they wouldn't be able to get back to the village before nightfall. Winston continued on alone and arrived at the tree just as the sun was setting.

He emptied his bladder on the poor goat in hopes that the faint human smell would cause the man-eater to intensify its attack once it began.

He slung the rifle over his shoulder and looked at the rope dangling down from one of the larger branches about thirty feet up. He began tying two prussic knots with some smaller cordettes around the larger rope as he began to shimmy up the rope. It was a slow process but he eventually came to the makeshift stand. He took a few minutes to get comfortable and eat the remaining dinner he had taken with him. Then he settled in for another long night in an uncomfortable tree.

The jungle seemed to come alive with the sounds of the evening. He had a favorable sighting with an opening between two branches on a small clearing just beyond the tree.

He always envisioned a perfect branch with support for his back, but never had found one in all his years of hunting man-eaters. For hours he sat there as various parts of his body ached and feel asleep. The only time he moved was when he absolutely had to, and he was very careful not to make a sound doing it.

At about two a.m., the goat began to bleat repeatedly. He became more focused as he stared into the night trying to make any sense of what was causing the problem. The gun was readied into a firing position as he listened for any sound.

He had been through this before and when the hair on the back of his neck began to rise he knew something was going to happen. It was instinct that he knew there was something out there. The question was whether or not it was the man-eater.

Winston continued to strain his eyes in the darkness, but whatever it was down there was taking its time.

The goat knew something was amiss and was bleating louder than ever.

Winston was well into the tree, but the opening between the two main branches was small and he couldn't see everything. He tried to allow his hearing to make out any distinct sound, but all he could hear was the goat.

Then he saw it for a brief moment as it attacked the goat. The soft white fur on the underside of the cat was just visible in the moonlight as he fired into the furry mass at less than twenty yards away. There was a loud roar and then it was gone. He was sure he had hit it, but without it lying there directly under the tree there was no way of knowing it was dead. He had to wait until first light to see anything.

The wait for the remaining hours of darkness to end was agonizing, but he dared not descend for if the animal was wounded it would surely kill him given the chance. At least he no longer had to keep quiet as he constantly changed positions in the tree. He was able to get in a few light snatches of sleep while waiting for the sunrise.

At last the rays began to beat down upon the eerie jungle and spread warmth and color to the landscape. He slowly opened his eyes as the warmth reached his face and looked immediately down under the tree. He could see that the goat was dead. Blood was everywhere.

He began to slide down the rope with the rifle slung over his shoulder, but upon hitting the ground he quickly removed the gun and had it cocked and ready. He was pretty sure he had hit it good, so he didn't expect an attack.

He saw the blood on the goat and on the ground and saw the trail it left going off into the jungle. He thought it prudent not to follow up but rather wait until the others arrived and they would then track it together. Inside he hoped against all hope that it was the man-eater.

He laid back on the trunk of the tree and lit his pipe. The smoke wafted upwards in a long steady stream. With the next breath he blew out a perfect smoke ring and then broke it with his finger.

It was only about ten minutes before the others arrived as they knew that Winston didn't like to hang out in the tree any longer than needed.

Winston pointed to the goat and said he got a shot off last night and they needed to track the animal and see if it was the striped beast they were looking for.

They set off almost immediately with the best tracker leading the way. They didn't have to go far before they came upon a beautiful male leopard dead in its tracks. Winston's heart sank as he knew it wasn't the killer and he had wasted a magnificent animal.

The shot was through the shoulder and the animal had not suffered long. It was one of the largest leopard's he had seen and they began the long process of skinning it.

Winston was pretty upset with himself, but with no indication otherwise he had to take the shot. There had been a chance that is was the man-eater.

He told the others he was taking one of the helpers back to the village and started back.

It was around 11 a.m. when he strolled back into the village and waiting there for him was Charles.

"You're a tough man to track down mate," said Charles.

"You think I'm hard, let me introduce you to a man-eater I know."

They both laughed and shook each other's hand vigorously.

"How is the minister?" asked Winston.

"Oh, he'll be fine. The viceroy is breathing down his neck, and of course he takes it out on me, but I can handle him. I'm sorry to hear about the hounds and happy you're still alive."

Winston replied, "It was luck and there's still a little left. We've got to get that bastard cat," Winston said, as he stared into the jungle like he had spotted something.

"Well, where do we start now?" asked Charles.

"Let's get some lunch first, you must be starving."

They went over to the hut of the best cook in the village and the woman, already anticipating that Winston would be eating, had cooked up some tender Gaur meat with rice. They sat down in her hut and devoured the entire meal like civilized savages, if that was even possible.

"The cats in the area, I can sense it," said Winston. "But the rains will be here soon. We don't have much time. If we're lucky we can possibly get one more chance before the rains come. I think it may strike near this or another close village soon. I'm very sure of it."

"So, do we wait until it strikes?" asked Charles.

"Well, the locals have caught on to my presence here and no one is going into the countryside to gather wood or get water unless they are in a group, can't say I blame them, and they also know that something is afoot. But that cat will need to eat soon. Do you have any suggestions?"

"I don't have much faith in the anything, but I was thinking as I was traveling up here, if we knew the cat was in an area, what if we made up a dummy that looked like a real person, with old clothes and everything, and set him up in a clearing close to the edge of the jungle. If he was set upright under a tree we could rig his arm to go up and down with a strong fishing line, like he's chopping wood or something. If we set up a log to receive the blows and put some weight on the arm the sound itself could attract the cat and we would be waiting to pick it off."

"Interesting, that is quite an elaborate plan," said Winston as he stroked his month-long beard. "I'm not sure it will work, but it couldn't hurt to try. It beats waiting around for the next victim. And if the cat's in the area like I think it is we just might get it with some luck," said Winston.

Charles was a little more enthusiastic than Winston, but Winston couldn't stand to tell Charles he didn't think it would work, and since he had no good reason to tell him no, he let him go on.

They finished their meal quickly and went over to the local leaders hut to solicit any help from him. The plan was told to the chieftain and he went with them over to a hut where a lady was known for her sewing abilities. They talked in the local language of what was wanted with the lady and she occasionally nodded her head in agreement. Soon old clothes were procured, and the sewing started.

Winston and Charles went to work on the arm contraption. They secured several pieces of stout bamboo and with the help of a primitive drill were able to secure the extended arm to a larger piece of bamboo. They then drilled a hole in one end and attaching it to the other larger piece with a long piece of a homemade hardwood dowel which easily slid through the holes and was attached with wire on both ends.

A local craftsman was helping them by this time and it was good to have him because he hammered out the finer details and made the arm look and act realistic.

Once they had the two-piece contraption done, they moved the arm section up and down until they were satisfied it was working well enough. A little coconut oil was needed at friction points, but it held solidly as some weight was added to the hollow section of the arm to add sound when it came down. A glove was secured to finish off the arm portion and a hat was obtained for the head with a mosquito net around the head and neck.

Within a few hours the clothing was stitched together, and the wooden bamboo hand and attachment was placed inside the dummy and it was filled with straw.

Winston had to admit that it looked fairly real from behind as they experimented with the chopping arm.

Since the sun had gone down by the time everything was ready, they were left with no choice but to wait until the morning to find a suitable place for the set up.

They retired to Winston's hut to look at the map again.

As they looked over the map Winston ran his fingers over the stitches still present in his forehead and throat. Charles asked him if he was alright. Having heard about the attack, Charles looked at the fresh scar but didn't ask him about it, he casually said that he heard it was a close one. Winston said he was very lucky this time but he was fine and that devil cat will answer for it.

Winston tried to remember where there was a good tree and lookout in the valley he thought the cat might be in.

"I think we should check out this area in the morning and set up in this valley," pointing to an area on the map.

It looked promising but he wasn't looking forward to another long night in a tree. At least this time he would have company.

With still no news from an attack, they had little other choice.

Charles enjoyed a wonderful slumber, and since time was not of the essence Winston let him sleep in because the night was going to be a long one.

Finally, when Charles arose Winston had breakfast brought to him quickly and he indicated that he wanted to get started once he was finished.

To Charles, Winston looked fresh and alive. With his clothes cleaned and ironed he looked like he had just left Bombay.

The women of the village had put some last-minute touches on the dummy and it did indeed look lifelike. They continued to play with the fake arm until Winston dismissed them for fear that too much playing might damage it.

While he was waiting for Charles to get ready he set it up next to him on a chair and watched people's reaction to the lifeless body. Some of them probably thought it was another victim of the man-eater. He was quite amused when Charles finally showed up ready to go.

They took a few locals who knew the area and trudged off to the valley Winston had chosen.

They decided to give the dummy a name on the way and some of the names that they came up with were Winston the 2nd, comangetit, tasty Sam, Glutounous Jake, Yokeuno (a local dialect name for delicious), and ToostiffCharley.

It took about an hour to get to the valley and another half an hour to find a suitable tree and clearing that offered a good shot.

They settled on a large sycamore with two large branches big enough to support each person and far enough off the ground to be out of reach of a jumping tiger.

They pulled a large downed log over to the spot where they wanted the mannequin set up and began working on its position and where the chopping hand should go.

They set up some ropes in the tree so that when they came back that night they could easily scramble up the tree.

Once they were satisfied, they took the dummy down and hid it in some thick brush, then made their way back to the village for lunch. They would eat their fill and try and get in as long a nap as was possible before returning just prior to sundown.

Everyone seemed to be in good spirits as they made their way back to the village.

By now everything was extremely dry and withered and the rains could be expected within a fortnight, if they came early. Winston was hoping they would be late this year to give him a few more chances. They knew that the cat was close.

The men found their hut and stretched out on the floor with a mat and Charles made for the hammock. They needed to get some sleep before the evening.

Things were quiet in the village, just a typical day with a man-eater on the loose in the area. There was a lot more chit-chat than usual, but people remained in groups of three or more for safety at all times unless they were in the village.

The cook had been cooking up some casavara. Having found out Winston loved it she wanted to surprise him.

A few hours later Winston was the first to get up and looking at his watch woke Charles too. Charles drew his suspenders back over his shoulders yawning the entire time as he followed Winston out into the village.

Dinner was ready for them and both men thought it was delicious.

Soon after the meal Winston lit his pipe as Charles made ready for the short hike to the clearing.

Within thirty minutes they were bidding farewell to the locals as if they were going on an expedition to the pole.

Neither man spoke much but hiked in the sultry heat towards their destination.

As they left the village they saw a large group of women gathering wood for their cooking fires. Within another half an hour they were well away from anyone and even though it was still light they found the countryside eerie.

Winston kept his rifle ready at all times, not knowing what to expect but preparing for the worst. Charles was a little more lackadaisical in his approach, with his gun slung over his shoulder.

Occasionally a flock of birds would instinctively flutter up and fly away, and each time they did Winston halted them both and examined the area of commotion before giving the signal to proceed.

When they got nearer to the tree they approached it carefully and uncovered the man-made dummy.

Everything had been set in the morning and all they needed to do was to set the fishing line on the hand and position the mannequin where it looked natural for a wood chopper. They had to nail the body section to a log, but it didn't take long before they were satisfied with the way the body was positioned and the way the arm worked up and down, a small hatchet attached to the hand.

Charles climbed up first and waited for Winston to throw the fishing line up, which he had attached to a stick that was lying around. Once Charles had the line, he threw it over a higher branch and grabbed the stick while Winston began climbing up into the tree.

Winston asked Charles to move since it was more likely that he would be the first shooter. Charles obliged and adjusted the stick to the desired height in order to make himself comfortable but still able to work the hand.

Winston suggested that he climb higher into the tree to make sure that the tiger didn't see his hand working the dummy. Charles looked up and there was a branch another twenty feet up which would be directly over the dummy. He climbed up to it while Winston threw him the extra line.

The noise from the chopping hand of the dummy was not loud but could be heard from a distance. Once it got dark one of them would have to descend and light a lamp in order to give the appearance of a wood chopper working late into the evening.

As darkness was beginning to fall Winston descended the rope and lit the lamp where it obscured the men in the tree.

Charles started practicing with the dummy arm.

Winston was unsure of this new trap. Surely it was promising, maybe even ingenious, but would it fool the tiger?

The wind picked up and the bushes around the tree waved from side to side.

Being apprehensive due to the circumstances Winston was concerned being on the ground. Before, he had for the most part always put himself in more favorable positions, areas where he was relatively safe, the high ground, and now if the cat was near it would be intense.

He began scaling the rope. Only after he was safely on his branch did he begin to slow his breathing and heart rate.

Not a word was spoken between the two men, but both understood what had happened and Charles, for one, finally thought that Winston was human after all.

Charles began to reflect on the events of the last couple of weeks while straining to see in the darkness. He found that he loved being here in nature as opposed to the office. He was quickly despising the shenanigans of the office and national politics.

His thoughts were that the great showman in America PT Barnum was a lot like the government of England they were both in it for the money. He thought of how much simpler things were out here in the country, and how, with a little money, you could truly live like a king.

Many thoughts came to his mind as he consistently raised and lowered the chopper hand, getting into a rhythm that he would need to sustain for the six hours the lamp would be lit.

Both men were attentive and watchful as the hours ticked off through the night.

It was somewhat of a brilliant plan, for no other cat except the man-eater would attack a man, yet they knew the tiger would have to be fairly close for the trap to work.

Sometimes a person can have a feeling that something is about to happen. Winston usually had such premonitions, but tonight he had no such feeling as they continued to watch and listen.

The winds were beginning to pick up and Winston did have a fore-boding that the monsoons were on their way. It was a sixth sense that it was coming and with it went all chances of getting the beast.

Occasionally Winston would think back to his childhood growing up in India and the joy he felt with nature and the outdoors.

The night stake-out was eerie for Charles. He had not been on many and it brought a very uneasy feeling to him, not having sight and hearing sounds that, to him were unfamiliar. It was an experience that he was very uneasy about. It reminded him of being uncomfortable on several occasions when he first served in the royal navy, putting in at questionable ports in the Caribbean.

Without thinking he began to lose rhythm with the chopping hand. It really didn't matter because it was more natural that way, but instinctively when he heard a sound he stopped until he realized he had slowed down and began up again.

The sounds from the jungle were a cacophony of diurnal animals throughout the night.

Hour after hour went by in what seemed like an eternity.

Charles could see his watch from the light of the lantern since he wore his watch upside down in the jungle, and it seemed to him as if the hands weren't moving at all. If Winston had known he would have chided him for the reflection it can give off.

At last the six hour lantern had burned out and they had seen nothing the entire night. Charles's arm was aching as if he had rowed the English Channel.

Now things turned even more sinister as shadows from clouds passing across the moon moved through the darkened sky. Sounds became more pronounced and seemed to intensify.

They still had about four hours before the sun would begin to rise, and it was starting to get very cold.

Not a word was spoken per Winston's instructions and it seemed to Charles that he hadn't moved an inch the entire time, but he was used to this sort of thing, waiting in uncomfortable trees entire nights whereas Charles had no experience.

Charles legs had fallen asleep again and he quietly moved them.

Winston knew from experience that most often, deadly cats visited a stake out between one and three in the morning, so there was still time for a visit from the striped beast.

As they quietly waited for anything to happen they were startled by a large owl that came to land on their branch without realizing they were humans or even that they were there. It quickly flew off into the night hardly making a sound at all.

Winston had wondered if he should have tethered a goat instead, but he knew this tiger had a taste for human flesh and that it rarely wavered from its unique diet.

Charles began to think how comforting the unpleasantness of the village was.

Just when Charles didn't think they were going to see anything, something came out of the bushes towards the great tree. Winston instinctively raised his rifle but the creature was the rarely seen Kaotao, a small deer that Winston knew was plentiful in the country of Nam Viet.

It didn't take Winston long to recognize it wasn't the big cat they were looking for. More importantly, just as the small deer had wondered off there was a strong breeze from the southwest that came in an instant. Charles didn't pay it any attention but Winston, through his experience, knew exactly what it was. With the breeze the monsoons would follow in a few days. The hunting would be over until the rains left again in four month's time. He was very saddened because he knew that the cat would go on killing and as many as forty people would lose their lives before he could get back and start hunting it again.

He said nothing to Charles as they continued to wait for the light to make it safe to return to the village. When it finally came, they lowered themselves down and began to disassemble the woodsman. Not much was said as the breeze slowly began to pick up in intensity.

On the way back they were met by others from the village to escort them. After a few hours of sleep Winston would inform them that the hunt was over until the rains left.

Both men slept easily following their all night stakeout. When they awoke Winston gathered everyone together in the largest hut and made the announcement that the rains would come within a couple of days and even if they knew where the cat was now they wouldn't be able to be on full alert. Hearing was as much an asset to seeing, and with the winds they would not be able to hear.

Charles asked Winston about the monsoons. Winston said that, as the scientists explained it to him, there was a high that developed over the high Himalayan plain with a low developing over the Indian ocean, "the difference," he explained, "creates a wind pattern where western winds come up from the ocean over the Himalayan plateau bringing warm moist air. As the air descends the plateau, it releases copious amounts of water on the Asiatic region. The rains will most definitely follow the strong winds."

He went on to mention that the failed monsoon of eighteen seventy-six caused millions to starve as the crops failed from needed rain. It sounded to Charles like a lecture from a prominent college.

Charles couldn't believe it. He wanted to continue, but deep down he knew Winston was right. He was always right.

Even as he thought about it, the winds outside were really picking up. The villagers, when they found out the news that the hunters were packing up, had a desperate look in their eyes as if their one hope for deliverance was going away never to return.

Within three days they would be back in civilization. Charles shuddered at what the director would think or do. It was as if they had failed and everyone knew it.

He stopped looking into the eyes of the villagers. They were all filled with longing as they served them a sumptuous meal in hopes that they would stay, little was said.

Charles couldn't bring himself to send a cable of their defeat and the oncoming monsoon. Those at the ministry might see the rain first hand and a day before themselves being in the southern part of the country. The entire group was depressed beyond measure.

The tiger had been patrolling the countryside like a dedicated policeman on a beat, taking things at a leisurely yet cautious pace. It was not where Winston and Charles had thought, but it was close only being about twenty miles distant.

It meandered along many of the paths that connected the villages or hamlets together. As it did so it heard a very unusual sound coming from the jungle itself. Every minute or two you could hear a loud thud echoing from the distance. It went to investigate the rare sound. As it did so, it left the path and continued on. Many birds and monkeys would call out an alarm once they discovered it prowling in the vicinity. The grasses gave way as it slid its body through and around the obstacles in its way.

After carefully making its way to the sound, it at first did not understand what could be making the noise. Beneath a large coconut tree lay several large coconuts on the ground which wasn't unusual until another one came crashing down making a large boom.

From cover the tiger instinctively looked up to see what was making the coconuts fall. In the top of the tree was an older man using a machete to lop off the coconuts as they fell to jungle floor.

The tiger rested on its haunches, observing the entire process. It realized at once that eventually the man must come down and that would give it a perfect chance to kill. It slowly made its way closer to the base of the tree with the existing cover and then patiently waited.

The man had only recently climbed this new tree when the cat happened upon what was going on and it took him a little while to clear out the ripened coconuts.

The man was aware that there were reports that the Katagi man-eater was in the area, but he needed to gather coconuts for his livelihood. Man-eater or not the work must go on eventually. He had waited in his hut for several days hoping that the cat would bypass this area. He was more alert and discerning about the area around him, especially when he moved between trees and walked to and from his hut each day. But there was no way to be quiet when he was about his work. He couldn't carry all the coconuts down the tree, and he couldn't drop them silently on the ground either.

A domesticated water buffalo chewing its cud was hitched to a small wagon with two wheels on a path that led into the area. The tiger had noticed it when it moved to get closer but paid no attention being solely concerned with the man in the tree.

At last, the man decided there were enough coconuts and began to descend the tree, oblivious to the danger that awaited him. The tiger was starting to drool at the very thought of human flesh as it began to study the man starting to descend. With each step having to be placed in a small groove which he had cut earlier, the descent required that the man look down for the next notch. The notches were cut some distance apart as the man was very limber from doing this for a living for the last seven years.

He was at about the halfway point in coming down when tiger began to rise and get ready. When he got within about fifteen feet of the ground the tiger made its move, covering the small distance in about two leaps.

The man was descending when something caught the corner of his eye. He heard the call of birds and as he looked around to see what it was, he saw an enormous paw coming straight for his face. There was no time to duck or move as the foreleg of the tiger hit him squarely in the face and with such force to knock him off the tree. He was spinning in the air with arms and legs flailing as blood rushed out the fresh cuts made by the paw on his face. He tried to land feet first but he was spinning so much that he landed on his head with the force of his body breaking his neck.

The tiger was on him the second he hit the ground and a vise like grip was applied to his neck which was already broken. The whole ordeal was over in less than thirty seconds as a still beating heart pumped blood through the wounds in the man's face which were beginning to stain the tiger's fur around its mouth.

Even with the victim it held, the tiger was still keenly aware of its surroundings, keeping a watchful eye for anything out of the ordinary.

After a few minutes it sensed through its whiskers that the pulse had stopped and it released its grip as the man's lifeless body slumped to the ground.

The tiger instinctively picked up the light body in its jaws and went for cover. Since the man lived alone it would be several days before news of the disappearance would be known.

With the death, the strong winds came up from the south and began to penetrate the interior. The monsoon was arriving.

Winston was back at his home when the monsoon hit with full fury. Charles had returned back to Bombay and the viceroy had scheduled a meeting for the following monday with a note for Charles that it was mandatory to attend, and he would be required to give a full report.

Charles was dreading the entire ordeal. He had retired to his cottage on the outskirts of town for peace and solitude, but the nagging thoughts of a job left undone haunted him. He tried to get back into his normal schedule, but it was of no use, he just wasn't into it.

Perhaps he should take some time off, he thought to himself. But where would he go and what would he do? The monsoon was bearing down with a ferocity that would wake Hades himself.

He began putting together his report but after several rough copies he decided to wing it verbally without forethought. Before long he was out cold, sleeping the night away in his front room. His servant put a warm blanket over him, not disturbing his sleep, as his snores resonated throughout the room.

With the speed of a courier, Monday morning had come and Charles was dreading the meeting with each passing hour.

Charles decided to arrive at the meeting early but as he entered the room there were several people already there none of whom he knew. Workers were bringing in extra chairs and he noted to himself that this meeting was going to be bigger than he thought.

He noticed the several additional flags on the map noting that the map had been moved from where it used to be and was now in the large conference room.

He had no desire to talk to anyone as he took his seat at one end of the table.

Within minutes of the meeting starting it seemed that the room was filled to capacity. When the viceroy strolled in murmurs began to quell.

George began to speak and as he did Charles couldn't help but wonder why he hated the man so much. Indeed, he thought that he must have picked it up a notch while out in the field.

Someone that Charles did not know was conducting the meeting and after opening up he indicated that the meeting was for discussion of the Katagi man-eater. George Smythe would be the first speaker followed by Charles Whent.

"Following those speakers we will openly discuss the menace at hand."

George elaborated on the problem, going into the details of what the ministry had tried to do to eradicate the problem. He spared few details and when he was done everyone was familiar with the issue.

George turned the time over to Charles to discuss what they were doing presently.

Charles didn't go into too much detail but did mention that they had a couple of good opportunities and that they were using Winston Jamison but luck was not on their side. He went on to mention that they were dealing with a very smart and intelligent creature that was all too wily. He continued to explain that due to the monsoon season they had been forced to abort the hunt until the spring rains abated, but he assured everyone that he felt confident that before long they would be able to lift the curfew in the tiger's regions and finally be rid of the beast.

Nearing the end of his speech questions began to be asked in earnest to the dismay of George, who wanted to field the questions himself. It became apparent quickly enough who the real expert on the man-eater was.

The usual questions were asked and Charles for one was beginning to grow weary of the same questions from months and weeks ago, but he was able to shed some light on the question of how big the man-eater was when he pulled out a plaster cast of one of the pug marks. It looked massive to everyone as they all stared at it.

Charles explained that this print was taken from soft soil near where a young girl was killed.

"With this we will be able to identify and confirm that a tiger killed is in fact the man-eater. Of course, there aren't many this size in all of India so it shouldn't be hard. But anyone claiming to have killed the man-eater will need to verify it with the plaster cast before any reward money is spent."

The next question naturally asked was regarding what size he thought the beast was. Charles answered that it was likely eleven feet over curves.

Charles was beginning to sense this was more of a news conference than a meeting. After answering and explaining for what seemed like half an hour there was an older gentleman, who looked and acted noble and had a long handlebar mustache, who raised his hand and when acknowledged stood up and began to pace around the table.

He began by saying, "Charles, we applaud your efforts." After a timed pause he continued, "But in talking with the viceroy this last week, perhaps there is something else that we can do, and as I mention this I must also ask that we expect to have the full cooperation of your office here" as he looked directly at George.

With that said George verbally spoke up in saying, "Yes, you do in every aspect."

Charles could see right through George as he was amply kissing the man's posterior.

The man went on to say that by indicating 'we' he was talking about the British government, and by the way, we also have the full support of the viceroy in the matter, and that we should be on the same page as to the fact that *we all* want the menace eliminated.

He was tapping his cane occasionally on the floor as he spoke.

It was apparent to Charles that this man was someone who was important and Smythe should have informed him who was going to be there at the meeting beforehand. He attributed this lack of communication to the incompetence of George and his general buffoonish nature.

The man continued, "We have taken the liberty of hiring another professional from the Transvaal in Africa, who is also very experienced and highly competent in these matters."

Charles immediately thought, Oh no, that's all we need, another professional out in the field competing against Winston.

The man continued, "He has already killed a man-eating lion and a rogue elephant and from what I understand is a crack shot, receiving the highest marks in marksmanship granted by the military. We've already sent for him over a fortnight ago and expect him in the country in about three weeks to a month."

Charles spoke up at this point and said that the monsoon rains wouldn't end for another twelve weeks.

"I'm sure Mr. Hawthorne will manage things nicely, after all he is a professional. As I mentioned before," looking straight at Charles, "we expect the full cooperation of the local government here and any resources you can provide."

George spoke up again saying, "We shall provide him with whatever he needs."

Charles couldn't help but think that Winston and himself had needed to get along with the barest of necessities. He also thought of how he was going to break the news to Winston that he had some competition. He put the thought out of his head for now and reasoned that he would deal with that later.

His mind was beginning to wander as the overstuffed peacock of a man rambled on and on. He looked again at the map and wondered how many more would succumb to the man-eater before someone could take it out.

The rain continued to patter along the slit panes of the office as he noticed men were beginning to file out one by one. Only Charles remained with the politician and George who were both making for the door.

When the other gentleman was halfway through the door the politician used his cane to remove the door stop and shut the door prior to Charles getting through.

"I sincerely hope, Mr. Whent that you will give us your full cooperation in this matter. I couldn't help but notice your body language which seemed to say, if I may, 'I don't give a rat's ass what they're doing.'"

"Mr. ..." Charles hadn't yet been introduced to the man, so he tilted his head to receive his name.

"Blygoth. Javier Blygoth," replied the man.

"Well, Mr. Blygoth, I'm sure you're a man of great intellect and fore-sight. Could you possible tell me, from your foresight who will kill the man-eater?"

The man puffed out his chest and said, "Candidly speaking, I have no doubt in my mind that Mr. Hawthorne will without question be the one who will be responsible for the creature's demise."

Charles responded, "I, on the other hand, place my faith in Mr. Jamison. Would you care for a wager on the matter?"

Mr. Blygoth had fallen into a trap set by Charles. He couldn't save face by not taking the bet after extolling Mr. Hawthorn's ability to kill the beast, yet he could extricate himself by requiring a large bet which Charles would be forced to refuse.

After a slight pause he said, "How about fifty pounds."

He tried to read Charles' astonishment, but Charles held a poker face giving no indication of the large wager. It was two month's salary for Charles and probably only a couple of weeks for the politician.

Charles didn't take long to decide himself and replied by saying, "That's a rather large amount of money which I do not have at the moment."

Javier breathed a sigh of relief, but it was premature.

"But I have something that's just as valuable as cash. When I was sta-tioned in the eastern province several years ago I happened to come across a deal that I could not pass on," he continued, "A man was in need of some quick cash and offered me a very large clear ruby of the most prized pigeon blood color for a bargain. I took the offer and when I returned to Calcutta, I had it appraised. Although it was singly refractive and turned out to be a spinel instead of a ruby its appraised price is fairly close to your fifty pounds. I can put it up for the wager, but if I do, I must insist that you put up the cash as well and we can have an impartial third party hold the goods and the money until the bet is settled. Agreed?"

Javier didn't like it but could not back out without losing face.

"Very well. We'll have Smythe here hold the goods for us."

"No, I don't think so. He's not exactly impartial. After a slight pause he told Blygoth to look out into the office and pick someone there,"

They opened the office door just as Sarkee was walking by.

"You sir, what is your name?"

"Sarkee Maslan, sir."

"Do you consider yourself an honest man?"

"Why of course! You can't get ahead in this world by cheating," replied Sarke.

"Good. I wish you would hold some goods and cash for us on a bet we've made. If Jamison kills the so called Katagi man-eater you are to give the gemstone and cash to Charles here and if Mr. Hawthorne kills the beast you are to deliver the goods to me, is that clear?"

"Sir, I don't know if I want the responsibility for such valuable commodities. I haven't a secure place"

"I can lend you a strong box, chain and padlock. You'll only need to keep the key safe," replied Charles.

"Very well," replied Sarkee, "You can bring the items to me tomorrow. Don't forget the strongbox Charles."

Charles didn't hesitate to mention that Mr. Sarkee will also act as the judge on the matter and both would need to defer to him for the final word. Bylgoth nodded and said "agreed" after that Charles then extended his hand to shake on it while there were witnesses and said, "the bet is on then," "Yes indeed" replied Javier.

Charles amazed himself at having taken such a large bet, but he didn't want to give the man the satisfaction he was looking for. He hated men like that. It would be worth it if he won.

The striped cat had moved south since its last kill, meandering slowly through the rains and the vegetation, which was quickly returning to its vibrant nature. It was again looking for food as it ventured into territory that was more open. It had always preferred the thick jungle which could easily hide its movements, but hunger had forced it here. If it had known the danger it was about to witness it would have never ventured into the open. But being unaccustomed to not having its way, it slowly prowled, knowing that the hunters had gone, and enjoying a bit of solitude.

There was, in the area, a large pack of hyena's which had come across the scent of the tiger, and being a strong pack of twenty-four animals, the group felt that they could perhaps pick up some scraps from a meal or even chase off the cat from a feeding. They were rarely challenged and had not had any competition for the majority of their lives.

The alpha female began a call that signaled the rest of the pack to follow and soon they were in a slow, steady pursuit of their quarry.

This pack had been very successful in most of their hunts and there was a considerable amount of experience among the older ones.

The pack is unique among animals. Like wolves the hyenas had a set of alpha parents and most of the group were descendants in one way or another. They were very efficient killers, being patient while eating many of their victims alive by disemboweling their victims while others held strangle holds or simply held the limbs of the victims. They feared nothing and at times had battled with leopards or tigers with impunity, only losing a couple members of the pack. Most predators gave them a wide berth. It was the bravado of the tiger or leopard that eventually lead to their deaths as they would rather stand their ground and fight than run. In this manner the pack would surround the victim and come in from all angles. It was really only a matter of time before superior numbers lead to death.

Stories were sometimes told of areas of death where great battles had been fought with some of the hyenas being disemboweled themselves or their skulls crushed. But more than likely a dead leopard or tiger would be found nearby having been killed but not eaten in order to eliminate competition, as well as several members of their own kind killed as well. It was Darwin's hypothesis to the fullest as only the strong survive.

With the tiger only casually looking for food and the hyenas bearing down on it, it was only a matter of time before they would cross paths.

The tiger disliked the new terrain and wanted to return to the dense foliage it preferred.

Within twenty minutes the tiger could hear the wails of the hyena pack closing in. It had no fear, not being intimidated at all throughout its life and when it was fearful, as when it had encountered other large male tigers and fights ensued, it had always remained victorious. So it remained unperturbed, to be mauled or to lose a battle badly was not something it was accustomed to.

It turned to investigate the unique sounds from an unknown foe.

As the calls from the pack were nearing, the tiger sensed that something was amiss and slowly began to return to denser cover. After a few minutes it turned around to see the full pack bearing down on it with the determination of a honey badger.

The big cat growled furiously in the hope of driving away the menace, but though its ears were laid back with fangs exposed the pack was not intimidated.

The distance closed within seconds and the tiger, realizing the full extent of the danger, immediately charged the pack and by doing so caused it to scatter to the four directions of the compass. Its speed was surprising and it caught the lead hyena by surprise, dispatching it with a blow to the head from its paw which knocked it out for the time being as blood ran down its jowls from the claws which had opened up the skull.

The other hyenas began circling the tiger and giving their hellish laugh. Whenever the tiger lunged at one of them the others were quick to press the attack from the other side.

A hyena's bite force is greater than a tiger's and with little effort they can crush a leg bone, but what it gains in bite force it loses in speed and quickness.

Two of the hyenas had gotten too close, and the tiger was able to lunge and slash their necks with a quick paw, but it was getting nicked in the flank each time. With each passing minute the circle was getting smaller and smaller and it realized it needed to break out if it was going to survive.

It quickly rushed one side, scattering all, then quickly did an about face and leaped over the group from the other side. It was chaos but when it landed it whirled about and caught one, then two hyenas off guard and dispatched another with a paw swath to the neck.

As another closed in from behind, it kicked violently with its hind legs connecting with the hyena right under its jaw. The resulting connection left the hyena bleeding badly from an opened mouth.

The tiger raced off again with the pack in hot pursuit.

It came to a large boulder and, doing another about-face, it used the stationary rock to launch itself into the melee again. This time all but one shot clear, but the one that was too slow was disemboweled right on its underside and intestines started to ooze out.

The attack was starting to make the tiger weary. Some of the attacks had started to show on the limbs of the tiger as blood began to trickle down from several wounds. The big cat charged through the pack again, this time unable to reach any of the hyenas. It ran down a path until it came to a large fallen cypress tree that was easily three feet in height. In the middle of the tree the side was deteriorating and offered a sort of concave opening to the tree. Here the tiger back up and faced the pack.

The hyenas could no longer attack from behind and from all sides, but they pressed on undeterred. The big cat was in a more favorable position now as it continued to swat at all comers. The top of the log was slippery, and the hyenas didn't like going up there from behind because they couldn't get away when they needed to.

There were by now another two wounded hyenas as they continued to press the attack. The tiger was constantly being attacked in the front with black and brown fur rushing in, but it dealt with each attack individually and singled out the hyena that it could reach. Within minutes another one was injured and had to pull out of the fray, badly wounded.

The tiger crouched in the cavity of the log and with two legs kicking and reaching, just doing whatever it could to wreak havoc among the hyenas. It was fighting for its life and with all the claws coming forth from that cat it was nothing short of hell's fury.

The attack never lessened but the hyena's bodies began to pile up in front or to the side of the tiger, making it difficult to get over or around.

The alpha male realized that they were getting no further in the fight and began to retreat, calling out to the others to hasten back where they had come.

The tiger was mauled in places with some of the wounds deep but was still able to walk without difficulty. It casually walked over to a severely wounded hyena which it dispatched quickly with a bite to the spine, severing the rigid bones.

The hyena pack had left about a third of their group behind, being either dead or dying. Some even limped away with minor wounds themselves. They had misjudged their enemy and would think twice before attacking a tiger again.

The tiger, though exhausted, had survived and roared constantly, alerting the jungle that it was supreme. The retreating hyenas could hear the roars and knew that they had been defeated for the first time as they continued their retreat.

The big cat found some shade and laid down for a rest as it licked its own wounds and cleaned the blood from its magnificent coat. It then fell into an exhausted slumber as a light rain continued to pour down.

In Bombay, the rains continued to fall as if they were never going to let up. The gutters and roads were constantly filled with rainwater. Locals waded through the liquid mess while others with money paid to use the rickshaws or other means of transportation.

Charles went into the office and put in his hours all the while bidding his time until he could continue the hunt. Sometimes he would try and gather information about the deaths as the reports came in and all he could do was watch additional flags being put on the map. It was noticeable how without much pressure the attacks were clumped together without much distance between them. He wondered if it was a lack of pressure or the rains that caused it.

He mused how he at first wanted nothing to do with the hunt and now it had been a complete reversal as he longed for the chase. The game that was begun was now in his veins, in his blood. He'd see it to the very end and follow that cat to the ends of the earth if need be.

He surprised himself with his thoughts and came to realize how much he'd changed, how much he'd grown in confidence and determination. Not that he was walking with a swagger or anything, but just a deep conviction that he had confidence that he can do hard and difficult things.

The rain continued to patter on the lush green plants outside his office. A knock from George Smythe released him from his daydream as he asked to come into his office. Without waiting for a reply, he strode in and George came straight to the point.

"Well, Charles I know you don't like it, working with anyone else, but those higher up want this to go down and I want you to use all your influence to make this happen. We need to put egos aside here and work for the common good. I know Winston is sort of a loose cannon and a maverick, but there's going to have to be cooperation on this from the beginning. I don't want the chances of a kill being thwarted by two prideful, egotistical, great white hunters. Remember Charles that I control you. You shan't eat, drink or piss without approval from me. Do you understand?"

"I understand," replied Charles, "But you also need to understand one thing."

"And what might that be?"

"I'm not going to be your puppet forever. They had a saying over in the Americas, 'don't tread on me!'"

With that said he remained as stoic as a statue.

Silence followed as George turned and walked out of his office and Charles reverted to his thousand yard stare out the window. Perhaps he should spend the weekend visiting Winston, he mused, after all, someone will need to inform him of the recent news.

He decided he needed some air and locked up his office to walk home in the rain. It was a long walk, but he had the time.

The monsoons continued to bring the rain as everything plantlike blossomed into every shade of green there was.

He grabbed his umbrella and began to take a leisurely stroll through the streets.

While Charles had to play the politics game, Winston on the other hand was enjoying a semi- holiday as he lounged in his covered hammock in his yard or slept in well past nine o'clock in the morning. He would eventually rise and go on a run or a long hike in the rain all the while thinking of new ways to kill the man-eater. Occasionally he would begin to feel his new scars and run his fingers over the coarse texture of the wounds, reminding himself that he had been lucky that time.

Most hours were spent waiting out the rains that came every day like clockwork. He had also used the time to write his memoirs of hunts of the past, of close calls and death as a constant companion. There was no need to embellish anything. It was all the truth and he realized he had led a wonderful life and had been blessed by a God who cared enough to send a few guardian angels to preserve his life. He wasn't much a spiritualist but he knew enough to know that someone was looking out for him.

He often thought about things and how different they would have been if he had gotten married and raised a family. He had all the comforts money could buy, yet there was something missing. Perhaps it was loneliness. *Maybe it's not too late*, he mused. He could find a wife now and settle down, give up the hunts. He had an eye on a daughter of one of his servants that sometimes came and helped her mother. He also missed Charles and hated to admit it to himself, but he had grown fond of him and realized he was a better friend than he had ever been to anyone. Maybe he should visit him on a weekend, he wouldn't be working.

With those thoughts dancing in his head he fell into an afternoon slumber as the jungle made no notice but went on as it always will.

Bart Hawthorne was a very large man by any standards; six foot two inches tall with a long handlebar mustache and long sideburns. He was built like a barrel and it came naturally. There were few willing to cross him or short him out of any change or deal. He had the temperament of a honey badger and was known to have a short fuse.

He had grown up in the Transvaal area of Africa, born to wealthy parents who had made their fortune finding diamonds in the region they had settled. Bart was spoiled from the day he was born and felt privileged above all others. He grew up a bully. He was selfish, manipulative, egotistical, churlish, and ugly. He had few friends. He was usually unkempt in appearance with the exception of his mustache and was sometimes known to be fond of his scotch.

He was a single parent who had a daughter who had obviously inherited her mother's looks. She was twenty-two and beautiful, she was unmarried due to the few courters and the domineering personality of her father.

Bart's daughter did a large portion of the chores around the home and was almost an exact opposite of her father. She was stunning, selfless, caring, generous to a fault, and often thought of others, especially at the market where she would give away a portion of the food allowance to the poor.

It was a strange relationship between father and daughter, but life in the Transvaal was always hard.

Bart had established himself as a great guide and an excellent hunter having killed several trophies and, in addition, a man-eating lioness that was responsible for killing over thirty people in just over a year. It was from this event that his fame spread and from which he was contacted and given an opportunity to kill the Katagi man-eater.

Visiting politicians from South Africa and England, aware of the menace and stories of the Katagi man-eater in India, made an effort to flatter him into taking the job. They failed to mention that there would be competition. Some of the details including how much he was being paid were known to only a select few.

Once he decided to take the job, he busied himself putting his affairs in order and making arrangements to leave for India on a steamship bound for the Indies with a stop in Bombay. It would take close to five weeks to make the voyage and the monsoons would still be in force for several months once he arrived. He was capable of doing the job, there was no doubt about that, but he was also careless at times and lacked the patience, which is needed to hunt in India. It wasn't like the plains of South Africa where you could see for miles and there was little cover.

He relished the thought of bagging a tiger, and a man-eater at that, and also wanted to kill an Indian rhino and elephant. It didn't matter to him that his daughter Victoria didn't want to go or that he never had her interests in mind. Not that she couldn't handle things, on the contrary, she could shoot with the best of them and was rugged to the core. You don't grow up in that region of Africa without learning a thing or two about survival. But she was a woman too, and when she fixed herself up, there was no doubt heads would turn no matter the age of the man. She could tame the black mamba. In fact the more she read up on India, the more excited she became about going there.

Her curiosity and wonder filled her dreams until she had done a complete turnaround from what she had originally told her father. She was also excited about bringing back some spices to liven up the diet of game they were used to. It seemed she was always experimenting with something new. Her father had put up with it enough and had even got quite ill when she tried feeding him aardvark steaks. Most the time the meals were tasteful, even delicious but there's only so much you can do with what you have.

The steamship at Capetown wasn't scheduled to arrive for another fortnight but they would have to leave no later than a week out to make sure they arrived on time and received their tickets.

Bart was controlling to the point where he was telling Victoria what she could bring and what she couldn't. Like most women she packed for the eventual need of everything and consequently the trunks began to pile up before her father put a stop to it.

Her reply to everything was, "They probably don't have it there."

It didn't matter anyway. With some ingenious packing she was able to condense four trunks into three with most of the things she felt she needed. Of course, she failed to tell her father that she had a craftsman hollow out compartments and remove separating drawers.

Without much fanfare they left at the appointed time for Capetown.

Not having traveled much, it was exciting for Victoria. Even though ladies were supposed to act and dress as such, her father relented into allowing her to dress in traveling clothes which included trousers.

They would have to travel overland for a few days by camel, then they could pick up the rail for the rest of the way to Capetown.

Bart looked at it as just another assignment or job. Victoria looked at it as the adventure of a lifetime.

The steamship was scheduled to arrive one month later in Bombay. It would be traveling through some of the most dangerous oceans in the world, but nothing could tame Victoria's enthusiastic approach to anything and everything. Once they arrived in Capetown she could be seen at the markets or bazaars making additional purchases until her father took away her money and only piecemealed it out to her so she wouldn't spend it all. They still had a few days before the ship left and she was determined to make the voyage as comfortable as possible.

When the time came to board she was as giddy as a young child on Christmas Eve.

After a few days at sea, there arose a big storm which made most of the passengers' sea sick, including Bart, but she was immune to the sickness and still enjoyed being on deck even when storms were their fiercest.

She continued to help carry dishes to the galley instead of letting workers clear the table.

Bart remained aloof for the most part just wishing they would make land soon. He was rude to the ship's employees and others. Sometimes you could hear him telling some of his exaggerated stories of himself in some daring adventure to other men in the smoke room.

Victoria started to keep a journal of the entire experience, realizing that it was a once in a lifetime opportunity.

The entire voyage was boring, mixed with brief moments of excitement to some and anxiety to others as the ship reeled to a fro in the storms.

At length they arrived in Bombay and as the signal cannon went off announcing their arrival, George Smythe, Javier Blygoth and their associates made ready to meet them at the quay. Bart of course was expecting them and Victoria had no idea what was going on.

George had left Charles a message to meet them as well, but since George hadn't spoken to him directly, he ignored it.

Both Javier Blygoth and George were excited to welcome Bart and were impressed by his manner, looks and intellect, although looks can be deceiving. The usual introductions were made and after recommending where they could stay, they made immediate dinner appointments.

Victoria was introduced as well and both men were immediately smitten by the young lady nearly half their age. She was still quite shy and slightly blushed as she was introduced.

Bart was asked to come over to the Ministry's Office prior to the dinner appointment so introductions could be made. He accepted and before long they were saying their goodbyes.

George had arranged to have some locals move their belongings as well as have a translator for Bart if needed. One of the first things out of Bart's mouth was what a filthy country it was and asked what that god-awful smell was. The locals could discern things well and his looks and mannerisms were of a superior nature which angered the locals.

Arrangements had been made to rent a home within the city for now, and they had the option of switching residences if they desired.

Hired rickshaws were waiting for them at the end of the dock as Victoria took in everything like a little child finding a new play place.

Within minutes everything was loaded. George noticed several gun cases being unloaded and asked Bart why he needed so many guns. Bart replied that he was going after other game after his business with the tiger was over. After that they boarded the rickshaws and they were off to clean up and rest before Bart would need to meet his appointment.

The entire country was completely different from the one they had come from even though it was also under British rule. On the way the translator pointed out the bank where money could be exchanged and other local sights or buildings. It was a port town for sure, but they would find an even more foreign country away from the city.

Victoria busied herself unpacking and making their new house a home, but the humidity was something she was not used to, and she tired easily. She sat down for a moment and fell fast asleep.

It continued to drizzle rain the whole day and there was a muggy wet feeling for anyone not used to the conditions of the monsoon.

Bart cleaned up, shaved and made ready to meet his appointment.

A messenger was sent to gather him at the appointed time and guide him through the city to the ministry's office. As they traveled, he took little notice of his new surroundings and just thought how much further Africa was in its development as a country. Within minutes of leaving, his shirt was already showing wet stains from the muggy heat and sweat, and though he didn't realize it yet this was the cool part of the season. He was constantly thirsty in this new country and he couldn't wait to be done with this job and headed back home.

When he arrived at the office one of the first things he noticed was the map showing the kills from the Katagi man-eater.

George met him immediately and was introducing him to everyone around the office. When they came to Charles' office, George politely knocked and opened the door as Charles was busy at his desk.

"Charles, I'd like to introduce you to Bart Hawthorne from Africa. He will be working with you and Winston on killing the Katagi man-eater."

Charles rose from his desk to shake Bart's hand.

As Bart extended his hand he said, "Ah yes, you're the one who was unsuccessful in killing the cat. What a pity, but I suspect things are in good hands now that a professional has arrived."

Charles replied, "We do have a professional here, his name is Winston Jamison. Perhaps you've heard of him."

Everyone who was anyone and could read would have heard of him in the English-speaking world.

But Bart replied, "No, I haven't, but I don't see how I could have as news probably doesn't get out of this little country of yours. By the way, I was informed that you hit the beast?"

"Yes, I did. Not a kill zone though. It seems the cat has resurrected another life."

"No doubt it would be dead if it had been I," replied Bart. "I plan to go after the beast as soon as possible and clear up this mess once and for all."

"The monsoons won't be gone for another two months at the very least," replied Charles.

"A little rain shan't stop me. It will be dead in a fortnight or two, you can bet on that."

Charles thought about cashing in on a large bet heavily placed in his favor but then thought better of it. He didn't like Bart right from the beginning, and it was probably best to keep away from him as much as possible. Anyway, he would already have to pay out a handsome sum if he lost his bet with Mr. Blygoth.

"Well, I think the rain here is quite a bit different than what you're used to in the South of Africa."

"It's rain, all the same," replied Bart, "and the beast will die with or without it, you mark my words young man. We have the brains and the firepower and that will always result in triumph. Do you know how many times I've had a brush with death? Whether it's stampeding hippos in the dark of the night sensing danger and trying to make it to the river, or stepping over the feared black mamba, it's all the same. All you need is courage and determination."

Charles replied by saying, "You know, the terrain is quite a bit different here as well. This isn't the open plain where you can see a beast bearing down on you. You may have only a second or two here, maybe ten if you're lucky, and if you miss you'll be dead."

Bart looked at Charles with a stoicism nobody could read and then said, "Your territory, nor your rains don't frighten me Mr. Whent, I perceive that a man like yourself doubts a man of my reputation and skill."

"No, I'm not doubting that at all, but I want to impress upon you as much as I can that this is a beast not to be trifled with nor underestimated."

Bart smoothed out his handlebar mustache and calmly stuffed some tobacco into his pipe and lit it.

"Three weeks and you'll be thanking me when it's over."

With that, Bart and George turned and walked out of his office.

Charles let out a large sigh. He was beginning to realize as he looked out the window at the rain, that Winston and Bart were not going to get along at all.

Bart followed George into his office and shut the door.

"That Mr. Whent is quite the chap."

"You don't know the half of it. He wants this position, I can tell you that. I've given him some leeway with the tiger, and he's created a monster. This thing has just been over the top."

"Well, I understand the reporters have had a field day with it," replied Bart. "What you need is a little positive publicity, something that you can give the people that shows them you're doing your job, and I'm the man that can help you with that."

"What's the angle," replied George.

"Didn't Mr. Whent say that he couldn't go hunting the beast until the rains left?"

"Yes, but I don't see your angle," replied George.

"Well you simply get a reporter or two," Bart paused for a second, "that you trust and you feed them information that I'm going into the jungle to track down the beast. You'll also mention to the reporters that Charles, and the other fellow Jamison, are sitting in their comfortable homes doing nothing while the man-eating tiger kills innocent women and children. You'll then get the local populace on your side and destroy the popular support for you competition at the same time."

"I like your thinking. The viceroy will believe I'm doing more than required," replied George while getting Bart a couple of drams of scotch.

With that said there was a distinct clank to their crystal glasses as they drank a toast to the demise of the wretched creature and the furthering of their careers.

While Bart was busy making preparation for his foray into the jungle during a monsoon, Victoria was making preparations to make their rented house more like home. Although she tended to be more male oriented at times than a traditional lady, she could still put a nice feminine touch to a home and make it quite cozy.

As she had few friends to talk to, she had a tendency to talk Bart's ear off until he yearned to be out of the house. He wanted to go up to the local shooting club to get some practice in before venturing out into the jungle and Victoria begged to go with him. With those doe-like eyes staring up at him, even he couldn't say no.

They made preparations to go out the following day. The gun club of Bombay specialized in shooting glass balls imported from Italy. They were specially made, hand blown glass, with different colors made to burst into a hundred pieces if shot. There was a mechanical device that had been made exactly for the purpose of launching the glass balls and was one of the first the world had seen. The idea was to mimic a bird in flight with the glass balls being thrown out and away from the shooter as well as to the sides.

As a coincidence Charles had also scheduled a time slot for around the same time as Bart had. Most affluent residents who shared a passion for shooting were members of the club and it was needed if you wanted to succeed at all in India as it was a very common thing to do.

The next day arrived and Bart had arrived with his guide and Victoria. As introductions were made, they eventually made their way to the shooting area where Charles was already engaged in shooting.

Charles was surprised to see a woman coming onto the course in male attire. It was the first time he had seen her but the shapely figure of a well-proportioned woman rarely missed his gaze. Her hair was pinned up and she seemed to walk with the confidence of a woman who knew exactly what she was doing. She was wearing tan khaki shorts which showed immaculate legs that were as tan as an african gazelle, with a green hunting vest that held all the shells and other items.

As she approached she noticed Charles as an attractive man with piercing blue eyes and slicked back hair. Charles reflected that she was with Bart and thought that the old man was truly robbing the cradle with this one.

Bart noticed Charles and even though Charles detested the man he went over to shake hands with him. It was at that time that Bart introduced Charles to his daughter Victoria. There seemed to be electricity in the air as Charles took her hand and kissed it while saying that it was a pleasure to see such a beautiful woman in India.

Victoria, who was naturally shy, blushed somewhat while making the reply, "Thank you, but I'm sure you tell all the ladies here in India the same thing." "That may be true, but I don't always believe it" replied Charles.

She couldn't tear herself from the piercing blue eyes that seem to captivate her gaze. It was as if she was in some kind of stupor, hypnotized by his eyes.

She turned back to her father and Bart was eying them with concern. Bart wanted to protect her and had been doing so for some time, but it was apparent that she had become a woman and there was no question of that in anyone's mind.

Bart thought Charles to be a man who hit on all the pretty women, and with those eyes probably found few who rejected him. He didn't want him getting to know his daughter any better.

Charles broke the silence when he said, "I believe they're ready for you."

Bart and Victoria looked over to see the ready flag up for their section of the course.

"So they are," replied Victoria.

She nimbly picked a shell from her vest and in one sweeping motion loaded and slapped the shotgun shut. She and Bart walked to the open deck and after a few moments Victoria stepped to the shooting position, pulled back the hammers and yelled, "Pull!"

A glass ball was immediately flung out at a quick pace, Victoria sighted the ball in flight, tracked it and squeezed the trigger. The ball was hit perfectly, spraying into a hundred pieces.

"Nice shot," said Charles still within hearing range.

It was apparent that she was a natural as women generally didn't find pleasure in shooting. She went through her series and hit nearly seventy percent of her shots, more than most male members of the club. Following her last shot she retired to the clubhouse to get something to eat, thinking she had talked enough to the strange new man.

Bart took over her section and began hitting the balls with ease. It was apparent that he was an even better shot than his daughter as he had hit six in a row. Charles knew that no one could keep up that record for long and began to move closer to Bart.

Between shots, Bart mentioned something that startled Charles.

"Charles," he said, "I couldn't help but notice you took a liking to my daughter Victoria."

Charles was surprised but responded quickly "She's a refined woman. Congratulations on raising her," replied Charles.

"I really don't want her to get involved with men like you," said Bart as he raised his gun, yelled 'pull,' and missed the shot.

"What's that supposed to mean?" said Charles.

Bart replied that he'd seen his kind a lot; womanizing men who seduce women for their own selfish pleasures, and then leave them high and dry. He only knew because he was one himself, although in his later years he had lost some interest.

"I'll tell you what. Let's shoot for twenty balls. If I win you will stay away from my daughter, and if you win you can court her if you like."

Bart was pretty sure of himself winning and had no idea the kind of shot Charles was with him having won the Bombay open championship three years ago.

"You're on with that one, but just to make it interesting let's throw in ten pounds as well," replied Charles.

Charles could consistently hit eighteen or nineteen balls out of twenty. He was one of the best shots in the city with his only match being Winston himself and a select few others.

Bart was a pretty good shot himself, but thinking he was better than everyone else was his flaw. He grew up in the South of Africa where missing a game bird meant that you likely would go hungry that night, so he became a good shot at an early age, but he was getting older and should have been wearing his spectacles.

The game was on and each would take a turn until all forty balls were used. The sun was starting to beat down on the men and Charles put on his specialty shooting glasses that blocked the glare. He had an inward smile and was confident, and yet he didn't fully understand his opponent, not knowing how good he really was and already being impressed with what he had done. On the one hand there was Charles who was confident yet humble and on the other was Bart who was confident and arrogant.

Victoria had no idea what was happening. The first five balls were hit by both players, although Bart had barely hit one of them with only a single spherical ball breaking the glass.

Charles was feeling more confident as they went along. He casually shot another, then he broke open his gun, the smoke rising in a small column through the humid air.

Bart had also hit his next two shots and both were at a perfect seven hits each.

Charles was the first to miss on his next shot as he pulled the trigger too soon. Bart hit his next two again but missed on his tenth shot evening the score.

They were halfway through the match and sweat was coming down both men's faces as the sun beat down on them. Bart missed the ball on his fourteenth shot, but Charles also missed two shots later. They only had four remaining shots each and it was getting pretty intense as the pressure was mounting.

One by one they were each hitting their shots calmly, although they were both quite pressured. The intensity was extreme for both men as Charles hit his next to last ball. Bart followed with a hit of his own and they were both up to where either one was apt to miss.

Charles took his last shot and barely hit it with only two small spherical balls. Now it was Bart's turn but rather than waiting the few seconds, he immediately called out the pull and quickly hit his ball as well. They had tied after the twenty balls each.

Charles broke the silence first as he said, "Sorry you couldn't come away with the win, ol chap."

Bart wanted to finish things off and he said, "Let's finish it with another round."

Charles knew he was lucky to get away with a tie. Although he was an expert shot he knew Bart was his equal and a loss would forever stall his pursuit of Victoria.

Not wanting to gamble any further he simply said, "Sorry, but you can keep your money today, perhaps another time."

Bart was incensed and turned a shade of red, so livid that he couldn't think of anything to say, and watched Charles grab his gun sheath and walk towards the main building.

Bart swore to himself as he brought his gun down hard and it knocked the table.

As Charles walked through the clubhouse he saw Victoria coming his way heading back out to the range.

He stopped as he said, "It was a pleasure meeting you today Miss Victoria, and I hope we shall see each other again."

She replied, "likewise Mr. Charles," and he kissed her hand and walked off.

She couldn't help but think he was a curious man indeed.

Bart was still livid as Victoria came up to do some more shooting. She surmised that something had happened between her father and Charles but was afraid to ask him what it was. Bart was in a hurry to pack up his things and leave the club. Victoria helped him where she could and they left in a hurry.

The tiger had been moving a lot ever since the monsoons began, making its way westward, still leaving bodies in a wake of blood and terror as it entered new territories and new hamlets.

The ministry's office continued to tally the deaths and try to keep tabs on its general whereabouts as best they could. The fact was that in about a month's time it had traveled to the far reaches of the western boundary of India and had now entered the Gir forest which was new to it as the jungle gave way to plants and trees other regions did not produce. But little did it know that it was on a collision course with destiny, for in the Gir forest lived a colony of Asiatic lions and although the males had somewhat less of a mane than their African counterparts they were as much their match.

The resident male of the colony was a fine specimen alone for it was also a freak of nature being only a hundred and fifty pounds lighter than the man-eater itself and having fought any and all comers just to hold its pride together. But at this time it was patrolling alone on the eastern boundaries of the pride's range seeing what was out there, ready to challenge anything which might disturb its paradise.

Scar's marked its face and it was no stranger to battles legendary with other male prides it had destroyed. It feared nothing and would take on all comers. Each step revealed lean muscles, ribbed to its body, made from the distances it traveled each day and the fights it had endured. It believed it was supreme and had no worthy opponent.

It was the tiger that first caught its mark and smelled something it had never encountered. The mark was high on the tree and the tiger itself could see the claw marks on the bark of the tree. It fletched as it sniffed the new smell, unlike the leopards or another tiger it could tell it was a foreign smell that it had never encountered.

It gave a disapproving snarl and then let out a roar that could be heard for miles. Instinctively it knew that it had to investigate this new smell and it knew that there was a formidable opponent out there. With confidence it sprayed over the day old marking on the tree and reached up to sharpen its claws reaching only slightly higher than the previously made marks.

The trail moved both north and south and it choose the north side to investigate further. It had entered a sparsely populated region where people were hard to find and villages turned into smaller hamlets. It had killed a few days previously, an older man, but it was hungry again and sought anything that would satisfy its insatiable appetite.

While following the trail it spied a tapir foraging for grass on the open meadow. This was highly unusual as these animals prefer dense vegetation and although the monsoon had brought abundant grasses to the Gir forest it was by no means dense. The rains, although constant, would consistently taper off in the afternoon.

The tiger crouched low and began the stalk to get within striking distance of the tapir. It didn't blend well in the new green grasses but it kept hidden enough for the beast with poor eyesight to not see it. Luckily the breeze was carrying away from the tiger otherwise the Tapir's excellent smell would send it off in an instant.

Slowly and steadily the tiger was creeping ever closer. When it was within twenty feet it stopped. The tiger's eyes were low and could barely see through the grass but luck was on its side as the tapir moved closer while it continued to feed. Within a few seconds the tiger had sprung from its concealed position and was on the tapir as it desperately tried to get away. But the tiger was on it and in a second the jaws crushed the neck bringing near instant death.

The tapir was big, nearly weighing in at two hundred and fifty pounds, and provided the meat necessary for the big cat so it wouldn't have to eat for several days. It feasted like a king in a palace as it ate its favorite parts first, and then went down to the brook for a drink and a soak before taking a long nap. It would eat again tomorrow and then resume its course for the unknown beast.

The next day came, and after getting one last drink it continued on. When it reached the next tree with the unmistakable scent it realized it was going the wrong way as the scent was several days older than previous markings, and so it turned around and began making its way south. Fortunately, it had only traveled a half days journey before discovering the error. It was eager and curious to find the new beast. The markings were about a week old.

After spending several days with the pride, the male lion was again making its rounds like a night watchman and it was on a collision course with the tiger. Each day the two titans moved closer and closer towards each other.

On the third day in the morning they met, and it was a meeting of the largest meat eaters on the Asian subcontinent. They spied one another from across an open meadow and as each beast saw the other, they slowly began to close the gap until they met at the middle of the field.

Each animal began to snarl and lay its ears back as they began to move in a circle, neither one wanting to avert its eyes from the other.

The tiger was larger and was more stout and stocky in the shoulders. It held the weight advantage. The Lion was a very large specimen itself, much larger than average and had its characteristic Asiatic mane which undoubtedly helped in fighting by concealing the throat area. It also had been in several scraps and was no foreigner to fights to the death having taking over the pride only a year before. Both beasts possessed confidence that they would emerge victorious.

It was the lion who made the first move by lunging in with paws outstretched and in front. The tiger parried the strikes with its own paws as it retreated, taking on the attack. The tiger was able to bring a paw swiftly down on the lion which caught a part of its nose with a claw as the first blood was drawn. The tiger now counter- attacked with an equal fury as the lion parried the blows from the tiger.

Dust arose from the battlefield as each beast tried to get traction in order to always be facing the enemy. Snarls and hisses could be heard a half mile away as the magnificent beasts fought on. Neither was willing to yield and the back and forth battle continued.

Within time it became apparent to the lion that the tiger was connecting more and more, and the blows more powerful. The lion's confidence began to wane as the tigers confidence began to grow with each encounter. The more powerful forelimbs of the tiger were giving it an advantage, but the mane of the lion kept the tiger from getting a death grip on the neck. Tails were raised and lowered with each attack as both animals displayed huge canines.

The tiger began to mount more and more attacks keeping the lion off-balance as it began to work a more defensive fight. Occasionally one would get a grip on the foreleg or neck of the other only to be thwarted with four paws kicking and scraping the opponents head until it let loose. Blood soaked the fur of both animals heads as equal wounds let out the precious lifeblood.

The tiger, being a bit more aggressive now, had pushed the lion up into the hillside and into thicker brush. Bamboo and other small trees were broken with each powerful encounter. Each cat was fighting for the high ground, occasionally one or the other would gain the high ground and had a distinct advantage. Snarls and debris continued unabated.

The fight had been going on now for more than fifteen minutes and the intensity and exertion was beginning to wear the cats down. Each cat instinctively knew that they needed to face the other at all times. When an attack came from one the other prepared for it by whirling around with its tail counter rotating to help it keep its balance and face the threat.

They had been, without knowing it, working their way further into the jungle from the plain and there was a fallen cypress log of considerable size that was in the way. The tiger was the first one on top of it and it turned itself to face the enemy who was coming up as well. The tiger used its rear claws for added traction as it lunged with all its might from the top of the log downward and into the lion which was midair in an attempt to get to the top. For a brief second the two beasts became one entangled ball of fur. The momentum of the tiger and its weight carried both cats downward into the ground with the weight of the tiger falling directly onto the lion as bones began to crunch.

The lion immediately put all four legs on the tiger and sprang it off. The claws had been extracted and the tiger had some serious under belly wounds. The tiger responded by attacking again with a ferocity the jungle rarely sees. By now each cat had at least one significant wound, but neither was willing to yield.

The additional weight of the tiger was starting to be more and more of a factor as the fight continued.

The cats had fought their way back to level ground, and the tiger was discovering that as it attacked, if it stood up on its hind legs and came down with its weight that the lion, being a little less tall, was receiving not only the brunt of the added weight but the more powerful forward stocky body of the tiger. The tiger began to use this to its own advantage as it rose again and again, pummeling the lion underneath it. Each forelimb of the tiger came down like an anvil and although the lion was fending the blows well, it was starting to sap its strength.

The tiger was in a little better shape as well, as it was used to traveling great distances, whereas the lion was usually only patrolling its own territory.

The tiger could sense the fight was getting to the lion and increased its tenacity with a vengeance. Both cats were baring fangs and snarling enough for the whole region to hear.

At last the tiger came down again on its adversary with a powerful blow that made it turn its face away, and in another instant the tiger was on the lion, pinning its head to the ground with a fore paw while biting hard on the lions own fore paw with enough force to have it let out an anguishing roar.

It was over now as the lion tried to retreat backwards while trying to defend itself with a wounded limb. The tiger didn't let up for a few minutes but kept on beating it down as it retreated. At last with both cats exhausted the lion returned to where it had come as the tiger stood where it was and let out a loud victorious roar. It was still lord of the jungle and at the moment, nothing could challenge it. It laid down casually licking its wounds with its rasping tongue as it watched the lion limp into the setting sun.

Reports of an occasional killing were still being made and the ministry's office could still track the big cat as it moved in a south-westerly direction. It could cover incredible distances and that was what made it so difficult to predict.

As Bart made his final preparations, he was informed of the latest whereabouts of the tiger. The rain continued to come to Bombay like clockwork, and if anything wasn't covered it was wet through and through. There were the usual reports of delays from mudslides onto the train tracks or towns and hamlets deluged by the water, even occasional bridges that had washed away, but for the most part it was normal for the monsoon and life went on.

Since the last report of the tiger's most recent kill was on the western part of the country, and since they were already stationed in a coastal city, Bart had opted to catch a ship bound for another port on the western side of the country and would then take the rail northward to intercept the tiger. This was suggested by Javier Blygoth who continued to run things in the ministries office and was even starting to annoy George who felt like he had lost all control.

Charles wasn't sure if Blygoth was really concerned for Bart or if he was simply doing everything in his power to ensure that he won his bet.

Charles was still coming into the office to catch up on things and was planning on calling on Victoria when Bart was away. He figured he had to be smart about this and one bad decision could ruin the whole courtship.

It didn't help things that he was thinking about her a lot and couldn't seem to get her out of his mind. The whole idea concerned him because he knew that Bart would probably bungle the planned hunt and he would be out in the field as soon as the rains let up and he needed to be one-hundred percent focused.

What he didn't know was that Victoria was thinking about him as well but was also smart not to ask her father about him for fear that he might insist that she not see him. She wanted to accompany Bart on the hunt too. She had occasionally done so in the past, but Bart knew instinctively that this time they would have few base camps with the luxuries she was used to. Although Bart had an inkling that by not taking her she would be seeing Charles, he put it at the back of his mind and focused on the task at hand which was getting supplies and people willing to accompany him on the trip.

The ministry was helping all they could and had to increase wages just to get someone to step up. Of course, Bart didn't know the language and would have to gesticulate half the time.

George knew that Charles was going back out after the rains with Winston but didn't dare ask him to go with Bart knowing that they didn't get along. Anyhow, it looked like things were coming together as the ship was sailing in two days anyway.

There were some bets being made in the office, and other places as well, on who was going to kill the man-eater, and it was Winston who was the favorite with the locals as they knew his previous record. Charles stayed away from the small betting as he already had a heavy one with Javier Blygoth.

The soonest they could expect the rains to end was still a month away. Winston would probably want Charles to come up to his bungalow in three weeks time.

Charles was envious of the seemingly endless supply of materials and funds which Bart was getting, and which he had earlier been denied, being forced to get by on a minimal number of supplies.

Charles would put in his time at the office and then take a rickshaw to his favorite restaurant, the Monsoon Café, where he would eat his dinner and plan the next day's mundane tasks. Occasionally Sarkee would join him but since he had a family it wasn't often, but he gave Charles important information about what Bart was doing and where he was going. That information would be helpful once he got back into the field.

The next day Charles would write a note to Winston asking him what day he wanted him up there and what gear to bring.

It looked as if Bart was planning a Himalayan expedition for months with the material he was gathering. One thing was for sure, he would have about everything he needed. The large feathered sleeping pads were a little much Charles thought. It was a hell of a lot of gear.

Everything was being stored just outside the ministry's office under a tarpaulin in the rain which wasn't letting up. Bart was secretly hoping that it would turn into a light mist to make things easier. They would load things down to the quay by tomorrow morning and be off the next day.

Whenever Bart came into the Ministry's Office, Charles would instinctively avoid him or take an early lunch, or even work after hours.

Charles was able to get Victoria's address through the help of Sarkee, how he got it was anyone's guess.

The final touches were being made that night and Bart was barking out orders like an Austrian artillery captain. At about midnight the final supplies had been brought in and it was just a matter of moving them to the ship tomorrow.

Some of the low-lying areas of the city were still inundated with water as the drainage was inadequate, and people who used those areas were forced to wade through ankle deep water. The proliferation of mosquitoes was an added annoyance of the monsoon as they seemed to be everywhere.

The morning dawned dark, with the sun trying to poke its way through the mist and rain. Porters were busy moving crates of supplies down to the quay and onto the ship before it set sail. Bart was already assuring Javier that the cat was already bagged and should be back within a fortnight as they said goodbye. Victoria accompanied Bart down to the quay and said goodbye.

The ship was ready to make way as soon as Bart got aboard. As the captain barked orders and sails were set by the seamen the big ship gently gained momentum, sailing on jibs and smaller sails to get clear of the bay.

Later on, the captain told Bart that they would need to sail further out to sea and then come around due to the monsoon.

The wind was high and it was raining. With the rolling waves it was just a matter of time before everyone on board was seasick except the sea hands. Bart was forced to come out on deck and heave over the side the contents of his early morning breakfast. The ship was much smaller than the one they had come over on and consequently it rolled much more with the waves.

It would be two days before Bart arrived at his port of destination and he was miserable already. He tried to lay down in a hammock that swung between two pillars, but the swinging tended to make things worse and he would curse every few minutes. There was also a stench from some cargo downside that reeked heavily a most unpleasant smell. He couldn't quite make it out, but it could have been the ginkgo biloba or some other foreign substance.

Rats had infested the boat and they could occasionally be seen scurrying around getting into food stores. The resident cat was excellent at catching and killing them but there were just too many. Bart thought to himself, *if only it were that easy with the tiger.*

With a few drinks from the cargo and a few from the hospitality of the captain, it wasn't long before he was out cold. The next day he awoke to the same conditions although he had a hangover now.

He started to think whether it was wise to leave Victoria behind knowing in the back of his mind that Charles was going to be courting her. He put the thought out of his mind.

The ship was getting old and it would only last a few more years until the worms would do enough damage to make it no longer a seaworthy vessel. It creaked and groaned like an old woman in pain in a rocking chair.

Bart hated the weather and longed for the hot dusty conditions of his African homeland. It seemed everything was either wet or damp, nothing was dry. The sailors went to work as usual whether it was raining or not. Tomorrow they would arrive at Gathow, a port on the western side of India, and then Bart could do his work.

Most of the passengers and crew spent a restless night being tossed by the waves as they started to head inland. In the afternoon the next day land was sighted and they began to make their way past the mangrove estuary and into the sheltered port. Word had already been sent by telegraph that Bart was expected and there were already porters and helpers arranged to meet and help him.

After a brief lunch Bart was anxious to get onto the afternoon train heading north. His baggage was loaded on the train and those traveling with him boarded the train. It was good to be on terra-firma and it wasn't long before the clack clack clack clack of the train's wheels passing over the joined steel rails put Bart soundly to sleep.

The rains were still apparent in this part of the country. Everyone longed for the sunshine that they had rarely seen for the better part of a month. The train had several stops that day, but in the morning it had arrived at Butana, the northernmost terminal of the rail. From there it would be all foot traffic through smaller trails and roads connecting the various villages and hamlets. It was a primitive part of the country.

In Bombay, Charles had received word that he would be expected in about a month's time at Winston's cottage with a list of items to bring. That gave him an entire month to begin courting Victoria, figuring that Bart would be gone at least that long trying to find the tiger in the densest foliage the country could produce.

He began by sending a dozen Indian purple orchids, a flower indigenous to lower India and available only during the rainy season. They were one of the world's most beautiful flowers with a fragrance known nowhere else. There was a note attached from Charles which said, "Dear Victoria, I hope that you will enjoy the orchids. They are a rare flower here in India and I think you are deserving of them being a rarity yourself. I would ask if you would join me in seeing the famed waterfalls of Chalati tomorrow. It will take the entire day to get there and back but it is a sight one must see if at all possible while in the country. Due to the rainy season I would advise dressing warmly. Please reply to the courier and if all is well, I'll plan on picking you up early at seven a.m."

She was excited to hear from Charles and her heart skipped a beat or two just thinking that he had actually asked her out. She looked again at the orchids and smelled them anew as the courier waited for her reply. She choose the words of her reply carefully as she wrote, "Charles, thank-you for the lovely flowers. They are beautiful. I look forward to seeing the falls of Chalati and will be ready at seven o'clock sharp. Victoria."

Charles somehow knew her reply before she had even given it. He also knew that they were destined to be together somehow, someway. It was just inevitable.

The next day dawned as any other during the rainy season as the constant drizzle beat upon the housetops and shops of Bombay. Charles was prompt as he arrived with a horse drawn buggy at the appointed hour.

Victoria was dressed for a hike with khaki trousers and a white shirt with multiple pockets and a red scarf she wore around her neck. She also had a foldable canvas hat similar to the ones the Australians used in war for their soldiers.

Charles greeted her at the door and told her it was great to see her again. She blushed a little. Within a few moments they were off making their way to the waterfalls.

Charles asked her about her homeland in Africa and what it was like, and although Victoria was nervous at first, talking of her home eased her somewhat and she opened up.

Charles had shaved all of his facial hair except for a mustache that shown out as the morning light shown through the half-opened window of the buggy.

The horses seem to like the light drizzle as they kept up a steady trot from a driver who was well equipped for the rain.

To get a chance to break away from the city was a treat for Victoria as she seemed to relish taking everything in from the jungle and the countryside. Charles was explaining everything he knew about the country as Victoria seemed to have a thousand questions about India. There was definitely something different about Victoria. Charles couldn't quite put his finger on it, but he definitely liked what he saw.

Once they arrived, they began hiking towards the falls with a single porter carrying their lunch and a few supplies. The mosquitoes were out in force as usual, but Charles had brought head nets for them as they climbed in and around obstacles on a well-worn trail that led to the falls. Everything around them was beginning to bloom as the rains had made everything blossom like some cocooned garden.

At last they heard the falling water and as they came around a corner there was the most beautiful waterfall Victoria had ever seen. It was over one hundred and fifty feet high, carrying a large volume of the monsoon rains over it. There was a mist everywhere and it made one feel as if they were in some sort of jungle fog.

Charles could see a large smile on Victoria's face as she removed the mosquito net and took everything in. Being from the Transvaal in Africa, there definitely wasn't anything like it. It was so lush and beautiful, even in the rain.

She looked back at Charles and their eyes met. She couldn't hold the gaze and turned away.

Butuna was a small, bustling city where the railroad terminated. As the locomotive came to a stop and expelled the hot steam from its tanks, Bart was aroused from his slumber as local servants, including a person who seemed to be in charge, told him that they were there to help in any way they could. George had hired the help by cable under the urging of Javier Blygoth.

Now they would have to track overland. Bart caught a glance out the window as he raised the curtain. He could see the rain continued to pour. He had been hoping against hope that the monsoon would be over by now.

The first thing he did was send someone to the telegraph station in the office of the rail house to see if there was any new information from George Smythe about the tiger's whereabouts. When word came back that there was no new information, he sent a small cable that they were starting off immediately to the last known attack location, which was still one hundred and forty miles distant in some of the most rugged country in all of India.

The porters began assembling the vast amount of necessary gear which was starting to get wet. Little did they know that wet gear weighed much much more.

Bart went into a local store to purchase some additional whiskey as he had consumed a large amount on the boat but there was none available. He walked back to the depot where everyone was waiting for him. He yelled orders like he was Fredrick the Great, and people began to move. Like a giant constrictor the team set out through the streets and soon disappeared on the road moving north.

A guide was there to make sure they didn't get lost. All the help was generously paid and knew they were going after the tiger. As they ventured further North the roads began to get narrower, and with the new growth machetes were sometimes needed to clear the paths. One had to beware especially while crossing swollen streams because leeches would gather inside of clothes and attach to the body. Also, mosquitoes were out in force due to the rain and day after day as they trudged on, the constant moistness contributed to a general feeling of complaint about everything and anyone.

After the fourth day they had arrived at Sinopo, a small village within the general radius Bart was looking for from the previous kill. The villagers were excited to see them as most had kept themselves indoors since the tiger was reported in the area. They came out and clamored to the men as if he were Moses himself.

Bart gathered as much local information as he could and sat down to a well-deserved break. He left additional details to his appointed right-hand man as he slumbered, snoring louder than a South American howler monkey. The information was scant, but they were able to determine that the tiger had killed a young woman about a week ago only fifteen miles distance to the east of where they were located. With the information from the kill before that, they were able to ascertain that the cat was moving back in a north-eastern direction similar to the way it had come.

Bart was a hard taskmaster and was beginning to be disliked among the porters. Instead of hiking the usual twenty-five miles a day, he would often push them to thirty-five miles and the strain was starting to show on the men. Often times at camp when things weren't exactly right, he would bark out at someone or reprimand someone for not performing fast enough. There were many complaints and the men were getting tired of the way he handled things. Many had been paid half up front and the other half was due when the job was done but there were some who had had enough already. Now that they were close Bart needed them more than ever, but he just did not win them over.

The rain was becoming burdensome and annoying. Bart had decided that a good night's sleep might be in order as they would probably be camping out in the jungle for the next while.

With the dawn of a new day, came an exited man with a few others into the village, telling of a recent killing by the man-eater only thirty miles distant. Bart was elated and ordered everyone to move out quickly. Like a seasoned circus, everything was packed up as they moved out in the direction of the killing. They would undoubtedly be there by nightfall.

There was only a small path that led to the nearest village where the young man had been killed, and they were forced to walk along it single file. As they got closer, anxiety among the men grew. Bart got concerned quickly and took the point as he held his rifle un-slung and ready for the unexpected. This action alone heightened the fear of the others.

Everything was wet and the visibility was only fifty yards at best due to the mist and the fog from the low clouds that hung around the higher mountains. The jungle was thick and Bart was unsure how to hunt in it. He quickly realized that even if he saw the cat, he was unlikely to get off a shot.

On they went, Bart was having to occasionally clear the path with his machete in one hand cutting the foliage. He knew it wasn't working and ordered someone else up front to clear the way. With every other step, each man was looking sideways or backways to see if they would be the first to see the danger. There were a total of eight men. Five were porters, and there was a tracker and a guide besides Bart.

Bart had never seen such thick cover, even on the path. Some of the porters held large jungle leaves over their heads to keep the rain off. The water continued to come down from above, sometimes from the low clouds and sometimes dripping off the trees or plants. It just wasn't any good and Bart knew it. Even on a clear day he probably wouldn't be able to get off a shot, let alone in these conditions. All he wanted now was to get to the nearest village and rethink things, but he couldn't hurry because he instinctively knew that if he got careless he would wind up dead.

To make matters worse the heavy rainfall had swollen the streams and rivers they had to cross and it required extra work. In many cases the water was up to the bottom of a bamboo bridge and when weight was put on it, the bridge dropped down into the swift current. Bart kept asking himself if anything was going to go right on this foray.

Some of the group got quite excited when one of them discovered some leopard tracks in the soft mud. Bart had to calm them down by indicating it was not the man-eater as the pug marks were much too small.

They pressed on slowly, still looking every way for signs of danger. Bart stopped to light his tobacco, but the rain had penetrated his snuff bag and it was too wet to light. In shear desperation he took his pipe and threw it against a rock with such force that it broke into four pieces.

Charles was having a grand time in Bombay. Never before had he so looked forward to being with someone. It seemed like the music was clearer, the flowers were brighter, and everything was just on a whole new level. He got along so well with Victoria. She seemed to laugh at even his most boring jokes.

They had been on several dates at this point and were seeing each other every night as Charles introduced her to new sights and places to eat in the city. The rain was still constant, but it didn't matter to him. He even longed for it to continue, because he knew once it stopped the work would begin again and he wouldn't see Victoria for awhile. Her smile, her hair, her eyes were ingrained in his thoughts and he knew he was in deep, deep enough that it could affect him in the field. Like two doves, they cozied up to each other often, feeling the warmth of each other's body heat.

The girls at the office could tell something was different with Charles as he was so pleasant to work with and always seemed to be in a good mood. He still managed to get in a full day's work and continued to keep abreast of the man-eater's whereabouts and where Bart was, but he did things now with an increase in enthusiasm that startled even George.

George had thought that Charles' reports which he had submitted to the office were sparse. Bart's were no more than two sentences at most, frustrating George to the point that he took it out on everyone else and was not pleasant to be around. People started to take their lunches early if a telegram came into the office.

Work at the office became more difficult for Charles as well, but when you're in love, nothing seems to get you down. Charles knew that he was going to have to leave in a couple of weeks to meet up with Winston and he wanted to spend as much time with Victoria as he could. His friend Sarkee knew why he wasn't spending time with him anymore. He was lucky to even get a lunch with him. But he was glad that Charles was happy and had never seen him like this before. Being married himself he knew what a good woman could be to a man.

Charles continued to track the tiger's latest killings, watching as it moved north east. It was still difficult to determine where exactly it was going. Sometimes it would completely change course and go south for a week or two and make a killing, and then suddenly change directions again. It was no use trying to predict, but you did have a twenty-five percent chance of being right.

With the inundation of rain the jungle was blossoming into its magnificent glory. Even though the rains would soon be over, it would still be another month before the jungle would begin the slow transformation of becoming drier and making visibility better, at least to a point where they would have a likelihood of a good shot at the man-eater. It was just a matter of time, but the waiting was usually the hardest point, at least for Charles. However, he was not complaining now.

Most of the dates they went on were not considered ladylike. They would go shooting at the gun club or on boat rides down the river. They would have rickshaw races, and they even went pea-fowl hunting in the rain on the backs of elephants, and the rain didn't matter to either one as they really enjoyed each other's company.

They had been on a dozen dates already but somehow the only kisses they had shared were the polite good night kisses on the cheek. Victoria was quite shy although she possessed a great confidence in herself, and each evening she managed to turn away and let Charles just give her a nice good night kiss. But this evening was destined for something special.

They had rented a small rowboat and had gone across a beautiful lake to have dinner on the shore of a small island. After dinner they needed to get back to the mainland before it got dark and so they got back into the rowboat just as the sun was beginning to set. Somehow the clouds had parted that evening and there was no rain. The sun was bigger than ever and was starting to shine its long red, orange and violet rays across the horizon.

Victoria sat on the main seat and offered to row a bit with one oar and Charles was apt to let her as he gathered up the other oar. They rowed independently, her a little awkward as the blade often missed the water and he a little more experienced.

The sun was now just above the mountains about to disappear when their eyes met for a brief second. Instinctively Charles made a move towards her. He gently touched her chin and raised her head somewhat as their eyes met again. A second later they were kissing.

Bart knew the cat was moving consistently in two directions more than the others, and he had set a course to intercept the tiger by choosing one of those directions and hoped to cut it off. He knew deep inside that with the rain and the low visibility of the terrain he had little chance of success, but he had been hired to do a job and he was going to do it.

By some sort of luck Bart had chosen the right direction and was indeed in the area where the man-eater was. He had decided to set up an ambush just outside the village of Terak where he thought the next attack might come. He was hoping the tiger might enter the village at night through the main trail leading into the village. By sheer coincidence rather than brilliant deductive reasoning he was in the right place and the right time. This was the only spot where it was open enough to give him a clear shot.

It was the second night they were waiting in ambush, and the tiger was approaching the village by the same main trail. It had waited until nightfall and the cover of darkness before approaching slowly. Due to the terrain of the surrounding hills the main trail leading into the village was from the east. As the tiger approached to within a half a mile, there was a new and distinct smell carried to it by the westerly winds of the monsoon. The smell was foreign to it and from what it had learned before, it could only mean one thing. Any new smell or any smell from men who had sweat during the day from long hikes or portages meant men intent on killing it.

Bart was having a hard time dealing with the humidity of India and to combat the constant feeling of wetness combined with the monsoon rains he had started using talcum powder all over his body. The unique smell combined with his sweat traveled with the wind into the sensitive nose of the man-eater. The tiger was suspicious of any new smells and had learned lessons well from anything out of the ordinary.

Upon sensing the new smell and recognizing the danger, the tiger decided to take a long way around the village to an approach that was unconventional. It took more than an hour to circumnavigate the village and it decided to wait on a small cliff overlooking the village to see if there was anything amiss. It could hear an occasional cough or covered up sneeze from the direction of the main entrance and knew that men were waiting for it there. If it was any other village, everyone would be locked into their huts by this time.

Bart had four men guarding the trail leading into the village and they were up in two mango trees which seemed to guard the entrance to the village. The moon was only at half-light and was covered most of the time due to the monsoon as a light drizzle continued to rain down on their positions.

The tiger itself was wet but it was also hungry and wanted to eat. Near the main entrance was a house built out of stone which had a somewhat modern roof of coconut trunks laid on top in an A-frame style with mud plugging the holes. The big cat had stealthily approached the main trail entrance by taking another half an hour to cover less than two hundred yards. It required slinking under vines and carefully stepping over plants in an area no one would have thought an animal could pass because it was so thick. The men in the trees were looking outwards towards the jungle and couldn't fathom the beast coming from anywhere else but that direction. The overall wetness nullified any sounds.

Once the tiger was within sight of the trees where it thought it had heard the muffled sneeze, it stopped and waited, looking and listening for anything out of the ordinary. It had lain down with its ears moving independently towards any sound coming from anywhere. Then it saw a movement in the tree about a hundred yards away. It was slight, but a movement just the same. It focused on the area and then saw it again as it discerned a leg hanging over a branch slowly and occasionally swaying. It knew it was human and somehow it knew it was meant for itself, to kill it.

It slowly got up and being very careful began to retreat back the way it had come. Once it got to the other side of the village it waited again to see if it could see any movement or anything out of the ordinary. It had the patience to wait and make sure.

The villagers were somewhat content that Bart, with his small contingent were watching the village entrance. In fact, they were given strict instructions not to come out of their huts, but to remain inside and to secure their doors. Even with the news that the Katagi man-eater was in the area they felt somewhat assured that, with Bart guarding the entrance, the tiger would meet its demise if it tried to come into the village.

The rains had made the air muggy with vapor, and inside the huts it was even worse, especially if all the openings were shut tight. One hut had slightly opened a bamboo window by propping it outward a little to let air circulate better. The occupants felt a little safer because Bart and his group were standing watch at the main opening to the village. The tiger could smell the occupants inside as it neared the hut and promptly jumped down from the side of the hill.

It slowly neared the hut on the side of the opened window. Within a few seconds it had stuck its head into the window and had placed its front paws inside, then with a big leap from its hind legs it was within the hut. It was nearly silent. All the occupants were already sound asleep, and it simply found the nearest person by smell and with a powerful bite to the neck, cracked vertebra as the cat held the bite to suffocate the victim.

The small rustling had awoken some of the relatives of the victim and there was a commotion. The tiger had by now killed the old woman and was dragging her to the window. With a final hold on the woman's shoulder it lifted her up and jumped out the window and within seconds was off into the blackness of the jungle.

The screams had brought Bart and his companions running to the hut, but it was too late. Some relatives went into hysterics and started to hit Bart. One of them was the victim's daughter and she continued to plead and hit Bart, insisting that he go after her mother. Bart had had enough and when she went to hit him again he took his hand and pushed her forehead forward with such force that she fell down into the mud. Bart's companions pulled the rest of the family away.

Bart could see the blood trail moving into the jungle and asked for a torch. When it was lit and brought to him, he quickly surveyed the scene and it didn't take long to realize that it would be suicide to follow the cat in the darkness. He could see how thick the vegetation was and he simply would have no shot before the cat would attack him. The villagers by this time were egging him to go after the beast but he refused and told them it would have to wait until daylight.

The tiger knew they would follow the kill in the morning. It had been done plenty of times before and it remembered. It knew that it would not only have a meal this evening but by tomorrow it was going to exact some revenge.

It feasted on the body only a few miles from the village in dense foliage. After getting a drink in the nearby creek, it retired to a point where it would wait for the recovery party. It had lain down under a large banana tree and slept the remainder of the night.

Bart woke early and got everyone up with him at first light. They had a light breakfast but were eager to get on the trail. The rain continued to pour down and Bart actually thought that it might help to muffle their sounds. They started out like a small army of Napoleons ready to take Moscow.

The trail was easy to follow with all the vegetation being either broken or matted down as they followed it cautiously. Some of the great hunters have a sixth sense when it comes to danger and Bart had it now as he slowed down and pulled the hammers back on his gun. The hair on the back of his neck was tingling. Something was about to happen and he knew it.

The rain poured off his hat as he looked this way and that for any danger. The men behind him although brave, were anxious to say the least. One thing the tiger had going for it on this day was that the rain had caused many of the other animals to seek cover, especially the ones that often gave out alarm calls to warn others it was approaching. In addition to that, the new growth of vegetation provided a perfect setting to prevent discovery.

It was the smell again that woke the big cat up, and it knew people were on the trail. It raised itself from the jungle floor and followed the scent to a point where it could easily see the trail but anyone coming up from the village would have a difficult time seeing it, and then waited.

The party of men were proceeding slowly and undoubtedly knew the cat had to be close. The tiger, after seeing them, ducked down into further cover and patiently waited for them to arrive, its tail slowly curling and releasing in anticipation of an attack.

In time the party arrived where the tiger was hiding, unaware of its presence but feeling something was amiss. Bart passed by the big cat, and although he was looking everywhere, he could not see the tiger in the under-brush. The second man came within a few feet of the tiger and it sprang on him before anyone knew what was happening. The momentum carried them off the trail and into the thick foliage on the opposite side. Within a second the tiger found its favorite part for killing humans and snapped down on the man's neck, instantly killing him.

Bart whirled around with the commotion and fired one barrel into the jungle at the noise that was being made. The bullet actually passed through the stomach of the man who was already dying. The tiger, after killing the man, disappeared like a phantom into the jungle, casually strolling away with its fur wet and matted and stained with blood at the mouth.

When the group got to the man they could see that the cat had done its job, but Bart's shot was clearly visible as well and they could not tell what had killed the man, the bullet or the tiger. The men could not believe the fact that Bart had fired into the jungle when a man was there and there was a good chance to hit him. Some of them resolved then and there to quit the hunt and return home, that it wasn't worth the money and dealing with Bart.

The tiger was believed to still be close, so they dragged his body back to the village. The striped cat had left after killing the man, but it extracted revenge when and where it wanted. After returning to the village many of Bart's group left and returned home. Those that decided to stay with him were too few in numbers.

Bart decided that Charles was right. There was no way to kill this man-eater during the monsoon. He began to pack his things and return to Bombay as soon as possible. It was hard to admit defeat. The cat was more cunning than he had expected, but he knew he would meet up with it again and it was just a matter of time.

The rains were beginning to be less and less each day and Winston knew from experience that they would stop within a week or two. He also knew that they would have to change hunting styles as well, for the summer heat would not begin to wilt the plants until a couple of months after that.

He stared out into the jungle day after day with a thousand-yard stare that few men possessed, as if he were deep in thought about some answer to the universe. He continued to keep himself in shape by hiking every day and performing his calisthenics as much as he could. People would still bring him daily news about what was happening, and thanks to Charles letters, he already knew about Bart. He thought the man a fool for attempting to hunt the beast during the monsoon, but recognized he knew nothing about India.

During the lazy afternoons when the rain subsided he was hard at work building a second bungalow for guests, just to keep himself busy. The rain had been a welcome respite from the hot days of summer, but it brought the dreaded mosquitoes as well. As the rain had continued for two months, now Winston was yearning for the hot dry summer again.

The rains had been wet enough this year that certain dens were inundated with water and some creatures were forced out to the surface. Just the other day a reticulated python over seventeen feet long was found slithering near Winston's cottage. Winston had retrieved a machete and quickly decapitated it, and the skin was stretched out on pegs underneath his large porch. The meat he had given to the local villagers to eat, although he kept a small portion for himself. The creature itself was probably responsible for some dog and goat disappearances over the last year.

Winston was an avid journal keeper and wrote about his experiences as often as he could, and now that he had the time he wrote of the most recent campaign against the Katagi man-eater.

Winston's maid was a woman in her mid-thirties who would come to clean his cottage every other day. She felt an obligation to Winston who had killed the leopard that had taken her husband from her. Winston still paid her a small allowance to help her out. As of late she had been bringing her daughter, who was in her early twenties and had not yet married. She could have passed as a contestant in a beauty contest and had striking features, especially her eyes which were dark and seductive. Although Winston was twice her age, he began to look at her more and more. She began to do little extra things for him, like peeling some fresh fruit and leaving it out for him or heating up the iron on the stove and ironing his shirts.

He had fallen in love once before and although it had not worked out he still had an innate desire to be with someone of the opposite sex. Winston had not yet acted on anything but there was some chemistry between the two of them. Sometimes one can wonder if you can truly love someone without touching them, without being physical, and with them it was like an energy of some unknown force. It certainly brightened his day when she came to the cottage.

Sometimes she would offer to soothe his weary muscles with a special pain reliving lotion and would work it into his neck and back muscles. He felt that the strokes, the kneading, were a little more than just working the lotion in, but he didn't complain, who would?

They both knew that with unfinished business at hand nothing could materialize at the moment, but there was always a hope of the future, and a smile here and there could be seen as something much more between the two of them.

Winston found that whether he liked it or not he was starting to enjoy seeing her. He was starting to dread having to go back into the jungle again, but he knew it had to be done. If the tiger wasn't killed, it could live another fifteen years in the wild, killing people the entire time. It would have to be his desires or an ongoing menace. He had had many close calls before and had always come out on top, but there was something different about this beast. It was an intelligent creature for sure, probably more so than any other he had hunted. At any rate he kept his knife sharpened and once the rains stopped he would be out there again.

Winston noticed that the tiger had gone as far west as the Gir forest, and based on the latest killings was making its way back into northern India. Winston studied the maps he had available to him, and even the terrain from that region. He wanted to know as much about the area as he could. What he found out was it was an area with dense vegetation and plenty of hills. The dense vegetation would definitely be a hindrance to him, but the hills would provide easier trails that the tiger could use, and if he could pick the right one he just may be able to gun the beast down.

George Smythe had just heard the news that Bart's group had disbanded and Bart was heading home. He had heard it through someone else besides Bart.

Charles' irregular but detailed reports months earlier were starting to look better every day.

Bart was no doubt taking the rail home after hiking fifty miles south to the nearest railway.

Smythe was more than mad about things. He was starting to lose faith in Bart and wondered if what Charles had said all along, that the beast could not be hunted during the monsoon, was true. He still kept the Viceroy and the prime minister apprised of the current situation, sometimes having to make things up because Bart wasn't giving him any information. They were anxious for results and the people continued to clamor at his office for news as each day he had to force his way through the door. It was just a big nuisance to say the least.

The pressure was starting to show and his hair was beginning to turn grey. What could he possibly explain to the crown's representative now? He didn't really care who killed the beast, as long as someone did it, because he felt that his job was on the line and he cared more for himself than anyone else. He was at his ends wit, and one day at work he sought out Charles in his office and closed the door as he sat down.

"Charles, do you realize my job is likely on the line with the problem of the Katagi man-eater?"

Charles and pretty much everyone else knew it, but no one dared say it. He decided to play it coy and replied, "No, but if you say so, perhaps."

George spoke up, "I've trusted you're instinct on this and given you a lot of latitude regarding the problem. You will be successful the next time you go out, because if I take the fall for this you will be coming down with me. Do I make myself clear?"

Charles could have attacked him by saying he was incompetent, or he could have chided him for not having any backbone against his superiors or he could have brought up the point that he hadn't helped him with his requested supplies in a timely manner, but he realized that George was his superior and it would likely only make things worse.

He had a lot of confidence in himself and felt somewhat sorry for George.

He decided to take a higher road and not defend his actions or what was said and simply replied, "If you're done, I have a lot of work to do."

It had taken George aback. He was fully expecting him to get defensive and come right back at him, for he was looking for verbal combat, but it wasn't there, and in an instant he realized he was the fool. He simply got up without saying a word and left the office.

Charles was smart enough to realize if he and Winston killed the beast, that George would take all the credit, saying that it was he who had decided to hire them, and if they failed he would blame the failure on him, so there was nothing Charles could do. But he was concerned about lives being lost and if there was a way to prevent it, then he was going to do all that he could. There was a cause and it was the right thing to do.

Sarkee came into Charles' office and asked how things were going. Charles just indicated that he wished things were over, but also that he was in love with Victoria and asked for Sarkee's advice. Sarkee knew that Victoria was Bart's daughter, so he said that it would be better to keep his mind and thoughts on the destruction of the katagi man-eater rather than deal with two complex issues at the same time. Sarkee always had the wisdom of Solomon and it was good advice.

They decided to get an early dinner at the Monsoon cafe.

Bart was having a difficult time getting back to Bombay. He didn't speak the language, he barely made the train station, the trek to the train station took days, the rain continued to pour down, his companions weren't getting along with him, and it just seemed that nothing was going right.

He finally boarded a train the next day but it lacked the comforts found on most of the trains in the south because this was a less dense area of population in India. This area got all the trains that were older ones sent up when newer trains were shipped in and assembled in the southern coastal cities.

He seemed in a foul mood all the time, ever since the last killing. What was worse was that he couldn't get used to all the rice and the other foods, and had a constant case of diarrhea forcing him to constantly visit the water closet. He also developed a nasty rash on his buttocks as he tried to wipe himself with a leaf in the jungle which turned out to be a skin irritant. This was one of the reasons he was in such a bad mood all the time.

He had sent a telegram to the Ministry's Office that he was returning as soon as he got to the rail station.

Charles was kept apprised of his situation and decided to have a talk with Victoria, he ended up telling her that he needed to focus on helping Winston kill the tiger, he explained that he wanted to be fully focused on the task and that he cared for her a lot and wanted to resume their relationship once the tiger was killed. Victoria wasn't ignorant of the situation with Charles and Winston and her dad. She understood things as they were and trusted Charles. If it ever came to having to choose her father or Charles she wouldn't hesitate to pick Charles. She believed her future was with him.

The rains stopped as quickly as they came, tapering off a little each day, until the full sun finally showed itself to India. It was a welcome sight and people's moods began to improve again. The growth the rains brought was extraordinary as everything began to bloom down to the smallest fern.

Winston had cabled Charles to meet him at his cottage within a few days as he could tell the rains were dying out.

Charles had one last night with Victoria since Bart had not returned yet, and it was marvelous. When he dropped her off that night he presented to her a keepsake pendant with a deep red Thai ruby. It wasn't large but it was exquisite. She was on such a high that nothing seemed to bother her. No one had ever given her something that meant so much, she was speechless.

Charles anticipated having to leave any day and was well prepared to leave at once. All the new gear and supplies were already bought and ready for transport. The ministry had allocated several men to help in the transport and could be called upon by Charles or Winston if they so desired. The pay was set at hazardous and was known to the workers. The people helping were asked by the ministry to help Charles but the better and more qualified workers were slated for Bart's future group.

Charles would leave in the morning after consulting with George Smythe on a few matters. He decided to retire early after his evening with Victoria and try and get as much sleep as possible.

The tiger had moved quite a bit north after killing the man from Bart's group. It was the end of July and the monsoon was winding down. It was on the prowl one day when it came across a tigress with two young cubs almost six months old. Normally the cubs will stay with the mother for about six months to a year before fending for themselves. This tigress was ready to defend her cubs to the death. The man-eater was a massive male and would not have a problem killing the tigress, but it had already learned that getting involved with a tigress defending her cubs might result in some serious wounds for itself.

The tigress was holding her ground and the cubs stayed low and close oblivious to the seriousness of the situation. The man-eater did not want to fight this day and was still recovering from a wound inflicted upon it by the lion a months before. The tigress growled and bared her teeth, hissing and growling the entire time. The man-eater began to give them a wide berth to avoid any trouble.

The cubs observed the whole ordeal and were safe as the man-eater passed around them. These cubs were already beginning to eat meat. Most tigresses gave birth in the spring just before the monsoon and would generally have one or two cubs that survived. The cubs were learning from their mother how life and death happened. At this stage the cubs were still learning, observing, and still playing, but soon they would be thrust out into the jungle where it's kill or be killed. It was generally kill for tigers as they were at the top of the food chain. Once the tigress would make a kill, the young cubs would come in and feast with her once she called for them. Little by little there were being weaned and each day they learned more and more.

The man-eater enjoyed the end of the rains, and with more cover to hide its movements, it began to become more aggressive in its attacks. There was so much blossoming from the native plants that only open areas offered a hunter a chance at a shot. It could and would go within fifteen feet of the main trail leading into a village without being noticed by even so much of a langur. It also was able to conceal itself enough to feast on other animals, although its taste for human flesh never wavered. It simply took meals where opportunity presented itself and as such the number of human kills went down. But it longed for the salty taste of human flesh and at least once a fortnight it was making a killing. Stealth was its constant companion and it was rarely surprised itself. This was the time it relished, being unseen and striking at will wherever and whenever it wanted.

The main wound from the lion last month was beginning to heal, but it was still unpleasant and bothersome to the tiger at times. It took comfort in water as all tigers do and would sometimes soak for hours in a small stream or a concealed section of a lake. After enjoying the water, it raised itself up, walked up onto the bank, and shook the excessive water from its beautiful coat. Then it was ready to eat again.

It was a lifelong struggle to eat, to survive, but it also realized that its appetite for certain flesh made it a hunted beast and although it didn't know it, man would not stop its pursuit of it until it was dead. Surely as the green reeds it was passing through must eventually wither and die, so it was with itself. Its days were numbered.

Bart arrived in Bombay within a few days of giving up on the hunt and he was not at all pleased with how things had gone. As soon as he excited the train some beggars came up to him and instead of giving what change he had or walking away he took the forehead of the woman and forced her backward, sending her into a puddle left over from the rains.

In doing so he had simply lashed out with the words "get away from me!"

Those that saw it felt sorry for the woman to the point of going over to help her up while looking back at Bart who was already walking away, oblivious to what he had done, or perhaps knowing what he had done and not caring at all.

He was also upset that no one was there at the train station to welcome him back, but the trains arrival, in fact any trains arrival in India, was not as accurate as he was used to in South Africa. Anything within two hours would be considered on time by many.

He stormed back to the ministry's office knowing that George would likely be working late.

He happened to notice that just as he arrived, when he could sleep comfortably under a roof away from the harsh jungle that the skies had opened up and the sun was shining for the first time since he had been in the country.

The fact that Bart went first to the Ministry's Office before going home to see his daughter showed how upset he was. When he arrived, there were no crowds to push through because most people were gone from the office, but George was there working late on some sort of media manipulation.

Bart stormed in and it wasn't long before an argument erupted and both men seemed to be at each other's throat. After a few minutes of neither man getting in any words edgewise, Bart stormed out of the office and went home.

Victoria was there waiting for him and offered to get his bath going, but she could tell he was in a foul mood and had already heard the news of what had happened. She longed to tell him so much, that she was in love for the first time in her life and everything was so grand, but he just wasn't approachable, nor was there a good time that presented itself. He was the only other person in her life that she loved so dearly. Why was it that she couldn't express her innermost joy?

Charles had written to her a few times and she had been careful to not leave the letters out where they would be discovered. She was as smart as she was beautiful, and the two traits rarely went together.

It took a few days for Charles to arrive at Winston's cottage because the roads were still muddy from the rains, but he arrived without incident and Winston was happy to see him.

"The prodigal son has returned! We had better kill the fatted calf and then the fatted tiger."

Both men laughed. It was good for them to be together again and Charles indicated that he had a good feeling about things this time. They sat up late that night, telling stories and getting caught up with the Ministry, and Charles told Winston about Bart. He did leave out the part about the large wager with Javier because he didn't want to put any pressure on Winston, and besides he knew he was going to do it, either himself or Winston, and most likely it was going to be Winston.

Like a couple of pirates that hadn't seen each other in years, on and on they went late into the night. They would not be leaving until the day after tomorrow, so they could sleep in, and it was likely going to be the last good sleep they got for awhile.

Before Charles finally went to bed, he roamed the cottage and looked around again at the stuffed mounts of previous man-eaters and instinctively knew the Katagi man-eater would soon be there.

The bed Winston had given him was more comfortable than his own having been personally stuffed with the down from the Eider duck and imported at great cost.

Winston woke him the next day at a reasonable hour and they began making their preparations for the field. As they did, Winston told him that the cover was still too thick to try and force it out into the open or through a certain area. Their best chance stood with drawing it in with a tethered animal somehow, like when he had killed the Janira tigress. He asked Charles what Bart was like and reiterated that he was only going to work with who he had choosen. Charles indicated that he was domineering, arrogant, prideful, foolish and vain and that he should get along well with him. Winston stared at Charles for a brief second before they started laughing together.

Secretly Charles was concerned, knowing Winston as well as he did, about how he was going to get along with Bart. They both had ego's the size of the moon, although Winston was a little more humble about things.

While they were packing, a native came running up to the cottage asking Charles where the sahib was. Winston shortly showed himself and the runner delivered the latest news of the last killing, which had only happened yesterday. Winston asked for his map to be given to him and as they looked it over they realized they could be in or near position within three days time. If they guessed correctly they may be in a very advantageous village where the next attack could possibly come.

Both men looked at each other thinking the same thing. Again they looked at the map. Winston pointed out where the last three attacks had come from, including the attack on Bart's group. It was clear the tiger was moving in a north eastern direction and the village of Baquune was only one hundred and fifty miles in an almost perfect north eastern direction. He mentioned that it would be a full moon in a week's time and it would give them excellent visibility at night. The question was, would the cat continue in the same direction or would it change course like it had in times past, occasionally mixing things up for no apparent reason. It had changed courses before and trying to predict when and where an attack was going to happen was a science in and of itself.

Winston studied the area. It was still quite hilly. He scratched his beard again and asked Charles for his opinion, respecting him. It meant a lot to Charles that he would ask his opinion, but he really didn't have an answer, so he told Winston that he was the one with the experience and whatever he thought, they should go with it. Winston said he would give it some thought when they headed out. It would still take them a couple of days to get there and he'd have a decision by then.

One thing had surprised Charles a lot before they left and that was that Winston had asked Charles to open with a prayer and invoke God's blessing on the hunt. Charles was touched as everyone bowed their heads.

He began, "Dear Father of heaven and earth, thank-you for the beauty that thou hast created here in India, thy footstool. We give thanks for thy holy words and inspiration, and for the lovely women that make our lives to be filled with joy." Winston immediately opened an eye and looked directly at Charles as he continued.

"Bless this hunt Lord, that we may be an instrument in thy hands to kill and rid this beast from this earth, that it can destroy no more, that peace may be restored to thy land here and children will no longer lose a parent or that parents will no longer lose a child. Guide us to fulfill a destiny, in the name of thy Son, Jesus Christ. Amen."

Winston had always believed that there was a higher power, for the heavens and the planets all seemed to be too much order for there not to be a God, but he was not a religious person, and for him to start the hunt with a prayer was surely unexpected. Charles on the other hand *was* a religious person and although he wasn't consistently seen at church on Sundays he did go as often as he could, and thought the gesture sincere and spiritual.

The small group of Winston, Charles, and two hired porters made their way to the train station.

Victoria had managed to keep clear of Bart due to his foul mood, which could last for days, and tried to do everything she could to help him and make things more pleasant around their temporary home, but he remained soured and the following day made his way back to the ministry's office again.

While walking briskly there, a few kids were running down the street rolling small old wooden wheels along with bamboo sticks and just being kids. One of the small wheels managed to hit Bart in the leg. The wheel was without spokes and was just the outer part. Bart set it up and smashed it with his foot and continued walking. The kids came together to examine the broken wheel and the small kid whose wheel it was started to sob, knowing that his toy was broken.

Bart shoved his way through the protesting crowd outside the ministry's office and as there were not a lot of people some of them fell down due to the shove he produced.

He found his way inside to see that Javier was meeting with George in his office. They quickly invited him in and asked when he was planning to get going, and that Charles and Winston were already heading to the area where the man-eater was. They mentioned that they had received Charles' telegram informing them they were officially starting up the spring hunt.

Bart wasn't aware they had already started but confidently informed them they he would be off in the next few days. He asked about the tiger's current whereabouts and other minor matters.

Before he left, Javier indicated that they had invested a lot in him, even just getting him there, and they hoped that he wouldn't let them down. They were counting on him. Bart sensed correctly that something else was afoot even though no one had told him of the large wager between Charles and Javier.

Bart indicated that he would be getting things ready and would be in touch before he left. The fact was that he hadn't started to organize anything yet and was caught unprepared.

Before he left he went and examined the map with the killings.

George asked Javier what he thought of Bart after he had left, and Javier told him that he was a bit churlish, but he was the right man for the job. George not sure himself nodded in agreement anyway.

Winston and Charles made it to the nearest train station as soon as they could. Since the train didn't arrive until later that night, and wasn't scheduled to leave until early the next morning, they took up residence in a primitive hotel with several rooms to rent and a thatched roof with bamboo pillars and an old colonial look.

That night after dinner, Charles proposed a new idea he had been thinking about.

He said, "I've got a radical new idea I'd like to propose to you."

"Well, we have the time. What is it?" replied Winston.

"A trap unlike any other we have ever done, this time with live human bait."

Winston's eyebrow instantly went up. He was intrigued and listened intently to Charles as he lit his pipe.

"Well we will need to build a very long rectangular trap with a trigger mechanism that trips two trap doors at once, one to trap the cat and the other to protect the person staying in the cage as live bait."

Charles showed Winston a rather crude drawing as he continued,

"The trap would need to be long enough to give the person acting as bait enough time for the trigger mechanism to trip. It would also need to be wide, so that the sides can be lined with plants or vines to make it look natural. I suspect the tiger will probably move in cautiously giving the person enough time for the second door to come down and protect them."

Winston thought about it, trying to envision it in his mind and then said without hesitation, "Would you be willing to test out your special trap?"

"Somehow, I knew you would be getting to that, and yes, I've given it a lot of thought and would be willing to be the human goat so to speak. After all, who else would ever agree to it?"

"Well, you may get that chance because with the vegetation as thick as it is right now, we may only have that chance, at least for another month or so. Let's decide where it's going to strike and set it up. It will be due for another kill in about two or three day's time."

"Excellent," replied Charles.

"We may need to work fast on this, and we need to be in the right area."

Charles went back to sketching his trap. He had thought about his simple mouse trap when he was at home and the thought expanded from there. Sure, it had never been tried before, but these were new times and with it came new ideas.

Winston had already put his hat over his face and lifted his feet onto the seat ahead of him and was quickly asleep, and Charles knew from experience that he wouldn't rouse until the train arrived.

Charles stopped his sketching and looked again at the jadeite figure of a tiger, perfectly carved in miniature and worn around his neck with a crude leather strap. It was cool to the touch as jadeite is and he remembered how it was given to him for luck from Victoria on their last night together. He would have loved anything from her, but this gift he truly loved and treasured, and he hoped it would give him the luck he needed. Perhaps this one time, while he was waiting for the train with nothing else to think about he could let his mind wander to the good times he had with her. The smell of her hair, her smile, her laugh, everything that made him feel great.

His mind changed to the thought of Winston meeting Bart and how well that was going to go down. There was nothing he could do about it. He had known it was inevitable, but whether they would end up killing each other was another consideration. Would he really be able to break things up between them? That would be left to the future he thought.

He looked out the window at the beautiful sunset. Everything was so lush and green, even the smell of the country was invigorating. He took a deep breath and relaxed.

The striped cat stayed in the area of its last kill for an additional day before moving on. It liked to cover large distances and was in a sense a rogue moving in and out of other tigers domains, never feeling threatened and occasionally meeting the challenger and vanquishing him, only to give the area back and explore new territory. It was heading north east and it had been in that area years before. Like an elephant, it remembered rivers and valleys it had traveled before.

After a day's travel it had come to the Baruzi river, a river fed from mountain glaciers far to the north. It was the largest river in the north of India and eventually it would make its way in a snakelike pattern out to the Bay of Bengal. The river was a natural barrier to many animals. The tiger had crossed it before but remembered that it was by no means an easy task with strong currents in some places. Where the river spread out and the current slowed it was infested with crocodiles some of which were fifteen feet long and still growing as they continued to grow throughout their lives. Many of the animals that tried to cross the mighty river became victims as the crocodiles were waiting, sometimes they would even attack each other, as weak members of their species would get injured or sick and were picked off by the strong and healthy. Although the tiger had had a few encounters with the cold-blooded beasts before, it was always wary of a crossing, for the water was where they were in their element. They would lay low in the slow parts of the river with their beady little eyes just above the surface, constantly looking for an opportunity to pluck a hapless animal from the river. The big ones usually fought aggressively and were the first on getting picks for food or forcing smaller crocs to abandon their meals. But tigers are known as great swimmers as well and are not intimidated too often.

The big cat came to a likely crossing of the massive river and could not see the crocodiles, but knew by instinct that they were there, waiting.

They had in times past stolen meals from it when it had killed a sambar in a lake when it was young and it never forgot it. It happened again a few weeks later and it was then that it decided to retrieve it successfully. That was how it became the beast that it was. It waited on the bank surveying the situation for any signs of danger.

The river at this point was fairly slow but it was at least three hundred yards across. At this time of year with the recent monsoons in the low country and snow in the mountains it swelled to a much greater volume than normal.

The cat moved its head down to get a drink of water crouching low. It lapped up the water efficiently with its long tongue with thousands of tiny ridges curving exactly in a position to retrieve the water through tension. It then rose up and sat on it haunches, looking out across the river with a determination that it would succeed. Then there was no longer any hesitation as it leaped from the bank into the water and began jumping at first, and then swimming powerfully when it became too deep.

It kept its head above water with its massive paws churning the water beneath its magnificent body. It would not look either to the left or the right, being focused on the opposite bank and the point it wanted to exit. The current was bringing it downstream somewhat, but it continued to cover the distance between the banks in great speed. The crocodiles near the bank where it had entered did not have time to gather or get in position but the crocodiles on the far bank had heard the splash and some were waiting for it.

The tiger was just reaching the shallow part of the far bank when one crocodile found itself perfectly positioned to grab the cat with its jaws. It was large enough to do so and managed to propel itself right up alongside the cat and reached out with its jaws clamping down on the tiger's rear leg. The bite was powerful and strong and although the teeth of a crocodile are not meant for ripping or tearing, they are meant to hold as they try to drown their victim in the water.

The crocodile was trying to roll the cat, but it was in shallow enough water that the striped cat was able to maintain footing and was trying to relieve pressure by somewhat going in the direction the crocodile was rolling. The crocodile wasn't one of the bigger ones but was still around twelve feet long. It continued to hold the tiger by its rear leg, and when it switched its weight to try and get a better grip, the crocodiles tail came within reach of the tiger turning back to try to release the pressure that held its leg. The tiger brought the tail in closer until it was able to bite down on it with a powerful force of its own, yet the crocodile would not release its hold.

In a desperate move to try and get a better grip where it could drag its victim into the deeper water and execute the death roll, it released its grip momentarily in order to get a better one, and when it did the cat whipped around and bit down on its head. The thick scales and the crocs head were not crushed but it wasn't taking any chances and began to roll with the tigers jaws still clamped tight like a bulldog that wouldn't let go. While it was turning, the croc exposed the most vulnerable part of its body, the whiter, softer, less scaly underside, and as it did so the tiger found an area just under its jaw with a fore-paw and with claws extended, with each tiny muscle stretched to its maximum, it dug deep inside the skin of the crocodile. Then with the full force of every muscle in its forward body it reached out and downward, cleanly opening up the underbelly of the crocodile as blood and organs began to ooze out into the water as if freed from a sewn sack of vegetables sold at the market.

The fight was over and the cold-blooded beast would be dead from the loss of blood in less than two minutes. No longer having the energy to fight, its life ebbed from its body as the light of day ebbs after the sun sets.

As other crocodiles started to smell death and began to move to the smell, the cat seized its scaly tail and began to tug and to pull with its might bringing the half ton beast to the shore, and after it did it let out a roar only a victor in such a fight could deliver.

It smelled the dead beast and struck its tongue out tasting the opened flesh, then ripped off a piece of soft underbelly with its massive jaws and quickly spat it out, not liking the taste and not being hungry enough to eat it. It abandoned the kill to encroaching crocs as it moved away from the river and into the jungle where it felt secure. The wound to its leg was not a serious one, but it still walked with a limp. As night set in, it moved with impunity into the darkness like a great fish moves into the deep.

Bart was busy making preparations for another month or two into the jungles of India as he called it and was behind schedule. He knew that Winston and Charles had already left two days ago and he would not be ready to leave until the next day. There was no word yet from Charles, but Bart knew they were most likely heading to an area within close proximity to the last kill, at least within fifty miles or so. But that could be fifty miles in any direction. He continued to have a surly attitude and was constantly barking orders again and again. He kept in touch with the Ministry's Office but didn't like their constant attention to the details of what he was planning or how he was going to accomplish this or that. He was starting to feel like they were managing him in a small way and felt more and more like a puppet figure to do their dirty work for them. Javier was worse than George, as he had a lot riding on the outcome and generally was like Napoleon in his later years, full of pride bordering on arrogance in everything he did or had an opinion on, including how to kill the tiger.

Late in the afternoon Bart went back to the Ministry's Office to see if there was any breaking news about the man-eater. He was planning on heading out the next day and wanted the latest news. George told him there was no news of any recent attacks. When he heard this he turned and was walking out when he met Javier coming in the front door. He had a military satchel on and it looked heavy.

He stopped Bart and told him, "I have something here for you that may help in your endeavor," and with that he carefully pulled out three military grade english grenades and handed them like eggs to Bart saying, "If you trap the beast somewhere or if it gets too close throw one of these at it and as long as your somewhat close, the cat will be pulverized."

Bart looked at one of the grenades and there were foreign markings he didn't recognize painted on it.

"Where did you get these?" asked Bart.

"It's better if you don't know," replied Javier.

Javier wasn't concerned so much with Bart's safety as he was at winning that bet of his.

Bart took the satchel carefully and turned around and left the office. He had a big day of traveling in the morning and he needed to get a good night's rest.

As much as he tried to sleep that night the pressure of the upcoming hunt and the details weighed heavy on Bart's mind. Victoria could hear him from the other room tossing and turning on a creaky old bed. When dawn came she noticed that he had already been up for a while seeing to last minute details. She asked if she could make him some breakfast and he replied yes.

She made his favorite Scottish biscuits with eggs over easy and tea. There was a new marmalade she also put out on the table, but Bart didn't bother to test it and wolfed down the food as quickly as it was served. There was so much on his mind that he forgot to thank Victoria.

He told her he needed to go or he would miss the train. A rickshaw was already waiting outside his bungalow, courtesy of Javier as he wanted Bart out there as quick as possible.

They embraced as father and daughter. Before he turned away she told him that she loved him, and he said that he loved her too and to take care of herself while he was gone. With that he turned, picked up his personal gear and walked out the gate. It was a surreal feeling as both knew that somehow, someway, things were never going to be the same.

Victoria had reached a milestone in her life and was passing from child to young woman and there was no looking back. Tears welled up in her eyes as she turned away, never feeling comfortable telling him of the love of her life.

Like the seasoned gladiators of old, the formidable Bart and Winston were about to clash as only two egotistical men could and no one could predict what would happen.

Winston, while traveling on the train and when he wasn't sleeping, looked over the map again and again. After a while he turned to Charles and said he had an inkling that the tiger would continue in the north easterly direction and would cross the Baruzi river and strike next at a hamlet called Nacaali. Charles knew he had the best mind for determining where the tiger would show, so he concurred.

They could be in the hamlet in two days time and set the trap up within a day if they had some villagers to help. That would put them about six days out from the last attack and the tiger should be hungry by then. The only question was whether the cat would cross the Baruzi river. Winston was very optimistic, and Charles was starting to have second thoughts on his decision to be the bait in the trap. He continued to rework his drawings of the trap and to modify it.

The train, like a giant constrictor, slowly snaked its way toward the northern provinces. Only Winston and Charles knew the danger they were going into.

After switching trains in Maderaa, they were able to catch the evening train heading directly north. By morning they would be able to hike the rest of the way to Nacaali. With a smaller party they would be able to travel faster and that was the way Winston preferred it.

The train ride went by without incident and by nine a.m. they were already unloading and getting a quick breakfast before trudging off to Nacaali.

The hike through the jungle along the primitive paths was cooler than normal due to the vegetation covering the trails and the cool spring air. There was nothing quite the same as a fresh jungle following a monsoon. In some places they needed to widen the path with machetes. Thanks to good local knowledge they were kept in the right direction, but the locals also knew that with Winston being there, there was a good chance the tiger couldn't be far. Only needed travel was done by the locals.

Even with the cool air, everyone started to lather up a good sweat because they were trying to get to Nacaali before sundown and they wanted to set up the trap as soon as possible. Winston was still in great shape having exercised through the wet season. Charles on the other hand had spent a little too much time with Victoria and he was struggling and panting quite a bit just to keep up, even though he was a lot younger than Winston.

Charles would occasionally reach up and feel the cool jade around his neck that Victoria had given him. It was a reassurance and a physical representation of their love.

He paused to catch his breath as Winston distanced himself from him. He took out his handkerchief and wiped the sweat from his brow and then with an audible sigh marched on. They had managed to cover the twenty-five miles in just under seven hours as they arrived in Nacaali. The people welcomed them like a liberating army and every sort of benefit available was offered to them. They quickly took them up on a dinner.

Winston knew they would not be in a position to do anything other than sleep after dinner and made no plans other than to ask for some help constructing a bamboo trap early the next morning. The chieftain agreed to help in any way he could.

The meal was ready within an hour. They could have been fed mangy dog and still devoured it, being as hungry as they were. Winston was glad to hear that there had been no attacks in the area recently. The tiger had to be getting hungry soon and it was just a matter of a day or two before it would kill again.

Following the dinner the men were given a large hut to sleep in. The usual occupants went over to relatives to sleep giving the entire hut to Winston and his small company.

Dawn came earlier than expected. Charles thought that he had only slept for a few hours, although his watch did indicate it was time to go.

They got a quick breakfast and the necessary supplies and headed off to a nearby valley that was close to the village, and in an area that Winston thought was promising as to where the tiger might enter. They had to get the trap done that day, and preferably before dark so that it could be set up.

Winston didn't want the trap too far away from the village because the village was likely where the cat would get its next victim, and he also didn't want it too far away so that the tiger would entirely bypass it.

They arrived at a valley that funneled up to the village which looked very promising. The bottom came from the south and that was supposedly the direction the man-eater was coming from. There was what looked like a perfect spot next to a large tree where vines could cover the sides of the trap.

Winston had purchased a goat that he indicated would attract the tiger with its bleating but likely would keep Charles up all night.

The locals had offered to help and Winston had instructed them to bring as many large and long bamboo poles as could be found. They began to deposit the poles near the tree as the construction began. Charles made the outer base with the longest poles and made sure that all the poles were securely tied and double tied, he did not want to take any chances with his life being on the line.

It was an immense trap as anyone could see. Charles had made it very long because he wanted as much distance between the man-eater and himself as possible. With each passing hour the trap began to take shape as locals pitched in to help as well.

The trigger mechanism was a large square shaped latched piece of bamboo with rope inter-woven between the outer poles so that not even a small hand could pass through. Into the lattice-like rope were strung twigs and grasses to simulate a natural jungle like floor. At the fulcrum of each side, a stout pole had been placed that ran the entire length of the contraption, with the ends of the poles passing through a second bamboo pole placed on top of the original ground poles. With weight on one side or the other the unit could be depressed either way about four inches. At the entrance and about ten feet past the floor trigger, two tracks were made with reinforced walls where the doors would slam down if the trigger floor was depressed. Coconut grease was used to facilitate the bamboo wall falling to the ground.

Both Winston and Charles were giving orders left and right. A trap of this size had probably never been built before, except possibly for elephants.

On the trigger floor mechanism were two fine wires that ran upwards and through small pulleys to both the sliding wall, which was supposed to protect Charles, and the opening wall that would trap the man-eater. Once the trigger floor was tripped both walls would slide down the guides and trap the tiger.

Pins were at the ends which held up the walls and these were greased excessively. If they failed Charles would be the evening meal. Weights were added to the sliding walls to facilitate a quick downward movement in addition to keeping the walls from being raised.

They had been at it for nearly seven hours when it was starting to take shape and to look like a trap. Many of the cross sections were tightly wrapped with vines and tied off. Vines were used to help hide the walls and the ends though openings could be seen clearly.

Winston and Charles tried the trigger mechanism several times and were satisfied that it would work. Vines were the last finishing touch done by the locals as Winston and Charles walked the entire trap looking for any signs of weaknesses. When they were satisfied they came under the tree for a breather and some calamanchi juice.

Winston spoke first, "You know, you'll only have a few seconds before that door reaches the floor. Any determined attitude from the cat to get you may mean that it trips the trigger and comes directly to you, beating the door."

"Yeah, I've thought a lot about that, and I'm betting my life that it will be cautious and that won't happen."

"Would you like me in the tree, just as a precaution?"

"No, I want everything to be as perfectly natural as it possibly can, but I'm glad we reinforced the wall between me and the cat"

"Well, I'll be guarding the approach to the village from the other side and will likely use a tethered goat, so if it comes up to the village both approaches will be covered. I'm going to need to get going before sunset. Good luck and Godspeed. I guess if the trap is successful, we'll be back in the morning. Until then you can conduct the first interview of a man-eater."

"Very funny. Hey, is there any food you can leave with me?"

"Yes, there are some mangos and some oranges left. I gather that you will be in the trap before sunset?"

"Yes, most likely as soon as you leave. I'll gather up some grass to sleep on and with any luck we'll catch a tiger by the tail, as they say."

"Good one Charles. If you fail as a big game hunter, you can always do comedy."

"Adieu."

"Caio, and good luck yourself."

Winston began to gather the locals and within a few minutes they were making their way back towards the village.

Charles had a premonition about this night that something was going to happen. He didn't know what but he just knew that there was some sort of mystique in the area.

Charles had gathered a lot of grass to sleep on. He had thrown it over the trigger mechanism and then carefully climbed the side cage wall and eased over into his area without tripping the trap. He began spreading out the grass where he would sleep and carefully choose the best area. He had been working hard all day in hopes that he would be extremely tired and would not have to deal with thoughts of a man-eater close by with himself as the bait.

The sweat he had exerted during the day had saturated his clothes. It was a scent that was unmistakable and if the tiger was in the area it could be picked up easily by its keen sense of smell if the wind favored the direction. What concerned him the most was whether the trap would work as designed? One thing was certain, he didn't want one door coming down and not the other where he would be dead for sure. He also realized that he was a loud snorer and the sounds of his snoring would be heard in the dead of the night.

The sun was setting in the west as it had through the eons of time, but this night was going to be different from all the others. Just as the sun was quickly disappearing over the horizon, he began with trepidation to try and get some sleep. Before laying down he urinated on the trigger mechanism hoping that the smell would entice the tiger onto it. As soon as the sun set he was already fast asleep despite the spartan circumstances.

The tiger was on the prowl the day the trap was set up and as luck would have it, was indeed moving towards the village of Naacali. The leisurely pace at which it was going put it within a few miles of Charles by the time the sun had gone down.

It was following the valley up towards the village and had been there before, so it knew the terrain and the hamlet. It had taken a victim from the village a few years previous and the inhabitants all shared an extreme dislike for the man-eater and were more cautious than most. They took no chances after the sun went down now that they knew the cat could possibly be in the area. That was why Winston had gotten so much local help, because they were willing to help in any way to exact revenge on the striped beast.

As the tiger had moved up the valley earlier in the day monkeys or langurs would give out alarm calls which were heard by no one except the animals in the valley. These creatures were the eyes of the jungle, being able to see full color they could pick out the orange coat from the tiger while the deer and other animals could not. But now that it was dark the calls had stopped and the tiger continued to move as quietly as the owl flies though the night. It was used to covering such vast distances which was one reason everyone else had underestimated it so many times.

Its body color was masking it in the darkness with only the white spots on the backs of its ears being the only visible sign indicating it was the feared tiger. Most all animals gave it a wide berth if they smelled it coming or caught a glimpse of it in the night. Any sound in the night was perceived by other animals as a predator and they quickly took to the trees or scampered away.

The trail the tiger was using would bring it within fifty yards of Charles so long as it maintained its course. Most people would be terrified of the prospect of sleeping as bait for a man-eating tiger, but Charles was already snoring loud enough to wake most people, and it could be heard from two hundred yards away. It was as if he was on some holiday, exhausted from a day's activity, sleeping the slumber of his life, oblivious to the danger he was in.

The cat snaked its way up the valley getting closer with each passing minute until the unmistakable scent of human sweat reached its nose. It stopped in its tracks beginning to salivate at the smell of the flesh it desired. It sensed its direction and cautiously approached the source.

There was a slight breeze that night that wafted the human scent into the air and carried it away. Only those animals with a keen sense of smell would be able to pick it up.

It was more careful now, having learned from past experiences to be wary of everything. It hadn't survived this long without learning a few things along the way. It slowed down its pace a little, and just to be cautious, it left the well-worn trail and made its way into the jungle going in the same direction. Although leaving the trail was more difficult, it felt it was safer. The grass on the hillside had grown long and fast following the monsoon season, and as it nudged itself through the tall grass it held its head high, still sniffing the air trying to get a direction from the wind as to where the distinct smell it craved so much was coming from.

There was no moon this night and it was emboldened by the absence of light. On nights like this it had always been successful.

After another hour it was very close, it could smell it. Within a few minutes it came to the small clearing with the large sycamore tree where the foot path ran beside it, and it watched the clearing with its excellent night sight for close to ten minutes. Nothing at all happened. It decided to investigate the smell and the noise and, being extremely careful on where it was placing its feet, moved around the clearing until it was near the tree. It could at this point make out some vines and a shape of some sort that looked like a small cave.

It could hear the snoring from Charles and knew right away that there was a human sleeping inside the cave. There were enough vines covering the cave that it couldn't quite see through and it slowly began to be more and more curious, but cautious at the same time. It could smell the sweat easily now and it began to salivate and lick its jowls. It finally decided to investigate closer and slowly made its way around the cage until it found the wide opening.

It was smart of Charles to insist on using all natural elements in the trap as the tiger sniffed the bamboo and the vines that held it together searching for anything out of the ordinary.

The muffled sounds of the snoring could be heard better from the opening, but the tiger was wary. Something was amiss but it couldn't figure out what. It stayed at the opening for another five minutes before it started to step inside the trap. One paw was placed inside, and the following paw was placed exactly where the first had left to avoid making any sound.

It wasn't recognized as a trap by the tiger because of its immense size. It had seen other traps and recognized them as such, but this had been built on such a grand scale that it seemed perfectly safe, like a cave or something.

It continued forward, pausing with each step, still hearing the loud snores coming from Charles who was oblivious to the danger. It took nearly seven minutes to cover the fifteen feet to the trigger mechanism. Here, in order to set the trap, the fake floor had been raised at an angle, where towards Charles' side there was a clearance on the floor of a good five inches, enough that if depressed the sliding walls would both come down.

The tiger put its front paw on it, then retrieved it. It smelled a strong human scent on that particular part of the floor. The lattice-like work with the vines had required the work of many hands of different people and the tiger's keen sense of smell picked up on the differences of human sweat. It realized at once all was not right and quickly retreated out of the cage and into the night as easily as it had come.

It was over. Charles had had a very good chance, but the tiger was smart, very smart. If the same trap had been placed a few years earlier, with the tiger less experienced, it would have been sprung, but like an oriental wood puzzle, the cat was beginning to be hard to figure out.

The tiger left the area and retreated back down the valley it had come up leaving the area completely.

As the sun began to rise basking the meadow and the trap in its rich warm yellow rays Charles awoke. Rubbing his eyes he at first thought nothing had transpired in the evening, and with all his efforts he had slept as sound as a baby. But looking over the trap trigger he could see even from his distance the large pug marks in the soft dirt of the floor. At first he couldn't believe it, then he stumbled over to get a closer look only to trip the trap and have both doors come sailing down to the earth in a flash. *No matter*, he thought, as he knew he could lift them up again, but he did get a closer look at the pug marks and knew instinctively that from the size of them it could only be the man-eater.

He looked around some more and after raising the outer door and putting a small bamboo pole to hold it up about four feet he shuffled under it and began to examine the pug marks again and could see how the tiger had circled the trap entirely and had even come in as far as the trigger. Why hadn't it come further? He was puzzled. He looked around and wondered if he was in danger. Was it still there somewhere, ready to pounce?

He looked again at the pug marks. There was no mistake about it. They were the biggest set of tracks he'd seen from a tiger and it looked exactly like the plaster one at his office. He wiped the sweat from his brow with his handkerchief, it was already getting sultry.

He barricaded himself in the trap. Maybe it had gone around and Winston had a shot, but then he didn't remember hearing a shot. He didn't want to be known as a coward for hiding within the safety of the cage, but better to be alive was what he was thinking.

There was no activity in the countryside as the people knew the tiger could be there. It was as if Winston and Charles were the only people operating outside the village. A group of people would venture out occasionally to gather wood as there was safety in numbers, but it was eerily quiet, even with the animals.

Winston and his company arrived within an hour and Charles was excited to tell him that the trap had nearly worked.

Before they had even said good morning, Charles had blurted out, "It was here, in the trap!"

Winston was astonished and replied, "It was here…" unsure of what Charles had said.

"It was here last night and even ventured part way into the trap. The pug marks are one and the same as the man-eater's. Look, see for yourself," as he pointed to the area of soft dirt around the far end of the trap, "It paid a visit last night."

Winston could hardly believe it.

"We'll let's have a look, but it's good to see you in one piece," and with that came a hearty slap on the back as the trap door was lifted and Charles emerged as the men began to chuckle silently to themselves.

Winston forbade anyone else to enter the area around the trap except for Charles.

Looking at the pug marks there was no mistake it was the tiger they were looking for, but he said, "Look here," and pointed at a well preserved print in the soft pumice like dirt.

"There's a split here in the pug from the front left. It's new as we haven't seen it in other casts. There's no doubt from the size that it's the same cat. It must have been in some sort of fight lately or cut it somehow, and it will take a few weeks for it to heal."

Charles looked closer and could see the slight split.

"It means it likely won't be traveling as far for the next few days, which gives us a better chance of locating it."

He paused for a few seconds stroking his several day old beard, then he spoke up.

"We'll send a tracker out a few miles and find the direction it took once it left the valley, and we'll be in perfect position next time. We had better get back to the village and make preparations to get going. There's not a moment to lose. It will probably strike tonight or tomorrow since it hasn't killed anything in about five days."

"Right, let's move," replied Charles.

Winston and Charles made for the village while the locals began to examine the pug marks. It didn't take long for them to realize that the sahibs had left with the guns and that a man-eater was in the area, and they were soon passing Winston at a brisk pace back to the village.

Winston's tracker had taken a brave lad to help in the tracking and once they got the general direction they would get the information to Winston.

Winston and Charles got into the village and immediately took out the map and began to consult about which village the tiger would most likely visit based on which direction it was heading. There were only three possible directions that had villages. Winston ruled out one due to the terrain which was very rough as it would be too difficult for the cat with a healing paw. After identifying the possible destinations all they could do was wait until the tracker determined the correct direction.

Rather than try and track the cat as they had sometimes done before, Winston had decided to try and ambush the cat before it arrived. They needed to travel quickly if they were going to be in position, so they began to inquire around for additional porters so they could travel light. There was only one in the village that was in good enough shape, but the chieftain said another could be obtained from a neighboring village and Winston made arrangements to get him straightway.

Winston mentioned to Charles that if he could take a nap to do so because he might need it, as the tracker would likely be back in a couple of hours. Charles was always keen to take Winston's advice and made for a hammock.

The tracking was in difficult terrain but that also made it easier to see broken pieces of foliage where the cat had gone. They were very careful, proceeding slowly in case the tiger wasn't as far ahead of them as they thought. It didn't take long to figure out that once it left the valley it was going in a south-westerly direction, and they made haste in getting back to Winston with the news.

When they arrived, Winston was already having lunch but put everything aside to examine the map once more. It was unfolded again and lain out on the table as various items of food or drink were moved and put on the corners. He didn't wake Charles, wanting him to get as much sleep as possible.

There were two villages some distance away in the south west direction and he had begun to examine the predetermined one. It just didn't seem like the right one. He had a gut feeling that the cat would bypass it and move onto the next one. It had already been spooked by the trap and the smell of a human inside and wanted to get back into its element.

Winston decided that the second village was going to be the prime target. He had a pretty good feeling about it anyway. It was about thirty-five miles distant, but they might be able to get there the next day just before sunset. He went to wake Charles.

Charles was a little groggy but was soon himself. They moved over to the map as Winston spoke.

"I believe it's going to strike here," pointing to the village of Hamlii. "We're going to have to cover a large distance as its thirty-five miles away, and for safety's sake we'll need to bypass the footpath that leads directly to it because the tiger may be in any part of the area."

He again pointed at the map.

"It left the area here and moved down and out the valley going in this direction. It could be anywhere between those two lines, but I think it will utilize these valleys here and strike at Hamlii from the north. If we move out quickly we can be in position by tomorrow night, and if it strikes tonight we can track it to the kill and make a stakeout. Otherwise we will try to ambush it as it comes into the village."

Charles spoke up by saying, "It looks like the topography is very dense around there. Will it give us much of a chance?"

"There's only one way to find out, and we need to move immediately."

Charles wrote a quick message to be delivered to the nearest cable station as soon as possible.

It read, TIGER IN NAACALI DISTRICT WILL CONTINUE TO TRACK CHARLES.

The cable was required by the ministry now that they had to relay critical information to Bart's group as well. Of course, Bart would not relay the information as he was supposed to, but Charles was asked to do it and he obeyed. Besides, with the cable station being some distance away the information would be stale in a few days anyway.

Bart and his group had arrived in a hamlet to the south of the last attack. Although he was at one of the last crime scenes, he was unaware of the habits of the cat and unlike Winston was not aware of the amount of distance it could cover after an attack. It was only luck that kept him in the general vicinity, if you could call being within fifty miles the general area. Although he had luck before there was no chance it would come again.

The others were waiting for him to make a decision on what to do and the fact of the matter was that he didn't know what to do. He hated to admit it but hunting in India was a whole other ball game than Africa. It was just too dense, especially now just after the monsoons. Why, you needed a machete just to get through to the next village! He didn't understand the nature of the hunt in these conditions, and so he called a conference with his party, and through competent individuals, he was able to take some new ideas and decide on what they could do.

He had decided to buy a few goats and tie them up on the outskirts of the hamlet and wait for the cat to come in as suggested. He made a purchase for two goats and within a few minutes of purchasing them was exchanging them as one of the men suggested that it would be difficult to see two black goats in the middle of the night, and so he had exchanged them for two white ones.

Little details like that was not his forte and the natives working for him began to wonder if the extra pay was worth their lives. Why he had chosen a hamlet so far away from the last attack was a question everyone had asked themselves. The people working for him were starting to have some serious doubts. Like a group of sailors who disliked the captain's orders they were about to mutiny, but the pay kept them on, although the complaining would not stop. The morale, like a slow leak from a cracked pitcher, was beginning to ebb away slowly with each passing day.

The hired hands had managed to tether the goats near the village and instructed Bart to get into the tree overlooking the goats. He had assumed he would be watching from the comfort of a chair or something, but they insisted this was how it was done so he wouldn't become the next victim. It was good advice because he probably would have fallen asleep anyway.

It was most uncomfortable for him in the tree and it didn't help that he had a robust overweight frame. He couldn't find a proper branch to sit on and was constantly moving and making noise.

He hadn't been in the tree more than a couple of hours when he heard one of the goats bleating as if its life was in danger. Bart quickly switched his torch on that he had fastened to the side of his gun and simultaneously fired both rounds at the animal attacking the goat. One shot passed through the goat's neck severing the jugular vein and the other found its mark on the attacking animal. Bart wanted to get down immediately but the man with him advised against it, saying that the animal might just be wounded and without light there was no way of knowing for sure.

He kept saying, "We need wait," over and over again.

Bart was upset about having to spend another five or six hours in the wretched tree. He had never done anything similar to it and was used to being in comfort.

When the first rays of dawn spread their light on the surrounding countryside, they slowly descended and went over to the scene of death. The goat lay there in its gore having lost most of its blood through the neck as its small heart continued to pump until there was none left.

The other animal was visible too and to Bart's horror he could see that it was a large dog of sorts that clearly had a frayed rope on its neck, its eyes were still open, but it was dead, and they seemed to be saying, why?

Bart tried to remember the sounds of the night before. Was it just a playful dog coming to romp with the goats? One thing was for sure, as soon as the owner found out they would not be welcomed anymore.

Bart instructed the other man to dig a grave and they would bury the beast, but what hurt most was Bart's pride, as this clearly would get out and he would be the laughing stock of the country to say the least.

He sat down under the tree and took a long break, not offering to help the other man dig in any way. Soon the rest of the party would arrive to pick them up and the news would be out. He thought to himself how he hated this country.

He could hear the sounds of villagers approaching and his thoughts quickly turned to frenzied and demented throngs approaching with pitchforks and torches, ready to hang the individual who had caused so much pain and suffering. He quickly got rid of the thought as they approached closer.

The grave had been dug and the animal had been put in with dirt covering the hole in a small mound. The rest of Bart's party began to ask what happened, and the sole witness besides Bart was eager to fill in the details as he motioned and gesticulated in Bart's direction and spoke in their native tongue so Bart couldn't understand. Finally, Bart had had enough and ordered everyone up and back to the village.

The trek back was without words between the men and Bart, although the men continued to yak to each other.

When they arrived at the village they could see an old man going around the various huts whistling and calling out a pets name. He was the obvious owner of the dog. Bart didn't do anything, but the other men in Bart's group sought him out and explained what had happened. The man fell to his knees and started sobbing uncontrollably at first and then started wailing and cursing. It was an emotional scene and one would have thought he had lost his wife or something. There was no consoling him and eventually he was led away.

Bart should have been the one to tell him what happened, or he could have been the one to purchase a new puppy and give it to him as penance for his deed, but he did nothing and like a lot of men who care for nothing except themselves, he pushed it aside like a thousand choices before that didn't affect him.

The villagers saw what had happened and it wasn't long before Bart was not welcomed anymore and the courtesies that had been afforded him were no longer forthcoming. It didn't take a genius to figure out the new attitude and so he simply picked up his things and moved on to the next village.

It was on route that a cable finally caught up to him that there had been a sighting or evidence that the tiger had been in Naacali. Bart broke out his map and studied it for a few minutes before a worker pointed out where the village was on the map. Bart was more than seventy five miles away, and to the south of Naacali, but he decided to change course and move north to the small village. Although it was a long distance away, Bart wanted to get there as soon as possible, and it didn't matter much to him that it would be a forced march beyond human capacity, with himself being a bit out of shape, it just wasn't possible. With the cat already moving south and Bart moving north it was just a matter of time before the two parties meet.

With Bart and his draconian tactics, the locals helping him were starting to get fed up with the whole situation. He had already had two men up and leave, even though the pay was great, and with this decision to march the fifty miles he had another three leave. He needed to hire some more locals in order to carry his baggage which was dropped on the trail. It forced him to go to the nearest village to summon help, but it took time, and time was something he couldn't afford to lose.

He didn't have much of a load before and now he dumped his light pack with the rest of the gear and ventured to the next village. There was a lot of grumbling from the others as they set off. After doing fifteen miles they stopped at a large stream to take a break and refill their canteens. Bart sat on a log that ran across the stream and took off his socks and boots to let his aching feet dangle in the cool water. They were there for about fifteen minutes and when he pulled his feet out of the water they were covered with leeches. Some of the men snickered under their breath, and it took him another ten minutes to get them all off with the help of several matches. Some of the wounds were bleeding and Bart did a final check in his crotch area to make sure none had made a migration north.

They made the nearest village within an hour and although they could hire porters in the local area to move their items to the village, none were willing to venture into an area close to where the man-eater was reported even with the much higher wages. There was only one thing to do until the Ministry could send him some replacements and that was to only take the bare essentials, and he would have to carry a heavy pack like the rest of the group.

He sat down in the village to make a list of the items they absolutely needed while the rest of the team and a few more locals went back to retrieve the gear that was left behind. The problem was that all the bags had to be opened to find certain items as there was no organization to them.

Instead of continuing to write down the essential items needed, he sat back and proceeded to take a nap while lowering his hat over his eyes.

The men returned about an hour later and Bart was still dozing, so the men began to unpack everything and get out just the essential gear that could be carried by the remaining men. Once Bart awoke, he found that his pack had already been assembled, and with him getting several bottles of scotch and adding them, his pack became heavier than he had wanted.

One thing they didn't know was that the information they had on the last kill was several days old and the tiger had been making its way south for over forty-eight hours. Their proximity to the tiger would increase as they continued to move north.

Most of the hired hands knew they would be going after the man-eater, but many thought they would simply ferry supplies to villages with the sahib. They thought that a select few would be the ones sitting in tree stands waiting for the cat to approach while they slumbered away in semi-fortified huts. No one knew how much danger they were about to be in.

The cat had not covered its usual distance in the two days since its last kill, but the area covered was still substantial as it had gone about thirty-five miles.

The long miles it managed to roll off like a newspaper coming off a press had toned and defined its muscles. With every step a visible ripple could be seen between shoulder and leg muscles. It was as if a wave was formed at the top of its shoulder and slowly with each step contorted and moved down its body, getting less perceptible until it reached the bottom of its leg.

Other tigers were indeed fit as well but the mere fact of covering so much territory and not having any space to settle down provided the means to develop such a specimen the world rarely sees. The steady diet of human flesh had given the tiger a unique diet. Somehow there was something in the flesh that contributed to a magnificent coat where the colors were more vivid, more saturated. The orange was dark, the white was like the driven snow and the black was darker than the darkest cavern. It was so vivid that the camouflage was slightly brighter than the surrounding foliage, especially this time of year when things were still as green as Ireland.

The wound in its foot was healing slowly and each time it stopped, it licked it, which cleaned it out somewhat and prevented infection. It was still a sore spot for it and Winston was right when he guessed that it would somewhat reduce its speed.

Winston and Charles had arrived in Hamlii after twelve hours of hard marching and were very exhausted. The good news was that there had been no news of an attack and if it was to come tonight they would be ready. But first everyone needed a heavy nap of a few hours. It didn't take long, as most everyone fell asleep where they had stopped in the village. Winston and Charles managed to make it into a hut that was graciously offered to them. They declined lunch at the time but indicated they would take some in a few hours.

Every village they visited was very accommodating and offered anything and everything to be at their disposal. It sure reduced the supplies they had to carry, and it was mostly for Winston as he was like a hero to the people. His fame had spread throughout the entire country, either with his exploits in the papers of killing man-eaters or by word of mouth to those who couldn't read.

Charles was asleep within a minute of laying down but Winston took a little longer. The children gathered around the outside of the hut to snicker at how loud the snoring was.

Both men slept a few hours and awoke with the help of Winston's servant who had been given instructions on exactly when to wake them. After a quickly eaten lunch they set about examining the small village.

Winston was of the opinion that the attack would come directly in the village and had spied a large mango tree on the south perimeter of the village where he expected an attack to come from. They went to the tree and realized that one branch would need to be trimmed in order to get a clear look at the pathway and surrounding area.

They instructed the locals that they needed to cut the limb off and although they were reluctant, with a little prodding from Winston they were convinced.

Some fire torches were set about on all the entrances to ward off the cat as was customary if it was in the area. Winston wanted some bigger ones on the South entrance so he could see a little better. There would be no goat tethered tonight. He was expecting the tiger to come into the village directly.

Winston didn't tell anyone, but he had a good feeling about tonight and optimism was evident in his attitude and countenance. Although his gut feelings were sometimes wrong, like the sun halo that brought rain within a few days, they were mostly correct.

He instinctively reached up and felt the new scar tissue on his neck. This time, he thought to himself, things would be different. It was still a little early to get into the tree as the sun had not set yet and the locals were picking off the mangos from the felled limbs before they were cut up for firewood. The people as usual felt more secure with Winston around.

As Winston and Charles waited for another long night to come, much as a convicted criminal awaits his execution, Charles asked the following question of Winston.

"Do you suppose that the tiger enjoys killing? I mean, it sometimes does it when it's not hungry just to do it. Is it due to circumstance or does it possess an intellect like, say Jack the Ripper, who seemed to kill just for the pleasure of it?"

Winston paused and looked like he was in deep thought, then said, "I think it kills people mostly for food, and when it doesn't, it's coincidence that caused the person's death. Either they surprised it or stumbled upon it, or it just acted naturally like any other killing. There is no doubt in my mind that it's learning and has acquired some important lessons that have managed to keep it alive thus far. It is by far the most elusive, intelligent and strongest cat I've ever encountered, and mark my word this cat will go down in history as the most efficient killing machine the world has known. There will be a note following any article about this cat which will read 'Killed by Charles Whent.'"

Both men started laughing. After the laughter died down Winston asked Charles how he felt about this night. Charles was always honest with his answers, at least he tried to be, and he told him, "I have no feelings one way or the other, but I think we do have an excellent chance tonight, and if we're lucky one of us will have a rather large tiger rug to put on the floor of our cottage and perhaps a world record to go along with it."

Bart and his group had been moving fast and as they continued to put on the miles, one thing was for sure, and that was that Bart was in no position to march that many miles in so short a time. But his dogged personality would not accept defeat and like a hound dog that pursues its quarry until it dies if not forced to rest, he, through his stubborn mind, would continue to hike as his mind was made up and there was no changing it.

With each passing mile he and the others carrying larger loads were sapped of energy and their strength began to wane. It was looking at this point that at their present pace they would be in the man-eater's territory by nightfall and continuing to hike at night, especially with torch supplies left behind, would be suicide. Everyone realized this but Bart, and with the porters and helpers a mutiny was beginning to develop. Not knowing the native language Bart could not tell what they were talking about, but the talk rose in decibels from whispers to loud discussions.

The hiking continued as the men pushed on. The heat was stifling to say the least and sweat was constantly being wiped from the forehead and the back of the neck. By late afternoon the men were getting extremely tired, especially Bart who was more out of shape, but his determined personality pushed everyone on and within an hour they were most definitely within the tiger's possible killing zone.

The porters who possessed any brains at all realized that they would come upon the village of Aknar within a few hours and if they pushed on would be between villages after the sun had gone down. There was increased chatter among them as they came to the conclusion that they would go no further than Aknar after the sun had gone down. It wasn't an easy decision, but they feared for their own lives and weren't ready to risk everything on a final push with a mad man. They were in the process of trying to convince the others to stage a sit down at the village. Most were for it, but some were still undecided.

The trek continued winding through valleys and over streams. If it weren't for the man-eater one could really enjoy the countryside with its lush vegetation. On they marched like a military regiment going to an unknown battle. Everyone was getting weary. The hot tropics and the forced march had sapped their strength. It was apparent to all, even to the supporters of Bart that it would be madness to continue.

They arrived at Aknar with the sun just setting through the hills. The next village was fifteen miles to the north and would take another eight hours at least to get there. The porters who were against going to the next village immediately staged a sit down, taking off their heavy packs and baskets and folded their arms, indicating that they were not continuing. Once they sat down others followed until all the porters but two were sitting down.

Bart came back and was yelling at them to get up and continue, but they remained stoic, not moving a muscle or even making eye contact. Bart had become at this point apoplectic. He ran over to some vegetation and broke off a small bamboo growth and came back and whacked the first guy he came to. The blow hurt the man and he yelled out in pain. It was then that the remaining porters who had sided with Bart pulled him away from the group as the porters who had staged the sit down were about to beat Bart to death themselves.

Bart realized what he had done and was starting to calm down as he was pushed and shoved further away from the group. There was nothing to do now. No amount of persuasion was going to change their minds. In fact, Bart would be doing well just to retain their services the next day.

Bart's right-hand man was able to diffuse the situation somewhat and separate the parties for the moment. Some of the villagers had witnessed what had happened and were also giving Bart disapproving looks. The chatter was incessant with the group who had staged the sit down and it seemed everyone was gesticulating and chatting rapidly which was common for them when they were upset. Trying to make sense of it all was madness, but one thing was apparent, they really did not like Bart.

Bart realized he was stymied without the supplies that were absolutely necessary. There was nothing he could do and he was mad to say the least. He was ranting himself and to the others he looked like he injured his toe when he tried to kick a coconut tree that was of course immovable. It was almost hysterical the way he was acting as if he were a small spoiled child who didn't get his way and threw a tantrum.

After a while Bart accepted the inevitable and made arrangements to stay the night in the village. It was a forced compromise.

The sun had slowly dipped beyond the horizon as both Winston and Charles stared at the last rays. They then looked at one another without speaking and knew the time had come. Within a few minutes the darkness would begin displacing the light and the prime killing time would be upon them.

They shouldered their weapons and began climbing the tree with the help of a ladder which, although crude, made the ascent easier. It was taken down after they were in position.

Winston had observed all the evidence of attacks in previous villages and from the pug marks knew exactly what the cat favored. With two main entrances to the village and with the south entrance so open he heavily favored the north entrance. So confident was he in his assurance that he didn't bother to station Charles at the other entrance.

Once in the tree the hair on the back of his neck started to rise. It was an eerie feeling that had mostly, but not always been the foreboding of an event of mayhem. There was a sense of excitement in the air.

Winston took the prime position on a large tree limb overlooking the entrance to the village thanks to the sacrifice of another limb. Charles took a higher branch, and although it didn't afford quite the open view Winston had it did give him a slight window to a small area Winston could not see. With both views of the entrance covered, they had a commanding view of about ninety percent of the opening. The chances were good with the light from the moon which should last most of the night and the lit torches, that if the cat were to come in this way, it would be finished. Winston continued to feel his scar with its newly heightened tissue. Some things are best forgotten, but that physical reminder demanded vengeance. He wondered if this was the night they would bag that cat from hell. Charles, although aware of the situation, didn't have enough experience to recognize the high chances of meeting the killer tonight.

Both men strained to see further than was possible, to try and get the first glimpse and get ready to fire. Once Winston chose a position to sit in, he would only change it once during the night and that was with utmost care in order to not make a sound.

The cacophony of noise from night creatures continued for a few hours until things started to settle down and get very quiet. The moon was making its way across the night sky, giving off enough light to see a short distance. It was easy to just shut the eyes and sleep a wink or two and Winston had already warned Charles about this the first time they were up in a tree. Within a few minutes a person would be completely out and then the balance would be off just a little, and before you knew it you would be eating dirt, if you didn't break your neck in the process. Winston was used to it, having done it dozens of times, but Charles was having a heck of a time and constantly needed to change up his head or bite his tongue to keep from dozing off. The fact that Winston even trusted him up there was something Winston had never allowed before and with that trust he wasn't going to let him down no matter how tired he was.

From detailed reports supplied by Charles to Winston, Winston knew that the tiger had nearly always attacked between dusk and about two in the morning, but nothing was for sure. Winston had already decided to make it to four am and had indicated such to Charles. Surely he could make it that far into the night.

After several hours of being in the tree, Winston was really straining to look into the jungle, he sensed something was afoot. Sometimes when you want to see something so badly your mind can play tricks on itself. It instinctively looks for what it wants to see, and that can make shapes or inanimate objects appear real. There were several times when Winston thought he had seen something move out there, but it wasn't near enough or clear enough to shoot. He had to make sure of his shot. The last thing they needed now was a wounded man-eating tiger. Occasionally sounds would come from one direction or another and the men would both turn their heads to look in the direction of the sound, knowing that it could have been an animal giving an alarm call for the lord of the jungle. The flies and mosquitoes were especially bothersome this evening and they would be for another month until the rains leftover from the monsoon abated. Rivers and lakes were at their full capacity and pools of stagnant water were everywhere contributing to a most annoying pest problem. The only thing the men could do was to slowly squish them to death as they felt their presence. Many times as they did so they would get more than one. They couldn't slap them because of the noise it would make, they just had to endure it. The minutes turned into hours as they patiently waited. In the village there was a particular man who knew what was going on but came out to check on them prematurely. As he walked down the main path between the huts he had a lantern that could direct the light out a distance in a certain direction. It was used in the mines of Scotland and had been imported to this country, and he had done some trading to get it when he was at a coastal city. The man was oblivious to Winston's instructions that no one should come out of their village hut during the night. Not only was he making too much noise but he had whispered up to Winston and

Charles asking if they had seen anything. Winston didn't bother to answer and Charles wouldn't dare answer if Winston wouldn't.

When the man didn't get an answer he directed his lantern out into the jungle and both Winston and Charles followed the light as its directional path swept the jungle. Just behind some grass, for a brief second, two yellow eyes were seen reflecting the light and looking directly back at him. They were big enough to belong to a tiger or a leopard.

Winston and Charles saw it and Winston instinctively raised his rifle while at the same time pulling both hammers back on the gun, but when the man moved the light back to where he had seen the eyes, they were gone.

It was eerie and it made everyone wonder if they had really seen them. But there was no mistake, something had been watching from just outside of sight. Was it the man-eater? Had it been stalking them? Did it know they were in the tree? So many questions and there were no answers. One thing was for sure, it was not a figment of their imagination. Winston wondered whether, if he had been more ready, he would have been able to get off a shot when the eyes appeared. But he hadn't expected it.

It was apparent that the man with the light was drunk on the local coconut wine. Winston wanted to suggest that he go get some firewood immediately and venture out into the night to his own doom.

The more Winston thought about it, he surmised that it had to have been the man-eater. The eyes were far apart indicating a very big cat and it had been watching the village, or them. He wasn't sure. It's possible it could have been ready to come into the village when it heard the drunkard yelling out and could have retreated back into cover. If that was the case it would have been a matter of a few feet before Winston or Charles would have seen it. Just another five minutes and what could have been. Or it could have just arrived at that time waiting to come in.

One thing could be verified, in the morning they should be able to view its pug marks to see if it was the man-eater. They might be able to ascertain which direction it was heading again and set up another ambush in the next village. The wait for daylight was agonizingly slow.

Bart had convinced his group to start moving again the following day after the sit down, but he continued to be in a foul mood. He had ordered additional supplies, and the loads for each porter were heavier with the men who had quit. The going was slower and Bart himself wouldn't carry a heavier load, so Bart and the stronger porters distanced themselves from the others, but would wait for them at stream crossings where the men would fill their canteens. As the day continued they were well within range of the man-eater.

Unbeknown to them the tiger had been near the village where Winston and Charles were waiting in ambush, and it was the same cat whose eyes they had seen. Once the light was shown on it, it melted back into the jungle and on to a different destination, moving southward. It had traveled most of the night in spite of its slightly injured paw even though it was healing well.

Bart's group had been moving northward getting closer with each mile, and in that region there were only a few roads or trails moving in a south/ north direction. They continued their forced march and as they did so the distance between the stragglers who were lagging behind began to grow more and more. At the next stream they waited until two of the last three men came to the stream, but the third man never showed up. He was a little heavier than the others and was more out of shape. He had started to lag behind as usual and since he had always caught up to the main group nobody was particularly worried. He thought the man-eater was much further to the north.

As the trail wound through the jungle terrain the man-eater had heard them coming with their noise and chatter and had come to investigate. The alarm calls from various animals announcing the presence of the tiger went unnoticed due to the heavy burdens and chatter among the men. The tiger had been shadowing them for close to a mile when it saw an opportunity as the heavier man fell behind, and just at a bend where nothing could be seen and little heard, the tiger had laid wait and in an instant had attacked the man with his bamboo basket full of supplies.

The man was knocked over by the initial attack, and the basket still attached to his back, had somehow saved him from the moment the tiger assailed him. But although it bought him some seconds, the sands of time were dropping through his hourglass of life.

The tiger in no time at all whirled around and enveloped the man in a streak of orange and white, and this time it proved fatal. The big cat dragged his body off the trail some distance to ensure some privacy. The area was thick with elephant grass and various other shrubs and bushes. Approaching without making a sound or moving the grass would have been impossible.

When two of the men were sent back to check on the missing man they saw a small pool of blood and the smears of crimson red marks on the elephant grass. They returned in haste to tell the sad fate of their friend which severely frightened everyone.

George Smythe had received a notice from Javier Blygoth saying that he wanted to see him first thing in the morning at the Viceroy's palace at nine a.m. George knew too well that such meetings never boded well and was antsy the entire night, tossing and turning and unable to sleep. At length he rose from his bed to open the wooden shutters of their country cottage.

His wife asked what was bothering him and he simply replied that the man-eater was beginning to be a real nuisance. He jokingly asked her if she wouldn't mind tracking down the beast and ridding the country of it. They both chuckled but deep down she could see how the problem had started to develop dark areas under his eyes. If there was anything she could have done to help him she would have done it. How many nights had she awoken only to find him gazing with a thousand yard stare out the window into the dead of night. She made a mental note to make him some roast Chinese pheasant tomorrow which was his favorite. But now she undid the neckties of her sheer nightgown and let it drop to the floor and went over to him wrapping her arms around him and pulling him close. Her warmth radiated to him as he turned to kiss her.

The next morning the streets of Bombay were as busy as London's on a monday morning. Everywhere people were either in the process of selling or buying some kind of service, merchandise or food. You could hear the various vendors yelling and trading. For some it was organized chaos.

George slowly made his way through the throngs of people in the streets and finally came to the Viceroy's palace. It was a lavish palace decorated with the finest materials India could offer, and what wasn't local was imported with no expense spared. There were some sentries guarding the entrance but George had been there enough that they knew his face and allowed him to enter.

In the foyer was the secretary. She was a very large boned woman who could have challenged most men to a wrestling match and probably would have won. George told her that he was meeting with Mr. Blygoth today and had an appointment. She said that he was expecting him and told him to go on in.

He started down the long hallway to Javier's office, his leather soled shoes clacking on the marble floor with each step until he arrived at the office at last. A small knock and a secretary told him to enter. Before she had a chance to say anything Javier was already opening his door and welcoming George to his office.

They went in and the door was shut behind them. The room was as much of an impression as the rest of the palace. Behind the large leather chair where Javier sat was a picture of the Queen. After a moment of somewhat awkward silence, Javier spoke up.

"George, I'll come straight to the point. The government has expressed some concerns that we aren't doing everything we can to get rid of the Katagi man-eater, and they want to ensure that the problem will be taken care of before the religious migrations this fall." There was a long pause before he spoke again.

"They have suggested that we use Punjab Frontier Force. As you may be aware, they are two-hundred of the top native soldiers the country has to offer trained by some of Britain's finest men. We are not talking just ordinary soldiers here. This is the best of the best. Many have graduated in the top of their class. Most of them have battle experience and are no strangers to death and war. I would like your honest opinion on the matter."

George was instantly caught between two extremes. If on the one hand he agreed with bringing in the elite troops, and it was something that he didn't agree with at all, then he would be caving to political pressure. On the other hand, if he said it was a bad idea he would probably be viewed as unaccepting of his superior's ideas. After all it was the Viceroy's and the governments suggestion.

All of this went through his mind in a matter of seconds before he spoke.

At last he said, "Well, that certainly is a different approach, but I think we have to look at the matter from another perspective. Here is a man-eating tiger, which up to this point has cheated death a number of times, eluded everything we have thrown at it, is very intelligent, and has most of India to work with. The beast at most times cannot even be seen unless you're within a few yards from it. In my opinion, if you send more men into its domain, some of them are going to be killed. That is a decision you are going to have to live with."

There was a long silence as Javier's pipe continued to puff out smoke. "How many people has it killed this year?" "Well, it's early in the year but I have thirty-two confirmed kills with another probable ten that are missing."

"Missing? What do you mean missing?" asked Javier.

"They've disappeared. We get a lot of reports of people who fail to show up at their village or haven't come home. No one knows for sure what's happened to them and it could be a number of things. Realistically the tiger probably takes a quarter of them, and the others, well who knows."

"How do you confirm the kills?" asked Javier.

"Well, it's usually an eyewitness or blood found at the scene or individual pieces of jewelry, that sort of thing."

"How many have actually survived an attack?"

"Not many. It's very brutal when it attacks, but we do have a couple of survivors, very unusual circumstances of course."

Javier then pulled out his ace card by slapping down the morning's paper. The tiger usually got bottom front page, and there in the bottom corner was a picture of the large trap Winston and Charles had built with a caption saying, "Hired professionals try to trap man-eater."

George looked at the article and wanted to immediately start reading it, but the damage was already done. Many believed the men hired by the government were wasting time. Finally, after a strategic pause Javier spoke up.

"George, don't you think the people would feel at ease with the troops in the area?"

"Well, I guess if I were a local, probably," replied George. "But some of the locals believe it's a were-tiger."

"A were-tiger? what the devil is that?"

"It's like a were-wolf but a tiger or a man, an entity that can transform itself. They believe that a person who has wronged someone in this life in a truly bad manner are reincarnated into a were-tiger which exacts its revenge on others."

"That's a lot of rubbish, don't you think? It just goes to show you how primitively these people think."

"Well, for the people, they truly believe in it."

George felt again that he should counsel against the troops coming into the area, and as he did so he was cut off by Javier when he said, "I appreciate your advice, George. I'll let you know what we decide. I hope it wasn't too much of an inconvenience to come over today, and I hope that you continue to keep me apprised of the situation."

The men shook hands and parted. George then began the long walk down the corridor and out the building. He decided to catch a rickshaw back to his office, which would give him time to think of the events that have transpired.

Javier had already made a decision to use the troops. He had always had no backbone and was just doing the bidding of the Viceroy. He immediately made arrangements for them to leave the next day and would send a message to George that they would be used.

When George arrived at his office his mood was perceived as bad since he didn't say good morning to anyone, but his rather attractive secretary said, "Good morning sir, the report you've been waiting for is on your desk."

It was psychic how she was able to tell exactly what he wanted and when. He was almost ashamed of his not so virtuous thoughts of her that occasionally crossed his mind. He asked her to get the morning paper as he entered his office and closed the door behind him so as not to be disturbed.

He hung up his hat and coat and went immediately to the report which was from Charles. He preferred Charles' reports over Bart's because they were a little more detailed and better written.

Although they were indeed in the area of the man-eater, the report said not much more. What bothered George the most was that the man-eater continued to sputter out life and he wanted it dead more than anything.

Charles was a lot more detailed in his letters to Victoria and told her everything that was happening. She longed for the letters that came on a weekly basis. Had George known the detail of the letters he probably would have confiscated them for his own purposes. She knew the situation with the man-eater would have to come to an end sooner or later and then things would be different. She still had anxiety about when she was going to tell her father about her love for Charles, but that would have to wait another day.

Winston had decided to move south to the next village about twenty miles away thinking that the tiger might have already moved south. The closest village was a small hamlet called Napith.

Bart was still oblivious to the missing man having been killed and wouldn't know for another hour when the men came running into the village with the news.

Bart wasn't sure what to do and his indecisiveness was seen by the others as weakness. The sun was beginning to set and he didn't have much time but he gave orders to move out. Most of his men remaining were scared, even to the point of trembling. When he told them that he would lead they still seemed hesitant until he cajoled them, and then he was able to get the two bravest to follow him.

He and the two others backtracked down the trail they had come moving quickly with the waning light. The men who had found the blood had said that it was about a forty minute walk. Slowly they made their way up the trail, cautious at every turn. It was still hot and sultry, and the jungle with a man-eater so close provided all kinds of sounds and shadowy sights that played on one's mind.

Bart was careful when he got close to look for the signs because he did not want to pass up the spot. Then just after turning a bend on the trail he came across the blood smears on the elephant grass just off the trail. The grass was trampled where the tiger had dragged the victim off. The man-eater had eaten for about an hour and then had gone off to get a drink and sleep, but it was very likely that it wouldn't be far.

Bart's heart began thumping twice as loud and hard as before and he paused to gather in the surroundings and take a deep breath. Then he slowly started to follow the trail as there was just enough light. As he moved forward he could see areas where blood had congealed when the tiger stopped for a rest.

It took him close to fifteen minutes to go forty yards as the sweat poured off his face even though the mountain air was chilly. His assistants followed closer than ever and there was no doubt in Bart's mind that they would run pell-mell back to the village at the first sign of trouble.

They continued to inch further on. Then they came upon the body, or what was left of it. It was like the scene of some operation gone bad as entrails were oozing out of the opened stomach area, and bare bones were sticking up into the air. The cat had been feeding on the buttock area and the flesh from the back of the legs. When that was finished it had turned the body over and had begun feeding on the stomach. The scene was ghastly.

Bart had stopped and was looking around for any signs of the tiger. The other two men were holding handkerchiefs over their mouths as the stench was hitting them.

Ironically it wasn't the slight sound of a cracking twig that woke the tiger a few hundred yards off, it was the smell of the men themselves that woke it. It instantly gave a silent snarl as it got to its feet sniffing the air trying to determine the direction of the smell. It could see easily in twilight as the moon rose over the horizon. Silently, like a Japanese ninja, it started back to its kill, always looking this way or that for any sign of danger, confident as the darkness was only minutes away.

Bart wasn't sure what to do. He had come this far and he didn't want to retreat, but it was the best thing to do under the circumstances. There was only a couple of hundred yards that separated the tiger from Bart, but while the tiger was able to gauge the distance based on the smell, the men had no idea where the cat was.

Just when things looked bad for Bart, some monkeys spotted the tiger on the prowl and gave their shrieking calls. At first it was to the south of them but soon the entire troop were calling from every direction, and it was impossible to hear anything. The tiger picked up its pace, confidently moving closer with every second. Bart knew it was close and had already pulled the hammers back on his gun and had it readied, trying to determine where the attack would come from. The two other men were ready to bolt at a moment's notice, and would have already if it weren't for the protection of Bart's gun. Then without notice the loudest roar any of them had heard was piercing the night as it came from within a hundred yards. It seemed to shake the very ground they were on. It was incredibly loud. The cat had decided to vocalize its displeasure.

The roar of a tiger, or any other big cat, produces an incredible sound wave capable of traveling for miles. The low bass sound is distinct, and every animal knows it. It drowned out the monkeys and even they stopped their alarm cries as they scampered to a safer distance. The tiger knew exactly where the men were. No one could describe the fear that came upon all men once the roar was heard. They knew exactly how close the cat was and that, coupled with the recent sight they had seen, drove fear into their very souls. Hearts were beating faster, nerves were on edge, sweat saturated their clothing and on one of the locals, pee ran down his leg.

The tiger kept a close but safe distance as they retreated back to the main trail. It wasn't long before one of the men couldn't take it any longer. The tension, the anxiety, the fear got to him and he turned and bolted back to the village as fast as he could run. Bart grabbed the other man to make sure he didn't bolt as well. Bart yelled at him that if he wanted to stay alive, they needed to keep together and work as a team. They were no longer the aggressor's looking to kill the man-eater, but now they were on the defensive, just trying to stay alive.

As they retreated, every noise, every movement real or unreal was indicated in the constant changing of heads to this way or that trying to see what was coming. But the tiger knew exactly where they were at all times. Bart knew instinctively that he was going to be lucky to get out of this alive. With a fear that suddenly grips those who know they are about to die, he was facing death with great fortitude, yet he still managed to work his retreat, trying to extricate himself from the danger.

They had now found the trail and could move more easily. They picked up the pace and began running and then walking when they needed to catch their breath. When they rounded a bend in the trail, they could see a slipped footprint where a man had fallen. When they got a little farther they came across a body lying in the middle of the trail. No doubt it was the servant who had bolted earlier. The tiger had followed him and picked him off easily. There was still enough light to see that red crimson blood was still oozing out of a large cut on his neck.

The men had stopped dead in their tracks, not knowing what to do, afraid of an ambush and paralyzed with fear. There was no decision on what to do, was it waiting for them? Or had it just made the kill and returned to the jungle as stealthily as it had come?

Bart had both hands on a death grip on the gun ready to fire at close quarters. Then they heard the snarl, a sound as if from hell itself, letting everyone know that it was still close and most certainly didn't approve of their presence. The men had their hearts take a double beat and sweat was pouring off their faces. They knew the cat was close and had them at its mercy.

The blood from the dead man was coagulating on the trail.

Bart needed to do something, anything, and quick or they were both dead men. He quickly told his servant to stand beside him at all times where possible since he was the only one with a gun. They moved towards the fallen man and quickly stepped over him and continued down the trail. Bart discharged his gun into the jungle where he thought he heard a sound. Deep inside he hoped the sound would scare away the striped cat. He quickly emptied the one empty chamber, as acrid gun smoke slowly wafted up to his nostrils, the smoke making a snake like movement visible in the night air.

As quickly as he could, he re-loaded the gun barrel inserting the large cartridge from a stitched row of them on his shirt. The gun was closed with a slight metallic click as he instinctively reached and felt his hunting knife on his hip. He pulled the released hammer back on the gun.

The tiger continued to prowl on the outskirts of the two men, occasionally making a noise here or there. It was unconcerned about the danger. It was in its element, jungle, semi- darkness, and it knew it had the upper hand. The men continued down the trail as quickly as they dared without turning to an all-out run. The cat continued to follow them. Sometimes they thought they had seen a black cat cross the trail in front of them, but it was difficult to tell for sure. The men could tell they were being followed for there were animal alarm calls from off the trail. It seemed like an eternity to them but they plodded on always looking for where the attack would come. Their shirts were soaked with sweat from the nerves. It was all Bart could do to keep from running for he knew they would be dead men if they did.

It seemed like it went on for eternity. The men were constantly looking into the shadows for an attack, and the anxiety of death on the doorstep caused them to almost give up from sheer exhaustion.

For some odd reason the tiger did not attack them, but allowed them to retreat. It was only when they saw the lights of the village that they realized they may have escaped death. As soon as they reached the village they both collapsed from exhaustion.

Winston had assumed that the cat would try to distance itself as much as possible from the village and the strange occurrences there, even with a slightly injured foot. He thought it might show itself further south and the hamlet of Napith sounded like a good start. He told Charles that they would start for the small hamlet as soon as possible.

While they were marching there Charles took the time to brief Winston about Bart, whom he knew they would meet sometime soon.

"Winston, I've got to tell you about Bart, the hunter from South Africa."

Winston spoke up, "Let me guess. The man is egotistical?"

"I would say so," replied Charles.

"Crotchety?" asked Winston.

"Most assuredly," replied Charles.

"Peevish?"

"Yes, I would say that too," replied Charles.

"Well I must say, a man just like myself. I think it would be wise to keep some distance between the two of us, don't you agree?"

"A prudent move, Winston, you're as wise to social matters as you are to the jungle."

"Thank-you, I'll take that as a compliment."

The march to Napith was a long one, but they were getting used to the long marches and it was important to try to keep abreast of the tiger. It had taken them most of the day to cover the distance they needed to get to Napith and when they arrived Bart and his men were still in the village having, returned last evening from the unfortunate accident.

Bart was aroused by curiosity as many villagers were running to meet Winston and thank him for coming. When he found out who it was, he knew that they would have to meet sometime, and the sooner the better. He got up and followed the throng to where Winston and Charles were coming into the village.

Charles saw him first and went over to say hi. Winston could see a large man who stood heads above everyone else and followed.

Charles shook hands with Bart and then introduced Winston by saying, "Bart Hawthorne, this is Winston Jamison the third."

The men shook hands and Winston's hand was immediately enveloped within the giant hand. Bart tried to squeeze his hand harder than normal as a show of strength, but Winston had anticipated such a move and held a tight grip as well. The grips were much tighter than usual.

Bart sought to establish who was in charge between the two of them by saying, "So, you're the man that's tried and failed to rid this country of the so called Katagi man-eater, I've heard of you, but I'll state right away that I'm the one who was hired to finish the job".

Winston had no time for such games and he answered in the only way he knew how, which was direct and to the point.

Everyone was watching what was going to happen next as Winston said,

"Look I understand you've got a big head because of a request for your assistance here to rid this country of a plague which is a very smart tiger, but you've got to get a few things straight in that thick skull of yours before you try to give out orders like your king George himself."

Bart began to speak but was immediately cut off by Winston again.

"First of all, I don't give a damn who in the hell you are, how far you've come, or what you have done to get this assignment. Second, you haven't got a clue as to what's going on here. This is not Africa, it is India and everything is different here. There's no open plains and there's certainly no savannah.

It's the true jungle and you sir, have no experience in hunting in this type of terrain. Third, I'm in charge here and if you don't like it get out of my way."

Sweat was coming off the forehead of Winston but he didn't care. Bart began ranting himself, but every time he brought something up, Winston was countering it with facts and figures or why that way would get someone killed. It was amazing he could think so quick while yelling at the same time.

Bart had rarely had anyone speak to him that way and it was apparent that he was baffled. His frustration was beginning to feed his temper. He had to save face somehow. With each sentence Winston was dishing out, he became more and more agitated. His face was actually turning red with rage.

Finally he grabbed Winston's heavy cotton jacket with his enormous hand pulling him closer to his face and said, "Look here professor, I've been sent here to do a job you couldn't do and I'll be damned if I take any orders from you."

He was in the process of saying more when Winston brought up his knee with all the force he possessed and slammed it into Bart's groin hard enough to have every man in sight who had seen it wince with sympathetic pain. Bart let out a long loud groan and instantly let go of Winston.

He was still doubled over when Winston raised himself up, pointed his finger at him and very forcibly said, "Don't ever touch me again," and began to walk away.

Bart was yelling at him and wanted to get to him, but he was still in a lot of pain and the people would have separated the two as well. Bart continued to yell out threats to Winston who kept walking.

Charles caught up to him and said, "Well, that went over well," as Winston eyed him and both men began laughing. Winston spoke up "You know the more I get to know people, the more I like man-eating tigers". Both men laughed again. Winston said that they needed to add cantankerous to the list of redeeming qualities Bart possessed. Winston went on to explain that Bart had him by fifty pounds and probably a four inch reach as well.

"But you've got to be like the honey badger," he said, "If you're going to go down, you may as well go down swinging, doing a bit of damage yourself. You'll respect yourself a lot more in the future.

"I was in Calcutta once, out too late, probably drinking too much. It was in my younger days," he glanced back towards Bart's direction, "anyway, walking home late one night, I came across a young serving waitress, probably no more than eighteen, being gang raped by four men. It was in a back alley, and I happened to glance down it and saw the whole thing happening by the light of the moon which was directly overhead. The girl's shirt was ripped off and she was trying to cover up as much as she could. I could have kept walking, minding my own business you know, but I just couldn't let that happen. The men were sailors, probably on leave from some sailing ship, just a step above pirates. I figured I would probably die but I was young and foolish…. well I got pretty angry, so I rushed in taking them on, trying always to keep myself on one side of the rest of them so I wouldn't be fighting on two fronts. Well, I knocked the first guy out, just clobbered him, but the others got me and beat me to a bloody pulp. Broke my nose and gave me two black eyes. In fact, my orbital lobe was severely cracked with my eye hanging out a bit, my jaw was broken, the girl, during the fray, had managed to escape and I was of course unconscious and never heard from her, but I respected myself for getting involved against overwhelming odds. I never regretted it."

Charles' only response was, "Wow, you've probably had more scraps than anyone I know."

"Well, probably not," replied Winston, "but I'll tell you this: it's not whether you win or lose, but that you do the best you can and you can respect yourself."

Charles later gathered information that two of Bart's men were killed by the tiger and that they had gone after it a day earlier. The cat was last seen or heard from about twelve miles to the south. Charles relayed the news to Winston who wasn't surprised.

They pulled out the map and began to look at it again. Winston said that it's likely no one was retrieving the bodies, so the tiger would likely feed on at least one of them for the next day or two. He began to say that they could bring in a tracker and track it out or maybe get a beat going and try to force it into the open somewhere, but in looking at the map there weren't a lot of clear openings as they were in an area that was pretty thick with the vegetation and much of it was still green. He was beginning to think the beat wasn't such a good idea.

"If we can track it, and maybe somehow get to it without it knowing, we could kill it when it's feasting, or if we're lucky when its sleeping during the day. The attack happened last night. If we hurry, we can get to the scene and get a chance at a shot before nightfall. We may have to find a tree for the rest of the night if we don't have time to get back, but if we're lucky we just might come across it while it's busy eating."

Charles was tired but agreed that it was a good plan as the tiger might just be hanging around the victim. They started to make plans immediately and asked for a local tracker, got a quick bite to eat and some food they could pack, and were off. Both men were very tired from the morning's hike but an opportunity like this didn't come around all that often.

They pretty much left in haste. Bart had seen them leave and was wondering what they were up to. He wanted desperately to get even with Winston, but that would have to wait now.

Winston and Charles had packed light for speed and were walking at a brisk pace. They still had several hours of daylight left and wanted to make the most of it. It wasn't long before they spotted the blood on the trail. Winston motioned for Charles and the tracker to follow him and they continued down the trail.

Not far down the trail, the tracker identified the spot of the first kill, and they left the well-worn trail to venture into the thick jungle. The grass was still matted down where the victim was dragged. It wasn't hard to follow the trail, so Winston took the lead and they proceeded very slowly in order to avoid causing any sound. Winston found it odd that there were also a second set of pug marks smaller than the man-eaters and was wondering if a leopard or another tiger was drawn by smell to the kill. Winston was still confident as the wind was against them and the scent of their sweating bodies was not being carried in the direction of the kill.

It took almost a half an hour to go 150 yards, but Winston wasn't taking any chances. They were very careful, and Winston told them by motioning his hands to step in exactly the same footsteps he was making so as to not make any noise. They knew that it wasn't far to the next kill from the description of Bart's servant. Winston instinctively pulled the hammers back on his gun while cupping his hands over them to muffle any clicks.

Winston would try to see ahead as much as possible through several blades of grass before advancing, trying to keep hidden, but yet trying to see or catch a glimpse of the tiger before it saw him. Something was going to happen, and Winston had the hair on the back of his neck stand on end. He peered through some blades of grass and could see the body of the first victim lying about twenty yards ahead of them. Charles was next in line and his heart was beating twice as fast as usual.

As Winston was trying to get a better look through the grass, he noticed something move near the body. As he caught the movement, he realized that the man-eater had been eating the victim from the far side. Due to the slight downward slope the cat had gone unnoticed when Winston first peered through the grass. Now it had raised its head which had been partway concealed as it was eating into the body and was covered with blood. It smelled the men and raised its head more and began a slow menacing snarl that stopped the men dead in their tracks.

Winston was at a disadvantage because he was not in a shooting position and wasn't sure if he could bring the gun to bear in time before the cat attacked him. He tried to bring it up slowly while kneeling. The cat snarled some more. Its head was huge, but it also wasn't more than twenty feet from them.

Winston decided to quickly bring the gun up for a shot and when he did so, the cat jumped up as well and made for dense cover to the side. The explosion of the gun was deafening to the ears and Winston didn't have a good shot as the cat was moving quickly to his left, but he took a chance firing off both barrels in quick succession. Normally he was a dead eye shot, but this time both bullets passed just over the cat by inches as Winston was still kneeling and the terrain had sloped downward where the man-eater had jumped.

Winston immediately jumped up and went forward quickly to see if there was any blood. He was there in a second, there was no sign of blood and the cover was thick. He ordered everyone back to the main trail as fast as they could. Once there he told them to look for a tree they could climb and to make it quick.

He guarded their backs as they moved down the trail. There was a large tree off the path about fifty yards and it didn't take long to decide it was the right one. They made for it quickly, knowing the cat could attack any moment. They had had the presence of mind to bring some rope with them. The tracker climbed up first with the rope since he was probably the best tree climber. It only took him a minute to get high enough but it seemed like an hour.

Winston and Charles both had their backs to the trunk of the tree and were looking for anything out of the ordinary. Charles went next and had the benefit of the lowered rope as he ascended about twenty-four feet up. Finally it was Winston's turn as he started climbing. Charles held his gun at the ready in case anything happened. Winston was finally up and they felt a lot safer for the moment.

It was difficult to determine whether the cat knew where they were, but Winston thought that it did and had been watching them. All of them took a deep breath as they tried to get comfortable in the tree. Winston figured they would have to spend the night at the very least to make sure the tiger had left the area and there was no guarantee on that point.

It had been a very close cal, Winston had been surprised at having glanced at the scene of the kill and initially not seeing anything had assumed the tiger wasn't there, but the tigers head was raised and looked directly at him which sent shivers down his spine. If only things were slightly different he could have had a better angle to shoot, but there always seemed to be "what if's".

The men's heart rates started to subside as they ate the remaining food from the small pack they had brought. It was going to be a long night. Winston seemed to be the only one able to catch any sleep while in a tree without falling. The other two had caught themselves just before losing their balance. Charles and the tracker used the rope they had brought to tie themselves in as a safety. They knew they wouldn't be able to keep from falling asleep that night.

Winston thought that there might be a slim chance that he could get a shot off if the tiger came closer to investigate but the foliage was just too thick.

It seemed to take forever for nightfall to come as they chatted about world events. The sun finally set, spreading its last rays throughout the sky. The night was passed in the safety of the branches, although the men shared it with a few monkeys who didn't know what to think of the new troop that had taken over their tree.

After a long night and what seemed like an eternity for Charles, who had never spent that much time in such an uncomfortable position, the sun began spreading its rays of light before showing itself. It was a beautiful sunrise and the men looked at its impressive beauty.

Winston wanted to wait at least a couple of hours just in case the tiger was still prowling the area, but after an hour they heard the unmistakable sound of many feet marching in cadence.

The elite Indian guard had made its way into the area and was marching north to the area nearest to where the tiger had last been reported, which information had been supplied by Bart in his last dispatch. They had already been traveling for two days when they had gotten the latest report by telegraph just the night before.

Winston and Charles began to descend from the tree with the sound of the approaching soldiers who were marching two abreast in perfect formation. There seemed to be a song they were singing that echoed throughout the jungle. Winston hurried over to the trail to try and find out what was going on.

The man in charge was in the front and when Winston halted them the man gave some orders for the men to take a rest. It was at this time that Winston and Charles found out that the Viceroy had ordered them up to the area to seek out and kill the man-eater. Both men could see that it was the imperial guard (from the patches on their sleeves) that had been sent out and Winston knew first hand that it would be impossible to convince them to turn around. Charles informed them that the man-eater was in the area last night and would likely be very close. The man in charge showed no concern about the news and was just determined to fulfill his orders.

The large group would at least offer Winston and Charles the protection of a large body in getting back to the village.

In asking the commander how the troops planned to kill the beast, they found out that they were planning a drive with the men and they would have the sharpshooters up on elephants. Winston knew that they would have to send for the elephants, and it would take at least a day or two.

They followed the troops back to the village arriving in the afternoon without incident.

The imperial guard commander met with Bart there, who had done nothing during the day, and somehow Bart convinced the commander to have a prime view as one of the shooters on the mahout atop one of the elephants.

The commander had felt they would use the village as a command center, so he had ordered his men to set up their tents just outside the village. The village itself could not hold all the men and Winston and Charles kept their hut, and Bart and his company had occupied the remaining available huts. Of course, the commander ordered one family out of their hut just for his officers and the family had to double up with friend just to find a place to sleep.

Messages had been relayed to bring in some working elephants from the sugar cane fields about forty miles away. It would take them at least a day to get there.

The troops had begun setting up camp with the military precision of a well organized unit. Many of the soldiers were seasoned and had fought together often. They did not fear the man-eater, probably because they found strength in the unit and in numbers, but they would soon find out what fear was.

The tiger had learned when and where to attack its victims. If it had learned one thing that had kept it alive, it was that the men who had tracked it down were trying to kill it. It had been surprised by Winston near its kill and that was something it wasn't used to. There seemed to be no rest for it from the previous year to now.

It moved in a western direction that day and although its foot was healing well, it didn't move fast, and it would probably be another week before it healed completely. It seemed that the quiet days of yester years were gone and it would continue to be hunted until it was eliminated.

The first night it did make some good distance and it had also managed to get some additional distance the day before. As it continued to move, it suddenly came across another menacing tigress that blocked its way to the west. It tried to move around her but she was very aggressive and a fight ensued. The man-eater was heavier and had more strength and experience, but it was a cat fight to the death. The tigress was constantly being the aggressor and after several encounters was starting to get some serious wounds. The man-eater itself was not devoid of serious wounds either as it was bleeding in several places where the tigress had scored with her claws.

It soon became apparent why the tigress had such fury as two mature cubs were seen watching through some Asian thorn bushes. The tigress was trying to protect them as they were older cubs but still too young to hunt on their own. The fight became vicious as each tiger went for the other. Both beasts were getting tired, but the man-eater had more stamina as it didn't have to share its kills with two nearly grown cubs. It didn't take much longer for the man-eater to end the fight. In moments, the tigress which had defended her cubs to her death , was being held by her throat in the death grip. Such is life in the jungle and if something can't survive, it will die. The tigress was doing what it should have knowing that the male was a threat to her cubs and she defended them to the very end. The man-eater finally released its hold on the tigress and dropped it to the ground lifeless as the dirt it fell on. The cubs looked on as the man-eater's eyes met theirs, but it had no fight with them and they, being inexperienced, wouldn't have a chance with it, and so the man-eater moved on, its face the color of red roses.

How many encounters had it had in its existence now? How many individuals had it sent to other worlds? Yet it prowled on, only thinking in the present, fearing nothing, not planning for a future as humans would, only contemplating one thing: survival. The cubs were barely starting to hunt and still relied on their mother. Whether they would survive no one knew, but they were at an extreme disadvantage now. If they learned quickly to kill perhaps they would defy the odds, but the jungle shows no mercy. Those that do live have learned to survive.

The military commander had sought out Bart because he was instructed to work with him, obviously from orders from Javier. Bart was pleased with the help but unsure on how to use the extra manpower. It was suggested to him that the troops could be used in a forced push to flush out the cat if they knew specifically where it was.

Winston instructed Charles to go over to where they were looking over a map to try and find out what was up. Since Charles and Winston were the last to see the cat, Bart needed the latest information from them as well. Charles had the ability to get along well with everyone, and although he really disliked Bart, he kept his feelings to himself. After all, if they all survived this ordeal, he may end up being his father-in-law.

Bart asked Charles exactly where he had last seen the tiger. Since this was by now common knowledge, he felt ok about telling him. After finding the spot on the map, Bart determined they had four choices from the compass to choose from and it was anyone's guess where the cat would head now.

As they were discussing where the cat would be next, Winston joined in on the group and spoke up, mentioning that the cat would most likely go to where it had been before. There was some awkward silence among the group as no one was sure what to say.

Charles picked up the cue and said, "Yes, it was in the area to the west here just two years ago, and it may favor the area because it's got knowledge of the terrain. There were several deaths there and it may find the killing easy as it has done it there before."

Winston and Bart were staring at each other being only separated by a table. Bart finally broke the silence by saying that the terrain certainly favored its going up one of the valleys.

Winston spoke again saying, "Mr. Hawthorne is correct. He must have coprolite in his brain, as the most likely path the cat would take would be up these two valleys," pointing to a section of the map.

He spoke again, as everyone valued his opinion.

"If you were to find out which of the two valleys it chose, you could organize a beat in that valley and perhaps come off with good chances for a shot or two."

Everyone seemed to be nodding at this point. The commander spoke next and said they could start first thing in the morning. He looked at the map for the nearest village to where the two valleys were and then said that Hataru would serve as their base camp.

Charles found it odd that Winston was helping them so much and, having come to know Winston as he had in the last few months and perhaps understanding him more than anyone else, wondered what angle he had.

Winston spoke up again and suggested that they get a couple of trackers to check out the soft sandy soil here and here, pointing again to areas on the map. They would need to get them going immediately because they would need the information as to which valley it was in by tomorrow morning.

The commander was no stranger to the legend Winston possessed and knew that his wisdom was greater than anyone else's in the jungle and in hunting man-eaters, so he suggested that he could spare a few soldiers with weapons to protect the trackers in the man-eaters territory. The arrangements were made but they had only the one tracker at hand. They would need to pick up another on the way in Hataru. Winston indicated they could rendezvous tomorrow afternoon at four o'clock at Hataru and then left.

Bart was unsure of what to make of the whole situation but was determined to get a prime shooters angle for the cat.

Charles left the group as well and followed Winston. After catching up to him he put his hand on his shoulder and asked what was up.

Winston, looking over his shoulder to ensure that no one was near, told him, "There's no use in discouraging them. They will be hunting the cat whether we like or not and we may yet use them to our advantage. In any event, it doesn't matter who kills the beast so long as it's dead. It's been killing a person every three or four days and the sooner we can rid the country of the cat the better. More families can rest assured that there will be no more killings, and like I said, we may still be able to use them to our advantage."

Charles replied, "You know, you surprise even me at times. Just when you think you know someone they go and surprise you. Let me ask you this: did you send me over to that group first to diffuse the situation with you and Bart?"

"Well, that may be partly true, but you do have to understand how to work together without letting others know you are working together, if you know what I mean. You'll perhaps learn these tricks for yourself and not make half the mistakes I've made."

Charles spoke again, "Well, if you're so wise Solomon, can you tell me what to do with Victoria?"

A sly smile came over Winston's face as he exclaimed, "Well, if you must ask, in all my fifty-five years of existence, I haven't quite figured women out yet."

Both men smiled and laughed.

The morning found the military camp in chaos and Bart's group not much better. Winston wanted to get to Hataru earlier but thought traveling in a smaller group to be unwise. They were going to tag along with the Viceroy's troops.

Before they left, Bart had managed to get a hold of the mail that the troops had brought up from Bombay. In the mail bag were several letters from Victoria addressed to Charles. Bart had told the deliverer that he would deliver the letters personally to Charles, and instead he had briefly held them to his nose as the sweet smell of lavender perfume wafted up through his nostrils. Without reading them he crushed them up and threw them into the evening fire where they were consumed.

Charles had no idea that the troops were carrying mail and so was oblivious as to what had been done. He had briefly thought that Victoria should have or would have written more than he had gotten already, but he put the thought aside thinking perhaps that she was not a letter writer.

The military troops were ready to move out at seven a.m. and were marching in cadence fifteen minutes later. There was safety in their numbers and it would allow everyone to reach Hataru safely that afternoon. There were some camp followers that also joined in bringing up the rear.

As they were hiking together, Winston pulled Charles aside and told him, "The beat is not going to work this time with the man-eater. It's very intelligent and will have learned from the last time we attempted it. We're going to use the beat and the soldiers to our advantage. They will most likely isolate the beast in one of the valleys, but I predict that it's going to try to break out early, probably as soon as it knows it's being pushed. It will wait for the right moment and break through the line. Our job is to try and figure out which side it will be on and try to intercept it. We can probably get on a mahout and position ourselves in the middle."

There was a pause as Winston was thinking.

"No, better yet, we can have a mahout on either side on the outskirts of the line towards the forward line. That way one of us is sure to get off a shot, and we'll have to make it count. There's a lot of cover in those valleys and the vegetation is still green. With any luck we'll probably only get one shot off."

Charles was preparing himself for the moment, trying to envision what was going to happen, getting himself mentally ready for the moment, as Winston had taught him. The thought of the perfect future shot came again and again to his mind and he rehearsed it over and over to make sure he would be ready.

There was no sign of Bart's group with the soldiers but there was no doubt he would be in the village as well. The soldiers kept formation and sang military songs as they hiked. They seemed like they enjoyed their work and were a tight knit unit, having worked years together. Everyone, including Winston, admired their discipline.

As the group was marching more and more people along the route fell in after them knowing that they could return that way in safety with the numbers.

Winston had more than the man-eater on his mind. He knew that it was far from over between himself and Bart and if it wasn't enough to try to outsmart the man-eater he had that imbecile as well. Secretly, he wondered if Bart had it in him to murder him if he had the chance and then try to say it was an accident. He kept his thoughts to himself.

Winston had the forethought to send a message ahead requesting two elephants on which he and Charles could be put on a mahout. Luckily this was a large agricultural area and working elephants were in large supply. They would most likely be pulled from the forests they were working, but the work would come to a standstill anyway once word got out that the man-eater was in the area. It seemed that news like that traveled much faster than anyone could carry it. Charles wondered to himself if that was how the director got his news before Charles reports.

As they marched along the narrow jungle path, they would at times have to be cut back foliage for a double passage of troops. The vines and trees still continued to dot the landscape they were in. The bright sunshine, the occasional pools of water and small streams all became part of a living jungle that was home to almost as many plants and animals as found anywhere else on earth.

There was a lot of ground to cover and the hike was quick paced. The military commander knew exactly the distance and how long it would take and set the pace accordingly.

The news had managed to travel throughout the region quickly and people were starting to gather in numbers for the beat. When the military group and the others arrived at Hataru that evening the trackers had already been there for several hours. They were lucky, for the tiger had gone the direction Winston indicated and the trackers had come back with some interesting news. They had found in the soft sand large pug marks which could only be the man-eater, indicating it had entered the south valley, but they also found fresh pug marks from another cat, possibly a tiger or a large leopard. From how fresh they thought the pugs were, they thought that both beasts might still be in the valley. The trackers had refused to enter the valley themselves.

There was a meeting held that night and everyone of importance was there. Many opinions were offered, and each person, having their own ego, was slowly raising their voices until they were near shouting. As the voices rose Winston had a long stout bamboo stick in his hand and without pausing in the least brought it down on the large map on the table. The whack was loud and distinct, and several men instinctively jumped back.

Winston spoke up and there was silence and respect. He said that due to the distance it had covered the tiger was likely to nap during the daylight hours in the valley, but if it was hungry enough it would prowl that night looking for the next victim, most likely at the nearest village. He gave his thoughts that the large military force in the village would discourage it from attacking. If it was still in the valley, they would need to have the beat at first light and suggested that they start at the high ground moving down the valley forcing it to continue on the path it had already chosen.

Winston had been over to talk to the trackers about the grass in the valley and how high it was. This was critical, he explained to Charles, because it would either give the cat as much cover as it wanted, thwarting any chance to see it, or on the other hand it would offer the men a better opportunity to see it at a distance. Winston thought that it would need to kill soon and wanted to get to the valley quickly before the cat went on the move and escaped the trap.

At the meeting Winston was showing deference in allowing Bart and his company and the military commander to have the most advantaged position at the bottom of the valley where the cat was expected to be flushed out. Winston suggested that he and Charles each take an elephant with a trainer and ride on the outside edges to make sure the line was kept and to guard against a breakout to the side. Winston thought, as he had mentioned to Charles, that as the cat had been through a couple of these beats already it would have learned that it needed to escape early. He knew that the cat was intelligent and would have learned from its mistakes.

After a few more minor points it seemed they were ready for the morning beat.

Villagers from around the area had been arriving in droves to the village. They were more than happy to be of service. As they were concluding the meeting Bart's right hand man came over to Charles and Winston and happened to mention that there was going to be a few boxing matches that night to keep the troops entertained, and asked if Winston would be willing to take on Bart for the final match. Charles began to oppose the idea based on weight alone as Bart had at least fifty pounds on Winston, but Winston stopped him immediately saying that he would accept.

"Queens rules I suppose."

"Yes, that's correct, but we will tape the hands with some padding. Be there by seven p.m."

Charles was aghast. After the man left he asked why he would accept such a match. Winston was at least twenty years older.

Winston thought a bit and said, "He's going to find me sooner or later. He's got a bigger ego than myself and he has a score to settle with me, and a man like him with all his pride won't sleep until he gets his revenge. There's no doubt he's been a boxer before and also that I'm out matched, but I hate those types and I'll do my damnedest to see that he's brought down to earth, literally, or I'll go down trying. You see Charles it's not whether you win or lose, its whether you can face yourself in the morning."

"If you say so, but what if you get hurt? Isn't the killing of the man-eater of utmost importance?"

"Sure, you have a great point, but look at the American civil war for example. A country divided cannot stand, I have to focus all my energies on killing the man-eater. I can't be watching my back all the time as well.

This way it will be over by tonight and we can get back to work. This cat is too smart to be trapped by the likes of those men. We're going to have to take it down and believe me it's not going to be easy. By the way, I'm sure the odds are in Bart's favor."

Winston pulled out his wallet and took out a ten pound note and handed it to Charles.

"Do something for me and put that on myself for me."

Charles raised an eyebrow but knew Winston well enough to know that there was no way he could change his mind, so he took the money and left. As he walked through the village, he could see out in the clearing a makeshift ring was being hastily constructed using two coconut trees. Charles thought about the ten pound note and why Winston had opted to bet on himself. Surely he didn't think he could win.

As he walked to the table where the bets were being made Bart was there as well. He asked for the odds, and when they came back to him as in Bart's favor he placed the note on the table before saying anything.

Bart spoke up and joked with him by saying, "Placing a wager tonight, huh, Charles?"

Charles told him flatly, "No, Winston asked me to put a ten pound on himself for the match tonight."

Bart was clearly upset but tried not to show it and stomped off.

Charles silently laughed within himself thinking, *that's clearly what he didn't want to hear.*

Charles couldn't help but notice that there were a lot of bets being placed on Winston. It looked like he was the favorite, being well known and liked in the country. There were far more bets being placed on that match than the others.

Charles went back to Winston's hut that was lent to him to see if he wanted to eat dinner before the match. When he got back there, Winston was sleeping like a bear in the middle of winter. He looked at his watch and there was still about three hours until the matches started, and since he was hungry and didn't want to disturb Winston, he went out looking for some food. He thought he would try something different and walked down to where the military personnel were cooking up their food. Since most of the men were native born they were having the usual rice.

The cook asked Charles if he wanted some and he said, "Sure, why not."

He had gotten used to the rice since arriving in the country, and although the other foreigners feigned to like it or at least tolerated it, he didn't mind having it although he preferred it fried, nevertheless, he ate it like everyone else. Some of the habits he picked up so easily that some would wonder if he had grown up in India.

He sat down with some of the red berets, as they all wore the same beret with their patch on the front. Many of them were educated and understood and could speak English, but they had a heavy accent.

After dinner he decided to write Victoria a letter. The words didn't come easily as there was a lot to say and putting his feelings into words was something that didn't come naturally. He looked out over the meadow as the torches were being lit and elephants milled at the far end of the clearing.

He thought he ought to wake Winston about an hour before his match and walked back to the hut. To his surprise Winston was up and eating and said that he didn't want to sleep too long for fear that he wouldn't be able to get to sleep that night. Deep down he knew that the fight would sap his strength and he would be out in minutes, probably nursing a massive headache.

"Should you be eating so close to your match?" asked Charles

"Not to worry, I'll be fine. Did you place my bet?"

"Yeah, right in front of Bart and I don't think he liked it."

"Well, at least he knows I think I can win."

"When do you want to head up to the ring?" asked Charles.

"About fifteen minutes before were scheduled to go out, but can you help me stretch in the mean time?"

"You know you're asking me to help you participate in activity designed to get you hurt?"

"Yeah, that's about it," replied Winston.

"Well, ok , I'm not going to babysit you."

In addition to the stretches that Charles helped him with, there was a local that came to the hut and offered a massage. Winston took her up on it and she worked wonders in loosening up worked muscles. In fact, the woman hadn't seen anyone Winston's age in such great shape physically.

Just before the fight someone came and asked if Winston needed an escort to the ring. He turned them away and told them that he would be there shortly.

Winston had stripped down to his khaki shorts as they were the only thing remotely proper for the fight. He did opt for coming to the ring in flip flops which he figured he would lose as the fight began because he was going to need to be fast on his feet and thought that bare feet would be better than his field boots. Charles had put the final touches on him by getting some coconut oil and lathering up his upper body so fists would glance off him.

Charles had forgotten how popular Winston was and when he walked into the area there was a great cheer from the men in the army and the locals who had gathered for the beat and the fight. There was no backing out now, not that Winston would do so anyway.

The earlier fight between the two military personnel was starting to finish up as Winston had his hands taped up. As the fight finished and one man was dragged out of the makeshift ring, Bart entered the ring to mild applause. He was shirtless and his barrel like upper body showed years of hard work as each muscle glimmered in the light of the torches. He was wearing his hiking boots as he probably had nothing else. He raised both hands over his head to try to gather support for himself and there was some applause as many of the men had bet on him looking at the weight difference as well as the reach he had. But when Winston ducked under the rope and entered the ring there was a much louder roar from men who supported him. He raised one hand to acknowledge them and went straight to his corner.

With a slow announcement of introductions the fight rules were explained and both men nodded that they understood them. There was a crude cow bell that announced when the fight began.

Winston began to come out slowly from his corner as Bart did so as well. When Winston was within about five feet he lunged, quicker than a mongoose, and landed a heavy right to Bart's jaw with the full force of his body. The blow was unexpected and knocked Bart to the ground, and raucous cheering erupted from the crowd. Bart felt his jaw and saw that there was blood on his hand. He wiped it off and got to his feet.

Winston knew he couldn't do that trick again but continued to dart in and out of reach as Bart tried to score a knockdown punch. Winston was quick on his feet as he was able to see the wind-up and anticipate the coming blow and get out of the way. Bart looked extremely sluggish compared to Winston as the first round came to a close.

When the cow bell signaled the start of the second round the crowd was already on its feet. They were here for the match and what a match it was turning out to be. There were a few blows to the body that Bart managed to land that showed Winston that he wasn't that young anymore. Bart seemed to put everything he had into each punch and as his weight came behind every one it was like a freight train.

Winston still managed to stay just out of harm's way for most of the time. He had clearly landed most of the punches and Bart's face was starting to bruise on the right side due to numerous quick blows. The second round had ended much the same as the first. They were only scheduled to go five and Bart was getting pretty exacerbated as time went on.

The third round came and people could see that both men were starting to get tired. Most people don't realize how much energy is used up in a single round and they had both done a pretty hardy hike in the morning as well.

Winston continued to dart in and out of Bart's range but he was starting to become a little less quick and a little more clumsy. Charles could see it and wondered how much longer he could last. The sweat from Winston's face was pouring from his forehead as he constantly wiped it away, and Bart was sweating even more as his shorts were nearly soaked.

Winston was trying to get as much water as possible but Charles wouldn't let him have too much.

The fourth round started and within a few seconds both men succumbed to fatigue as they had already spent their reserves. It was late in the round and Winston was connecting at will on Bart's face and body when Bart finally connected with a wild roundhouse that Winston didn't see coming. It hit him squarely in the side of the head and had enough force in it to knock Winston out and to the ground. There was a hush that fell over the crowd and people waited to see if Winston could recover, but it was not to be. Winston was running on reserves as it was, and the blow was enough to knock him out for a few minutes, enough for the count.

Charles rushed to his side with some water that relieved him. As he came to, he was jabbering and wondering if he had won. Bart was raising his hands in triumph though his puffy bloodied face surely looked like the losing end of the deal. Winston asked Charles to help him to the hut as the hunt was still scheduled to go on in the morning. He mentioned that he was really tired, and who could blame him as Charles put an arm around his neck and lead him away.

As he was leaving the crowd saw him and began chanting 'Winston, Winston, Winston,' first in a slow, barely perceptible chant, but then it grew louder to the bewilderment of Bart. Only a hero in his adopted country could still win the hearts of the people even when he had lost.

The money that was bet was distributed and the military men began to return to their tents as the locals dispersed as well. The rest of the evening was relatively quiet, although half the village was partially drunk.

The tiger had settled down during the day in the same valley the trackers had determined it had entered. It was a valley it had frequented early in its life soon after becoming a man-eater, and it was an area it was familiar with; a place where it felt comfortable, almost like a home. As it moved through the valley there was something that just didn't seem right to it, something different, something it could sense. It kept looking back where it had come from but it couldn't hear or smell anything out the ordinary. The valley was thick and full of vegetation and provided all the cover it desired and needed. After getting a long drink from the stream that slowly meandered down the valley, it retreated to a clump of bamboo where it weaved its way in and out of stalks until it was in the heart of the grove. Inside, there was just enough room to lay down in the cool shade the bamboo provided and sleep the day away. As it slept its tail instinctively recoiled back and forth shooing the flies away from its body. It had no idea that trackers had found its tracks and danger was converging on it with each passing hour. At twilight it would arise and search the nearest village for something to satisfy its hunger. The hours ticked away like sand falling through an hourglass and at last, it knew from the shadows that the time was right.

It was hungry and the prospect of another victim was making it salivate at the mouth. Like the ancient ninja warrior the tiger moved through the night without making hardly a sound. Each step brought it closer the village. The smoke from the cooking fires wafted through the jungle air and it could pick up the smell from miles around. With its keen sense of smell, it followed it, taking its time for there was no hurry.

The moon was just a slit in the night sky and darkness reigned. Within a couple of hours the cat was on the outskirts of a small village that only had twenty-two occupants in six rounded huts. It had learned to never venture in at first look, and so it patiently waited to see if anything looked out of the ordinary. It was patience, it had learned, that had managed to keep it alive all these years.

The minutes ticked by, one by one, until everything looked and smelled right. It began by prowling the back, in darker recesses of the huts, keeping hidden as much as possible. Some of the men of the small village had left to help in the beat that was scheduled for the next morning. There was little sound as most of the people were asleep. The last hut though still had a light on as one of the older women was still mending clothes under the light of a single candle. The tiger could smell the burning wax and came to investigate.

There were a couple of dogs in the village but they had been brought into the hut for fear of losing them to the tiger. Unaccustomed to spending the night indoors the dogs loved it and did not hear or smell the cat as it prowled close to the huts.

The big cat stopped at each hut and smelled to see what was inside. When it came to the last hut the light was visible through the slats. The old woman suddenly had a feeling that something was amiss and looked around her hut, but nothing seemed out of the ordinary so she continued on mending clothes. The tiger had been watching her in the candlelight and as it had not been discovered yet, continued to watch her.

She inadvertently dropped a needle onto her mat and cursed, knowing that it would be difficult to see with just the one candle as she grabbed it to give her more light. As she got down on her knees she instinctively looked out through the very small opening in the bamboo floor and she could see another eye looking in.

At first she thought she was seeing things but then it blinked and she knew it was real. There was nothing else it could be; the man-eater was looking in, staring at her. Before she could scream the cat was forcing its way into the hut. Slivers of bamboo were flying everywhere as it gnashed at any barrier preventing it. Its head first appeared poking its way in, teeth bared, and then the head turned to see her. Within a few seconds the body came through as well, like a snake shedding its skin. It had somehow brought its massive body through an opening just barely bigger than its head. The extreme fright had brought the old woman into a stoic trance as the cat pounced on her and quickly broke her neck and opened up her stomach with its rear claws.

The noise from the breaking up of the hut had woken up some people but with most of the men gone from the village, and no one with enough courage to venture out, the tiger was left alone. It picked up the woman in its jaws and laid her down next to the opening of the hut. It then went out head first and when it had done so, it reached back with a paw, with claws bared, and brought the woman's body closer to the opening. Finally it grasped her in its jaws again, and because she was so small it had no difficulty raising her off the ground, and moving with a graceful ease, it disappeared into the night like a thief makes off with stolen jewels.

Normally the man-eater would only drag its victim a short distance, but because the woman was so light, it took her further into the jungle. The wound on her stomach was fully opened and it made for a sight as the small intestine had protruded out and was being dragged behind the tiger. It was hungry and ate as much as could be eaten from the unfortunate victim. Within hours the deed was done and nothing but bones and the palms of the hands and soles of the feet were all that was left.

It was thirsty now and needed water. The only stream was in its favorite valley as it meandered down the hills and eventually into a small river about ten miles to the East. It didn't take long to get back to the valley, for it had spent a lot of time there, and after getting its fill of water it retired further up the valley to get some sleep. Little did it know that it was the same valley that had been designated for the beat the next day. The cat began to lick its fur from the blood that had discolored it and then stretched out in a bamboo thicket for a well-deserved rest.

The night hours in the village that was attacked dragged on like a watch mechanism that was always ticking but yet time seemed to stand still. Not that anyone had courage enough to venture out into the night and let Winston know of an attack. The tiger had eaten and had its fill, but that wouldn't make it so that it couldn't attack again if someone were to cross its path. Besides, the only ones with courage enough to make a small hike like that had already volunteered to help with the beat. So Winston and all the others had no idea an attack occurred that night.

Winston was awakened by his servant who always seemed to know when to wake him and at what time. People were starting to stir as they needed to get up and going before first light. There wasn't a lot of noise as everyone seemed to have a job to do and went about doing it.

There was a large black mark over Winston's eye, but Bart fared much worse. Not only did he also have a shiner, but his other eye was nearly shut as the swelling had forced it closed. His face looked like it had expanded as well, and looking at the two no one could tell you that Winston had been on the losing end of things. Everyone who saw Bart did a double take, but he barked orders to the others like he was in charge just the same.

Winston and Charles still had some time so they took a breakfast offered to them as the military commander and his sniper and Bart's group got going.

Winston thought that there was a good chance the tiger would be in the valley but had severe doubts about whether this group had what was necessary to kill the man-eater. Even with those doubts he wasn't so cocky as to think that he alone could kill it, it just needed to be someone in the right place at the right time. Besides, it didn't matter who killed it as long as it was dead. He alone had seen the heartache for a spouse or loved one who had been taken by a man-eater. The facts were that he had already killed two man-eating tigers, a man-eating tigress, and a man-eating leopard, and although many called him arrogant, Charles had seen him as a man who was not proud but humble and treated people the same as he himself was treated.

The hour of waiting time had passed for the first group to get into position and now it was time to move out. Winston and Charles both mounted their elephants before the handlers and were heading out along with an enthusiastic crowd. It didn't matter that they needed to be quiet as they would approach the valley coming from the opposite direction. But the others would need to make some noise in the beat to drive the tiger out.

It took them only an hour and a half to get to the top of the valley. The idea was to set up the men on foot with anything they could get their hands on and space them out about five to seven feet apart. Then they would all walk in a line as straight as possible down the valley, beating the brush and yelling as they went along to try to drive the cat out and down the funnel to the narrow end of the valley.

There was one path that ran along the side of the hill and another at the other side of the valley where the stream was. They could get an elephant on one trail, but they couldn't get another on the other side of the hill because it was too steep. Winston decided to send Charles and his elephant to the valley floor, and he would take the other on the trail and hopefully one of them could get a shot off.

The vegetation was still green in the valley and was thicker than they had hoped. As soon as everyone was in position a horn was sounded and the beat was begun. Bart and his company, and the military commander and his two best snipers were presumably already in position at the bottom of the valley guarding the escape routes.

The line was progressing slower than usual due to the difficult terrain, but nothing was getting through and it was starting to push animals ahead of it. The tiger had awoken as soon as it heard the horn blast, and having experienced this twice before, instinctively knew what was about to happen. It smelled the air for anything that was out of the ordinary. It looked in the direction of the blast but could not see anything yet as the distance was too great. It left the edge of the bamboo grove and darted to the next cover. There were other animals in the valley as well, and the push down the hills began funneling most of the animals present. As in other beats, the animals would only number a few at the beginning but after an hour there would be a constant number of various beasts running the gamut into Bart and the military commander's position. With their limited experience with the man-eater, it was likely that any big cat that ran into their view would be shot at.

It was still early in the beat and Winston didn't expect anything to happen for at least another hour when things got a little tighter for the tiger. It would have been better for it to try to escape earlier as the hills were higher and it was more difficult to keep the line together. It was a sheer coincidence that the man-eater had returned to this valley, the same valley that was chosen for the beat.

The push down the valley was now in the second hour and hills had become less steep and there were fewer obstacles to deal with. The military group stayed together on the western side of the valley and the locals mostly held the eastern side as they moved together down the slope. The tiger knew from experience the gap would get tighter and tighter and it knew it couldn't wait much longer. It had waited perhaps too long to escape as the men were coming on it now and there wasn't as much cover as before. It decided to wait on the outside edge of the valley in some dense elephant grass before making its move to escape.

There wasn't much distance separating the end of the valley from the beaters and many of the animals were running through the opening between Bart's group and the commander's group. Tensions were at the height when a young tiger burst into the opening going at a slower speed while looking back. Bart was closest and saw it first. He lowered his sights and put the bead just on its chest as it was still moving. Everything had seemed to him to slow down as moments went by with repeated instinct forming each and every move he had made. There was a sense of relief when the cat went down from his first shot and he felt that he had accomplished his mission. The shot was heard from everyone as it rang into the morning air like a cannon blast. The tiger fell forward collapsing on its front paws and rolling over head long into the soft, sun baked dirt. Death was instantaneous as Bart was a crack shot. Only Bart's group and the commander and his sharp shooters witnessed the scene as it unfolded. With the cat down and blood oozing from its fatal wound, guns were lowered and tensions eased. It was then, without warning, that something unexpected happened, surprising Bart and the commander with his sharpshooters. Seemingly out of nowhere there appeared a second tiger as it sprinted past the dead tiger. It was as if it had a second sense for the situation because it briefly paused and looked directly at Bart for a small millisecond before guns were raised again. Before a shot could be fired it looked like it had gone into a bamboo thicket, but there was a lot of elephant grass too so they weren't sure.

The shot has caused everyone to momentarily stop. There were still animals running the gauntlet and coming into view and both Bart and the commander with his men stayed on the elephants and readied themselves focusing on the bamboo clump.

The man-eater had waited in the cover of the bamboo and had not made any attempt to escape, it knew from previous experience not to run, and so it waited. It wasn't long before the beat continued and the sounds became clearer and closer. Within a few minutes the man-eater would be able to see the men making the snakelike line come into view. It was on the far end of the valley and the military men had that point of the line, and Charles was on his elephant on that side as well. The sounds were growing louder still and instead of making the man-eater run from them, it began to agitate it as it paced back and forth in the bamboo, still concealed but trying to look at what was coming. With such a large clump of bamboo, there was no doubt that some men would inspect it to make sure nothing was hiding in it. As the valley opened up Winston mounted his elephant and continued just behind the line of men making the beat.

The men and the noises were drawing much closer to the tiger and it could see some of the men now. It stopped pacing and just focused on what it saw. Bart tried to get them to focus on the bamboo where he saw the tiger enter. The men were just slightly ahead of Winston and his handler with the elephant. As they approached to within twenty yards of the bamboo, the man-eater had no choice but to attack. It came out of the grove with lightning speed and was already on one man within a few seconds. Many were expecting nothing because most of the animals were running ahead of them from the noise, so it was a complete surprise. The man that was attacked was already badly mauled, and panic and fear spread across the line from those closest to the victim.

Bart could not fire without endangering the men as flashes of tiger and men mixed like rain and snow.

Winston heard the commotion but from his angle behind the elephant's head could not get in a good position to shoot. The tiger left the first man as he crumbled to the earth, lifeless, and in a split second seized upon the next hapless soldier in the line. The frenzy and chaos that ensued caused some of the men to open fire at the tiger, not aiming but just getting a shot off as their fear engulfed them. Each bullet narrowly missed the big cat, but with more than one bullet whizzing through the air, there was an accident waiting to happen. As shots went flying one of them hit a soldier on the other side of the tiger as the line of men were still somewhat close and he happened to be on the opposite side of the tiger as the firing started. For a few seconds it was mayhem and pandemonium as soldiers jockeyed to get out of the way and were running away.

The tiger left the second man and made for the hill where cover was abundant. It had broken through the line and was running as fast as it could run. It darted first one way then another as it leaped over bushes or downed trees. It still had about thirty yards to cover before it came to thicker brush. By this time Winston had got the handler to calm the elephant down and had put himself in a better position for a shot before the man-eater reached the thicker foliage.

Winston carefully put the bead of his gun on the breast of the man-eater as it was darting for cover, careful to lead it with the speed it was covering. Just as he was squeezing the trigger the elephant changed positions again as the shot rang out. It was just enough of a movement to place the bullet just between the outstretched legs of the tiger. The next shot a second later hit the rear leg on the man-eater and passed clean through, having hit it in a fleshly part between the tendons and doing little damage other than to let the blood come out. But the impact made the tiger reel and tumble. Winston thought he had got it even though the second shot was rushed. To his dismay the tiger got up immediately after going down and darted into cover just as several shots rang out from the military men, but none were well placed and all were a little slow as they fell harmless to the rear of where the tiger had entered the cover.

Winston knew from the size of the cat that it was the man-eater. The rest of the military men were tending to the three wounded men. The man in the first attack was already dead with a broken neck. The second man was holding on and the third man, who was wounded by the bullet, looked like he might survive as it had missed his heart, however he was in a lot of pain.

Everything was over within a few seconds and took most of the group by surprise. Winston had thought something like this might happen. He had already dismounted from the elephant and was rushing to inspect the spot of the hit. The grass was a little high and it was still possible the tiger could be close. Winston inspected the spot where the shot had found its mark and discovered some splattering of blood on the grass. This was bad news for him as it indicated a shot that had passed clear through carrying much of the blood as it went. He followed the trail for a little while, seeing a drop of blood here and there, but the terrain was beginning to get thicker and it just didn't feel good to continue. He had a bad vibe about pressing on.

He realized with the blood being more and more spotty the cat probably just had a superficial wound. The chances were that it could still travel well and wasn't as hurt as he had hoped. There was a very good possibility that it would survive, and to make matters worse a wounded tiger was a lot more dangerous as well. He concluded from the speed it had kept moving into the cover that it was going to be fine within a few days. The whole beat had produced more than he thought would actually happen and he was surprised at the outcome, although disappointed.

He rejoined Charles at the bottom of the valley as he had come over as soon as the shots started firing. When they met up, Winston told him that he had missed on the first barrel and hit it with the second, but that it was only slightly wounded. Charles was amazed that he had missed at all and asked what happened on the first shot, knowing that they were good enough friends and that he would tell him the truth.

"On, the elephant, its bloody head was in the way and by the time we got it turned around the cat was going at a pretty good pace. I still may have gotten it if the elephant hadn't shifted slightly and threw off the aim just at the last second. Anyway, I wasn't expecting a shot at all."

"Well, should we follow the men down to see what the other shot was all about?" asked Charles.

"It was probably Bart mistaking the man-eater for a monkey that had bared its teeth," said Winston.

They walked down to where most of the men were and it was no surprise to see that Bart had left already.

At first, he was excited to have killed the man-eater, but when he saw the second cat he had some doubts. When he got down to inspect the killed tiger, he knew from the smallness of the beast that it could not possibly be the man-eater. The adrenaline had gotten to him and in the excitement he had killed an unsuspecting tiger. He didn't want to stick around and have people point out his mistakes, so he just up and left, and his assistants left with him.

Winston eventually got to where the cat was laying and looked over the beautiful beast. He was told what had happened and that another tiger was spotted soon after this one was shot, but that it had escaped. Winston explained to the others that it was a young cat, probably just a year old. The orange colors were still vivid in its coat and the canines were still growing and were only about two and a half inches long.

He started the long process of skinning the cat, which only a few individuals present knew how to do properly. Later they would peg out the skin to let it dry at the village.

The military commander had remained to let Winston know what had happened. It was pretty much as Winston had expected and nothing came as a surprise. The commander was concerned about his men who had died or were hurt and was telling Winston that he was pulling back to the village kartuew near where he can resupply by rail. They would be unavailable for the next week, after that time he would be happy to help Winston where he could if he could. Winston thanked him for their help. The commander asked Winston if there was anything else his troops could do for him. Winston thought about it and could see that he really wanted to help but couldn't think of anything and told him so. They shook hands with the forearms being grasped in the Indian custom and parted ways for the time being. It seemed that the commander had a lot more respect for Winston than Bart.

Charles was asking Winston about the tiger and how it could be mistaken for the man-eater. Winston said that in the heat of the moment it was easy to make a mistake.

"And what if you thought that it wasn't the man-eater and it turned out to be it." "Better to be safe and make the shot" replied Winston.

Charles asked if they would track the wounded tiger tomorrow and Winston said no. It was too dangerous with the cover it had and it was wounded as well. They would need to retire to the village and perhaps try to guess which village or area would be the next target. He thought the cat would spend a few days recuperating before making another kill.

The locals left in a group bearing the skin of the tiger and marched back to the village. The body was buried where it had fallen. The reproductive organs and the gall bladder were retrieved by the locals in order to make some sort of ancient aphrodisiac.

Although they should have been discouraged from another near miss on bagging the man-eater, Winston at least was upbeat and always seemed to possess a positive attitude.

"We're getting closer and I can just feel it. We are going to get a very good chance to see this to the end, and that end involves the death of the Katagi man-eater. I can sense it."

Charles knew that with all the resources being thrown at it that it was just a matter of time before it made a mistake that would cost it its life.

The hike back to the village was somber, but not overbearing. There would be another opportunity. The fireball of the sun was just starting to set over the hills, bathing the countryside in the long stretched out rays that brought out the colors of the far end of the spectrum.

Back at the village there was some commotion as Bart was arguing vehemently with someone. As they got closer Charles realized it was Victoria who had traveled up to the village where they were by gathering bits of information from the ministry and locals. Bart had already been in a foul mood when she had showed up. He yelled and berated her in front of everyone. Charles' and Victoria's eyes met and they both yearned to run and hold one another tightly as they were still very much in love but the current circumstances prevented such things. After a few minutes Charles wouldn't take it any longer.

He went over and simply said, "Victoria, our dinner's ready. Would you care to join me?"

The words were like a warden giving parole to a seasoned inmate. "Why thank-you, Charles, I believe I'll take you up on that offer." With that said she gave Bart a look that could have killed a grown death adder. As she got up, Bart had become more bellicose than ever, yelling at her to sit down and yelling to Charles to stay out of family affairs. He marched over in an attempt to physically restrain her.

Charles moved between them and in a stern voice told him, "I wouldn't do that if I were you."

Bart wouldn't stand for it and was about to lay some fists on Charles when Winston stepped into the developing fray. "What's the trouble here?" he asked, while pushing Charles away from Bart.

"Nothing at all," replied Charles, "I was just escorting Miss Victoria to some dinner."

Bart was fuming mad, but he possessed enough intelligence to know that he couldn't whip both Winston and Charles. His face was red with anger and he was sweating profusely.

With Winston still standing there, Charles and Victoria left together.

When they had gone Bart came over to Winston who was already on guard and said, "I wouldn't meddle in my affairs if I were you."

Winston looked him straight in the eye and said, "You know Bart, I'll meddle anywhere I damn well please," and with that he gave a brief stern look into Bart's eyes and turned and walked away.

Bart turned away too and after walking a short distance drop kicked the local dog who happened to be in close proximity. The yelp could be heard throughout the village.

When Charles and Victoria were alone, Charles was the first to speak.

"Victoria, what are you doing here? I thought we agreed that you would stay in Bombay until this was finished?"

"I know, but I couldn't sleep another night without seeing you. I miss you!"

Charles was touched because he missed her as well.

"I know darling, but I can't focus when you're here."

"You don't want me here, do you? Do you even love me?"

"Yes, I do love you and want to be there for you. But you have to under-stand that I can't work or concentrate one hundred percent when your here, because I'll think of you and it could be at a critical time and it could cost me my life or someone else's. You understand that, don't you?"

"Why can't this be over? Why can't we get on with our lives?"asked Victoria as they held one another tight. "Don't worry darling, it will soon be over and when it is we'll celebrate and have the rest of our lives to be with one another."

"I'm worried about my father too. Did you see how upset he was? It seems like I'm going to have to choose between the two of you and I know he needs me now."

"Don't worry yourself about it. Family always forgives, you'll just have to give him a little time."

"You're right, you always are, but before I head back to Bombay, I'm going to try to set things right. If something were to happen to him and we haven't forgiven one another, it would affect me for the rest of my life. I'm going to go see him later tonight after he's had a chance to cool down a bit, and I'll leave first thing in the morning."

"I would like for you to travel with the military group. Their leaving in the morning as well and there is strength in numbers as the cat could still be in the area. Will you promise me that?"

"Yes, whatever you say," With that they kissed, and it didn't matter that Charles smelled like he had been in the jungle for weeks.

Winston was too hungry to wait for Charles or even to expect that he would come to dinner with his girlfriend there. Winston valued Charles' opinion and knew he wouldn't need to let him know that a beautiful woman in camp would be a distraction. The two men had become a formidable team and they needed each other to see this through to the end.

After Charles and Victoria had talked for another hour, Victoria went back to Bart's hut to try to patch things up with her father. Luckily for her he had calmed down a bit, and like a dog which had found his favorite bone, was glad to see her, although he hid his feelings as he always did. He had to show her that he was right.

She told him that she was leaving in the morning with the military group and going back to Bombay. Bart remained stoic, showing no emotion. The memories of what had happened earlier came flooding back to his mind and he could feel himself getting angry again. The remembrance caused him to have a lapse and he told her to get out and he would speak to her when he returned to Bombay. She was hurt and knew him well enough to know that it was futile to try and reconcile at that moment, so she turned and left as tears were streaming down her face.

As she left, she said, "I love you father and I'm truly sorry."

Bart remained unmoved. She then left and went to the military leader.

The villagers were pegging the tiger skin in the main common area of the village when Bart emerged from his hut still fuming over what had happened and how he thought he should have reconciled with Victoria.

"That's mine!" he bellowed as he stormed up to the locals pegging out the skin. "Don't you forget that skin is mine and I'll be claiming it later."

An interpreter translated and no one dared challenge him as he seemed to be in a foul mood. After another hour he cooled off and went and found Victoria still in tears, he said that he was sorry for treating her the way that he did and that he loved her. She had never heard him apologize and she rushed to hug him tightly causing him an uncomfortable moment. But she was glad they had patched things up as she was and had always been the peacemaker.

The man-eater hadn't gone far. Although the wound was superficial it still created pain when it walked. It would move about a mile or so and then stop to rest and lick its wound clean. It was more of a nuisance than anything else, but it would have to eat in the next few days.

The moon wasn't in its fullest state at this time which would undoubtedly help it. It would often times think it was being followed but every time it would turn around, there was nothing. Once, despite its slight pain, it even tried to circle around hoping to catch the culprit, and that was when it whiffed the smell of another tiger. It was now very cautious and knew that men were trying to kill it and as a result took many more precautions to ensure its safety. It took pleasure knowing that the thick foliage was creating enough cover to keep it mostly hidden. Even the monkeys didn't cry an alarm until it was directly under them.

It traveled a lot more at night now and was sleeping more during the day with its injury. Each day it survived, it became more and more healthy, but it would need to kill soon as it had been several days since its last attack. The smaller game in the area were too fast for such a big beast and besides, it fancied humans. That salty flesh that it craved as its favorite food would have it sniffing the air constantly, trying to determine where the next village was or who was in the area.

After a few days it was traveling early in the morning when it came across a reticulated python spread out across the trail. It was a fully grown snake stretching nearly twenty-one feet as it slithered across the trail. The tiger was hungry and as it had encountered the mid-section of the snake it instinctively struck at it with its paw. The outstretched claws snagged the diamond designed skin and caused the snake to recoil and turn back to where the pain was. Its head moved back and forth with its tongue moving in and out of its mouth sensing the air for danger. The heat pits on its nose could sense the warm body before it. The tiger had also seen it change position from a long straight mass of flesh to coiled aggressiveness, and it was being careful to keep its distance from its head.

The snake was bleeding slightly from the claw wound in its midsection. It recoiled back waiting for the right moment to strike, its jaw agape showing several sharp but non-venomous teeth arranged in a row, beginning with the longest sharpest tooth and getting smaller and smaller as they went back into the throat of the snake. A snake this size could easily swallow a full-grown antelope. All it had to do was secure a bite hold and then coil itself around its victim, slowly and methodically squeezing tighter and tighter until the victim could no longer breathe.

The tiger was constantly moving from one place to another, occasionally making a swath with its paw and retreating back out of range of the snake's bite. The snake was standing its ground and had probably never had to retreat from anything anyway. The tiger was trying to get the tail uncoiled but the snake was having none of it. The snarl from the tiger could be heard for a quarter mile away as the hissing continued. The snake had made several lunges at the striped cat but each time the tiger was just out of reach. When it lunged again the tiger jumped out of the way and knocked its head to the ground with a powerful swath of its paw. The python recovered quickly and recoiled back. The snake was still somewhat dazed from the tiger's blow and wanted to get away, so it tried to slither into some dense cover but the tiger snagged its mid-section again and pulled it back out of the foliage. The snake had to somewhat straighten itself in order to slither away. As it tried to get into cover, the big cat snagged it with its claws and pulled it out as more wounds were created. At last the tiger got a little too close and it lunged at it, catching its paw in its powerful jaws. The tiger was surprised and leaped backward, for the snake was trying to coil itself around it. The big cat answered with a massive bite of its own just behind the head as it was still attached to its forward limb. The snake, with quick reflexes, tried again and again to coil itself around the tiger. The tiger constantly moved in the opposite direction of the snake making it difficult to get a coil around it. The big cat pulled the snake out into the open with its mouth still attached to its limb and the cat still holding the back of the head. Neither was willing to let go. With the snakes head still attached to the tiger it finally succeeded in getting a coil started around the tiger's body, but with the tiger's bite becoming more and more forceful it was unable to breathe. Without oxygen it slowly succumbed to temporarily blacking out, and as it did, it lost the advantage of the coil it had started. The bite from the tiger was enough to not only suffocate it but to break the snake's neck, making it unable to fully recover. The python continued to writher on the ground as its strength slowly ebbed away. The tiger was wet with sweat from the exertion of the entire fight and was lucky it had got a hold of the snake where it did or things might have turned out differently. It simply walked away looking for a stream to drink from and wash itself clean.

After finding a stream and cleaning itself, it returned to the area to eat some of the snake, for it was hungry and there was not a village near it. There was not a lot to eat and it would have to eat again in a day or two, but it was enough to sustain it.

That night it rested and continued to nurse the wound on its rear leg from the gunshot and now the new wound on its fore paw from the snake. Like all the big cats it was always cleaning itself and rarely received contamination from bad bacteria because it cleaned its wounds constantly, making sure that nothing was left inside the wound as it healed. Although nothing was broken it would take a week before the pain would subside and perhaps two to three before it was fully healed.

For Charles, the next morning came too soon. He and Victoria hadn't talked much the night before, he could see that she was upset and tried to console her as best he could but she needed some time alone. The military group began to break camp, So Charles went over to where Victoria was staying to say goodbye. Bart was there and wasn't letting either of them out of his sight, and it would have been fruitless to carry on that something was going on more than mere friendship. Charles said goodbye without a kiss, but Victoria did leave her handkerchief with him with the sweet smell of his favorite perfume still wafting through the stench of the village.

Bart went over to talk to the military commander and make sure that his daughter was in good hands. Charles turned and walked back to Winston's hut, and as soon as he came in Winston could smell the perfume. He told Charles that he was going to have to wash up to get rid of the smell on him because the tiger would no doubt pick it up.

Charles wasn't aware he was smelling so sweet and replied, "After breakfast, in the meantime, can you tell me what our plans are?"

"Sure, follow me", they both picked up their coats and left the hut together.

As they walked to get breakfast Winston said, "That was wise to send her off. She's a beautiful woman and you'll make a wonderful couple when this is over."

Winston lit up his pipe and puffed a few breaths. They sat outside at a bamboo table and were fed a wonderful breakfast by the locals, after they had a few bites, Winston spoke up.

"We're going to take a tracker back to the scene of where it disappeared into the thick brush and see if we can see what direction it's headed."

"Won't that be pretty dangerous, with the brush and all?" asked Charles.

Winston waited a few seconds before answering.

"The cat should be long gone by now. It has, most the time, moved on after finishing a kill or getting shot at, so I don't anticipate that we'll have a problem. We'll find out which direction it's headed and then we'll plot the next probable village where it will attack. We'll need an expert tracker who's willing to come with us. Can you see about that after breakfast for me?"

"Sure, I'll see what I can do," replied Charles. "It seems a lot quieter around here without the military."

"Yeah, but if we don't get this beast soon, they will be back in force."

Bart was busy with his remaining group trying to figure out where the cat would end up as well, but they had no concrete plans and he had formulated a plan to try to find out where Winston was going. Then he was going to try and beat him there. He was using a small wiry spy to get the information from either Charles or Winston or whoever they were going to use for tracking. Both Winston and Charles knew the small man couldn't be trusted. The questions he was asking seemed to point out that he wanted some information. Winston was too smart to give up his plans and Charles was too, so he was getting nowhere. But a half an hour later he spied Charles talking to one of the trackers that had come up to help and offer his services. After Charles had left, he casually went over as if he was going somewhere to do something and struck up a conversation with the tracker. He found out that he had been asked to help track some day old pug marks from yesterday.

Like a child before Christmas, the rat was beaming with the new information as he hurried over to Bart's camp to divulge the juicy gossip.

When Bart heard the news he continued to puff on his pipe, his head playing out scenarios and thinking what they could possibly be doing going back to that area knowing the cat would be gone. Then, like he had just put together the London crossword puzzle in a few seconds, he surmised that they were picking up the trail to see what direction it was heading. He promptly paid his spy and the spy, eager to spend his easy money, left seeking the fermented Jaiba-jaiba juice.

After he left, Bart gathered his only two trusted servants around him and told them that Winston and Charles were trying to find out what direction the man-eater was going. Bart was intent on waiting until they got back and then follow the lead to the tiger and get their first and kill the beast before they did.

It didn't take long for the tracker to determine which way the cat was headed, but he also discovered another set of pug marks that nearly overlapped the man-eater's. The tracks, after rounding the top of the hill, headed west even though the terrain was not conducive to that direction, and based on those facts Winston was fairly certain it was headed that way.

They made for the village as quickly as possible as it was going to be another long hot day. As soon as they got to the village they were a bit surprised to see Bart's group still there, but it wasn't long before the tracker, unaware of giving out information, told some people that the cat was headed west. Bart had already prepared for a quick departure and hurried away as if he knew where a treasure was.

Winston was keen to notice the quick departure and put two and two together. He looked at his map and saw that the major village of Samtiona was only twenty-five miles to the west. It was very likely that Bart was headed there.

After a hearty lunch, Winston and Charles and their small group headed out as well.

Bart and his group arrived in Samtiona several hours ahead of Winston and Charles. Bart had tried to cajole the wealthy rubber plantation owner to give up his home as a base camp to Bart, but the owner had refused all attempts. It was a mansion compared to everything else and all the materials used in construction had been brought in by either men or elephants. Such lavishness was rare, the area was very remote.

When Winston arrived just before sunset, the wealthy landowner offered to share his home with the sahib who had killed the man-eating leopard which was responsible for the death of his cousin. Winston and Charles accepted. Once inside the home and after a sumptuous dinner, Winston got out his map and laid it out on the table that had just been cleared.

"Things are looking up here," Winston said. "We know it's headed due west and it's got to be in this area. The plan will be to wait until it kills again. When it does, Bart will try and get there before us, and as he does it may prove his undoing, for the man-eater will try to kill him and we'll be able to use the situation to get close enough to the man-eater to kill it."

As he spoke there was the thousand yard stare in his eyes.

Charles spoke up.

"We simply can't let a man die like that."

Winston thought for a moment then spoke up.

"He's likely to get killed by this thing one way or another. You know he's hell bent on taking the fame and the fortune and he will stop at nothing to get it done. His ambition will prove his undoing and the cat will get him in the end, it's just a matter of time."

"But we can't let him die like that," replied Charles.

"Well, what would you like to do? Do you want to go over there and tell that piss-for-brains man that he's going to get killed? He won't listen to you, and we're trying to predict the future here based on intelligence and reason. Its the same way God sees a drunkard's son and can predict the future jail cell which will hold him. It's all a matter of probability. We need someone or something to divert its attention just long enough for us to make the kill. He's already been spying on us, gathering our intelligence on the animal and stealing it for his own use. He has a little spy that feeds him the info after we've gathered it."

Charles asked how he knew that and Winston put the pieces together for him by saying, "Have you wondered how he has ended up in the same village just half a day ahead of us? Have you wondered why he waited before departing the morning we tracked which direction the pug marks led? The tracker most likely spilled the information to someone else in Bart's employ. He's using the information for himself and waiting for us to make the right move, and then he storms the castle ahead of us and claims the victory.

"Look, to be honest I don't care for him at all and neither do you for that matter. All we want is for the beast to be killed and the slaughter to stop, He's surely capable, otherwise he wouldn't be here. We'll simply feed him correct information and if he's got it in him, he'll kill the beast."

"But you know as well as I do that he's green in this country, its foreign to him. He's going to get killed!" said Charles.

"We can infer that but we don't have a crystal ball to tell us for sure, and besides do you think that he would listen to anything we warned him about? He's like that American named Custer, the one that had two of the American Gatling guns at his disposal but refused to bring them up because of the time involved, and look what he got. He went out with guns a blazing, I'll give him that, but he's dead all the same.

"He'll get the information one way or another, there's no stopping it. But if it makes you feel better, why don't you go have a chat with him and see what happens. I've seen guys like that ten times over and they usually get licked or end up dead one way or another."

Charles was deep in thought as he left the mansion.

Bart's spy later informed him that Winston and Charles were staying at the Karish mansion and Bart became livid, as was seen in the color of his face. It wasn't long after that when Charles showed up at his hut and asked to have a word. Bart seemed surprised because they had remained aloof ever since they had left Bombay.

Charles came straight to the point.

"Bart, I sense that you're indifferent to me and that you definitely hate Winston, but is there any truth to the rumor that your gathering information gleaned from us to get the upper hand on being first to kill the man-eater?"

Charles' frankness and honesty took Bart by surprise and he was in a trap either way. If he answered truthfully, it would indicate he had violated an unwritten code at the very least and was conniving at the most. On the other hand, if he answered negatively, he would be lying. In the time it takes a cobra to strike he had played out both scenarios. For a moment he thought of telling the truth but it was a small moment at that.

After a slight pause he said, "No, why do you think such a thing?"

"Oh, Winston was thinking it was pretty coincidental that we both ended up here in the same village. Anyway, I have no other way to say this, but I hope you're taking all the precautions necessary to keep you and your group safe and not to pursue the beast in too much haste. After all, we don't want a pyrrhic victory."

"Charles, I haven't known you for long but you don't strike me as the concerned type. If there's something you're not telling me, come out with it and quit beating around the bush!"

Charles had thoughts race through his mind of telling him how much he was in love with his daughter, which if he was a smart man he would already have figured out by now.

"Winston thinks you're using the intelligence we gather to get to the cat first, as I mentioned."

He did leave out the part of Bart possibly being the bait, and continued by saying, "Let me tell you a quick story which won't take long. A couple hundred years ago there was another man-eater that ended up killing hundreds, just like the Katagi man-eater, but back then there was no newspapers reporting the story, just the story as I've heard it passed down through generations from the locals. At that time there was no gunpowder available and the weapons that a few possessed were no match for the tiger. It prowled a large area at will, taking victims as it became hungry, and of course the people tried just about everything they could think of to kill it, all to no avail as it was a wily cat. Eventually it was given the respect it deserved, and earned I might add, because of its reputation and skill. In some places it was even deified, and people worshiped it and made sacrifices to it.

"It lived in the mangrove swamps near the eastern border and so the only way to get to it was to go in on its watery territory by boat or canoe, the waterway snaking its way deeper and deeper into its territory. It brought down a few who tried to go after it. The few who survived said it was a stealthy swimmer and had the ability to leap up out of the water. Eventually after about fifteen years the killings stopped. Most likely explanation was that it died of natural causes, but no one knows for sure. I'm telling you this because the cat had earned everyone's respect and with that respect, people proceeded with caution and kept in numbers, traveling and working, and so the killings weren't as many as they could have been. I hope that you give this man-eater the same kind of respect that it deserves."

"You came over here tonight to tell me this? To give the man-eater some respect? What do you think I am, a school boy going after some cat in the tree? You need to give me some respect! Get the hell out!"

Charles realized it was pointless to try to continue and so he got up and walked out. He thought about telling him to take a rhino horn and shove it up his rectum, but he came to his senses and realized it wouldn't accomplish anything.

He walked back into the plantation owner's mansion and the first thing Winston said was, "Well, how did it go?"

"Not well, I suppose," was Charles reply.

"Well, you didn't expect anything else, did you?"

"No, I suppose not. But I do feel better for at least trying."

"You didn't tell him everything, did you?"asked Winston.

"No, he wouldn't really let me, and I guess he brings out the worst in anyone."

"Now that's the honest way of saying he's a real bitch."

That brought a smile to Charles face.

"Let's get some sleep. We may have a few very long days ahead us."

"Are you sure we can sleep in these accommodations?" Charles said.

"Ah yes, we may have to get use to these, and the food as well. He has a very good cook."

With that said they laid down their heads on pillows made from the eider duck of Scandinavia and Charles thought that it had to be the softest, most comfortable pillow he had ever encountered. Within minutes they were both fast asleep.

When they awoke the next morning there was a sumptuous breakfast laid out before them in the dining hall which had been prepared for them by the servants. When they were about halfway through the meal a messenger came knocking at the door to say that the Katagi man-eater had struck last night at a remote hut in the countryside not far from the village.

Winston immediately made eye contact with Charles and said, "We better get ready".

The news wasn't exactly fresh as Bart had heard about it before Winston and was already close to an hour ahead of him. Both Winston and Charles knew he was heading into Hades itself as the cat would most certainly still be in the area.

They made more haste in order to get to the site. The tracker was ready to go as well but would only lead them to the scene of the crime, the hut where the attacked had occurred. They prepared their packs for a few days in the jungle if necessary.

As soon as Bart heard the news he was ready to go and off he went with his followers. He figured he had at least a forty-five minute head start on Winston and Charles and wanted to get there first. One of the men who had brought news to the village was only willing to lead them part of the way to the dead man's hut, but when he got close, he also got scared and opted to stay with Bart and his men rather than return to the safety of the village alone. Once they could see the hut, he pointed to it and quickly got in the back of the line of men. Bart now led the way and was cautious every step not knowing what he would encounter.

They got to the hut and everyone could see a gaping hole with blood stains soaking one side of it. There was some coagulated blood on the ground just under the hole as well and the whole scene gave off an eerie feeling to all who were there. When Bart first saw the scene, he had to admit that he was not only concerned, but a bit scared along with everyone else, but yet no one was willing to admit it.

They surveyed the scene for a few minutes and then the tracker indicated that he had dragged the victim into the jungle and pointed the way. They really didn't need the tracker as the trail of blood was easy to see. What made everyone on edge was that the blood hadn't yet dried up.

Bart reached out to a long piece of elephant grass and touched the crimson blood. He looked at his fingers and could see that the blood was still wet and fresh. It must have mixed with the early morning dew and become wet again, because surely it would have been dried since the killing was the night before. Still, they were extremely agitated, but Bart was eager to continue and feared Winston and Charles would show up any moment and get ahead of him.

The jungle slowly got thicker and thicker with more and more elephant grass and the visibility was reduced to only about twenty feet in any direction. In their haste to track the kill they forgot to check the wind and see what direction it was blowing. Had they done so, they would probably not have proceeded following the trail, for the wind carried their human smell into the air ever so slightly. It was just enough to be picked up by any animal with a sensitive nose at least three hundred yards before they even arrived.

Bart's men could see the places where the tiger had stopped briefly as pools of coagulated blood stained the jungle dirt. The tracker's realized they were close enough to warrant Bart being in the lead with his gun. Bart was careful after that, as there was no way to know if the cat was ready to pounce at any time. After thirty-five minutes of slowly following the trail they could hear flies buzzing around an object that they could barely discern about twenty yards ahead in a sort of a clearing. At that moment they could make out the shape of a man, covered with blow flies, which appeared to have several major bones and ribs poking up in the air.

Bart looked around carefully to see if he could see anything but there was nothing but flies. The soft sandy soil revealed the huge pug marks of the enormous tiger as it had dragged its hapless victim. Sweat began to bead up in large droplets on his head and neck, sliding down his face or neck like a squirrel runs down a tree. There was no time to wipe them for it was unknown what could happen at any moment. There was only one thing to do and that was to go forward to check out the victim. The tracker would be able to tell how long it had been there and how long ago the cat had vacated the kill.

As if there was a sense of foreboding in the air, Bart proceeded more cautiously than ever, looking around everywhere, turning his head in the direction of any sound. His gun was ready to fire at a second's notice and his hand was on the stock with his finger on the trigger. Slowly he inched forward with the men behind him following too close as they were as afraid as he was.

The stench of decaying flesh had already set in and could be whiffed from several yards back. As Bart moved closer he became more and more fixated on the dead corpse, which was an eerie sight in and of itself. The fingers were curled up and the face showed a terrible distortion. The body was half eaten and certain sections looked like they had just been picked off the bone. It looked as if the cat had vacated the kill not that long ago. Perhaps it had gone down to get a drink, thought Bart. The rest of the men began to slowly release their tension as they got closer and realized that with each passing second the chance for an attack was disappearing.

The corpse was starting to putrefy as the smell was very strong, maybe the bowels had been opened up. The tracker came forward to examine the pug marks around the body and suddenly became ghastly white. He indicated with hand signals that the pug marks were very fresh. No words were spoken but everyone looked around to see if they could see anything. Bart got down on one knee and was poised to receive an attack. The thoughts that came to his mind were, *did it smell them coming and left for good or was it disturbed while eating the victim?* Nobody knew for sure, but there was no doubt that it had been there very recently. The focus was no longer on the corpse but the surrounding area with thick elephant grass. The pug marks led out of the small clearing, but no one made any effort to follow them.

Bart examined the pug marks and they showed that it had not run away, they indicated that it had casually left the kill, probably to get a drink in the brook at the bottom of the hill. He could either wait for it to come back and position himself for a good shot or he could track it down to the brook and perhaps surprise it and get a good shot at it. He thought about Winston and Charles and wondered how far they were behind him. When he thought about that he made the decision to try and track it down to the brook. He looked over once more at the grotesque body and motioned for everyone to follow him.

The tracks still led in a direction that was with the wind which carried their scent before them.

As it turned out Winston and Charles were both hot on the trail and had already arrived at the hut and could see the scene where the death had taken place. The trail wasn't hard to find as all they had to do at this point was follow several men's tracks which were still fresh. Winston looked at Charles, and although no words were spoken they were both thinking the same thing, that Bart's group was in danger.

The tiger, after eating a good portion of the body, had only left the scene about thirty minutes prior to Bart's arrival. As predicted by Bart it had gone down the hill to get a drink at the brook and wasn't completely full so it was intending to come back. The cool water was clean and the brook, although slow, meandered down the hill.

After slaking its thirst, it ventured into the small stream to wet its coat and to take a few steps and exit the brook a few feet away. It was its usual practice and it found that it helped throw off the scent if anything was tracking it. The tiger then found a bamboo grove not far from the small creek and sheltered from the sun laid down for a mid-day nap. It was awoken not by noise from Bart's group but by the smell that it had come to know only too well. It sniffed the air again and again and there was no mistake about what was coming. It got to its feet but remained hidden in the bamboo.

Bart remained in the lead and followed the pug marks when he could see them. When he couldn't, he would defer to the tracker who would take a look and point which direction they were going. He was being careful, but going too fast, for he could hear the trickling water of the brook but failed to slow down at all.

The tiger could see them approaching the brook. Within Bart's group of four men, only Bart had a big gun. Another man had a small caliber pistol, the tracker had no gun at all and neither did the forth man; all they carried were spears. They cautiously approached the brook where the pug marks clearly showed where the big cat entered. The trail at that time was momentarily lost. The tracker started looking upstream for any pug marks and Bart walked a few paces downstream. It didn't take long for him to find the exit point. He gave out an imitation bird call he had mimicked in Africa as a youth that was close enough to the original that he was able to get the native male birds to come close to him. Once he got the others attention, he motioned to them without saying a word. Instead of waiting for them he started following the trail and could see that it led to the bamboo clump before him.

The man-eater had been watching the entire time since they had come into view. Bart looked at the bamboo and tried to peek inside without moving any closer. As he continued to focus his eyes, he could see two large eyes staring straight back at him. He raised his gun to fire but the cat was already out of the bamboo, and within a single bound it was on Bart as he simultaneously fired and let out a blood curling scream.

Bart had misjudged the height of the leap and the bullet had passed just under the tiger singeing its underside. The full force of its body knocked Bart to the ground and he lost his grip on the gun as he tried to fend off the large cat with both his forearms. The two front paws with claws extended landed on his head and shoulder. The claws that landed on his face raked downward opening up skin like a filleting knife opens a tuna.

The attack had so unnerved the other men that they dropped what weapons they had and fled while Bart was being attacked.

The blow to Bart's head had knocked him out and when the tiger came around it shook Bart like he was a rag doll. The tiger displaced that much weight like it was yarn. Some of the wounds were deep enough that Bart would die from the loss of blood within minutes, never regaining conscience. The tiger was aware of the other men who had fled but held Bart in its jaws by his neck, crunching the vertebrae with a sound that reverberated around the area. It was still hungry and had not experienced a person with this much weight for some time, and so it sat down and began feasting on its favorite parts.

Winston and Charles had been examining the hut and the scene of the attack when they heard the other men running for their lives. They had stopped yelling but had not stopped running desperately for a couple of miles, occasionally tripping and falling, still having a dazed look in their eyes. Charles tried to stop them but there was only death on their faces and nothing could stop them from running. After they frantically passed, Winston looked at Charles.

As both their eyes met Winston said, "Let's finish the bastard."

They moved as quickly as they dared, with Winston in the lead following the well-worn trampled grass the other men had conveniently created. They were trying to move as silently as possible under the circumstances. Bart hadn't been with the group and so it was assumed he had been a victim. They didn't even know how far it was to where whatever had happened, but with the men still running all out, it couldn't have been far, so on they went as silently as they could.

They saw the brook and they slowed further, sensing with instinct that there was danger in and around the area. They both scanned the area before making any move, and then Winston spotted Bart's body and silently pointed it out to Charles.

The hammers on both guns had long since been set and they were ready for whatever would happen next. Life hung in the balance as they slowly crept forward to the body. When they got close they could see that it had been partially eaten. Intestines and blood were spread about around the body like Jack the Ripper had just been there. The stomach area of Bart was opened up and pieces of flesh looked like they were still hanging on the rib cage. Winston didn't look too long at the sight, because he knew by instinct that the tiger was still around and like a warrior facing the enemy, he had all his senses trained for anything out of the ordinary. He whispered to Charles to go back to back and it didn't take Charles long to figure out what he wanted. He immediately moved his back against Winston's so they had two sides covered at all times in case of an attack. Charles knew Winston enough to follow his movements as they slowly spun around and half walked at the same time.

Just at a point when the tension was at an all-time high Winston whispered that he was going to yell, and within seconds the loudest peacock alarm Charles had ever heard reverberated throughout the jungle. The ear-piercing screech prompted the man-eater to attack from the cover that concealed it. It had broken cover from only fifteen feet away, but in that time it had already bounded once and was in the air coming straight for Winston with its paws outstretched emitting a snarl that would banish Satan himself back to the underworld.

Winston instinctively moved the gun upwards. There was no time to bring his head in line with the sights, so he just pointed the barrel at the blur before him. Everything seemed to transpire to a slow motion action. The gun fired, and in the millisecond it took, a small flame could be seen coming out of the barrel. The bullet was slightly low, hitting the cat in its underside without a vital hit. A fraction of a second later a second blast raced through the tiger's outstretched whiskers, passing harmlessly into the jungle beyond.

Charles had felt Winston's movement to fire and had whirled oppo-site of Winston just in time to fire once at point blank range at what was a striped blur. Charles bullet had passed under the tiger's jaw and entered its brain. The full weight of the cat with its still outstretched claws came down on Winston and Charles knocking them over with the cat crumpling to the ground after them. Charles had lost his grip on his gun but Winston still had a death grip on his. Still breathing hard, Charles pulse was racing like a thoroughbred. They quickly recovered and turned to face the deadly beast ready to fight for their lives, but they were staring at the huge beast before them, the Katagi man-eater died the moment the bullet entered its brain, no longer breathing, no longer a threat. A rare specimen, much bigger than an ordinary tiger, something Winston already knew from the pug marks, but a fact that caused Charles to stare. Both men had hit the man-eater but it was Charles' lucky shot that ran true, killing the man-eater immediately. Had Charles shot missed, it was most probable that, both men would have been pushing up daisies.

Charles helped Winston to his feet as Winston slowly felt his face with a new cut from one of the outstretched claws. He wiped the blood off his face and embraced Charles as both men gave a strong hug to the other. Winston uttered the famous words of Julius Ceasar, "Veni, vedi, vece," and Charles was educated enough to understand 'we came, we saw, we conquered.'

The famous Katagi man-eater lay at their feet. They scrutinized their kill. Truly it was a magnificent beast. It was the largest tiger Winston had ever seen and he had killed dozens. He reached down and its paw alone spread out as far as his hat. He extracted a claw out of its natural sheath with his knife and it was as thick and long as his own thumb. He looked for any evidence of porcupine quills which have often contributed to tigers turning man-eaters but found none. The original gunshot wound that forced it to eat man was covered with fur and could not be seen.

The tiger would need to be transported and skinned at the nearby village and there would be a need to get the two bodies buried as well. They were going to have to hike out and get some help from the village in order to transport the tiger and the bodies there.

After covering Bart's body with a blanket, Charles brought out his portable camera and Winston asked him to give it to him and he would take a picture of Charles with the beast. Winston managed to roll the beast into a position that was photogenic as he snatched a few shots. He then opened its blood laced jaws and Charles was amazed at the size of the canines. Both men stroked the beautiful coat with its vivid orange against white with black stripes blacker than the darkest night. They would need to hike back to the village to ask the natives to help with the transport of the beast to the village and to haul Bart out as well and give him a proper burial.

After Charles took a few more pictures with his brownie camera, Winston turned to him and said, "If it weren't for you mate, I'd be dead right now. It's a good thing I insisted on you coming along."

"No, it was your instructions to be ready for the moment when the moment came. It allowed me the courage to fire without showing fear, to control my emotions. Of course I hadn't mastered it, and I'm not ashamed to say I was about to bolt with fright, but I wanted to support and help you as you were in a fix as well. With each foray into the bush, I've been able to get better at trying to control my fear the way you taught me. The shot came from the side and with a head only a few feet away it was hard to miss, but it was without a doubt the teacher that taught me what was needed to have to pull such a shot off. Your own courage inspired me. You had faith in me, and I began to believe and have courage myself. Thank-you and by the way, just between you and I, it was a lucky shot" Both men looked at one another and began laughing. After a slight pause Winston spoke up "You know you're going to be famous now, don't you? The man who killed the Katagi man-eater! Charles Whent. I've been there. You'll have your name in all the English speaking newspapers and couple dozen non-speaking ones. They'll have a parade for you back in Bombay and you'll be promoted beyond your wildest dreams."

"Perhaps so," said Charles, "but when you do come to visit me, you and only you, will know that I haven't changed one iota."

"Let's go see if we can find me a drink in that hut we passed earlier before finding some help," said Winston. Winston leaned his rifle up against the nefarious beast as Charles dusted his gun off and leaned it up against the beast as well. And with that they left their belongings on the ground and casually walked back to the isolated hut.

Before heading back to the hut Winston took out another blanket and draped it over Bart's body fully covering it.

They could walk casually back now, with no fear of where the tiger was. It seemed like they were always in its vicinity, always on guard, but now the country was safe again.

They reached the small hut and Winston climbed up into what was left of the wall, but all he could find was some fruit juice and water. He found some homemade cups carved from mango trees and they poured themselves a well-deserved drink. After quenching their thirst they started back to the village to find some help and it was only a mile or two before they found two men. They were a bit surprised to see them and asked if they weren't aware that the Katagi man-eater was in the area. They became ghastly white and replied that they didn't know, as they lived in the countryside and didn't come to the village but once a week. Winston told them not to worry, that this chap, pointing at Charles, had killed it just an hour before. He asked them to summon enough help from the village to transport the large cat and two humans back to the village, or what was left of them. They replied with great pleasure and took to calling Charles, "Sahib."

Winston and Charles slowly started to make their way back to the kill. Winston was leading and when he came into the small clearing there was an unmistakable snarl which stopped Winston in his tracks as Charles sidled up next to him unaware of the danger. There staring right at them with blood on its fangs was a smaller tiger crouched right behind Bart's body. Charles looked instinctively over to where the guns were leaning against the man-eaters body, obviously out of reach. Winston told Charles in a whisper not to move. The blankets had been removed from Bart's body and as Winston looked closer he could see that more remains of what was left of Bart had been eaten. Winston then gleaned the facts and everything seemed to make sense. The smaller pug marks they had seen everywhere, was this tiger coming to clean up after the Katagi man-eater had eaten its fill. It had learned how to scavenge from it, how to live and how to survive. It had shadowed them for who knows how long. Winston told Charles to slowly back away. Charles could also see the situation and was already doing what Winston had told him to do. Except for once looking at his gun, Winston never took his eyes off the tiger, but yet he didn't look directly into them either. They continued to back away as the tiger continued to snarl its disapproval. Eventually they were out of sight and began to run back towards the hut. They had almost never been without their guns and now with none, they lacked the courage to forge ahead on bravery alone.

They made it back to the hut and looked inside for any weapon they could find but only found one machete. They took it and continued back towards the village briskly. On the way back they met a large party coming down the trail, all of them chanting something that translated loosely as, "all praise the tiger's dead, all praise the tiger's dead." Winston immediately asked if anyone had a gun with them. One man had an old musket which Winston thought was inadequate for the job, but then a beat came to his mind which would likely force the tiger to retreat. Winston quickly dismissed the idea as too time consuming. He explained to the locals that Charles had indeed killed the Katagi man-eater, but there was another tiger in the area not letting them know that they had seen it eating the remains of Bart. Suddenly, most everyone had lost interest in getting the tiger. Winston took the ancient musket and verified that it was in working condition and then had the owner load it and coaxed the others into following him to the kill. A dispirited but anxious group followed Winston as word was spread that the man-eater was dead but there was another tiger in the area. When they started back to the kill, Winston had asked everyone to make as much noise as possible. There were only six people including Charles who ventured forth with Winston as he was cautious as a fox. They came near to the scene as Winston slowly approached alone with the antiquated musket which could hardly do anything. As Winston got very close he parted the grass obstructing the view to the kill area and as he did he noticed nothing and could see no tiger present. There in front of him was the macabre scene with a huge downed tiger and a body not far off with blood and internal parts spread about. Winston slowly approached the scene, but it was apparent the smaller tiger had left. He retrieved his own gun and quickly loaded it, but it was apparent the tiger had left. The villagers began to cut a bamboo pole to transport the tiger back to the village. It was suggested that they get an official photograph of everyone together with the tiger propped up on a rock in the foreground and Winston and Charles on either side with the natives behind them. Charles showed one of them how to depress the shutter on the small brownie camera and with that a historic picture was taken. As it happened it turned out very well and was the one sent out for the papers across the globe. It took several men to lift the tiger up on the bamboo as it was too large to tie just the legs. They had to tie the entire body to the poles, but they managed it well with extra rope. They continued their little chant as everyone began heading back to the village. Both Winston and Charles felt an enormous weight lift off their shoulders but inwardly Winston was both intrigued and concerned about the new tiger.

Winston shook off the thought and told Charles that he would be sleeping well tonight. He said that he was officially retiring from professional hunting except for an occasional royal command hunt. Charles understood and told him he was surprised himself to have even talked him into coming into on this one. Winston replied, "Well, I guess I'll always have this to remember it." He then pulled down his handkerchief that was around his neck and showed the months old scars that were still healing. Both Winston and Charles slept well that night. Bart's men didn't hang around knowing that everyone thought they were cowards.

Winston and Charles both sent word by a messenger to the nearest telegram office to inform the minister that the Katagi man-eater was dead. Charles sent a special telegram to Victoria, saying how sorry he was for her father, that he had been killed by the man-eater and that he had tried to do everything he could to prevent the disaster. He asked her to meet him in New Delhi in three days time, knowing that it would take him at least three to get there. If he was late he thought there was *no harm in having her wait a little.* She would no doubt want to visit to see her father's grave and probably pay for a more suitable headstone. They could take their time as Charles's telegram to George Smythe indicated that he would be taking a few well-deserved holidays and wouldn't return to the office until the following Monday where he will deliver the full report.

"You had also better get used to a new promotion" said Winston. "I know how things work there and if you know all the right people and don't rub people the wrong way, you might even get George's job if you play your cards right."

"That's absurd," said Charles.

"No, it's not, you wait and see. In fact, by the time we reach New Delhi there will be several reporters there asking for the story, and its going global," said Winston.

Charles wasn't thinking about that at all. He was just excited to see Victoria again and couldn't wait to meet up with her. It would still take Winston and Charles a few days to get to New Delhi.

As they arrived a few days later, as predicted, Charles was bombarded with reporters wanting to know the details of the kill. Charles told them the truth which was essentially that Winston had hit the tiger first and his shot had slowed it down quite a bit. He knew that Winston's shot was non-lethal, but he didn't mind sharing the credit.

Winston was then sought out for his side of the story, but he refused to take any credit, indicating that it was Charles' shot which killed the beast and his alone. In the papers around the world, there would either be the one variation or the other but most would be somewhere near the truth. It was an incredible story and had a climatic ending to it.

Charles, at Winston's suggestion, would have a taxidermist stuff the beast and it would later go on display at the Department of Natural Disasters and then on to the National Museum of India.

As expected, Victoria was waiting at the rail station in New Delhi for Charles. She had gone out of her way to look good for Charles, and she was in fact a stunning sight to see. They embraced and kissed, a lot longer than necessary.

While they waited for the luggage to unload, Charles went over to Winston.

"Headed home?" asked Charles.

"Yes, it's time to retire again. Don't be a stranger now."

Looking over at Victoria he said, "I'll expect a wedding invitation soon."

"You'll get one," replied Charles.

Charles extended a hand. Winston took a look at it, then immediately raised his arms and embraced Charles with a hearty hug that pulled the two of them together. It was an embrace of two wearied warriors.

"You take care of that girl. She's got spunk and that's something you need?"

Both men were smiling.

"And another thing, I couldn't have done this without you. I owe you my life."

"And I owe you mine," replied Charles.

And with that they parted, and Charles went with Victoria to retrieve his luggage as Winston lit up his pipe with some fresh tobacco.

It took Charles a few days to get back to Bombay and when he did, he was immediately summoned to the Viceroy's office. Apparently, informants had given out his arrival to others.

When he arrived at the Viceroy's office in the morning of the next day, he was surprised to see George Smythe there as well. They were both asked to come into the Viceroy's office at the same time. As they came in and were seated, they both looked at each other. The Viceroy entered and thanked them for coming. He started speaking immediately.

"I'll cut straight to the chase here," he said. "I have received orders from England to replace you, George as the director of natural Resources and have been granted permission to replace you with my choice."

There was stunned silence before he continued, "Apparently others have felt that the time to resolve the Katagi man-eater took too much time and the die was cast before your most recent success. I'm granting your choice of assignments to Overseer of Antarctic Research at the base at Mcmurdo Sound, or if you would like you can take a lesser position subservient to Charles here at the division of Natural Resources."

Charles couldn't believe his ears and began to smile. Smythe was speechless, but what could he say.

"You can have the week to decide which one you want," said the Viceroy, but Smythe spoke up sheepishly.

"There's no need to wait sir. I'll take the position here under, Mr. Whent."

There was a slight pause as he mentioned Charles name.

"Fine," said the Viceroy, "I'd like to ask you to wait outside as I have a private conversation with Mr. Whent."

"Yes, yes of course," replied George and he got up and excused himself. The Viceroy came straight to the point. "Charles, congratulations, the position is yours, and with the job you've done with the Katagi man-eater I have every bit of confidence you can handle any problem that you'll encounter. I'll expect a tight ship in that department, I'll be watching you". "You can count on it, sir, and I won't let you down. I will need a week or two off in the coming months for a honeymoon though." "Congratulations. Its good you're finally settling down, and I'm sure she's a lovely lady." They shook hands and Charles left the Viceroy's office.

As Charles left the office he said to George, "George, I'll need that desk cleared out by Tuesday morning. I believe there's an open office down the hall."

There was another pause before George said, "Sure," and left down the hall without waiting for Charles to walk with him.

Charles was enjoying every minute of it. George was walking quickly, befuddled by the turn of events. Charles stopped by to see Javier Blygoth. He found his office and asked his temporary secretary if he was in. She said that he was and he asked if he could see Charles Whent. She left and went into his office. Blygoth was dreading the meeting, but wished to delay it no longer and told the secretary to send him in. The men shook hands cordially and Blygoth mentioned that he had read the papers and understood that it was quite an experience.

He said, "I hope you understand that there will be no payment on the bet since it was officially you who killed the dreadful beast. You understand, don't you?"

Charles knew that he would try to weasel out of the wager somehow.

"It was Winston's party that killed the tiger of which I was a part, and you'll have to remember that Winston hit the beast as well and so contributed to its demise. I'll have the witnesses give testimony on the matter and a impartial committee will be formed by Sarkee to rule on the matter which is his prerogative and will let you know of the decision."

With that said, Charles got up and left saying, "Good day, sir."

He decided to take the rest of the day off and celebrate with Victoria in a nice cafe overlooking the bay. As he sat there staring at a stunning woman, with a promotion in hand, he thought that yes, things had turned out dandy.

Winston returned to his home, just as he had left it, but his girlfriend was waiting there on the front porch. No imported powder on her face, just God given beauty. That to him made the most beautiful woman in the world. When she saw him, she dropped everything and ran into his arms. They kissed like never before. Like two lovers whose love for one another transcended everything. He too had missed her. Although he wouldn't admit it, he had grown to love her, not only for her beauty but for her companionship as well.

It seemed that the time away from each other had transformed a love that knew no physicality before into something that would last a lifetime. It was then that he decided it was time in his life to retire, settle down, and get married. He couldn't believe the thoughts that were coming to him. Yes, he thought, life is full of difficulties but at times it was grand.

He thought about how things had played out and had to admit that the Katagi man-eater had created an experience where he had established a great relationship with a true friend in Charles. He also realized that his absence from his girlfriend had created love for himself. A love that he had never experienced before, a love that he would not have recognized had he not been away from it, and so he concluded that the man-eater had also created a new life for himself.

Just months after the man-eater was killed there was another report of a disappearance of a young girl in a far-flung providence, but it would take years before a new man-eater was given its credit.